Legends

Stephen King
Terry Goodkind
Orson Scott Card
Robert Silverberg
Ursula K. LeGuin
Raymond E. Feist

LEGENDS

**New works by the
Masters of Modern Fantasy**

THE DARK TOWER
THE SWORD OF TRUTH
TALES OF ALVIN MAKER
MAJIPOOR
EARTHSEA
THE RIFTWAR SAGA

Voyager

LEGENDS

edited by Robert Silverberg

◆

STEPHEN KING
TERRY GOODKIND
ORSON SCOTT CARD
ROBERT SILVERBERG
URSULA K. LE GUIN
RAYMOND E. FEIST

HarperCollins*Publishers*

Voyager
An Imprint of HarperCollins*Publishers*
77–85 Fulham Palace Road,
Hammersmith, London W6 8JB

The *Voyager* website address is:
www.voyager-books.com

Special overseas edition 2000
This paperback edition 2000
1 3 5 7 9 8 6 4 2

First published in Great Britain in one volume with LEGENDS:
Discworld, Pern, Song of Ice and Fire, Memory, Sorrow and Thorn,
Wheel of Time by *Voyager* 1998

The Little Sisters of Eluria Copyright © 1998 Stephen King
Debt of Bones Copyright © 1998 Terry Goodkind
Grinning Man Copyright © 1998 Orson Scott Card
The Seventh Shrine Copyright © 1998 Agberg, Ltd.
Dragonfly Copyright © 1998 Ursula K. Le Guin
The Wood Boy Copyright © 1998 Raymond E. Feist
Introductions Copyright © 1998 Agberg, Ltd.

A catalogue record for this book
is available from the British Library

ISBN 0 00 648393 3

Typeset in Stone Serif
by Palimpsest Book Production Limited, Polmont, Stirlingshire
Printed and bound in Great Britain by
Caledonian International Book Manufacturing Ltd, Glasgow

For Marty and Ralph
Who certainly know why

Contents

INTRODUCTION

Here is a book of visions and miracles – eleven rich, robust new stories by the best known and most accomplished modern creators of fantasy fiction, each one set in the special universe of the imagination that made that writer famous throughout the world.

Fantasy is the oldest branch of imaginative literature – as old as the human imagination itself. It is not difficult to believe that the same artistic impulse that produced the extraordinary cave paintings of Altamira and the Chauvet Cave, fifteen and twenty and even thirty thousand years ago, also probably produced astounding tales of gods and demons, of talismans and spells, of dragons and werewolves, of wondrous lands beyond the horizon – tales that fur-clad shamans recited to fascinated audiences around the campfires of Ice-Age Europe. So, too, in torrid Africa, in the China of prehistory, in ancient India, in the Americas: everywhere, in fact, on and on back through time for thousands or even hundreds of thousands of years. I like to think that the storytelling impulse is universal – that there have been storytellers as long as there have been beings in this world that could be spoken of as 'human' – and that those storytellers have in particular devoted their skills and energies and talents, throughout our long evolutionary path, to the creation of extraordinary marvels and wonders.

We will never know, of course, what tales the Cro-Magnon storytellers told their spellbound audiences on those frosty nights in ancient France. But surely there were strong components of the fantastic in them. The evidence of the oldest stories that *have* survived argues in favour of that. If fantasy can be defined as literature that depicts the world beyond that of mundane reality, and mankind's struggle to assert dominance over that world, then the most ancient story that *has* come down to us – the Sumerian tale of the hero Gilgamesh, which dates from about 2500 BC – is fantasy, for its theme is Gilgamesh's quest for eternal life.

Homer's *Odyssey*, abounding as it does in shapeshifters and wizards and sorceresses, in Cyclopses and many-headed man-eating creatures, is rich with fantastic elements too, as are any number of other Greek and Roman tales. As we come closer to our own times we meet the dread monster Grendel of the Anglo-Saxon *Beowulf*, the Midgard serpent and the dragon Fafnir and the apocalyptic Fenris-wolf of the Norse sagas, the hapless immortality-craving Dr Faustus of German legend, the myriad enchanters of *The Thousand and One Nights*, the far-larger-than-life heroes of the Welsh *Mabinogion* and the Persian *Shah-Nameh*, and an infinity of other strange and wonderful creations.

Nor did the impulse towards the creation of the fantastic disappear as the modern era, the era of microscopes and tele-scopes, of steam engines and railway systems, of telegraphs and phonographs and electric light, came into being. Our fascination with the unseen and the unseeable did not end simply because so many things previously thought impossible now had become realities. What is more fantastic, after all, than having the sound of an entire symphony orchestra rise up out of a flat disc of plastic? Or to speak into a device that one holds in one's hand, and be heard and understood ten thousand miles away? But the same century that gave us the inventions of Thomas Alva Edison and Alexander Graham Bell gave us Lewis Carroll's two incomparable tales of Alice's adventures in other realities, H. Rider Haggard's innumerable novels of lost civilizations, and Mary Wollstonecraft Shelley's *Frankenstein*.

Nor did the twentieth century – the century of air travel and atomic energy, of television and computers, of open-heart surgery and sex-change operations – see us losing our taste for tales of the extraordinary. A host of machine-age fantasists –

James Branch Cabell and A. Merritt and Lord Dunsany, E. R. Eddison and Mervyn Peake and L. Frank Baum, H. P. Lovecraft and Robert E. Howard and J. R. R. Tolkien, to name a few of the best-known ones – kept the world well supplied with wondrous tales of the fantastic.

One change of tone did occur in the twentieth century, though, with the rise to popularity of science fiction – the branch of fantasy that applies immense ingenuity to the task of making the impossible, or at least the implausible, seem altogether probable. As science fiction – which was given its essential nature well over a hundred years ago by Jules Verne and H. G. Wells, and developed in modern times by such writers as Robert A. Heinlein, Isaac Asimov and Aldous Huxley – came to exert its immense appeal on the atomic-age reading public – 'pure' fantasy fiction, that is, fantasy that makes no attempt at empirical explanation of its wonders – came to be thought of as something largely reserved for children, like myths and fairy tales.

The older kind of fantasy never disappeared, of course. But in the United States, at least, it went into eclipse for nearly fifty years. Science fiction, meanwhile, manifested itself to the reading public in the form of magazines with names like *Amazing Stories* and *Astounding Science Fiction* and readerships composed largely of boys and earnest young men with an interest in gadgets and scientific disputation. The only American magazine dealing in the material we define as fantasy fiction was *Weird Tales*, founded in 1923, but that magazine published not only fantasy but a great many other kinds of genre fiction that might not be thought of as fantasy today – tales of pure terror, for example, with no speculative content.

The separation between fantasy and science fiction is not always easy to locate, but some distinctions are fairly clear-cut, if not entirely rigid. Stories that deal with androids and robots, spaceships, alien beings, time machines, viruses from outer space, galactic empires, and the like, usually can be described as science fiction. These are all matters that are *conceptually possible* within the framework of scientific law as we currently understand it. (Although such things as time machines and faster-than-light vehicles certainly stretch that framework to its limits, and perhaps beyond them.) Fantasy, meanwhile, uses as its material that which is *generally believed to be impossible or nonexistent* in our culture: wizards and warlocks, elves and goblins, werewolves and vampires, unicorns and enchanted princesses, efficacious incantations and spells.

Fantasy fiction *per se* did not have a real magazine of its own until 1939, when John W. Campbell, Jr, the foremost science-fiction editor of his time, brought *Unknown* (later called *Unknown Worlds*) into being in order to allow his writers greater imaginative latitude than his definitions of science fiction would permit. Many of the same writers who had turned Campbell's *Astounding Science Fiction* into the most notable magazine of its type yet published – Robert A. Heinlein, L. Sprague de Camp, Theodore Sturgeon, Lester del Rey, Jack Williamson – also became mainstays of *Unknown*, and the general structural approach was similar: postulate a far-out idea and develop all its consequences to a logical conclusion. The stories about being nasty to water gnomes or selling your soul to the devil wound up in *Unknown*; those about travelling in time or voyaging to distant planets were published in *Astounding*.

But *Unknown*, though it was cherished with great fondness by its readers and writers, never attained much of a public following, and when wartime paper shortages forced Campbell to choose between his two magazines in 1943, *Unknown* was swiftly killed, never to reappear. Postwar attempts by nostalgic ex-contributors to *Unknown* to recapture its special flavour were largely unsuccessful; H. L. Gold's *Beyond* lasted ten issues, Lester del Rey's *Fantasy Fiction* managed only four. Only *The Magazine of Fantasy*, edited by Anthony Boucher and J. Francis McComas, succeeded in establishing itself as a permanent entity, and even that magazine found it wisest to change its name to *Fantasy and Science Fiction* with its second issue. When science fiction became a fixture of paperback publishing in the 1950s, fantasy once again lagged behind: few fantasy novels were paperbacked, and most of them – Jack Vance's *The Dying Earth* and the early reprints of H. P. Lovecraft and Robert E. Howard are good examples – quickly vanished from view and became collector's items.

It all began to change in the late 1960s, when the sudden availability of paperback editions of J. R. R. Tolkien's *Lord of the Rings* trilogy (previously kept from paperback by an unwilling hardcover publisher) aroused a hunger for fantasy fiction in millions of readers that has, so far, been insatiable. Tolkien's books were such an emphatic commercial success that publishers rushed to find writers who could produce imitative trilogies, and the world was flooded with huge Hobbitesque novels, many of which sold in extraordinary quantities themselves. Robert Howard's *Conan* novels, once admired only by a small band of ardent cultists, began to win vast numbers of new readers about the same time. And a few years later Ballantine Books, Tolkien's paperback publishers, brought out an extraordinary series of books in its Adult Fantasy series, edited by Lin Carter, which made all the elegant classic masterpieces of such fantasists as E. R. Eddison, James Branch Cabell, Lord Dunsany and Mervyn Peake available to modern readers. And, ever since, fantasy has been a dominant factor in modern publishing. What had been a neglected step-sibling of science fiction fifty years ago is, today, an immensely popular genre.

In the wake of the great success of the Tolkien trilogy, newer writers have come along with their own deeply imagined worlds of fantasy, and have captured large and enthusiastic audiences themselves. In the late 1960s, Ursula Le Guin began her searching and sensitive Earthsea series, and Anne McCaffrey co-opted the ancient fantastic theme of the dragon for her Pern novels, which live on the borderline between fantasy and science fiction. Stephen King, some years later, won a readership of astounding magnitude by plumbing the archetypical fears of humanity and transforming them into powerful novels that occupied fantasy's darker terrain. Terry Pratchett, on the other hand, has magnificently demonstrated the comic power of satiric fantasy. Such writers as Orson Scott Card and Raymond E. Feist have won huge followings for their Alvin Maker and Riftwar books. More recently Robert Jordan's mammoth Wheel of Time series, George R. R. Martin's Song of Ice and Fire books, and Terry Goodkind's Sword of Truth tales have taken their place in the pantheon of modern fantasy, as has Tad Williams' Memory, Sorrow and Thorn series.

And here is the whole bunch of them, brought together in one huge anthology in which fantasy enthusiasts can revel for weeks. A new Earthsea story, a new tale of Pern, a new Dark Tower adventure, a new segment in Pratchett's playful Discworld series, and all the rest that you'll find herein – there has never been a book like this before. Gathering such an elite collection of first-magnitude stars into a single volume has not been an easy task. My gratitude herewith for the special assistance of Martin H. Greenberg, Ralph Vicinanza, Stephen King, John Helfers and Virginia Kidd, who in one way or another made my editorial task immensely less difficult than it otherwise would have been. And, too, although it goes without saying that I'm grateful to my wife, Karen, for her inestimable help in every phase of this intricate project, I think I'll say it anyway – not just because she's a terrific person, but because she came up with what unquestionably was the smartest idea of the whole enterprise.

Robert Silverberg
December 1997

THE DARK TOWER

STEPHEN KING

THE DARK TOWER

STEPHEN KING

The Gunslinger (1982)
The Drawing of the Three (1987)
The Waste Lands (1991)
Wizard and Glass (1997)

These novels, using thematic elements from Robert Browning's poem *'Childe Roland to the Dark Tower Came'*, tell the saga of Roland, last of the gunslingers, who embarks on a quest to find the Dark Tower for reasons that the author has yet to reveal. Along the way, Roland encounters the remains of what was once a thriving society, feudal in nature but technologically quite advanced, that now has fallen into decay and ruin. King combines elements of fantasy with science fiction into a surreal blend of past and future.

The first book, *The Gunslinger*, introduces Roland, who is chasing the Dark Man, an enigmatic sorcerer figure, across a vast desert. Through flashbacks, the reader learns that Roland was a member of a noble family in the Dark Tower world, and that that world may or may not have been destroyed with help from the Dark Man. Along the way, Roland encounters strange inhabitants of this unnamed world, including Jake, a young boy who, even though he is killed by the end of the first book, will figure prominently in later volumes. Roland does catch up with the Dark Man, and learns that he must seek out the Dark Tower to find the answers to the questions of why he must embark on this quest and what is contained in the Tower.

The next book, *The Drawing of the Three*, shows Roland

recruiting three people from present-day Earth to join him on his way to the Dark Tower. They are Eddie, a junkie 'mule' working for the Mafia; Suzannah, a paraplegic with multiple personalities; and Jake, whose arrival is startling to Roland, who sacrificed Jake in his own world during his pursuit of the Dark Man. Roland saves Jake's life on Earth, but the resulting schism nearly drives him insane. Roland must also help the other two battle their own demons, Eddie's being his heroin addiction and guilt over not being able to save his brother's life, and Suzannah's the war between her different personalities, one a kind and gentle woman, the other a racist psychopath. Each of the three deals with their problems with the help of the others, and together the quartet set out on the journey to the Tower.

The third book, *The Waste Lands*, chronicles the first leg of that journey, examining the background of the three Earth-born characters in detail. The book reaches its climax when Jake is kidnapped by a cult thriving in the ruins of a crumbling city, led by a man known only as Flagg (a character who has appeared in several of King's other novels as the embodiment of pure evil). Roland rescues Jake and the group escapes the city on a monorail system whose artificial intelligence program has achieved sentience at the cost of its sanity. The monorail challenges them to a riddle-contest, with their lives as the prize if they can stump the machine, who claims to know every riddle ever created.

Wizard and Glass, the fourth volume in the series, finds Roland, Jake, Eddie and Suzannah continuing their journey towards the Dark Tower, moving through a deserted part of Mid-World that is eerily reminiscent of twentieth-century Earth. During their travels they encounter a *thinny*, a dangerous weakening of the barrier between different times and places. Roland recognizes it and realizes that his world is breaking down faster than he had thought. The *thinny* prompts him to recall the first time he encountered it, many years before on a trip out west with his friends Cuthbert and Alain, when Roland had just earned his gunslinger status. It is this story – of the three boys uncovering a plot against the ruling government and of Roland's first love, a girl named Susan Delgado – that is the central focus of the book. While the three manage to destroy the conspirators, Susan is killed during the fight by the townspeople of Hambry. The story gives Jake, Eddie and Suzannah new insight into Roland's background and why he may sacrifice them to attain his ultimate goal of saving his world. The book ends with the foursome moving onward once more towards the Tower.

◆

THE LITTLE SISTERS
OF ELURIA

BY STEPHEN KING

[Author's Note: The Dark Tower books begin with Roland of Gilead, the last gunslinger in an exhausted world that has 'moved on', pursuing a magician in a black robe. Roland has been chasing Walter for a very long time. In the first book of the cycle, he finally catches up. This story, however, takes place while Roland is still casting about for Walter's trail. A knowledge of the books is therefore not necessary for you to understand – and hopefully enjoy – the story which follows. S.K.]

I. Full Earth. The Empty Town. The Bells. The Dead Boy. The Overturned Wagon. The Green Folk.

On a day in Full Earth so hot that it seemed to suck the breath from his chest before his body could use it, Roland of Gilead came to the gates of a village in the Desatoya Mountains. He was travelling alone by then, and would soon be travelling afoot, as well. This whole last week he had been hoping for a horse-doctor, but guessed such a fellow would do him no good now, even if this town had one. His mount, a two-year-old roan, was pretty well done for.

The town gates, still decorated with flowers from some festival or other, stood open and welcoming, but the silence beyond them was all wrong. The gunslinger heard no clip-clop of horses, no rumble of wagon-wheels, no merchants' huckstering cries from the marketplace. The only sounds were the low hum of crickets (some sort of bug, at any rate; they were a bit more tuneful than crickets, at that), a queer wooden knocking sound, and the faint, dreamy tinkle of small bells.

Also, the flowers twined through the wrought-iron staves of the ornamental gate were long dead.

Between his knees, Topsy gave two great, hollow sneezes – *K'chow! K'chow!* – and staggered sideways. Roland dismounted, partly out of respect for the horse, partly out of respect for himself – he didn't want to break a leg under Topsy if Topsy chose this moment to give up and canter into the clearing at the end of his path.

The gunslinger stood in his dusty boots and faded jeans under the beating sun, stroking the roan's matted neck, pausing every now and then to yank his fingers through the tangles of Topsy's mane, and stopping once to shoo off the tiny flies clustering at the corners of Topsy's eyes. Let them lay their eggs and hatch their maggots there after Topsy was dead, but not before.

Roland thus honoured his horse as best he could, listening to those distant, dreamy bells and the strange wooden tocking sound as he did. After a while he ceased his absent grooming and looked thoughtfully at the open gate.

The cross above its centre was a bit unusual, but otherwise the gate was a typical example of its type, a western commonplace which was not useful but traditional – all the little towns he had come to in the last tenmonth seemed to have one such where you came in (grand) and one more such where you went out (not so grand). None had been built to exclude visitors, certainly not this one. It stood between two walls of pink adobe that ran into the scree for a distance of about twenty feet on either side of the road and then simply stopped. Close the gate, lock it with many locks, and all that meant was a short walk around one bit of adobe wall or the other.

Beyond the gate, Roland could see what looked in most respects like a perfectly ordinary High Street – an inn, two saloons (one of which was called The Bustling Pig; the sign over the other was too faded to read), a mercantile, a smithy, a Gathering Hall. There was also a small but rather lovely wooden building with a modest bell-tower on top, a sturdy fieldstone foundation on bottom, and a gold-painted cross on its double doors. The cross, like the one over the gate, marked this as a worshipping place for those who held to the Jesus-man. This wasn't a common religion in Mid-World, but far from unknown; that same thing could have been said about most forms of worship in those days, including the worship of Baal, Asmodeus, and a hundred others. Faith, like everything else in the world these days, had moved on. As far as Roland was concerned, God o' the Cross was just another religion which taught that love and murder were inextricably bound together – that in the end, God always drank blood.

Meanwhile, there was the singing hum of insects which sounded *almost* like crickets. The dreamlike tinkle of the bells. And that queer wooden thumping, like a fist on a door. Or on a coffin top.

Something here's a long way from right, the gunslinger thought. *'Ware, Roland; this place has a reddish odour.*

He led Topsy through the gate with its adornments of dead flowers and down the High Street. On the porch of the mercantile, where the old men should have congregated to discuss crops, politics, and the follies of the younger generation, there stood only a line of empty rockers. Lying beneath one, as if dropped from a careless (and long-departed) hand, was a charred corncob pipe. The hitching-rack in front of The Bustling Pig stood empty; the windows of the saloon itself were dark. One of the batwing doors had been yanked off and stood propped against the side of the building; the other hung ajar, its faded green slats splattered with maroon stuff that might have been paint but probably wasn't.

The shopfront of the livery stable stood intact, like the face of a ruined woman who has access to good cosmetics, but the double barn behind it was a charred skeleton. That fire must have happened on a rainy day, the gunslinger thought, or the whole damned town would have gone up in flames; a jolly spin and raree for anyone around to see it.

To his right now, halfway up to where the street opened into the town square, was the church. There were grassy borders on both sides, one separating the church from the town's Gathering Hall, the other from the little house set aside for the preacher and his family (if this was one of the Jesus-sects which allowed its shamans to have wives and families, that was; some of them, clearly administered by lunatics, demanded at least the appearance of celibacy). There were flowers in these grassy strips, and while they looked parched, most were still alive. So whatever had happened here to empty the place out had not happened long ago. A week, perhaps. Two at the outside, given the heat.

Topsy sneezed again – *K'chow!* – and lowered his head wearily.

The gunslinger saw the source of the tinkling. Above the cross on the church doors, a cord had been strung in a long, shallow arc. Hung from it were perhaps two dozen tiny silver bells. There was hardly any breeze today, but enough so these small bells were never quite still . . . and if a real wind should rise, Roland thought, the sound made by the tintinnabulation of the bells would probably be a good deal less pleasant; more like the strident parley of gossips' tongues.

'Hello!' Roland called, looking across the street at what a large false-fronted sign proclaimed to be the Good Beds Hotel. 'Hello, the town!'

No answer but the bells, the tunesome insects, and that odd wooden clunking. No answer, no movement . . . but there were folk here. Folk or *something*. He was being watched. The tiny hairs on the nape of his neck had stiffened.

Roland stepped onward, leading Topsy towards the centre of town, puffing up the unlaid High Street dust with each step. Forty paces further along, he stopped in front of a low building marked with a single curt word: LAW. The Sheriff's office (if they had such this far from the Inners) looked remarkably similar to the church – wooden boards stained a rather forbidding shade of dark brown above a stone foundation.

The bells behind him rustled and whispered.

He left the roan standing in the middle of the street and mounted the steps to the LAW office. He was very aware of the bells, the sun beating against his neck, and of the sweat trickling down his sides. The door was shut but unlocked. He opened it, then winced back, half-raising a hand as the heat trapped inside rushed out in a soundless gasp. If all the closed buildings were this hot inside, he mused, the livery barns would soon not be the only burned-out hulks. And with no rain to stop the flames (and certainly no volunteer fire department, not any more), the town would not be long for the face of the earth.

He stepped inside, trying to sip at the stifling air rather than taking deep breaths. He immediately heard the low drone of flies.

There was a single cell, commodious and empty, its barred door standing open. Filthy skin-shoes, one of the pair coming unsewn, lay beneath a bunk sodden with the same dried maroon stuff which had marked The Bustling Pig. Here was where the flies were, crawling over the stain, feeding from it.

On the desk was a ledger. Roland turned it towards him and read what was embossed upon its red cover:

REGISTRY OF MISDEEDS & REDRESS
IN THE YEARS OF OUR LORD
ELURIA

So now he knew the name of the town, at least – Eluria. Pretty, yet somehow ominous, as well. But any name would have seemed ominous, Roland supposed, given these circumstances. He turned to leave, and saw a closed door secured by a wooden bolt.

He went to it, stood before it for a moment, then drew one of the big revolvers he carried low on his hips. He stood a moment longer, head down, thinking (Cuthbert, his old friend, liked to say that the wheels inside Roland's head ground slow but exceedingly fine), and then retracted the bolt. He opened the door and immediately stood back, levelling his gun, expecting a body (Eluria's Sheriff, mayhap) to come tumbling into the room with his throat cut and his eyes gouged out, victim of a MISDEED in need of REDRESS –

Nothing.

Well, half a dozen stained jumpers which longer-term prisoners were probably required to wear, two bows, a quiver of arrows, an old, dusty motor, a rifle that had probably last been fired a hundred years ago, and a mop . . . but in the gunslinger's mind, all that came down to nothing. Just a storage closet.

He went back to the desk, opened the register, and leafed through it. Even the pages were warm, as if the book had been baked. In a way, he supposed it had been. If the High Street layout had been different, he might have expected a large number of religious offences to be recorded, but he wasn't surprised to find none here – if the Jesus-man church had coexisted with a couple of saloons, the churchfolk must have been fairly reasonable.

What Roland found were the usual petty offences, and a few not so petty – a murder, a horse-thieving, the Distressal of a Lady (which probably meant rape). The murderer had been removed to a place called Lexingworth to be hanged. Roland had never heard of it. One note towards the end read *Green folk sent hence*. It meant nothing to Roland. The most recent entry was this: *12/Fe/99. Chas. Freeborn, cattle-theef to be tryed.*

Roland wasn't familiar with the notation *12/Fe/99*, but as this was a long stretch from February, he supposed *Fe* might stand for Full Earth. In any case, the ink looked about as fresh as the blood on the bunk in the cell, and the gunslinger had a good idea that Chas. Freeborn, cattle-theef, had reached the clearing at the end of his path.

He went out into the heat and the lacy sound of bells. Topsy looked at Roland dully, then lowered his head again, as if there were something in the dust of the High Street which could be cropped. As if he would ever want to crop again, for that matter.

The gunslinger gathered up the reins, slapped the dust off them against the faded no-colour of his jeans, and continued on up the street. The wooden knocking sound grew steadily louder as he walked (he had not holstered his gun when leaving LAW, nor cared to holster it now), and as he neared the town square, which must have housed the Eluria market in more normal times, Roland at last saw movement.

On the far side of the square was a long watering trough, made of ironwood from the look (what some called 'seequoiah' out here), apparently fed in happier times from a rusty steel pipe which now jutted waterless above the trough's south end. Lolling over one side of this municipal oasis, about halfway down its length, was a leg clad in faded grey pants and terminating in a well-chewed cowboy boot.

The chewer was a large dog, perhaps two shades greyer than the corduroy pants. Under other circumstances, Roland supposed the mutt would have had the boot off long since, but perhaps the foot and lower calf inside it had swelled. In any case, the dog was well on its way to simply chewing the obstacle away. It would seize the boot and shake it back and forth. Every now and then the boot's heel would collide with the wooden side of the trough, producing another hollow knock. The gunslinger hadn't been so wrong to think of coffin tops after all, it seemed.

Why doesn't it just back off a few steps, jump into the trough, and have at him? Roland wondered. *No water coming out of the pipe, so it can't be afraid of drowning.*

Topsy uttered another of his hollow, tired sneezes, and when the dog lurched around in response, Roland understood why it was doing things the hard way. One of its front legs had been badly broken and crookedly mended. Walking would be a chore for it, jumping out of the question. On its chest was a patch of dirty white fur. Growing out of this patch was black fur in a roughly cruciform shape. A Jesus-dog, mayhap, hoping for a spot of afternoon communion.

There was nothing very religious about the snarl which began to wind out of its chest, however, or the roll of its rheumy eyes. It lifted its upper lip in a trembling sneer, revealing a goodish set of teeth.

'Light out,' Roland said. 'While you can.'

The dog backed up until its hindquarters were pressed against the chewed boot. It regarded the oncoming man fearfully, but clearly meant to stand its ground. The revolver in Roland's hand held no significance for it. The gunslinger wasn't surprised – he guessed the dog had never seen one, had no idea it was anything other than a club of some kind, which could only be thrown once.

'Hie on with you, now,' Roland said, but still the dog wouldn't move.

He should have shot it – it was no good to itself, and a dog that had acquired a taste for human flesh could be no good to anyone else – but he somehow didn't like to. Killing the only thing still living in this town (other than the singing bugs, that was) seemed like an invitation to bad luck.

He fired into the dust near the dog's good forepaw, the sound crashing into the hot day and temporarily silencing the insects. The dog *could* run, it seemed, although at a lurching trot that hurt Roland's eyes . . . and his heart, a little, too. It stopped at the far side of the square, by an overturned flatbed wagon (there looked to be more dried blood splashed on the freighter's side), and glanced back. It uttered a forlorn howl that raised the hairs on the nape of Roland's neck even further. Then it turned, skirted the wrecked wagon, and limped down a lane which opened between two of the stalls. This way towards Eluria's back gate, Roland guessed.

Still leading his dying horse, the gunslinger crossed the square to the ironwood trough and looked in.

The owner of the chewed boot wasn't a man but a boy who had just been beginning to get his man's growth – and that would have been quite a large growth indeed, Roland judged, even setting aside the bloating effects which had resulted from being immersed for some unknown length of time in nine inches of water simmering under a summer sun.

The boy's eyes, now just milky balls, stared blindly up at the gunslinger like the eyes of a statue. His hair appeared to be the white of old age, although that was the effect of the water; he had likely been a towhead. His clothes were those of a cowboy, although he couldn't have been much more than fourteen or sixteen. Around his neck, gleaming blearily in water that was slowly turning into a skin stew under the summer sun, was a gold medallion.

Roland reached into the water, not liking to but feeling a certain obligation. He wrapped his fingers around the medallion and pulled. The chain parted, and he lifted the thing, dripping, into the air.

He rather expected a Jesus-man sigil – what was called the crucifix or the rood – but a small rectangle hung from the chain, instead. The object looked like pure gold. Engraved into it was this legend:

James
Loved of Family, Loved of GOD

Roland, who had been almost too revolted to reach into the polluted water (as a younger man, he could never have brought himself to that), was now glad he'd done it. He might never run into any of those who had loved this boy, but he knew enough of *ka* to think it might be so. In any case, it was the right thing. So was giving the kid a decent burial . . . assuming, that was, he could get the body out of the trough without having it break apart inside the clothes.

Roland was considering this, trying to balance what might be his duty in this circumstance against his growing desire to get out of this town, when Topsy finally fell dead.

The roan went over with a creak of gear and a last whuffling groan as it hit the ground. Roland turned and saw eight people in the street, walking towards him in a line, like beaters who hope to flush out birds or drive small game. Their skin was waxy green. Folk wearing such skin would likely glow in the dark like ghosts. It was hard to tell their sex, and what could it matter – to them or anyone else? They were slow mutants, walking with the hunched deliberation of corpses reanimated by some arcane magic.

The dust had muffled their feet like carpet. With the dog banished, they might well have gotten within attacking distance if Topsy hadn't done Roland the favour of dying at such an opportune moment. No guns that Roland could see; they were armed with clubs. These were chair-legs and table-legs, for the most part, but Roland saw one that looked made rather than seized – it had a bristle of rusty nails sticking out of it, and he suspected it had once been the property of a saloon bouncer, possibly the one who kept school in The Bustling Pig.

Roland raised his pistol, aiming at the fellow in the centre of the line. Now he could hear the shuffle of their feet, and the wet snuffle of their breathing. As if they all had bad chest-colds.

Came out of the mines, most likely, Roland thought. *There are radium mines somewhere about. That would account for the skin. I wonder that the sun doesn't kill them.*

Then, as he watched, the one on the end – a creature with a face like melted candle-wax – *did* die . . . or collapsed, at any rate. He (Roland was quite sure it was a male) went to his knees with a low, gobbling cry, groping for the hand of the thing walking next to him – something with a lumpy bald head and red sores sizzling on its neck. This creature took no notice of its fallen companion, but kept its dim eyes on Roland, lurching along in rough step with its remaining companions.

'Stop where you are!' Roland said. ''Ware me, if you'd live to see day's end! 'Ware me very well!'

He spoke mostly to the one in the centre, who wore ancient red suspenders over rags of shirt, and a filthy bowler hat. This gent had only one good eye, and it peered at the gunslinger with a greed as horrible as it was unmistakable. The one beside Bowler Hat (Roland believed this one might be a woman, with the dangling vestiges of breasts beneath the vest it wore) threw the chair-leg it held. The arc was true, but the missile fell ten yards short.

Roland thumbed back the trigger of his revolver and fired again. This time the dirt displaced by the slug kicked up on the tattered remains of Bowler Hat's shoe instead of on a lame dog's paw.

The green folk didn't run as the dog had, but they stopped, staring at him with their dull greed. Had the missing folk of Eluria finished up in these creatures' stomachs? Roland couldn't believe it . . . although he knew perfectly well that such as these held no scruple against cannibalism. (And perhaps it wasn't cannibalism, not really; how could such things as these be considered human, whatever they might once have been?) They were too slow, too stupid. If they had dared come back into town after the Sheriff had run them out, they would have been burned or stoned to death.

Without thinking about what he was doing, wanting only to free his other hand to draw his second gun if the apparitions didn't see reason, Roland stuffed the medallion which he had taken from the dead boy into the pocket of his jeans, pushing the broken fine-link chain in after.

They stood staring at him, their strangely twisted shadows drawn out behind them. What next? Tell them to go back where they'd come from? Roland didn't know if they'd do it, and in any case had decided he liked them best where he could see them. And at least there was no question now about staying to bury the boy named James; that conundrum had been solved.

'Stand steady,' he said in the low speech, beginning to retreat. 'First fellow that moves –'

Before he could finish, one of them – a thick-chested troll with a pouty toad's mouth and what looked like gills on the sides of his wattled neck – lunged forward, gibbering in a high-pitched and peculiarly flabby voice. It might have been a species of laughter. He was waving what looked like a piano-leg.

Roland fired. Mr Toad's chest caved in like a bad piece of roofing. He ran backwards several steps, trying to catch his balance and clawing at his chest with the hand not holding the piano-leg. His feet, clad in dirty red velvet slippers with curled-up toes, tangled in each other and he fell over, making a queer and somehow lonely gargling sound. He let go of his club, rolled over on one side, tried to rise, and then fell back into the dust. The brutal sun glared into his open eyes, and as Roland watched, white tendrils of steam began to rise from his skin, which was rapidly losing its green undertint. There was also a hissing sound, like a gob of spit on top of a hot stove.

Saves explaining, at least, Roland thought, and swept his eyes over the others. 'All right; he was the first one to move. Who wants to be the second?'

None did, it seemed. They only stood there, watching him, not coming at him . . . but not retreating, either. He thought (as he had about the crucifix-dog) that he should kill them as they stood there, just draw his other gun and mow them down. It would be the work of seconds only, and child's play to his gifted hands, even if some ran. But he couldn't. Not just cold, like that. He wasn't that kind of killer . . . at least, not yet.

Very slowly, he began to step backwards, first bending his course around the watering trough, then putting it between him and them. When Bowler Hat took a step forward, Roland didn't give the others in the line a chance to copy him; he put a bullet into the dust of High Street an inch in advance of Bowler Hat's foot.

'That's your last warning,' he said, still using the low speech. He had no idea if they understood it, didn't really care. He guessed they caught this tune's music well enough. 'Next bullet I fire eats up someone's heart. The way it works is, you stay and I go. You get this one chance. Follow me, and you all die. It's too hot to play games and I've lost my –'

'Booh!' cried a rough, liquidy voice from behind him. There was unmistakable glee in it. Roland saw a shadow grow from the shadow of the overturned freight wagon, which he had now almost reached, and had just time to understand that another of the green folk had been hiding beneath it.

As he began to turn, a club crashed down on Roland's shoulder, numbing his right arm all the way to the wrist. He held on to the gun and fired once, but the bullet went into one of the wagon-wheels, smashing a wooden spoke and turning the wheel on its hub with a high screeching sound. Behind him, he heard the green folk in the street uttering hoarse, yapping cries as they charged forward.

The thing which had been hiding beneath the overturned wagon was a monster with two heads growing out of his neck, one with the vestigial, slack face of a corpse. The other, although just as green, was more lively. Broad lips spread in a cheerful grin as he raised his club to strike again.

Roland drew with his left hand – the one that wasn't numbed and distant. He had time to put one bullet through the bush-whacker's grin, flinging him backwards in a spray of blood and teeth, the bludgeon flying out of his relaxing fingers. Then the others were on him, clubbing and drubbing.

The gunslinger was able to slip the first couple of blows, and there was one moment when he thought he might be able to spin around to the rear of the overturned wagon, spin and turn and go to work with his guns. Surely he would be able to do that. Surely his quest for the Dark Tower wasn't supposed to end on the sun-blasted street of a little far-western town called Eluria, at the hands of half a dozen green-skinned slow mutants. Surely *ka* could not be so cruel.

But Bowler Hat caught him with a vicious sidehand blow, and Roland crashed into the wagon's slowly spinning rear wheel instead of skirting around it. As he went to his hands and knees, still scrambling and trying to turn, trying to evade the blows which rained down on him, he saw there were now many more than half a dozen. Coming up the street towards the town square were at least thirty green men and women. This wasn't a clan but a damned *tribe* of them. And in broad, hot daylight! Slow mutants were, in his experience, creatures that loved the dark, almost like toadstools with brains, and he had never seen any such as these before. They –

The one in the red vest *was* female. Her bare breasts swinging beneath the dirty red vest were the last things he saw clearly as they gathered around and above him, bashing away with their clubs. The one with the nails studded in it came down on his lower right calf, sinking its stupid rusty fangs in deep. He tried again to raise one of the big guns (his vision was fading, now, but that wouldn't help them if he got to shooting; he had always been the most hellishly talented of them; Jamie DeCurry had once proclaimed that Roland could shoot blindfolded, because he had eyes in his fingers), and it was kicked out of his hand and into the dust. Although he could still feel the smooth sandalwood grip of the other, he thought it was nevertheless already gone.

He could smell them – the rich, rotted smell of decaying meat. Or was that only his hands, as he raised them in a feeble and useless effort to protect his head? His hands, which had been in the polluted water where flecks and strips of the dead boy's skin floated?

The clubs slamming down on him, slamming down all over him, as if the green folk wanted not just to beat him to death but to tenderize him as they did so. And as he went down into the darkness of what he most certainly believed would be his death, he heard the bugs singing, the dog he had spared barking, and the bells hung on the church door ringing. These sounds merged together into strangely sweet music. Then that was gone, too; the darkness ate it all.

II. Rising. Hanging Suspended. White Beauty. Two Others. The Medallion.

The gunslinger's return to the world wasn't like coming back to consciousness after a blow, which he'd done several times before, and it wasn't like waking from sleep, either. It was like rising.

I'm dead, he thought at some point during this process . . . when the power to think had been at least partially restored to him. *Dead and rising into whatever afterlife there is. That's what it must be. The singing I hear is the singing of dead souls.*

Total blackness gave way to the dark grey of rainclouds, then to the lighter grey of fog. This brightened to the uniform clarity of a heavy mist moments before the sun breaks through. And through it all was that sense of *rising*, as if he had been caught in some mild but powerful updraught.

As the sense of rising began to diminish and the brightness behind his eyelids grew, Roland at last began to believe he was still alive. It was the singing that convinced him. Not dead souls, not the heavenly host of angels sometimes described by the

Jesus-man preachers, but only those bugs. A little like crickets, but sweeter-voiced. The ones he had heard in Eluria.

On this thought, he opened his eyes.

His belief that he was still alive was severely tried, for Roland found himself hanging suspended in a world of white beauty – his first bewildered thought was that he was in the sky, floating within a fair-weather cloud. All around him was the reedy singing of the bugs. Now he could hear the tinkling of bells, too.

He tried to turn his head and swayed in some sort of harness. He could hear it creaking. The soft singing of the bugs, like crickets in the grass at the end of day back home in Gilead, hesitated and broke rhythm. When it did, what felt like a tree of pain grew up Roland's back. He had no idea what its burning branches might be, but the trunk was surely his spine. A far deadlier pain sank into one of his lower legs – in his confusion, the gunslinger could not tell which one. *That's where the club with the nails in it got me*, he thought. And more pain in his head. His skull felt like a badly cracked egg. He cried out, and could hardly believe that the harsh crow's caw he heard came from his own throat. He thought he could also hear, very faintly, the barking of the cross-dog, but surely that was his imagination.

Am I dying? Have I awakened once more at the very end?

A hand stroked his brow. He could feel it but not see it – fingers trailing across his skin, pausing here and there to massage a knot or a line. Delicious, like a drink of cool water on a hot day. He began to close his eyes, and then a horrible idea came to him: suppose that hand were green, its owner wearing a tattered red vest over her hanging dugs?

What if it is? What could you do?

'Hush, man,' a young woman's voice said . . . or perhaps it was the voice of a girl. Certainly the first person Roland thought of was Susan, the girl from Mejis, she who had spoken to him as *thee*.

'Where . . . where . . .'

'Hush, stir not. 'Tis far too soon.'

The pain in his back was subsiding now, but the image of the pain as a tree remained, for his very skin seemed to be moving like leaves in a light breeze. How could that be?

He let the question go – let all questions go – and concentrated on the small, cool hand stroking his brow.

'Hush, pretty man, God's love be upon ye. Yet it's sore hurt ye are. Be still. Heal.'

The dog had hushed its barking (if it had ever been there in the first place), and Roland became aware of that low, creaking sound again. It reminded him of horse-tethers, or something – *hangropes* – he didn't like to think of. Now he believed he could feel pressure beneath his thighs, his buttocks, and perhaps . . . yes . . . his shoulders.

I'm not in a bed at all. I think I'm above *a bed. Can that be?*

He supposed he could be in a sling. He seemed to remember once, as a boy, that some fellow had been suspended that way in the horse-doctor's room behind the Great Hall. A stablehand who had been burned too badly by kerosene to be laid in a bed. The man had died, but not soon enough; for two nights, his shrieks had filled the sweet summer air of the Gathering Fields.

Am I burned, then, nothing but a cinder with legs, hanging in a sling?

The fingers touched the centre of his brow, rubbing away the frown forming there. And it was as if the voice which went with the hand had read his thoughts, picking them up with the tips of her clever, soothing fingers.

'Ye'll be fine if God wills, sai,' the voice which went with the hand said. 'But time belongs to God, not to you.'

No, he would have said, if he had been able. *Time belongs to the Tower.*

Then he slipped down again, descending as smoothly as he had risen, going away from the hand and the dreamlike sounds of the singing insects and chiming bells. There was an interval that might have been sleep, or perhaps unconsciousness, but he never went all the way back down.

At one point he thought he heard the girl's voice, although he couldn't be sure, because this time it was raised in fury, or fear, or both. 'No!' she cried. 'Ye can't have it off him and ye know it! Go your course and stop talking of it, do!'

When he rose back to consciousness the second time, he was no stronger in body, but a little more himself in mind. What he saw when he opened his eyes wasn't the inside of a cloud, but at first that same phrase – *white beauty* – recurred to him. It was in some ways the most beautiful place Roland had ever been in his life . . . partially because he still *had* a life, of course, but mostly because it was so fey and peaceful.

It was a huge room, high and long. When Roland at last turned his head – cautiously, so cautiously – to take its measure as well as he could, he thought it must run at least two hundred yards from end to end. It was built narrow, but its height gave the place a feeling of tremendous airiness.

There were no walls or ceilings such as those he was familiar with, although it was a little like being in a vast tent. Above him, the sun struck and diffused its light across billowy panels of thin white silk, turning them into the bright swags which he had first mistaken for clouds. Beneath this silk canopy, the room was as grey as twilight. The walls, also silk, rippled like sails in a faint breeze. Hanging from each wall-panel was a curved rope bearing small bells. These lay against the fabric and rang in low and charming unison, like wind-chimes, when the walls rippled.

An aisle ran down the centre of the long room; on either side of it were scores of beds, each made up with clean white sheets and headed with crisp white pillows. There were perhaps forty on the far side of the aisle, all empty, and another forty on Roland's side. There were two other occupied beds here, one next to Roland on his left. This fellow –

It's the boy. The one who was in the trough.

The idea ran goosebumps up Roland's arms and gave him a nasty, superstitious start. He peered more closely at the sleeping boy.

Can't be. You're just dazed, that's all; it can't be.

Yet closer scrutiny refused to dispel the idea. It certainly *seemed* to be the boy from the trough, probably ill (why else would he be in a place like this?) but far from dead; Roland could see the slow rise and fall of his chest, and the occasional twitch of the fingers which dangled over the side of the bed.

You didn't get a good enough look at him to be sure of anything, and after a few days in that trough, his own mother couldn't have said for sure who it was.

But Roland, who'd had a mother, knew better than that. He also knew that he'd seen the gold medallion around the boy's neck. Just before the attack of the green folk, he had taken it from this lad's corpse and put it in his pocket. Now someone – the proprietors of this place, most likely, they who had sorcerously restored the lad named James to his interrupted life – had taken it back from Roland and put it around the boy's neck again.

Had the girl with the wonderfully cool hand done that? Did she in consequence think Roland a ghoul who would steal from the dead? He didn't like to think so. In fact, the notion made him more uncomfortable than the idea that the young cowboy's bloated body had been somehow returned to its normal size and then reanimated.

Further down the aisle on this side, perhaps a dozen empty beds away from the boy and Roland Deschain, the gunslinger saw a third inmate of this queer infirmary. This fellow looked at least four times the age of the lad, twice the age of the gunslinger. He had a long beard, more grey than black, that hung to his upper chest in two straggly forks. The face above it was sun-darkened, heavily lined, and pouched beneath the eyes. Running from his left cheek and across the bridge of his nose was a thick dark mark which Roland took to be a scar. The bearded man was either asleep or unconscious – Roland could hear him snoring – and was suspended three feet above his bed, held up by a complex series of white belts that glimmered in the dim air. These crisscrossed each other, making a series of figure eights all the way around the man's body. He looked like a bug in some exotic spider's web. He wore a gauzy white bed-dress. One of the belts ran beneath his buttocks, elevating his crotch in a way that seemed to offer the bulge of his privates to the grey and dreaming air. Further down his body, Roland could see the dark shadow-shapes of his legs. They appeared to be twisted like ancient dead trees. Roland didn't like to think in how many places they must have been broken to look like that. And yet they appeared to be *moving*. How could they be, if the bearded man was unconscious? It was a trick of the light, perhaps, or of the shadows . . . perhaps the gauzy singlet the man was wearing was stirring in a light breeze, or . . .

Roland looked away, up at the billowy silk panels high above, trying to control the accelerating beat of his heart. What he saw hadn't been caused by the wind, or a shadow, or anything else. The man's legs were somehow moving without moving . . . as Roland had seemed to feel his own back moving without moving. He didn't know what could cause such a phenomenon, and didn't want to know, at least not yet.

'I'm not ready,' he whispered. His lips felt very dry. He closed his eyes again, wanting to sleep, wanting not to think about what the bearded man's twisted legs might indicate about his own condition. But –

But you'd better get ready.

That was the voice that always seemed to come when he tried to slack off, to scamp a job, or take the easy way around an obstacle. It was the voice of Cort, his old teacher. The man whose stick they had all feared, as boys. They hadn't feared his stick as much as his mouth, however. His jeers when they were weak, his contempt when they complained or tried whining about their lot.

Are you a gunslinger, Roland? If you are, you better get ready.

Roland opened his eyes again and turned his head to the left again. As he did, he felt something shift against his chest.

Moving very slowly, he raised his right hand out of the sling that held it. The pain in his back stirred and muttered. He stopped moving until he decided the pain was going to get no worse (if he was careful, at least), then lifted the hand the rest of the way to his chest. It encountered finely-woven cloth. Cotton. He lowered his chin to his breastbone and saw he was wearing a bed-dress like the one draped on the body of the bearded man.

Roland reached beneath the neck of the gown and felt a

fine chain. A little further down, his fingers encountered a rectangular metal shape. He thought he knew what it was, but had to be sure. He pulled it out, still moving with great care, trying not to engage any of the muscles in his back. A gold medallion. He dared the pain, lifting it until he could read what was engraved upon it:

James
Loved of family, Loved of GOD

He tucked it into the top of the bed-dress again and looked back at the sleeping boy in the next bed – *in* it, not suspended over it. The sheet was only pulled up to the boy's ribcage, and the medallion lay on the pristine white breast of his bed-dress. The same medallion Roland now wore. Except . . .

Roland thought he understood, and understanding was a relief.

He looked back at the bearded man, and saw an exceedingly strange thing: the thick black line of scar across the bearded man's cheek and nose was gone. Where it had been was the pinkish-red mark of a healing wound . . . a cut, or perhaps a slash.

I imagined it.

No, gunslinger, Cort's voice returned. *Such as you was not made to imagine. As you well know.*

The little bit of movement had tired him out again . . . or perhaps it was the thinking which had really tired him out. The singing bugs and chiming bells combined and made something too much like a lullaby to resist. This time when Roland closed his eyes, he slept.

III. Five Sisters. Jenna. The Doctors of Eluria.
The Medallion. A Promise of Silence.

When Roland awoke again, he was at first sure that he was still sleeping. Dreaming. Having a nightmare.

Once, at the time he had met and fallen in love with Susan Delgado, he had known a witch named Rhea – the first real witch of Mid-World he had ever met. It was she who had caused Susan's death, although Roland had played his own part. Now, opening his eyes and seeing Rhea not just once but five times over, he thought: *This is what comes of remembering those old times. By conjuring Susan, I've conjured Rhea of the Coos, as well. Rhea and her sisters.*

The five were dressed in billowing habits as white as the walls and the panels of the ceiling. Their antique crones' faces were framed in wimples just as white, their skin as grey and runnelled as droughted earth by comparison. Hanging like phylacteries from the bands of silk imprisoning their hair (if they indeed had hair) were lines of tiny bells which chimed as they moved or spoke. Upon the snowy breasts of their habits was embroidered a blood-red rose . . . the sigil of the Dark Tower. Seeing this, Roland thought: *I am not dreaming. These harridans are real.*

'He wakes!' one of them cried in a gruesomely coquettish voice.

'Oooo!'

'Ooooh!'

'Ah!'

They fluttered like birds. The one in the centre stepped forward, and as she did, their faces seemed to shimmer like the silk walls of the ward. They weren't old after all, he saw – middle-aged, perhaps, but not old.

Yes. They are *old. They changed.*

The one who now took charge was taller than the others, and with a broad, slightly bulging brow. She bent towards Roland, and the bells which fringed her forehead tinkled. The sound made him feel sick, somehow, and weaker than he had felt a moment before. Her hazel eyes were intent. Greedy, mayhap. She touched his cheek for a moment, and a numbness seemed to spread there. Then she glanced down, and a look which could have been disquiet cramped her face. She took her hand back.

'Ye wake, pretty man. So ye do. 'Tis well.'

'Who are you? Where am I?'

'We are the Little Sisters of Eluria,' she said. 'I am Sister Mary. Here is Sister Louise, and Sister Michela, and Sister Coquina –'

'And Sister Tamra,' said the last. 'A lovely lass of one-and-twenty.' She giggled. Her face shimmered, and for a moment she was again as old as the world. Hooked of nose, grey of skin. Roland thought once more of Rhea.

They moved closer, encircling the complication of harness in which he lay suspended, and when Roland shrank away, the pain roared up his back and injured leg again. He groaned. The straps holding him creaked.

'Ooooo!'

'It hurts!'

'Hurts him!'

'Hurts so fierce!'

They pressed even closer, as if his pain fascinated them. And now he could smell them, a dry and earthy smell. The one named Sister Michela reached out –

'Go away! Leave him! Have I not told ye before?'

They jumped back from this voice, startled. Sister Mary looked particularly annoyed. But she stepped back, with one final glare (Roland would have sworn it) at the medallion lying on his chest. He had tucked it back under the bed-dress at his last waking, but it was out again now.

A sixth sister appeared, pushing rudely in between Mary and Tamra. This one perhaps *was* only one-and-twenty, with flushed cheeks, smooth skin, and dark eyes. Her white habit billowed like a dream. The red rose over her breast stood out like a curse.

'Go! Leave him!'

'Oooo, my *dear!*' cried Sister Louise in a voice both laughing and angry. 'Here's Jenna, the baby, and has she fallen in love with him?'

'She has!' laughed Tamra. 'Baby's heart is his for the purchase!'

'Oh, so it *is!*' agreed Sister Coquina.

Mary turned to the newcomer, lips pursed into a tight line. 'Ye have no business here, saucy girl.'

'I do if I say I do,' Sister Jenna replied. She seemed more in charge of herself now. A curl of black hair had escaped her wimple and lay across her forehead in a comma. 'Now go. He's not up to your jokes and laughter.'

'Order us not,' Sister Mary said, 'for we never joke. So you know, Sister Jenna.'

The girl's face softened a little, and Roland saw she was afraid. It made him afraid for her. For himself, as well. 'Go,' she repeated. ''Tis not the time. Are there not others to tend?'

Sister Mary seemed to consider. The others watched her. At last she nodded, and smiled down at Roland. Again her face seemed to shimmer, like something seen through a heat-haze. What he saw (or thought he saw) beneath was horrible and watchful. 'Bide well, pretty man,' she said to Roland. 'Bide with us a bit, and we'll heal ye.'

What choice have I? Roland thought.

The others laughed, birdlike titters which rose into the dimness like ribbons. Sister Michela actually blew him a kiss.

'Come, ladies!' Sister Mary cried. 'We'll leave Jenna with him a bit in memory of her mother, who we loved well!' And with that, she led the others away, five white birds flying off down the centre aisle, their skirts nodding this way and that.

'Thank you,' Roland said, looking up at the owner of the cool hand . . . for he knew it was she who had soothed him.

She took up his fingers as if to prove this, and caressed them. 'They mean ye no harm,' she said . . . yet Roland saw she believed not a word of it, nor did he. He was in trouble here, very bad trouble.

'What is this place?'

'Our place,' she said simply. 'The home of the Little Sisters of Eluria. Our convent, if 'ee like.'

'This is no convent,' Roland said, looking past her at the empty beds. 'It's an infirmary. Isn't it?'

'A hospital,' she said, still stroking his fingers. 'We serve the doctors . . . and they serve us.' He was fascinated by the black curl lying on the cream of her brow – would have stroked it, if he had dared reach up. Just to tell its texture. He found it beautiful because it was the only dark thing in all this white.

The white had lost its charm for him. 'We are hospitallers . . . or were, before the world moved on.'

'Are you for the Jesus-man?'

She looked surprised for a moment, almost shocked, and then laughed merrily. 'No, not us!'

'If you are hospitallers . . . nurses . . . where are the doctors?'

She looked at him, biting at her lip, as if trying to decide something. Roland found her doubt utterly charming, and he realized that, sick or not, he was looking at a woman *as* a woman for the first time since Susan Delgado had died, and that had been long ago. The whole world had changed since then, and not for the better.

'Would you really know?'

'Yes, of course,' he said, a little surprised. A little disquieted, too. He kept waiting for her face to shimmer and change, as the faces of the others had done. It didn't. There was none of that unpleasant dead-earth smell about her, either.

Wait, he cautioned himself. *Believe nothing here, least of all your senses. Not yet.*

'I suppose you must,' she said with a sigh. It tinkled the bells at her forehead, which were darker in colour than those the others wore – not black like her hair but charry, somehow, as if they had been hung in the smoke of a campfire. Their sound, however, was brightest silver. 'Promise me you'll not scream and wake the pube in yonder bed.'

'Pube?'

'The boy. Do ye promise?'

'Aye,' he said, falling into the half-forgotten patois of the Outer Arc without even being aware of it. Susan's dialect. 'It's been long since I screamed, pretty.'

She coloured more definitely at that, roses more natural and lively than the one on her breast mounting in her cheeks.

'Don't call pretty what ye can't properly see,' she said.

'Then push back the wimple you wear.'

Her face he could see perfectly well, but he badly wanted to see her hair – hungered for it, almost. A full flood of black in all this dreaming white. Of course it might be cropped, those of her order might wear it that way, but he somehow didn't think so.

'No, 'tis not allowed.'

'By who?'

'Big Sister.'

'She who calls herself Mary?'

'Aye, her.' She started away, then paused and looked back over her shoulder. In another girl her age, one as pretty as this, that look back would have been flirtatious. This girl's was only grave. 'Remember your promise.'

'Aye, no screams.'

She went to the bearded man, skirt swinging. In the dimness, she cast only a blur of shadow on the empty beds she passed. When she reached the man (this one was unconscious, Roland thought, not just sleeping), she looked back at Roland once more. He nodded.

Sister Jenna stepped close to the suspended man on the far side of his bed, so that Roland saw her through the twists and loops of woven white silk. She placed her hands lightly on the left side of his chest, bent over him . . . and shook her head from side to side, like one expressing a brisk negative. The bells she wore on her forehead rang sharply, and Roland once more felt that weird stirring up his back, accompanied by a low ripple of pain. It was as if he had shuddered without actually shuddering, or shuddered in a dream.

What happened next almost *did* jerk a scream from him; he had to bite his lips against it. Once more the unconscious man's legs seemed to move without moving . . . because it was what was *on* them that moved. The man's hairy shins, ankles, and feet were exposed below the hem of his bed-dress. Now a black wave of bugs moved down them. They were singing fiercely, like an army column that sings as it marches.

Roland remembered the black scar across the man's cheek and nose – the scar which had disappeared. More such as these, of course. And they were on *him*, as well. That was how he could shiver without shivering. They were all over his back. *Battening* on him.

No, keeping back a scream wasn't as easy as he had expected it to be.

The bugs ran down to the tips of the suspended man's toes, then leaped off them in waves, like creatures leaping off an embankment and into a swimming hole. They organized themselves quickly and easily on the bright white sheet below, and began to march down to the floor in a battalion about a foot wide. Roland couldn't get a good look at them, the distance was too far and the light too dim, but he thought they were perhaps twice the size of ants, and a little smaller than the fat honeybees which had swarmed the flowerbeds back home.

They sang as they went.

The bearded man didn't sing. As the swarms of bugs which had coated his twisted legs began to diminish, he shuddered and groaned. The young woman put her hand on his brow and soothed him, making Roland a little jealous even in his revulsion at what he was seeing.

And was what he was seeing really so awful? In Gilead, leeches had been used for certain ailments – swellings of the brain, the armpits, and the groin, primarily. When it came to the brain, the leeches, ugly as they were, were certainly preferable to the next step, which was trepanning.

Yet there *was* something loathsome about them, perhaps only because he couldn't see them well, and something awful about trying to imagine them all over his back as he hung here, helpless. Not singing, though. Why? Because they were feeding? Sleeping? Both at once?

The bearded man's groans subsided. The bugs marched away across the floor, towards one of the mildly rippling silken walls. Roland lost sight of them in the shadows.

Jenna came back to him, her eyes anxious. 'Ye did well. Yet I see how ye feel; it's on your face.'

'The doctors,' he said.

'Yes. Their power is very great, but . . .' She dropped her voice. 'I believe that drover is beyond their help. His legs are a little better, and the wounds on his face are all but healed, but he has injuries where the doctors cannot reach.' She traced a hand across her midsection, suggesting the location of these injuries, if not their nature.

'And me?' Roland asked.

'Ye were ta'en by the green folk,' she said. 'Ye must have angered them powerfully, for them not to kill ye outright. They roped ye and dragged ye, instead. Tamra, Michela, and Louise were out gathering herbs. They saw the green folk at play with ye, and bade them stop, but –'

'Do the muties always obey you, Sister Jenna?'

She smiled, perhaps pleased he remembered her name. 'Not always, but mostly. This time they did, or ye'd have now found the clearing in the trees.'

'I suppose so.'

'The skin was stripped almost clean off your back – red ye were from nape to waist. Ye'll always bear the scars, but the doctors have gone far towards healing ye. And their singing is passing fair, is it not?'

'Yes,' Roland said, but the thought of those black things all over his back, roosting in his raw flesh, still revolted him. 'I owe you thanks, and give it freely. Anything I can do for you –'

'Tell me your name, then. Do that.'

'I'm Roland of Gilead. A gunslinger. I had revolvers, Sister Jenna. Have you seen them?'

'I've seen no shooters,' she said, but cast her eyes aside. The roses bloomed in her cheeks again. She might be a good nurse, and fair, but Roland thought her a poor liar. He was glad. Good liars were common. Honesty, on the other hand, came dear.

Let the untruth pass for now, he told himself. *She speaks it out of fear, I think.*

'Jenna!' The cry came from the deeper shadows at the far end of the infirmary – today it seemed longer than ever to the gunslinger – and Sister Jenna jumped guiltily. 'Come away! Ye've passed words enough to entertain twenty men! Let him sleep!'

'Aye!' she called, then turned back to Roland. 'Don't let on that I showed you the doctors.'

'Mum is the word, Jenna.'

She paused, biting her lip again, then suddenly swept back her wimple. It fell against the nape of her neck in a soft chiming of bells. Freed from its confinement, her hair swept against her cheeks like shadows.

'*Am* I pretty? *Am* I? Tell me the truth, Roland of Gilead – no flattery. For flattery's kind only a candle's length.'

'Pretty as a summer night.'

What she saw in his face seemed to please her more than his words, because she smiled radiantly. She pulled the wimple up again, tucking her hair back in with quick little finger-pokes. 'Am I decent?'

'Decent as fair,' he said, then cautiously lifted an arm and pointed at her brow. 'One curl's out . . . just there.'

'Aye, always that one to devil me.' With a comical little grimace, she tucked it back. Roland thought how much he would like to kiss her rosy cheeks . . . and perhaps her rosy mouth, for good measure.

'All's well,' he said.

'*Jenna!*' The cry was more impatient than ever. 'Meditations!'

'I'm coming just now!' she called, and gathered her voluminous skirts to go. Yet she turned back once more, her face now very grave and very serious. 'One more thing,' she said in a voice only a step above a whisper. She snatched a quick look around. 'The gold medallion ye wear – ye wear it because it's yours. Do'ee understand . . . James?'

'Yes.' He turned his head a bit to look at the sleeping boy. 'This is my brother.'

'If they ask, yes. To say different would be to get Jenna in serious trouble.'

How serious he did not ask, and she was gone in any case, seeming to flow along the aisle between all the empty beds, her skirt caught up in one hand. The roses had fled from her face, leaving her cheeks and brow ashy. He remembered the greedy look on the faces of the others, how they had gathered around him in a tightening knot . . . and the way their faces had shimmered.

Six women, five old and one young.

Doctors that sang and then crawled away across the floor when dismissed by jingling bells.

And an improbable hospital ward of perhaps a hundred beds, a ward with a silk roof and silk walls . . .

. . . and all the beds empty save three.

Roland didn't understand why Jenna had taken the dead boy's medallion from his pants pocket and put it around his neck, but he had an idea that if they found out she had done so, the Little Sisters of Eluria might kill her.

Roland closed his eyes, and the soft singing of the doctor-insects once again floated him off into sleep.

IV. A Bowl of Soup. The Boy in the Next Bed. The Night-Nurses.

Roland dreamed that a very large bug (a doctor-bug, mayhap) was flying around his head and banging repeatedly into his nose – collisions which were annoying rather than painful. He swiped at the bug repeatedly, and although his hands were eerily fast under ordinary circumstances, he kept missing it. And each time he missed, the bug giggled.

I'm slow because I've been sick, he thought.

No, ambushed. Dragged across the ground by slow mutants, saved by the Little Sisters of Eluria.

Roland had a sudden, vivid image of a man's shadow growing from the shadow of an overturned freight-wagon; heard a rough, gleeful voice cry, 'Booh!'

He jerked awake hard enough to set his body rocking in its complication of slings, and the woman who had been standing beside his head, giggling as she tapped his nose lightly with a wooden spoon, stepped back so quickly that the bowl in her other hand slipped from her fingers.

Roland's hands shot out, and they were as quick as ever – his frustrated failure to catch the bug had been only part of his dream. He caught the bowl before more than a few drops could spill. The woman – Sister Coquina – looked at him with round eyes.

There was pain all up and down his back from the sudden movement, but it was nowhere near as sharp as it had been before, and there was no sensation of movement on his skin. Perhaps the 'doctors' were only sleeping, but he had an idea they were gone.

He held out his hand for the spoon Coquina had been teasing him with (he found he wasn't surprised at all that one of these would tease a sick and sleeping man in such a way; it only would have surprised him if it had been Jenna), and she handed it to him, her eyes still big.

'How speedy ye are!' she said. ''Twas like a magic trick, and you still rising from sleep!'

'Remember it, sai,' he said, and tried the soup. There were tiny bits of chicken floating in it. He probably would have considered it bland under other circumstances, but under these, it seemed ambrosial. He began to eat greedily.

'What do 'ee mean by that?' she asked. The light was very dim now, the wall-panels across the way a pinkish-orange that suggested sunset. In this light, Coquina looked quite young and pretty . . . but it was a glamour, Roland was sure; a sorcerous kind of make-up.

'I mean nothing in particular.' Roland dismissed the spoon as too slow, preferring to tilt the bowl itself to his lips. In this way he disposed of the soup in four large gulps. 'You have been kind to me –'

'Aye, so we *have*!' she said, rather indignantly.

'– and I hope your kindness has no hidden motive. If it does, Sister, remember that I'm quick. And, as for myself, I have not always been kind.'

She made no reply, only took the bowl when Roland handed it back. She did this delicately, perhaps not wanting to touch his fingers. Her eyes dropped to where the medallion lay, once more hidden beneath the breast of his bed-dress. He said no more, not wanting to weaken the implied threat by reminding her that the man who made it was unarmed, next to naked, and hung in the air because his back couldn't yet bear the weight of his body.

'Where's Sister Jenna?' he asked.

'Oooo,' Sister Coquina said, raising her eyebrows. 'We like her, do we? She makes our heart go . . .' She put her hand against the rose on her breast and fluttered it rapidly.

'Not at all, not at all,' Roland said, 'but she was kind. I doubt she would have teased me with a spoon, as some would.'

Sister Coquina's smile faded. She looked both angry and worried. 'Say nothing of that to Mary, if she comes by later. Ye might get me in trouble.'

'Should I care?'

'I might get back at one who caused me trouble by causing little Jenna trouble,' Sister Coquina said. 'She's in Big Sister's black books, just now, anyway. Sister Mary doesn't care for the way Jenna spoke to her about ye . . . nor does she like it that Jenna came back to us wearing the Dark Bells.'

This was no sooner out of her mouth before Sister Coquina put her hand over that frequently imprudent organ, as if realizing she had said too much.

Roland, intrigued by what she'd said but not liking to show it just now, only replied: 'I'll keep my mouth shut about you, if you keep your mouth shut to Sister Mary about Jenna.'

Coquina looked relieved. 'Aye, that's a bargain.' She leaned forward confidingly. 'She's in Thoughtful House. That's the little cave in the hillside where we have to go and meditate when Big Sister decides we've been bad. She'll have to stay and consider her impudence until Mary lets her out.' She paused, then said abruptly: 'Who's this beside ye? Do ye know?'

Roland turned his head and saw that the young man was awake, and had been listening. His eyes were as dark as Jenna's.

'Know him?' Roland asked, with what he hoped was the right touch of scorn. 'Should I not know my own brother?'

'Is he, now, and him so young and you so old?' Another of the sisters materialized out of the darkness: Sister Tamra, who had called herself one-and-twenty. In the moment before she reached Roland's bed, her face was that of a hag who will never see eighty again . . . or ninety. Then it shimmered and was once more the plump, healthy countenance of a thirty-year-old matron. Except for the eyes. They remained yellowish in the corneas, gummy in the corners, and watchful.

'He's the youngest, I the eldest,' Roland said. 'Betwixt us are seven others, and twenty years of our parents' lives.'

'How sweet! And if he's yer brother, then ye'll know his name, won't ye? Know it very well.'

Before the gunslinger could flounder, the young man said: 'They think you've forgotten such a simple hook as John Norman. What culleens they be, eh, Jimmy?'

Coquina and Tamra looked at the pale boy in the bed next to Roland's, clearly angry . . . and clearly trumped. For the time being, at least.

'You've fed him your muck,' the boy (whose medallion undoubtedly proclaimed him 𝕵𝖔𝖍𝖓, 𝕷𝖔𝖛𝖊𝖉 𝖔𝖋 𝕱𝖆𝖒𝖎𝖑𝖞, 𝕷𝖔𝖛𝖊𝖉 𝖔𝖋 𝕲𝖔𝖉) said. 'Why don't you go, and let us have a natter?'

'Well!' Sister Coquina huffed. 'I like the gratitude around here, so I do!'

'I'm grateful for what's given me,' Norman responded, looking at her steadily, 'but not for what folk would take away.'

Tamra snorted through her nose, turned violently enough for her swirling dress to push a draught of air into Roland's face, and then took her leave. Coquina stayed a moment.

'Be discreet, and mayhap someone ye like better than ye like me will get out of hack in the morning, instead of a week from tonight.'

Without waiting for a reply, she turned and followed Sister Tamra.

Roland and John Norman waited until they were both gone, and then Norman turned to Roland and spoke in a low voice. 'My brother. Dead?'

Roland nodded. 'The medallion I took in case I should meet with any of his people. It rightly belongs to you. I'm sorry for your loss.'

'Thankee-sai.' John Norman's lower lip trembled, then firmed. 'I knew the green men did for him, although these old biddies wouldn't tell me for sure. They did for plenty, and cotched the rest.'

'Perhaps the Sisters didn't know for sure.'

'They knew. Don't you doubt it. They don't say much, but they know *plenty*. The only one any different is Jenna. That's who the old battle-axe meant when she said "your friend". Aye?'

Roland nodded. 'And she said something about the Dark Bells. I'd know more of that, if would were could.'

'She's something special, Jenna is. More like a princess – someone whose place is made by bloodline and can't be refused – than like the other Sisters. I lie here and look like I'm asleep – it's safer, I think – but I've heard 'em talking. Jenna's just come back among 'em recently, and those Dark Bells mean something special . . . but Mary's still the one who swings the weight. I think the Dark Bells are only ceremonial, like the rings the old Barons used to hand down from father to son. Was it she who put Jimmy's medal around your neck?'

'Yes.'

'Don't take it off, whatever you do.' His face was strained, grim. 'I don't know if it's the gold or the God, but they don't like to get too close. I think that's the only reason I'm still here.' Now his voice dropped all the way to a whisper. 'They ain't human.'

'Well, perhaps a bit fey and magical, but –'

'No!' With what was clearly an effort, the boy got up on one elbow. He looked at Roland earnestly. 'You're thinking about hubber-women, or witches. These ain't hubbers, nor witches, either. *They ain't human!*'

'Then what are they?'

'Don't know.'

'How came you here, John?'

Speaking in a low voice, John Norman told Roland what he knew of what had happened to him. He, his brother, and four other young men who were quick and owned good horses had been hired as scouts, riding drogue-and-forward, protecting a long-haul caravan of seven freight-wagons taking goods – seeds, food, tools, mail, and four ordered brides – to an unincorporated township called Tejuas some two hundred miles further west of

Eluria. The scouts rode fore and aft of the goods-train in turn and turn about fashion; one brother rode with each party because, Norman explained, when they were together they fought like . . . well . . .

'Like brothers,' Roland suggested.

John Norman managed a brief, pained smile. 'Aye,' he said.

The trio of which John was a part had been riding drogue, about two miles behind the freight-wagons, when the green mutants had sprung an ambush in Eluria.

'How many wagons did you see when you got there?' he asked Roland.

'Only one. Overturned.'

'How many bodies?'

'Only your brother's.'

John Norman nodded grimly. 'They wouldn't take him because of the medallion, I think.'

'The muties?'

'The Sisters. The muties care nothing for gold or God. These bitches, though . . .' He looked into the dark, which was now almost complete. Roland felt lethargy creeping over him again, but it wasn't until later that he realized the soup had been drugged.

'The other wagons?' Roland asked. 'The ones not overturned?'

'The muties would have taken them, and the goods, as well,' Norman said. 'They don't care for gold or God; the Sisters don't care for goods. Like as not they have their own food-stuffs, something I'd as soon not think of. Nasty stuff . . . like those bugs.'

He and the other drogue riders galloped into Eluria, but the fight was over by the time they got there. Men had been lying about, some dead but many more still alive. At least two of the ordered brides had still been alive, as well. Survivors able to walk were being herded together by the green folk – John Norman remembered the one in the bowler hat very well, and the woman in the ragged red vest.

Norman and the other two had tried to fight. He had seen one of his pards gutshot by an arrow, and then he saw no more

– someone had cracked him over the head from behind, and the lights had gone out.

Roland wondered if the ambusher had cried 'Booh!' before he had struck, but didn't ask.

'When I woke up again, I was here,' Norman said. 'I saw that some of the others – *most* of them – had those cursed bugs on them.'

'Others?' Roland looked at the empty beds. In the growing darkness, they glimmered like white islands. 'How many were brought here?'

'At least twenty. They healed . . . the bugs healed 'em . . . and then, one by one, they disappeared. You'd go to sleep, and when you woke up there'd be one more empty bed. One by one they went, until only me and that one down yonder was left.'

He looked at Roland solemnly.

'And now you.'

'Norman,' Roland's head was swimming. 'I –'

'I reckon I know what's wrong with you,' Norman said. He seemed to speak from far away . . . perhaps from all the way around the curve of the earth. 'It's the soup. But a man has to eat. A woman, too. If she's a natural woman, anyway. These ones ain't natural. Even Sister Jenna's not natural. Nice don't mean natural.' Further and further away. 'And she'll be like them in the end. Mark me well.'

'Can't move.' Saying even that required a huge effort. It was like moving boulders.

'No.' Norman suddenly laughed. It was a shocking sound, and echoed in the growing blackness which filled Roland's head. 'It ain't just sleep-medicine they put in their soup; it's can't-move-medicine, too. There's nothing much wrong with me, brother . . . so why do you think I'm still here?'

Norman was now speaking not from around the curve of the earth but perhaps from the moon. He said: 'I don't think either of us is ever going to see the sun shining on a flat piece of ground again.'

You're wrong about that, Roland tried to reply, and more in that vein, as well, but nothing came out. He sailed around to the black side of the moon, losing all his words in the void he found there.

Yet he never quite lost awareness of himself. Perhaps the dose of 'medicine' in Sister Coquina's soup had been badly calculated, or perhaps it was just that they had never had a gunslinger to work their mischief on, and did not know they had one now.

Except, of course, for Sister Jenna – *she* knew.

At some point in the night, whispering, giggling voices and lightly chiming bells brought him back from the darkness where he had been biding, not quite asleep or unconscious. Around him, so constant he now barely heard it, were the singing 'doctors'.

Roland opened his eyes. He saw pale and chancy light dancing in the black air. The giggles and whispers were closer. Roland tried to turn his head and at first couldn't. He rested, gathered his will into a hard blue ball, and tried again. This time his head *did* turn. Only a little, but a little was enough.

It was five of the Little Sisters – Mary, Louise, Tamra, Coquina, Michela. They came up the long aisle of the black infirmary, laughing together like children out on a prank, carrying long tapers in silver holders, the bells lining the forehead-bands of their wimples chiming little silver runs of sound. They gathered about the bed of the bearded man. From within their circle, candleglow rose in a shimmery column that died before it got halfway to the silken ceiling.

Sister Mary spoke briefly. Roland recognized her voice, but not the words – it was neither low speech nor the High, but some other language entirely. One phrase stood out – *can de lach, mi him en tow* – and he had no idea what it might mean.

He realized that now he could hear only the tinkle of bells – the doctor-bugs had stilled.

'*Ras me! On! On!*' Sister Mary cried in a harsh, powerful voice. The candles went out. The light which had shone through the wings of their wimples as they gathered around the bearded man's bed vanished, and all was darkness once more.

Roland waited for what might happen next, his skin cold. He tried to flex his hands and feet, and could not. He had been able to move his head perhaps fifteen degrees; otherwise he was as paralysed as a fly neatly wrapped up and hung in a spider's web.

The low jingling of bells in the black . . . and then sucking sounds. As soon as he heard them, Roland knew he'd been waiting for them. Some part of him had known what the Little Sisters of Eluria were, all along.

If Roland could have raised his hands, he would have put them to his ears to block those sounds out. As it was, he could only lie still, listening and waiting for them to stop.

For a long time – for ever, it seemed – they did not. The women slurped and grunted like pigs snuffling half-liquefied feed out of a trough. There was even one resounding belch, followed by more whispered giggles (these ended when Sister Mary uttered a single curt word – *'Hais!'*). And once there was a low, moaning cry – from the bearded man, Roland was quite sure. If so, it was his last on this side of the clearing.

In time, the sound of their feeding began to taper off. As it did, the bugs began to sing again – first hesitantly, then with more confidence. The whispering and giggling recommenced. The candles were re-lit. Roland was by now lying with his head turned in the other direction. He didn't want them to know what he'd seen, but that wasn't all; he had no urge to see more on any account. He had seen and heard enough.

But the giggles and whispers now came his way. Roland closed his eyes, concentrating on the medallion which lay against his chest. *I don't know if it's the gold or the God, but they don't like to get too close*, John Norman had said. It was good to have such a thing to remember as the Little Sisters drew nigh, gossiping and whispering in their strange other tongue, but the medallion seemed a thin protection in the dark.

Faintly, at a great distance, Roland heard the cross-dog barking.

As the Sisters circled him, the gunslinger realized he could smell them. It was a low, unpleasant odour, like spoiled meat. And what else *would* they smell of, such as these?

'Such a pretty man it is.' Sister Mary. She spoke in a low, meditative tone.

'But such an ugly sigil it wears.' Sister Tamra.

'We'll have it off him!' Sister Louise.

'And then we shall have kisses!' Sister Coquina.

'Kisses for all!' exclaimed Sister Michela, with such fervent enthusiasm that they all laughed.

Roland discovered that not *all* of him was paralysed, after all. Part of him had, in fact, arisen from its sleep at the sound of their voices and now stood tall. A hand reached beneath the bed-dress he wore, touched that stiffened member, encircled it, caressed it. He lay in silent horror, feigning sleep, as wet warmth almost immediately spilled from him. The hand remained where it was for a moment, the thumb rubbing up and down the wilting shaft. Then it let him go and rose a little higher. Found the wetness pooled on his lower belly.

Giggles, soft as wind.

Chiming bells.

Roland opened his eyes the tiniest crack and looked up at the ancient faces laughing down at him in the light of their candles – glittering eyes, yellow cheeks, hanging teeth that jutted over lower lips. Sister Michela and Sister Louise appeared to have grown goatees, but of course that wasn't the darkness of hair but of the bearded man's blood.

Mary's hand was cupped. She passed it from Sister to Sister; each licked from her palm in the candlelight.

Roland closed his eyes all the way and waited for them to be gone. Eventually they were.

I'll never sleep again, he thought, and was five minutes later lost to himself and the world.

V. Sister Mary. A Message. A Visit from Ralph.
Norman's Fate. Sister Mary Again.

When Roland awoke, it was full daylight, the silk roof overhead a bright white and billowing in a mild breeze. The doctor-bugs were singing contentedly. Beside him on his left, Norman was heavily asleep with his head turned so far to one side that his stubbly cheek rested on his shoulder.

Roland and John Norman were the only ones here. Further down on their side of the infirmary, the bed where the bearded man had been was empty, its top sheet pulled up and neatly tucked in, the pillow neatly nestled in a crisp white case. The complication of slings in which his body had rested was gone.

Roland remembered the candles – the way their glow had combined and streamed up in a column, illuminating the Sisters as they gathered around the bearded man. Giggling. Their damned bells jingling.

Now, as if summoned by his thoughts, came Sister Mary, gliding along rapidly with Sister Louise in her wake. Louise bore a tray, and looked nervous. Mary was frowning, obviously not in good temper.

To be grumpy after you've fed so well? Roland thought. *Fie, Sister.*

She reached the gunslinger's bed and looked down at him. 'I have little to thank ye for, sai,' she said with no preamble.

'Have I asked for your thanks?' he responded in a voice that sounded as dusty and little-used as the pages of an old book.

She took no notice. 'Ye've made one who was only impudent and restless with her place outright rebellious. Well, her mother was the same way, and died of it not long after returning Jenna to her proper place. Raise your hand, thankless man.'

'I can't. I can't move at all.'

'Oh, cully! Haven't you heard it said "fool not your mother 'less she's out of face"? I know pretty well what ye can and can't do. Now raise your hand.'

Roland raised his right hand, trying to suggest more effort than it actually took. He thought that this morning he might be strong enough to slip free of the slings . . . but what then? Any real walking would be beyond him for hours yet, even without another dose of 'medicine' . . . and behind Sister Mary, Sister Louise was taking the cover from a fresh bowl of soup. As Roland looked at it, his stomach rumbled.

Big Sister heard and smiled a bit. 'Even lying in bed builds an appetite in a strong man, if it's done long enough. Wouldn't you say so, Jason, brother of John?'

'My name is James. As you well know, Sister.'

'Do I?' She laughed angrily. 'Oh, la! And if I whipped your little sweetheart hard enough and long enough – until the blood jumped out her back like drops of sweat, let us say – should I not whip a different name out of her? Or didn't ye trust her with it, during your little talk?'

'Touch her and I'll kill you.'

She laughed again. Her face shimmered; her firm mouth turned into something that looked like a dying jellyfish. 'Speak not of killing to us, cully, lest we speak of it to you.'

'Sister, if you and Jenna don't see eye to eye, why not release her from her vows and let her go her course?'

'Such as us can never be released from our vows, nor be let go. Her mother tried and then came back, her dying and the girl sick. Why, it was we nursed Jenna back to health after her mother was nothing but dirt in the breeze that blows out towards End-World, and how little she thanks us! Besides, she bears the Dark Bells, the sigil of our sisterhood. Of our *ka-tet*. Now eat – yer belly says ye're hungry!'

Sister Louise offered the bowl, but her eyes kept drifting to the shape the medallion made under the breast of his bed-dress. *Don't like it, do you?* Roland thought, and then remembered Louise by candlelight, the freighter's blood on her chin, her ancient eyes eager as she leaned forward to lick his spend from Sister Mary's hand.

He turned his head aside. 'I want nothing.'

'But ye're hungry!' Louise protested. 'If'ee don't eat, James, how will'ee get'ee strength back?'

'Send Jenna. I'll eat what she brings.'

Sister Mary's frown was black. 'Ye'll see her no more. She's been released from Thoughtful House only on her solemn promise to double her time of meditation . . . and to stay out of the infirmary. Now eat, James, or whoever ye are. Take what's in the soup, or we'll cut ye with knives and rub it in with flannel poultices. Either way, makes no difference to us. Does it, Louise?'

'Nar,' Louise said. She still held out the bowl. Steam rose from it, and the good smell of chicken.

'But it might make a difference to you.' Sister Mary grinned humourlessly, baring her unnaturally large teeth. 'Flowing blood's risky around here. The doctors don't like it. It stirs them up.'

It wasn't just the bugs that were stirred up at the sight of blood, and Roland knew it. He also knew he had no choice in the matter of the soup. He took the bowl from Louise and ate slowly. He would have given much to wipe out the look of satisfaction he saw on Sister Mary's face.

'Good,' she said after he had handed the bowl back and she had peered inside to make sure it was completely empty. His hand thumped back into the sling which had been rigged for it, already too heavy to hold up. He could feel the world drawing away again.

Sister Mary leaned forward, the billowing top of her habit touching the skin of his left shoulder. He could smell her, an aroma both ripe and dry, and would have gagged if he'd had the strength.

'Have that foul gold thing off ye when yer strength comes back a little – put it in the *pissoir* under the bed. Where it belongs. For to be even this close to where it lies hurts my head and makes my throat close.'

Speaking with enormous effort, Roland said: 'If you want it, take it. How can I stop you, you bitch?'

Once more her frown turned her face into something like a thunderhead. He thought she would have slapped him, if she had dared touch him so close to where the medallion lay. Her ability to touch seemed to end above his waist, however.

'I think you had better consider the matter a little more fully,' she said. 'I can still have Jenna whipped, if I like. She bears the Dark Bells, but I am the Big Sister. Consider that very well.'

She left. Sister Louise followed, casting one look – a strange combination of fright and lust – back over her shoulder.

Roland thought, *I must get out of here – I must.*

Instead, he drifted back to that dark place which wasn't quite sleep. Or perhaps he did sleep, at least for a while; perhaps he dreamed. Fingers once more caressed his fingers, and lips first kissed his ear and then whispered into it: 'Look beneath your pillow, Roland . . . but let no one know I was here.'

At some point after this, Roland opened his eyes again, half-expecting to see Sister Jenna's pretty young face hovering above him, and that comma of dark hair once more poking out from beneath her wimple. There was no one. The swags of silk overhead were at their brightest, and although it was impossible to tell the hours in here with any real accuracy, Roland guessed it to be around noon. Perhaps three hours since his second bowl of the Sisters' soup.

Beside him, John Norman still slept, his breath whistling out in faint, nasal snores.

Roland tried to raise his hand and slide it under his pillow. The hand wouldn't move. He could wiggle the tips of his fingers, but that was all. He waited, calming his mind as well as he could, gathering his patience. Patience wasn't easy to come by. He kept thinking about what Norman had said – that there had been twenty survivors of the ambush . . . at least to start with. *One by one they went, until only me and that one down yonder was left. And now you.*

The girl wasn't here. His mind spoke in the soft, regretful tone of Alain, one of his old friends, dead these many years now. *She wouldn't dare, not with the others watching. That was only a dream you had.*

But Roland thought perhaps it had been more than a dream.

Some length of time later – the slowly shifting brightness overhead made him believe it had been about an hour – Roland tried his hand again. This time he was able to get it beneath his pillow. This was puffy and soft, tucked snugly into the wide sling which supported the gunslinger's neck. At first he found nothing, but as his fingers worked their slow way deeper, they touched what felt like a stiffish bundle of thin rods.

He paused, gathering a little more strength (every movement was like swimming in glue), and then burrowed deeper. It felt like a dead bouquet. Wrapped around it was what felt like a ribbon.

Roland looked around to make sure the ward was still empty and Norman still asleep, then drew out what was under the pillow. It was six brittle stems of fading green with brownish reed-heads at the tops. They gave off a strange, yeasty aroma that made Roland think of early-morning begging expeditions to the Great House kitchens as a child – forays he had usually made with Cuthbert. The reeds were tied with a wide white silk ribbon, and smelled like burned toast. Beneath the ribbon was a fold of cloth. Like everything else in this cursed place, it seemed, the cloth was of silk.

Roland was breathing hard and could feel drops of sweat on his brow. Still alone, though – good. He took the scrap of cloth and unfolded it. Printed painstakingly in blurred charcoal letters, was this message:

> *NIBBLE HEDS. Once each hour. Too*
> *much, CRAMPS or DETH.*
> *TOMORROW NITE. Can't be sooner.*
> *BE CAREFUL!*

No explanation, but Roland supposed none was needed. Nor did he have any option; if he remained here, he would die. All they had to do was have the medallion off him, and he felt sure Sister Mary was smart enough to figure a way to do that.

He nibbled at one of the dry reed-heads. The taste was nothing like the toast they had begged from the kitchen as boys; it was bitter in his throat and hot in his stomach. Less than a minute after his nibble, his heart-rate had doubled. His muscles awakened, but not in a pleasant way, as after good sleep; they felt first trembly and then hard, as if they were gathered into knots. This feeling passed rapidly, and his heartbeat was back to normal before Norman stirred awake an hour or so later, but he understood why Jenna's note had warned him not to take more than a nibble at a time – this was very powerful stuff.

He slipped the bouquet of reeds back under the pillow, being careful to brush away the few crumbles of vegetable matter which had dropped to the sheet. Then he used the ball of his thumb to blur the painstaking charcoaled words on the bit of silk. When he was finished, there was nothing on the square but meaningless smudges. The square he also tucked back under his pillow.

When Norman awoke, he and the gunslinger spoke briefly of the young scout's home – Delain, it was, sometimes known jestingly as Dragon's Lair, or Liar's Heaven. All tall tales were said to orginate in Delain. The boy asked Roland to take his medallion and that of his brother home to their parents, if Roland was able, and explain as well as he could what had happened to James and John, sons of Jesse.

'You'll do all that yourself,' Roland said.

'No.' Norman tried to raise his hand, perhaps to scratch his nose, and was unable to do even that. The hand rose perhaps six inches, then fell back to the counterpane with a small thump. 'I think not. It's a pity for us to have run up against each other this way, you know – I like you.'

'And I you, John Norman. Would that we were better met.'

'Aye. When not in the company of such fascinating ladies.'

He dropped off to sleep again soon after. Roland never spoke with him again ... although he certainly heard from him. Yes. Roland was lying above his bed, shamming sleep, as John Norman screamed his last.

Sister Michela came with his evening soup just as Roland was getting past the shivery muscles and galloping heartbeat that resulted from his second nibble of brown reed. Michela looked at his flushed face with some concern, but had to accept his assurances that he did not feel feverish; she couldn't bring herself to touch him and judge the heat of his skin for herself – the medallion held her away.

With the soup was a popkin. The bread was leathery and the meat inside it tough, but Roland demolished it greedily, just the same. Michela watched with a complacent smile, hands folded in front of her, nodding from time to time. When he had finished the soup, she took the bowl back from him carefully, making sure their fingers did not touch.

'Ye're healing,' she said. 'Soon you'll be on yer way, and we'll have just yer memory to keep, Jim.'

'Is that true?' he asked quietly.

She only looked at him, touched her tongue against her upper lip, giggled, and departed. Roland closed his eyes and lay back against his pillow, feeling lethargy steal over him again. Her speculative eyes . . . her peeping tongue. He had seen women look at roast chickens and joints of mutton that same way, calculating when they might be done.

His body badly wanted to sleep, but Roland held on to wakefulness for what he judged was an hour, then worked one of the reeds out from under the pillow. With a fresh infusion of their 'can't-move-medicine' in his system, this took an enormous effort, and he wasn't sure he could have done it at all, had he not separated this one reed from the ribbon holding the others. Tomorrow night, Jenna's note had said. If that meant escape, the idea seemed preposterous. The way he felt now, he might be lying in this bed until the end of the age.

He nibbled. Energy washed into his system, clenching his muscles and racing his heart, but the burst of vitality was gone almost as soon as it came, buried beneath the Sisters' stronger drug. He could only hope . . . and sleep.

When he woke it was full dark, and he found he could move his arms and legs in their network of slings almost naturally. He slipped one of the reeds out from beneath his pillow and nibbled cautiously. She had left half a dozen, and the first two were now almost entirely consumed.

The gunslinger put the stem back under the pillow, then began to shiver like a wet dog in a downpour. *I took too much*, he thought. *I'll be lucky not to convulse –*

His heart, racing like a runaway engine. And then, to make matters worse, he saw candlelight at the far end of the aisle. A moment later he heard the rustle of their gowns and the whisk of their slippers.

Gods, why now? They'll see me shaking, they'll know –

Calling on every bit of his willpower and control, Roland closed his eyes and concentrated on stilling his jerking limbs. If only he had been in bed instead of in these cursed slings, which seemed to tremble as if with their own ague at every movement!

The Little Sisters drew closer. The light of their candles bloomed red within his closed eyelids. Tonight they were not giggling, nor whispering amongst themselves. It was not until they were almost on top of him that Roland became aware of the stranger in their midst – a creature that breathed through its nose in great, slobbery gasps of mixed air and snot.

The gunslinger lay with his eyes closed, the gross twitches and jumps of his arms and legs under control, but with his muscles still knotted and crampy, thrumming beneath the skin. Anyone who looked at him closely would see at once that something was wrong with him. His heart was larruping away like a horse under the whip, surely they must see –

But it wasn't him they were looking at – not yet, at least.

'Have it off him,' Mary said. She spoke in a bastardized version of the low speech Roland could barely understand. 'Then t'other 'un. Go on, Ralph.'

'U'se has whik-sky?' the slobberer asked, his dialect even heavier than Mary's. 'U'se has 'backky?'

'Yes, yes, plenty whisky and plenty smoke, but not until you have these wretched things off!' Impatient. Perhaps afraid, as well.

Roland cautiously rolled his head to the left and cracked his eyelids open.

Five of the six Little Sisters of Eluria were clustered around the far side of the sleeping John Norman's bed, their candles raised to cast their light upon him. It also cast light upon their own faces, faces which would have given the strongest man nightmares. Now, in the ditch of the night, their glamours were set aside, and they were but ancient corpses in voluminous habits.

Sister Mary had one of Roland's guns in her hand. Looking at her holding it, Roland felt a bright flash of hate for her, and promised himself she would pay for her temerity.

The thing standing at the foot of the bed, strange as it was, looked almost normal in comparison to the Sisters. It was one of the green folk. Roland recognized Ralph at once. He would be a long time forgetting that bowler hat.

Now Ralph walked slowly around to the side of Norman's bed closest to Roland, momentarily blocking the gunslinger's view of the Sisters. The mutie went all the way to Norman's head, however, clearing the hags to Roland's slitted view once more.

Norman's medallion lay exposed – the boy had perhaps wakened enough to take it out of his bed-dress, hoping it would protect him better so. Ralph picked it up in his melted-tallow hand. The Sisters watched eagerly in the glow of their candles as the green man stretched it to the end of its chain . . . and then put it down again. Their faces drooped in disappointment.

'Don't care for such as that,' Ralph said in his clotted voice. 'Want whik-sky! Want 'backky!'

'You shall have it,' Sister Mary said. 'Enough for you and all your verminous clan. But first, you must have that horrid thing off him! Off both of them! Do you understand? And you shan't tease us.'

'Or what?' Ralph asked. He laughed. It was a choked and gargly sound, the laughter of a man dying from some evil sickness of the throat and lungs, but Roland still liked it better than the giggles of the Sisters. 'Or what, Sisser Mary, you'll drink my bluid? My bluid'd drop'ee dead where'ee stand, and glowing in the dark!'

Mary raised the gunslinger's revolver and pointed it at Ralph. 'Take that wretched thing, or you die where *you* stand.'

'And die after I've done what you want, likely.'

Sister Mary said nothing to that. The others peered at him with their black eyes.

Ralph lowered his head, appearing to think. Roland suspected his friend Bowler Hat *could* think, too. Sister Mary and her cohorts might not believe that, but Ralph *had* to be trig to have survived as long as he had. But of course when he came here, he hadn't considered Roland's guns.

'Smasher was wrong to give them shooters to you,' he said

at last. 'Give 'em and not tell me. Did u'se give him whik-sky? Give him 'backky?'

'That's none o' yours,' Sister Mary replied. 'You have that goldpiece off the boy's neck right now, or I'll put one of yonder man's bullets in what's left of yer brain.'

'All right,' Ralph said. 'Just as you wish, sai.'

Once more he reached down and took the gold medallion in his melted fist. That he did slow; what happened after, happened fast. He snatched it away, breaking the chain and flinging the gold heedlessly into the dark. With his other hand he reached down, sank his long and ragged nails into John Norman's neck, and tore it open.

Blood flew from the hapless boy's throat in a jetting, heart-driven gush more black than red in the candlelight, and he made a single bubbly cry. The women screamed – but not in horror. They screamed as women do in a frenzy of excitement. The green man was forgotten; Roland was forgotten; all was forgotten save the life's blood pouring out of John Norman's throat.

They dropped their candles. Mary dropped Roland's revolver in the same hapless, careless fashion. The last the gunslinger saw as Ralph darted away into the shadows (whisky and tobacco another time, wily Ralph must have thought; tonight he had best concentrate on saving his own life) was the Sisters bending forward to catch as much of the flow as they could before it dried up.

Roland lay in the dark, muscles shivering, heart pounding, listening to the harpies as they fed on the boy lying in the bed next to his own. It seemed to go on for ever, but at last they had done with him. The Sisters re-lit their candles and left, murmuring.

When the drug in the soup once more got the better of the drug in the reeds, Roland was grateful . . . yet for the first time since coming here, his sleep was haunted.

In his dream he stood looking down at the bloated body in the town trough, thinking of a line in the book marked REGISTRY OF MISDEEDS & REDRESS. *Green folk sent hence*, it had read, and perhaps the green folk *had* been sent hence, but then a worse tribe had come. The Little Sisters of Eluria, they called themselves. And a year hence, they might be the Little Sisters of Tejuas, or of Kambero, or some other far-western village. They came with their bells and their bugs . . . from where? Who knew? Did it matter?

A shadow fell beside his on the scummy water of the trough. Roland tried to turn and face it. He couldn't; he was frozen in place. Then a green hand grasped his shoulder and whirled him about. It was Ralph. His bowler hat was cocked back on his head; John Norman's medallion, now red with blood, hung around his neck.

'Booh!' cried Ralph, his lips stretching in a toothless grin. He raised a big revolver with worn sandalwood grips. He thumbed the hammer back –

– and Roland jerked awake, shivering all over, dressed in skin both wet and icy cold. He looked at the bed on his left. It was empty, the sheet pulled up and tucked about neatly, the pillow resting above it in its snowy sleeve. Of John Norman there was no sign. It might have been empty for years, that bed.

Roland was alone now. Gods help him, he was the last patient of the Little Sisters of Eluria, those sweet and patient hospitallers. The last human being still alive in this terrible place, the last with warm blood flowing in his veins.

Roland, lying suspended, gripped the gold medallion in his fist and looked across the aisle at the long row of empty beds. After a little while, he brought one of the reeds out from beneath his pillow and nibbled at it.

When Mary came fifteen minutes later, the gunslinger took the bowl she brought with a show of weakness he didn't really feel. Porridge instead of soup this time . . . but he had no doubt the basic ingredient was still the same.

'How well ye look this morning, sai,' Big Sister said. She looked well herself – there were no shimmers to give away the ancient *wampir* hiding inside her. She had supped well, and her meal had firmed her up. Roland's stomach rolled over at the thought. 'Ye'll be on yer pins in no time, I'll warrant.'

'That's shit,' Roland said, speaking in an ill-natured growl. 'Put me on my pins and you'd be picking me up off the floor directly after. I've started to wonder if you're not putting something in the food.'

She laughed merrily at that. 'La, you lads! Always eager to blame yer weakness on a scheming woman! How scared of us ye are – aye, way down in yer little boys' hearts, how scared ye are!'

'Where's my brother? I dreamed there was a commotion about him in the night, and now I see his bed's empty.'

Her smile narrowed. Her eyes glittered. 'He came over fevery and pitched a fit. We've taken him to Thoughtful House, which has been home to contagion more than once in its time.'

To the grave is where you've taken him, Roland thought. *Mayhap that is a Thoughtful House, but little would you know it, sai, one way or another*.

'I know ye're no brother to that boy,' Mary said, watching him eat. Already Roland could feel the stuff hidden in the porridge draining his strength once more. 'Sigil or no sigil, I know ye're no brother to him. Why do you lie? 'Tis a sin against God.'

'What gives you such an idea, sai?' Roland asked, curious to see if she would mention the guns.

'Big Sister knows what she knows. Why not 'fess up, Jimmy? Confession's good for the soul, they say.'

'Send me Jenna to pass the time, and perhaps I'd tell you much,' Roland said.

The narrow bone of smile on Sister Mary's face disappeared like chalk-writing in a rainstorm. 'Why would ye talk to such as her?'

'She's passing fair,' Roland said. 'Unlike some.'

Her lips pulled back from her overlarge teeth. 'Ye'll see her no more, cully. Ye've stirred her up, so you have, and I won't have that.'

She turned to go. Still trying to appear weak and hoping he would not overdo it (acting was never his forte), Roland held out the empty porridge bowl. 'Do you not want to take this?'

'Put it on your head and wear it as a nightcap, for all of me. Or stick it in your ass. You'll talk before I'm done with ye, cully – talk till I bid you shut up and then beg to talk some more!'

On this note she swept regally away, hands lifting the front of her skirt off the floor. Roland had heard that such as she couldn't go about in daylight, and that part of the old tales was surely a lie. Yet another part was almost true, it seemed: a fuzzy, amorphous shape kept pace with her, running along the row of empty beds to her right, but she cast no real shadow at all.

VI. Jenna. Sister Coquina. Tamra, Michela, Louise. The Cross-Dog. What Happened in the Sage.

That was one of the longest days of Roland's life. He dozed, but never deeply; the reeds were doing their work, and he had begun to believe that he might, with Jenna's help, actually get out of here. And there was the matter of his guns, as well – perhaps she might be able to help there, too.

He passed the slow hours thinking of old times – of Gilead and his friends, of the riddling he had almost won at one Wide Earth Fair. In the end another had taken the goose, but he'd had his chance, aye. He thought of his mother and father; he thought of Abel Vannay, who had limped his way through a life of gentle goodness, and Eldred Jonas, who had limped his way through a life of evil . . . until Roland had blown him loose of his saddle, one fine desert day.

He thought, as always, of Susan.

If you love me, then love me, she'd said . . . and so he had.

So he had.

In this way the time passed. At rough hourly intervals, he took one of the reeds from beneath his pillow and nibbled it. Now his muscles didn't tremble so badly as the stuff passed into his system, nor his heart pound so fiercely. The medicine in the reeds no longer had to battle the Sisters' medicine so fiercely, Roland thought; the reeds were winning.

The diffused brightness of the sun moved across the white silk ceiling of the ward, and at last the dimness which always seemed to hover at bed-level began to rise. The long room's western wall bloomed with the rose-melting-to-orange shades of sunset.

It was Sister Tamra who brought him his dinner that night – soup and another popkin. She also laid a desert lily beside his hand. She smiled as she did it. Her cheeks were bright with colour. All of them were bright with colour today, like leeches which had gorged until they were full almost to bursting.

'From your admirer, Jimmy,' she said. 'She's so sweet on ye! The lily means "Do not forget my promise". What has she promised ye, Jimmy, brother of Johnny?'

'That she'd see me again, and we'd talk.'

Tamra laughed so hard that the bells lining her forehead jingled. She clasped her hands together in a perfect ecstasy of glee. 'Sweet as honey! Oh, yes!' She bent her smiling gaze on Roland. 'It's sad such a promise can never be kept. Ye'll never see her again, pretty man.' She took the bowl. 'Big Sister has decided.' She stood up, still smiling. 'Why not take that ugly gold sigil off?'

'I think not.'

'Yer brother took his off – look!' She pointed, and Roland spied the gold medallion lying far down the aisle, where it had landed when Ralph threw it.

Sister Tamra looked at him, still smiling.

'He decided it was part of what was making him sick, and cast it away. Ye'd do the same, were ye wise.'

Roland repeated: 'I think not.'

'So,' she said dismissively, and left him alone with the empty beds glimmering in the thickening shadows.

Roland hung on, in spite of growing sleepiness, until the hot colours bleeding across the infirmary's western wall had cooled to ashes. Then he nibbled one of the reeds and felt strength – real strength, not a jittery, heart-thudding substitute – bloom in his body. He looked towards where the castaway medallion gleamed in the last light and made a silent promise to John Norman: he would take it with the other one to Norman's kin, if *ka* chanced that he should encounter them in his travels.

Feeling completely easy in his mind for the first time that

day, the gunslinger dozed. When he awoke it was full dark. The doctor-bugs were singing with extraordinary shrillness. He had taken one of the reeds out from under the pillow and had begun to nibble on it when a cold voice said, 'So – Big Sister was right. Ye've been keeping secrets.'

Roland's heart seemed to stop dead in his chest. He looked around and saw Sister Coquina getting to her feet. She had crept in while he was dozing and hidden under the bed on his right side to watch him.

'Where did ye get that?' she asked. 'Was it –'

'He got it from me.'

Coquina whirled about. Jenna was walking down the aisle towards them. Her habit was gone. She still wore her wimple with its forehead-fringe of bells, but its hem rested on the shoulders of a simple checkered shirt. Below this she wore jeans and scuffed desert boots. She had something in her hands. It was too dark for Roland to be sure, but he thought –

'*You*,' Sister Coquina whispered with infinite hate. 'When I tell Big Sister –'

'You'll tell no one anything,' Roland said.

If he had planned his escape from the slings which entangled him, he no doubt would have made a bad business of it, but, as always, the gunslinger did best when he thought least. His arms were free in a moment; so was his left leg. His right caught at the ankle, however, twisting, hanging him up with his shoulders on the bed and his leg in the air.

Coquina turned on him, hissing like a cat. Her lips pulled back from teeth that were needle-sharp. She rushed at him, her fingers splayed. The nails at the ends of them looked sharp and ragged.

Roland clasped the medallion and shoved it out towards her. She recoiled from it, still hissing, and whirled back to Sister Jenna in a flare of white skirt. 'I'll do for ye, ye interfering trull!' she cried in a low, harsh voice.

Roland struggled to free his leg and couldn't. It was firmly caught, the shitting sling actually wrapped around the ankle somehow, like a noose.

Jenna raised her hands, and he saw he had been right: it was his revolvers she had brought, holstered and hanging from the two old gunbelts he had worn out of Gilead after the last burning.

'Shoot her, Jenna! Shoot her!'

Instead, still holding the holstered guns up, Jenna shook her head as she had on the day when Roland had persuaded her to push back her wimple so he could see her hair. The bells rang with a sharpness that seemed to go into the gunslinger's head like a spike.

The Dark Bells. The sigil of their ka-tet. *What* –

The sound of the doctor-bugs rose to a shrill, reedy scream that was eerily like the sound of the bells Jenna wore. Nothing sweet about them now. Sister Coquina's hands faltered on their way to Jenna's throat; Jenna herself had not so much as flinched or blinked her eyes.

'No,' Coquina whispered. 'You *can't*!'

'I *have*,' Jenna said, and Roland saw the bugs. Descending from the legs of the bearded man, he'd observed a battalion. What he saw coming from the shadows now was an army to end all armies; had they been men instead of insects, there might have been more than all the men who had ever carried arms in the long and bloody history of Mid-World.

Yet the sight of them advancing down the boards of the aisle was not what Roland would always remember, nor what would haunt his dreams for a year or more; it was the way they coated the *beds*. These were turning black two by two on both sides of the aisle, like pairs of dim rectangular lights going out.

Coquina shrieked and began to shake her own head, to ring her own bells. The sound they made was thin and pointless compared to the sharp ringing of the Dark Bells.

Still the bugs marched on, darkening the floor, blacking out the beds.

Jenna darted past the shrieking Sister Coquina, dropped Roland's guns beside him, then yanked the twisted sling straight with one hard pull. Roland slid his leg free.

'Come,' she said. 'I've started them, but staying them could be a different thing.'

Now Sister Coquina's shrieks were not of horror but of pain. The bugs had found her.

'Don't look,' Jenna said, helping Roland to his feet. He thought that never in his life had he been so glad to be upon them. 'Come. We must be quick – she'll rouse the others. I've put your boots and clothes aside up the path that leads away from here – I carried as much as I could. How are ye? Are ye strong?'

'Thanks to you.' How long he would stay strong Roland didn't know . . . and right now it wasn't a question that mattered. He saw Jenna snatch up two of the reeds – in his struggle to escape the slings, they had scattered all over the head of the bed – and then they were hurrying up the aisle, away from the bugs and from Sister Coquina, whose cries were now failing.

Roland buckled on his guns and tied them down without breaking stride.

They passed only three beds on each side before reaching the flap of the tent . . . and it *was* a tent, he saw, not a vast pavilion. The silk walls and ceiling were fraying canvas, thin enough to let in the light of a threequarters Kissing Moon. And the beds weren't beds at all, but only a double row of shabby cots.

He turned and saw a black, writhing hump on the floor where Sister Coquina had been. At the sight of her, Roland was struck by an unpleasant thought.

'I forgot John Norman's medallion!' A keen sense of regret – almost of mourning – went through him like wind.

Jenna reached into the pocket of her jeans and brought it out. It glimmered in the moonlight.

'I picked it up off the floor.'

He didn't know which made him gladder – the sight of the medallion or the sight of it in her hand. It meant she wasn't like the others.

Then, as if to dispel that notion before it got too firm a hold on him, she said: 'Take it, Roland – I can hold it no more.' And, as he took it, he saw unmistakable marks of charring on her fingers.

He took her hand and kissed each burn.

'Thankee-sai,' she said, and he saw she was crying. 'Thankee, dear. To be kissed so is lovely, worth every pain. Now . . .'

Roland saw her eyes shift, and followed them. Here were bobbing lights descending a rocky path. Beyond them he saw the building where the Little Sisters had been living – not a convent but a ruined *hacienda* that looked a thousand years old. There were three candles; as they drew closer, Roland saw that there were only three sisters. Mary wasn't among them.

He drew his guns.

'Oooo, it's a gunslinger-man he is!' Louise.

'A *scary* man!' Michela.

'And he's found his ladylove as well as his shooters!' Tamra.

'His slut-whore!' Louise.

Laughing angrily. Not afraid . . . at least, not of *his* weapons.

'Put them away,' Jenna told him, and when she looked, saw that he already had.

The others, meanwhile, had drawn closer.

'Ooo, see, she cries!' Tamra.

'Doffed her habit, she has!' Michela. 'Perhaps it's her broken vows she cries for.'

'Why such tears, pretty?' Louise.

'Because he kissed my fingers where they were burned,' Jenna said. 'I've never been kissed before. It made me cry.'

'Ooooo!'

'*Luv*-ly!'

'Next he'll stick his thing in her! Even *luv*-lier!'

Jenna bore their japes with no sign of anger. When they were done, she said: 'I'm going with him. Stand aside.'

They gaped at her, counterfeit laughter disappearing in shock.

'No!' Louise whispered. 'Are ye mad? Ye know what'll happen!'

'No, and neither do you,' Jenna said. 'Besides, I care not.' She half-turned and held her hand out to the mouth of the ancient hospital tent. It was a faded olive-drab in the moonlight, with an old red cross drawn on its roof. Roland wondered how many towns the Sisters had been to with this tent, which was so small and plain on the outside, so huge and gloriously dim on the inside. How many towns and over how many years.

Now, cramming the mouth of it in a black, shiny tongue, were the doctor-bugs. They had stopped their singing. Their silence was somehow terrible.

'Stand aside or I'll have them on ye,' Jenna said.

'Ye never would!' Sister Michela cried in a low, horrified voice.

'Aye. I've already set them on Sister Coquina. She's a part of their medicine, now.'

Their gasp was like cold wind passing through dead trees. Nor was all of that dismay directed towards their own precious hides. What Jenna had done was clearly far outside their reckoning.

'Then you're damned,' Sister Tamra said.

'Such ones to speak of damnation! Stand aside.'

They did. Roland walked past them and they shrank away from him . . . but they shrank from her more.

'Damned?' he asked after they had skirted the *haci* and reached the path beyond it. The Kissing Moon glimmered above a tumbled scree of rocks. In its light Roland could see a small black opening low on the scarp. He guessed it was the cave the Sisters called Thoughtful House. 'What did they mean, damned?'

'Never mind. All we have to worry about now is Sister Mary. I like it not that we haven't seen her.'

She tried to walk faster, but he grasped her arm and turned her about. He could still hear the singing of the bugs, but faintly; they were leaving the place of the Sisters behind. Eluria, too, if the compass in his head was still working; he thought the town was in the other direction. The husk of the town, he amended.

'Tell me what they meant.'

'Perhaps nothing. Ask me not, Roland – what good is it? 'Tis done, the bridge burned. I can't go back. Nor would if I could.' She looked down, biting her lip, and when she looked up again, Roland saw fresh tears falling on her cheeks. 'I have supped with them. There were times when I couldn't help it, no more than you could help drinking their wretched soup, no matter if you knew what was in it.'

Roland remembered John Norman saying *A man has to eat . . . a woman, too*. He nodded.

'I'd go no further down that road. If there's to be damnation, let it be of my choosing, not theirs. My mother meant well by bringing me back to them, but she was wrong.' She looked at him shyly and fearfully . . . but met his eyes. 'I'd go beside ye on yer road, Roland of Gilead. For as long as I may, or as long as ye'd have me.'

'You're welcome to your share of my way,' he said. 'And I am –'

Blessed by your company, he would have finished, but before he could, a voice spoke from the tangle of moonshadow ahead of them, where the path at last climbed out of the rocky, sterile valley in which the Little Sisters had practised their glamours.

'It's a sad duty to stop such a pretty elopement, but stop it I must.'

Sister Mary came from the shadows. Her fine white habit with its bright red rose had reverted to what it really was: the shroud of a corpse. Caught, hooded in its grimy folds, was a wrinkled, sagging face from which two black eyes stared. They looked like rotted dates. Below them, exposed by the thing's smile, four great incisors gleamed.

Upon the stretched skin of Sister Mary's forehead, bells tinkled . . . but not the Dark Bells, Roland thought. There was that.

'Stand clear,' Jenna said. 'Or I'll bring the *can tam* on ye.'

'No,' Sister Mary said, stepping closer, 'ye won't. They'll not stray so far from the others. Shake your head and ring those damned bells until the clappers fall out, and still they'll never come.'

Jenna did as bid, shaking her head furiously from side to side. The Dark Bells rang piercingly, but without that extra, almost psychic tone-quality that had gone through Roland's head like a spike. And the doctor-bugs – what Jenna had called the *can tam* – did not come.

Smiling ever more broadly (Roland had an idea Mary herself hadn't been completely sure they wouldn't come until the experiment was made), the corpse-woman closed in on them, seeming to float above the ground. Her eyes flicked towards him. 'And put that away,' she said.

Roland looked down and saw that one of his guns was in his hand. He had no memory of drawing it.

'Unless it's been blessed or dipped in some sect's holy wet – blood, water, semen – it can't harm such as I, gunslinger. For I am more shade than substance . . . yet still the equal to such as yerself, for all that.'

She thought he would try shooting her, anyway; he saw it in her eyes. *Those shooters are all ye have,* her eyes said. *Without 'em, you might as well be back in the tent we dreamed around ye, caught up in our slings and awaiting our pleasure.*

Instead of shooting, he dropped the revolver back into its holster and launched himself at her with his hands out. Sister Mary uttered a scream that was mostly surprise, but it was not a long one; Roland's fingers clamped down on her throat and choked the sound off before it was fairly started.

The touch of her flesh was obscene – it seemed not just alive but *various* beneath his hands, as if it was trying to crawl away from him. He could feel it running like liquid, *flowing*, and the sensation was horrible beyond description. Yet he clamped down harder, determined to choke the life out of her.

Then there came a blue flash (not in the air, he would think later; that flash happened inside his head, a single stroke of lightning as she touched off some brief but powerful brainstorm), and his hands flew away from her neck. For one moment his dazzled eyes saw great wet gouges in her grey flesh – gouges in the shapes of his hands. Then he was flung backwards, hitting the scree on his back and sliding, striking his head on a jutting rock hard enough to provoke a second, lesser, flash of light.

'Nay, my pretty man,' she said, grimacing at him, laughing with those terrible dull eyes of hers. 'Ye don't choke such as I, and I'll take ye slow for yer impertinence – cut ye shallow in a hundred places to refresh my thirst. First, though, I'll have this vowless girl . . . and I'll have those damned bells off her, in the bargain.'

'Come and see if you can!' Jenna cried in a trembling voice, and shook her head from side to side. The Dark Bells rang mockingly, provokingly.

Mary's grimace of a smile fell away. 'Oh, I can,' she breathed. Her mouth yawned. In the moonlight, her fangs gleamed in her gums like bone needles poked through a red pillow. 'I can and I –'

There was a growl from above them. It rose, then splintered into a volley of snarling barks. Mary turned to her left, and in the moment before the snarling thing left the rock on which it was standing, Roland could clearly read the startled bewilderment on Big Sister's face.

It launched itself at her, only a dark shape against the stars, legs outstretched so it looked like some sort of weird bat, but even before it crashed into the woman, striking her in the chest above her half-raised arms and fastening its own teeth on her throat, Roland knew exactly what it was.

As the shape bore her over on to her back, Sister Mary uttered a gibbering shriek that went through Roland's head like the Dark Bells themselves. He scrambled to his feet, gasping. The shadowy thing tore at her, forepaws on either side of her head, rear paws planted on the grave-shroud above her chest, where the rose had been.

Roland grabbed Jenna, who was looking down at the fallen Sister with a kind of frozen fascination.

'Come on!' he shouted. 'Before it decides it wants a bite of you, too!'

The dog took no notice of them as Roland pulled Jenna past. It had torn Sister Mary's head mostly off. Her flesh seemed to be changing, somehow – decomposing, very likely – but whatever was happening, Roland did not want to see it. He didn't want Jenna to see it, either.

They half-walked, half-ran to the top of the ridge, and when they got there paused for breath in the moonlight, heads down, hands linked, both of them gasping harshly.

The growling and snarling below them had faded, but was still faintly audible when Sister Jenna raised her head and asked him, 'What was it? You know – I saw it in your face. And how could it attack her? We all have power over animals, but she has – had – the most.'

'Not over that one.' Roland found himself recalling the unfortunate boy in the next bed. Norman hadn't known why the medallions kept the Sisters at arm's length – whether it was the gold or the God. Now Roland knew the answer. 'It was a dog. Just a town-dog. I saw it in the square, before the green folk knocked me out and took me to the Sisters. I suppose the other animals that could run away *did* run away, but not that one. It had nothing to fear from the Little Sisters of Eluria, and somehow it knew it didn't. It bears the sign of the Jesus-man on its chest. Black fur on white. Just an accident of its birth, I imagine. In any case, it's done for her now. I knew it was lurking around. I heard it barking two or three times.'

'Why?' Jenna whispered. 'Why would it come? Why would it stay? And why would it take on her as it did?'

Roland of Gilead responded as he ever had and ever would when such useless, mystifying questions were raised: '*Ka*. Come on. Let's get as far as we can from this place before we hide up for the day.'

As far as they could turned out to be eight miles at most . . . and probably, Roland thought as the two of them sank down in a patch of sweet-smelling sage beneath an overhang of rock, a good deal less. Five, perhaps. It was him slowing them down; or rather, it was the residue of the poison in the soup. When it was clear to him that he could not go farther without help, he asked her for one of the reeds. She refused, saying that the stuff in it might combine with the unaccustomed exercise to burst his heart.

'Besides,' she said as they lay back against the embankment of the little nook they had found, 'they'll not follow. Those that are left – Michela, Louise, Tamra – will be packing up to move on. They know to leave when the time comes; that's why the Sisters have survived as long as they have. As *we* have. We're strong in some ways, but weak in many more. Sister Mary forgot that. It was her arrogance that did for her as much as the cross-dog, I think.'

She had cached not just his boots and clothes beyond the top of the ridge, but the smaller of his two purses, as well. When she tried to apologize for not bringing his bedroll and the larger purse (she'd tried, she said, but they were simply too heavy), Roland hushed her with a finger to her lips. He thought it a miracle to have as much as he did. And besides (this he did not say, but perhaps she knew it, anyway), the guns were the only things which really mattered. The guns of his father, and his father before him, all the way back to the days of Arthur Eld, when dreams and dragons had still walked the earth.

'Will you be all right?' he asked her as they settled down. The moon had set, but dawn was still at least three hours away. They were surrounded by the sweet smell of the sage. A purple smell, he thought it then . . . and ever after. Already he could feel it forming a kind of magic carpet under him, which would soon float him away to sleep. He thought he had never been so tired.

'Roland, I know not.' But even then, he thought she had known. Her mother had brought her back once; no mother would bring her back again. And she had eaten with the others, had taken the communion of the Sisters. *Ka* was a wheel; it was also a net from which none ever escaped.

But then he was too tired to think much of such things . . . and what good would thinking have done, in any case? As she had said, the bridge was burned. Even if they were to return to the valley, Roland guessed they would find nothing but the cave the Sisters had called Thoughtful House. The surviving Sisters would have packed their tent of bad dreams and moved on, just a sound of bells and singing insects moving down the late night breeze.

He looked at her, raised a hand (it felt heavy), and touched the curl which once more lay across her forehead.

Jenna laughed, embarrassed. 'That one always escapes. It's wayward. Like its mistress.'

She raised her hand to poke it back in, but Roland took her fingers before she could. 'It's beautiful,' he said. 'Black as night and as beautiful as forever.'

He sat up – it took an effort; weariness dragged at his body like soft hands. He kissed the curl. She closed her eyes and sighed. He felt her trembling beneath his lips. The skin of her brow was very cool; the dark curve of the wayward curl like silk.

'Push back your wimple, as you did before,' he said.

She did it without speaking. For a moment he only looked at her. Jenna looked back gravely, her eyes never leaving his. He ran his hands through her hair, feeling its smooth weight (like rain, he thought, rain with weight), then took her shoulders and kissed each of her cheeks. He drew back for a moment.

'Would ye kiss me as a man does a woman, Roland? On my mouth?'

'Aye.'

And, as he had thought of doing as he lay caught in the silken infirmary tent, he kissed her lips. She kissed back with the clumsy sweetness of one who has never kissed before, except perhaps in dreams. Roland thought to make love to her then – it had been long and long, and she was beautiful – but he fell asleep instead, still kissing her.

He dreamed of the cross-dog, barking its way across a great open landscape. He followed, wanting to see the source of its agitation, and soon he did. At the far edge of that plain stood the Dark Tower, its smoky stone outlined by the dull orange ball of a setting sun, its fearful windows rising in a spiral. The dog stopped at the sight of it and began to howl.

Bells – peculiarly shrill and as terrible as doom – began to ring. Dark bells, he knew, but their tone was as bright as silver. At their sound, the dark windows of the Tower glowed with a deadly red light – the red of poisoned roses. A scream of unbearable pain rose in the night.

The dream blew away in an instant, but the scream remained, now unravelling to a moan. That part was real – as real as the Tower, brooding in its place at the very end of End-World. Roland came back to the brightness of dawn and the soft purple smell of desert sage. He had drawn both his guns, and was on his feet before he had fully realized he was awake.

Jenna was gone. Her boots lay empty beside his purse. A little distance from them, her jeans lay as flat as discarded snakeskins. Above them was her shirt. It was, Roland observed with wonder, still tucked into the pants. Beyond them was her empty wimple, with its fringe of bells lying on the powdery ground. He thought for a moment that they were ringing, mistaking the sound he heard at first.

Not bells but bugs. The doctor-bugs. They sang in the sage, sounding a bit like crickets, but far sweeter.

'Jenna?'

No answer . . . unless the bugs answered. For their singing suddenly stopped.

'Jenna?'

Nothing. Only the wind and the smell of the sage.

Without thinking about what he was doing (like play-acting, reasoned thought was not his strong suit), he bent, picked up the wimple, and shook it. The Dark Bells rang.

For a moment there was nothing. Then a thousand small dark creatures came scurrying out of the sage, gathering on the broken earth. Roland thought of the battalion marching down the side of the freighter's bed and took a step back. Then he held his position. As, he saw, the bugs were holding theirs.

He believed he understood. Some of this understanding came from his memory of how Sister Mary's flesh had felt under his hands . . . how it had felt *various*, not one thing but many. Part of it was what she had said: *I have supped with them.* Such as them might never die . . . but they might *change*.

The insects trembled, a dark cloud of them blotting out the white, powdery earth.

Roland shook the bells again.

A shiver ran through them in a subtle wave, and then they began to form a shape. They hesitated as if unsure of how to go on, regrouped, began again. What they eventually made on the whiteness of the sand there between the blowing fluffs of lilac-coloured sage was one of the Great Letters: the letter C.

Except it wasn't really a letter, the gunslinger saw; it was a curl.

They began to sing, and to Roland it sounded as if they were singing his name.

The bells fell from his unnerved hand, and when they struck

the ground and chimed there, the mass of bugs broke apart, running in every direction. He thought of calling them back – ringing the bells again might do that – but to what purpose? To what end?

Ask me not, Roland. 'Tis done, the bridge burned.

Yet she had come to him one last time, imposing her will over a thousand various parts that should have lost the ability to think when the whole lost its cohesion . . . and yet she *had* thought, somehow – enough to make that shape. How much effort might that have taken?

They fanned wider and wider, some disappearing into the sage, some trundling up the sides of rock overhang, pouring into the cracks where they would, mayhap, wait out the heat of the day.

They were gone. *She* was gone.

Roland sat down on the ground and put his hands over his face. He thought he might weep, but in time the urge passed; when he raised his head again, his eyes were as dry as the desert he would eventually come to, still following the trail of Walter, the man in black.

If there's to be damnation, she had said, *let it be of my choosing, not theirs*.

He knew a little about damnation himself . . . and he had an idea that the lessons, far from being done, were just beginning.

She had brought him the purse with his tobacco in it. He rolled a cigarette and smoked it hunkered over his knees. He smoked it down to a glowing roach, looking at her empty clothes the while, remembering the steady gaze of her dark eyes. Remembering the scorch-marks on her fingers from the chain of the medallion. Yet she had picked it up, because she had known he would want it; had dared that pain, and Roland now wore both around his neck.

When the sun was fully up, the gunslinger moved on west. He would find another horse eventually, or a mule, but for now he was content to walk. All that day he was haunted by a ringing, singing sound in his ears, a sound like bells. Several times he stopped and looked around, sure he would see a dark following shape flowing over the ground, chasing after as the shadows of our best and worst memories chase after, but no shape was ever there. He was alone in the low hill country west of Eluria.

Quite alone.

The Sword
of Truth

TERRY GOODKIND

THE SWORD
OF TRUTH

TERRY GOODKIND

Wizard's First Rule (1994)
Stone of Tears (1995)
Blood of the Fold (1996)
Temple of the Winds (1997)

Terry Goodkind burst on to the fantasy scene in 1994 with the publication of *Wizard's First Rule*, which tells the story of Richard Cypher, a young man who learns that he is the key to defeating the evil sorcerer Darken Rahl, who threatens to subjugate all lands and peoples. Three succeeding novels in the series have brought Goodkind to the bestseller lists.

Little does Richard know when he happens across Kahlan, an alluring but secretive woman being chased by four assassins, that his life as a woods guide is about to be for ever altered. Richard, a man with his own troubling secrets, helps Kahlan find the wizard she seeks, but as the boundary between the lands begins to fail, discovers himself caught up not only in a strange new world, but in Kahlan's quest for a way to stop Darken Rahl, the charismatic and cunning leader of the far-off land of D'Hara. Darken Rahl has launched a war of arms as well as persuasion against the people of the Midlands as he searches for the power to control them entirely. For Richard and Kahlan, time is running out to find the repository of this power before Darken Rahl can impose a merciless fate on them. Richard, who comes to care deeply for Kahlan, must confront timeless lessons about the encroachment of evil on an unsuspecting world. The series becomes an inner quest as much as it is a struggle for destiny and freedom. In the course of obtaining the essential weapon – the Sword of Truth – he learns that the stakes are higher than simple life and death, and that the dividing line between moral choices and evil ones is often shrouded by apathy, ignorance, and greed.

In *Stone of Tears*, Richard strives to master the magic power that is his birthright, but finds that the effort of wielding such magic threatens his life. To save him, Kahlan, in desperation, sends him away with the Sisters of the Light. The Sisters, who promise to teach him to control his power, spirit him away beyond the Valley of the Lost to the Palace of the Prophets in the Old World. Kahlan undertakes an arduous journey to find their friend and mentor, Zedd, the First Wizard. Along the way she discovers the people of a city that has been attacked by the Imperial Order, and must forge an army of young recruits into a force that will not only stop this new threat to the Midlands but will exact vengeance. Richard's teachers turn out to include some who are sworn to the Keeper of the Underworld and intend to use Richard to free their master. Richard has already unwittingly helped them by using his gift, which tore the veil that separates the realm of the dead from the world of the living. Richard's only hope to save everyone is to find the Stone of Tears, but to do that, he must escape his imprisonment at the Palace of the Prophets. And to have any hope of escape, he must learn to use his gift before the Sisters of the Dark, who would destroy him, can turn him to their purposes.

In *Blood of the Fold*, the third novel, the emperor of the Imperial Order in the Old World lusts to conquer the Midlands. To that end, he tries to use an army of anti-magic zealots to purge the Midlands of those born with the gift of magic. The emperor, a dream-walker with magic of his own, captures the Sisters of the Dark and uses them against Richard and Kahlan, while the people who call themselves the Blood of the Fold plot their own conquest of the Midlands. Unless Richard can seize power and mould the fragmented Midlands into one, the Imperial Order will sweep across the land, shadowing the Midlands in an age of slavery, and freedom's last flames will die for ever.

In *Temple of the Winds*, Emperor Jagang sends an assassin to kill Richard, and in the process unleashes a deadly plague. The conflagration of disease claims more people with each passing day as Richard and Kahlan desperately search for a cure. Trust and love are tested in a twisting trail of devotion and betrayal. With hundreds and then thousands of their people perishing each day, Richard and Kahlan must find the Temple of the Winds, and then decide if they will pay the terrible price required to enter.

DEBT OF BONES

BY TERRY GOODKIND

'What do you got in the sack, dearie?'

Abby was watching a distant flock of whistling swans, graceful white specks against the dark soaring walls of the Keep, as they made their interminable journey past ramparts, bastions, towers and bridges lit by the low sun. The sinister spectre of the Keep had seemed to be staring back the whole of the day as Abby had waited. She turned to the hunched old woman in front of her.

'I'm sorry, did you ask me something?'

'I asked what you got in your sack.' As the woman peered up, she licked the tip of her tongue through the slot where a tooth was missing. 'Something precious?'

Abby clutched the burlap sack to herself as she shrank a little from the grinning woman. 'Just some of my things, that's all.'

An officer, trailed by a troop of assistants, aides, and guards, marched out from under the massive portcullis that loomed nearby. Abby and the rest of the supplicants waiting at the head of the stone bridge moved tighter to the side, even though the soldiers had ample room to pass. The officer, his grim gaze unseeing as he swept by, didn't return the salute as the bridge guards clapped fists to the armour over their hearts.

All day soldiers from different lands, as well as the Home Guard from the vast city of Aydindril below, had been coming and going from the Keep. Some had looked travel-sore. Some wore uniforms still filthy with dirt, soot, and blood from recent battles. Abby had even seen two officers from her homeland of Pendisan Reach. They had looked to her to be little more than boys, but boys with the thin veneer of youth shedding too soon, like a snake casting off its skin before its time, leaving the emerging maturity scarred.

Abby had also seen such an array of important people as she could scarcely believe: sorceresses, councillors, and even a Confessor come up from the Confessor's Palace down in the city. On her way up to the Keep, there was rarely a turn in the winding road that hadn't offered Abby a view of the sprawling splendour in white stone that was the Confessor's Palace. The alliance of the Midlands, headed by the Mother Confessor herself, held council in the palace, and there, too, lived the Confessors.

In her whole life, Abby had seen a Confessor only once before. The woman had come to see Abby's mother and Abby, not ten years at the time, had been unable to keep from staring at the Confessor's long hair. Other than her mother, no woman in Abby's small town of Coney Crossing was sufficiently important to have hair long enough to touch the shoulders. Abby's own fine, dark brown hair covered her ears but no more.

Coming through the city on the way to the Keep, it had been hard for her not to gape at noble women with hair to their shoulders and even a little beyond. But the Confessor going up to the Keep, dressed in the simple, satiny, black dress of a Confessor, had hair that reached halfway down her back.

She wished she could have had a better look at the rare sight of such long luxuriant hair and the woman important enough to possess it, but Abby had gone to a knee with the rest of the company at the bridge, and like the rest of them feared to raise her bowed head to look up lest she meet the gaze of the other. It was said that to meet the gaze of a Confessor could cost you your mind if you were lucky, and your soul if you weren't. Even though Abby's mother had said it was untrue, that only the deliberate touch of such a woman could effect such a deed, Abby feared, this day of all days, to test the stories.

The old woman in front of her, clothed in layered skirts topped with one dyed of henna and mantled with a dark draping shawl, watched the soldiers pass and then leaned closer. 'Do better to bring a bone, dearie. I hear that there be those in the city who will sell a bone such as you need – for the right price. Wizards don't take no salt pork for a need. They got salt pork.' She glanced past Abby to the others to see them occupied with their own interests. 'Better to sell your things and hope you have enough to buy a bone. Wizards don't want what some country girl brung 'em. Favours from wizards don't come easy.' She glanced to the backs of the soldiers as they reached the far side of the bridge. 'Not even for those doing their bidding, it would seem.'

'I just want to talk to them. That's all.'

'Salt pork won't get you a talk, neither, as I hear tell.' She eyed Abby's hand trying to cover the smooth round shape beneath the burlap. 'Or a jug you made. That what it is, dearie?' Her brown eyes, set in a wrinkled leathery mask, turned up, peering with sudden, humourless intent. 'A jug?'

'Yes,' Abby said. 'A jug I made.'

The woman smiled her scepticism and fingered a lick of short grey hair back under her wool head-wrap. Her gnarled fingers closed around the smocking on the forearm of Abby's crimson dress, pulling the arm up a bit to have a look.

'Maybe you could get the price of a proper bone for your bracelet.'

Abby glanced down at the bracelet made of two wires twisted together in interlocking circles. 'My mother gave me this. It has no value but to me.'

A slow smile came to the woman's weather-cracked lips. 'The spirits believe that there is no stronger power than a mother's want to protect her child.'

Abby gently pulled her arm away. 'The spirits know the truth of that.'

Uncomfortable under the scrutiny of the suddenly talkative woman, Abby searched for a safe place to settle her gaze. It made her dizzy to look down into the yawning chasm beneath the bridge, and she was weary of watching the Wizard's Keep, so she pretended that her attention had been caught as an excuse to turn back towards the collection of people, mostly men, waiting with her at the head of the bridge. She busied herself with nibbling on the last crust of bread from the loaf she had bought down in the market before coming up to the Keep.

Abby felt awkward talking to strangers. In her whole life she had never seen so many people, much less people she didn't know. She knew every person in Coney Crossing. The city made her apprehensive, but not as apprehensive as the Keep towering on the mountain above it, and that, not as much as her reason for being there.

She just wanted to go home. But there would be no home, at least nothing to go home to, if she didn't do this.

All eyes turned up at the rattle of hooves coming out under the portcullis. Huge horses, all dusky brown or black and bigger than any Abby had ever seen, came thundering towards them. Men bedecked with polished breastplates, chain-mail, and leather, and most carrying lances or poles topped with long flags of high office and rank, urged their mounts onward. They raised dust and gravel as they gathered speed crossing the bridge, a wild rush of colour and sparkles of light from metal flashing past. Sanderian lancers, from the descriptions Abby had heard. She had trouble imagining the enemy with the nerve to go up against men such as these.

Her stomach roiled. She realized she had no need to imagine and no reason to put her hope in brave men such as those lancers. Her only hope was the wizard, and that hope was slipping away as she stood waiting. There was nothing for it but to wait.

Abby turned back to the Keep just in time to see a statuesque woman in simple robes stride out through the opening in the massive stone wall. Her fair skin stood out all the more against straight dark hair parted in the middle and readily reaching her shoulders. Some of the men had been whispering about the sight of the Sanderian officers, but at the sight of the woman everyone fell to silence. The four soldiers at the head of the stone bridge made way for the woman as she approached the supplicants.

'Sorceress,' the old woman whispered to Abby.

Abby hardly needed the old woman's counsel to know it was a sorceress. Abby recognized the simple flaxen robes, decorated at the neck with yellow and red beads sewn in the ancient symbols of the profession. Some of her earliest memories were of being held in her mother's arms and touching beads like those she saw now.

The sorceress bowed her head to the people and then offered a smile. 'Please forgive us for keeping you waiting out here the whole of the day. It is not from lack of respect nor something we customarily do, but with the war on our hands such precautions are regrettably unavoidable. We hope none took offence at the delay.'

The crowd mumbled that they didn't. Abby doubted there was one among them bold enough to claim otherwise.

'How goes the war?' a man behind asked.

The sorceress's even gaze turned to him. 'With the blessings of the good spirits, it will end soon.'

'May the spirits will that D'Hara is crushed,' beseeched the man.

Without response, the sorceress appraised the faces watching her, waiting to see if anyone else would speak or ask a question. None did.

'Please, come with me, then. The council meeting has ended, and a couple of the wizards will take the time to see you all.'

As the sorceress turned back to the Keep and started out, three men strode up among the supplicants and put themselves at the head of the line, right in front of the old woman. The woman snatched a velvet sleeve.

'Who do you think you are,' she snapped, 'taking a place before me, when I've been here the whole of the day?'

The oldest of the three, dressed in rich robes of dark purple with contrasting red sewn inside the length of the slits up the sleeves, looked to be a noble with his two advisors, or perhaps guards. He turned a glare on the woman. 'You don't mind, do you?'

It didn't sound at all to Abby like a question.

The old woman took her hand back and fell mute.

The man, the ends of his grey hair coiled on his shoulders, glanced at Abby. His hooded eyes gleamed with challenge. She swallowed and remained silent. She didn't have any objection, either, at least none she was willing to voice. For all she knew, the noble was important enough to see to it that she was denied an audience. She couldn't afford to take that chance now that she was this close.

Abby was distracted by a tingling sensation from the bracelet. Blindly, her fingers glided over the wrist of the hand holding the sack. The wire bracelet felt warm. It hadn't done that since her mother had died. In the presence of so much magic as was at a place such as this, it didn't really surprise her. The crowd moved out to follow the sorceress.

'Mean, they are,' the woman whispered over her shoulder. 'Mean as a winter night, and just as cold.'

'Those men?' Abby whispered back.

'No.' The woman tilted her head. 'Sorceresses. Wizards, too. That's who. All those born with the gift of magic. You better have something important in that sack, or the wizards might turn you to dust for no other reason than that they'd enjoy it.'

Abby pulled her sack tight in her arms. The meanest thing her mother had done in the whole of her life was to die before she could see her granddaughter.

Abby swallowed back the urge to cry and prayed to the dear spirits that the old woman was wrong about wizards, and that they were as understanding as sorceresses. She prayed fervently that this wizard would help her. She prayed for forgiveness, too – that the good spirits would understand.

Abby worked at holding a calm countenance even though her insides were in turmoil. She pressed a fist to her stomach. She prayed for strength. Even in this, she prayed for strength.

The sorceress, the three men, the old woman, Abby, and then the rest of the supplicants, passed under the huge iron portcullis and on to the Keep grounds. Inside the massive outer wall Abby was surprised to discover the air warm. Outside it had been a chill autumn day, but inside the air was spring-fresh and warm.

The road up the mountain, the stone bridge over the chasm, and then the opening under the portcullis appeared to be the only way into the Keep, unless you were a bird. Soaring walls of dark stone with high windows surrounded the gravel courtyard inside. There were a number of doors around the courtyard, and ahead, a roadway tunnelled deeper into the Keep.

Despite the warm air, Abby was chilled to the bone by the place. She wasn't sure that the old woman wasn't right about wizards. Life in Coney Crossing was far removed from matters of wizards.

Abby had never seen a wizard before, nor did she know anyone who had, except for her mother, and her mother never spoke of them except to caution that where wizards were concerned, you couldn't trust even what you saw with your own eyes.

The sorceress led them up four granite steps worn smooth over the ages by countless footsteps, through a doorway set back under a lintel of pink-flecked black granite, and into the Keep proper. The sorceress lifted an arm into the darkness, sweeping it to the side. Lamps along the wall sprang to flame.

It had been simple magic – not a very impressive display of the gift – but several of the people behind fell to worried whispering as they passed on through the wide hall. It occurred to Abby that if this little bit of conjuring would frighten them, then they had no business going to see wizards.

They wended their way across the sunken floor of an imposing anteroom the likes of which Abby could never even have imagined. Red marble columns all around supported arches below balconies. In the centre of the room a fountain sprayed water high overhead. The water fell back to cascade down through a succession of ever larger scalloped bowls. Officers, sorceresses, and a variety of others sat about on white marble benches or huddled in small groups, all engaged in seemingly earnest conversation masked by the sound of the water.

In a much smaller room beyond, the sorceress gestured for them to be seated at a line of carved oak benches along one wall. Abby was bone-weary and relieved to sit at last.

Light from windows above the benches lit three tapestries hanging on the high far wall. The three together covered nearly the entire wall and made up one scene of a grand procession through a city. Abby had never seen anything like it, but with the way her dreads careened through her thoughts, she could summon little pleasure in seeing even such a majestic tableau.

In the centre of the cream-coloured marble floor, inset in brass lines, was a circle with a square inside it, its corners touching the circle. Inside the square sat another circle just large enough to touch the insides of the square. The centre circle held an eight-pointed star. Lines radiated out from the points of the star, piercing all the way through both circles, every other line bisecting a corner of the square.

The design, called a Grace, was often drawn by those with the gift. The outer circle represented the beginnings of the infinity of the spirit world out beyond. The square represented the boundary separating the spirit world – the underworld, the world of the dead – from the inner circle, which represented the limits of the world of life. In the centre of it all was the star, representing the Light – the Creator.

It was a depiction of the continuum of the gift: from the Creator, through life, and at death crossing the boundary to eternity with the spirits in the Keeper's realm of the underworld. But it represented a hope, too – a hope to remain in the Creator's Light from birth, through life, and beyond, in the underworld.

It was said that only the spirits of those who did great wickedness in life would be denied the Creator's Light in the underworld. Abby knew she would be condemned to an eternity with the Keeper of darkness in the underworld. She had no choice.

The sorceress folded her hands. 'An aide will come to get you each in turn. A wizard will see each of you. The war burns hot; please keep your petition brief.' She gazed down the line of people. 'It is out of a sincere obligation to those we serve that the wizards see supplicants, but please try to understand that individual desires are often detrimental to the greater good. By pausing to help one, then many are denied help. Thus, denial of a request is not a denial of your need, but acceptance of greater need. In times of peace it is rare for wizards to grant the narrow wants of supplicants. At a time like this, a time of a great war, it is almost unheard-of. Please understand that it has not to do with what we would wish, but is a matter of necessity.'

She watched the line of supplicants, but saw none willing to abandon their purpose. Abby certainly would not.

'Very well then. We have two wizards able to take supplicants at this time. We will bring you each to one of them.'

The sorceress turned to leave. Abby rose to her feet.

'Please, mistress, a word if I may?'

The sorceress turned an unsettling gaze on Abby. 'Speak.'

Abby stepped forward. 'I must see the First Wizard himself. Wizard Zorander.'

One eyebrow arched. 'The First Wizard is a very busy man.'

Abby reached into her sack and pulled out the neck band from her mother's robes. She stepped into the centre of the Grace and kissed the red and yellow beads on the neck band.

'I am Abigail, born of Helsa. On the Grace and my mother's soul, I must see Wizard Zorander. Please. It is no trivial journey I have made. Lives are at stake.'

The sorceress watched the beaded band being returned to the sack. 'Abigail, born of Helsa.' Her gaze rose to meet Abby's. 'I will take your words to the First Wizard.'

'Mistress.' Abby turned to see the old woman on her feet. 'I would be well pleased to see the First Wizard, too.'

The three men rose up. The oldest, the one apparently in charge of the three, gave the sorceress a look so barren of timidity that it bordered on contempt. His long grey hair fell forward over his velvet robes as he glanced down the line of seated people, seeming to dare them to stand. When none did, he returned his attention to the sorceress.

'I will see Wizard Zorander.'

The sorceress appraised those on their feet and then looked down the line of supplicants on the bench. 'The First Wizard has earned a name: the wind of death. He is feared no less by many of us than by our enemies. Anyone else who would bait fate?'

None of those on the bench had the courage to gaze into her fierce stare. To the last they all silently shook their heads. 'Please wait,' she said to those seated. 'Someone will shortly be out to take you to a wizard.' She looked once more to the five people standing. 'Are you all very, very sure of this?'

Abby nodded. The old woman nodded. The noble glared.

'Very well then. Come with me.'

The noble and his two men stepped in front of Abby. The old woman seemed content to take a station at the end of the line. They were led deeper into the Keep, through narrow halls and wide corridors, some dark and austere and some of astounding grandeur. Everywhere there were soldiers of the Home Guard, their breastplates or chain-mail covered with red tunics banded around their edges in black. All were heavily armed with swords or battle-axes, all had knives, and many additionally carried pikes tipped with winged and barbed steel.

At the top of a broad white marble stairway the stone railings spiralled at the ends to open wide on to a room of warm oak panelling. Several of the raised panels held lamps with polished silver reflectors. Atop a three-legged table sat a double-bowl cut-glass lamp with twin chimneys, their flames adding to the mellow light from the reflector lamps. A thick carpet of ornate blue patterns covered nearly the entire wood floor.

To each side of a double door stood one of the meticulously dressed Home Guard. Both men were equally huge. They looked to be men more than able to handle any trouble that might come up the stairs.

The sorceress nodded towards the dozen thickly tufted leather chairs set in four groups. Abby waited until the others had seated themselves in two of the groupings and then sat by herself in another. She placed the sack in her lap and rested her hands over its contents.

The sorceress stiffened her back. 'I will tell the First Wizard that he has supplicants who wish to see him.'

A guard opened one of the double doors for her. As she was swallowed into the great room beyond, Abby was able to snatch a quick glimpse. She could see that it was well lighted by glassed skylights. There were other doors in the grey stone of the walls. Before the door closed, Abby was also able to see a number of people, men and women both, all rushing hither and yon.

Abby sat turned away from the old woman and the three men as with one hand she idly stroked the sack in her lap. She had little fear that the men would talk to her, but she didn't want to talk to the woman; it was a distraction. She passed the time going over in her mind what she planned to say to Wizard Zorander.

At least she tried to go over it in her mind. Mostly, all she could think about was what the sorceress had said, that the First Wizard was called the wind of death, not only by the D'Harans, but also by his own people of the Midlands. Abby knew it was no tale to scare off supplicants from a busy man. Abby herself had heard people whisper of their great wizard, 'the wind of death'. Those whispered words were uttered in dread.

The lands of D'Hara had sound reason to fear this man as their enemy; he had laid waste to countless of their army, from what Abby had heard. Of course if they hadn't invaded the Midlands, bent on conquest, they would not have felt the hot wind of death.

Had they not invaded, Abby wouldn't be sitting there in the Wizard's Keep – she would be at home, and everyone she loved would be safe.

Abby marked again the odd tingling sensation from the bracelet. She ran her fingers over it, testing its unusual warmth. This close to a person of such power it didn't surprise her that the bracelet was warming. Her mother had told her to wear it always, and that someday it would be of value. Abby didn't know how, and her mother had died without ever explaining.

Sorceresses were known for the way they kept secrets, even from their own daughters. Perhaps if Abby had been born gifted . . .

She sneaked a peek over her shoulder at the others. The old woman was leaning back in her chair, staring at the doors. The noble's attendants sat with their hands folded as they casually eyed the room.

The noble was doing the oddest thing. He had a lock of sandy-coloured hair wound around a finger. He stroked his thumb over the lock of hair as he glared at the doors.

Abby wanted the wizard to hurry up and see her, but time stubbornly dragged by. In a way, she wished he would refuse. No, she told herself, that was unacceptable. No matter her fear, no matter her revulsion, she must do this. Abruptly, the door opened. The sorceress strode out towards Abby.

The noble surged to his feet. 'I will see him first.' His voice was cold threat. 'That is not a request.'

'It is our right to see him first,' Abby said without forethought. When the sorceress folded her hands, Abby decided she had best go on. 'I've waited since dawn. This woman was the only one waiting before me. These men came at the last of the day.'

Abby started when the old woman's gnarled fingers gripped her forearm. 'Why don't we let these men go first, dearie? It matters not who arrived first, but who has the most important business.'

Abby wanted to scream that her business was important, but she realized that the old woman might be saving her from serious trouble in accomplishing her business. Reluctantly, she gave the sorceress a nod. As the sorceress led the three men through the door, Abby could feel the old woman's eyes on her back. Abby hugged the sack against the burning anxiety in her abdomen and told herself that it wouldn't be long, and then she would see him.

As they waited, the old woman remained silent, and Abby was glad for that. Occasionally, she glanced at the door, imploring the good spirits to help her. But she realized it was futile; the good spirits wouldn't be disposed to help her in this.

A roar came from the room beyond the doors. It was like the sound of an arrow zipping through the air, or a long switch whipping, but much louder, intensifying rapidly. It ended with a shrill crack accompanied by a flash of light coming under the doors and around their edges. The doors shuddered on their hinges.

Sudden silence rang in Abby's ears. She found herself gripping the arms of the chair.

Both doors opened. The noble's two attendants marched out, followed by the sorceress. The three stopped in the waiting room. Abby sucked a breath.

One of the two men was cradling the noble's head in the crook of an arm. The wan features of the face were frozen in a mute scream. Thick strings of blood dripped on to the carpet.

'Show them out,' the sorceress hissed through gritted teeth to one of the two guards at the door.

The guard dipped his pike towards the stairs, ordering them ahead, and then followed the two men down. Crimson drops splattered on to the white marble of the steps as they descended. Abby sat in stiff, wide-eyed shock.

The sorceress wheeled back to Abby and the old woman.

The woman rose to her feet. 'I believe that I would rather not bother the First Wizard today. I will return another day, if need be.'

She hunched lower towards Abby. 'I am called Mariska.' Her brow drew down. 'May the good spirits grant that you succeed.'

She shuffled to the stairs, rested a hand on the marble railing, and started down. The sorceress snapped her fingers and gestured. The remaining guard rushed to accompany the woman, as the sorceress turned back to Abby.

'The First Wizard will see you now.'

Abby gulped air, trying to get her breath as she staggered to her feet.

'What happened? Why did the First Wizard do that?'

'The man was sent on behalf of another to ask a question of the First Wizard. The First Wizard gave his answer.'

Abby clutched her sack to herself for dear life as she gaped at the blood on the floor. 'Might that be the answer to my question, if I ask it?'

'I don't know the question you would ask.' For the first time, the sorceress's expression softened just a bit. 'Would you like me to see you out? You could see another wizard or, perhaps, after you've given more thought to your petition, return another day, if you still wish it.'

Abby fought back tears of desperation. There was no choice. She shook her head. 'I must see him.'

The sorceress let out a deep breath. 'Very well.' She put a hand under Abby's arm as if to keep her on her feet. 'The First Wizard will see you now.'

Abby hugged the contents of her sack as she was led into the chamber where waited the First Wizard. Torches in iron sconces were not yet burning. The late afternoon light from the glassed roof windows was still strong enough to illuminate the room. It smelled of pitch, lamp oil, roasted meat, wet stone, and stale sweat.

Inside, confusion and commotion reigned. There were people everywhere, and they all seemed to be talking at once. Stout tables set about the room in no discernible pattern were covered with books, scrolls, maps, chalk, unlit oil lamps, burning candles, partially eaten meals, sealing wax, pens, and a clutter of every sort of odd object, from balls of knotted string to half-spilled sacks of sand. People stood about the tables, engaged in conversations or arguments as others tapped passages in books, pored over scrolls, or moved little painted weights about on maps. Others rolled slices of roasted meat plucked from platters and nibbled as they watched or offered opinions between swallows.

The sorceress, still holding Abby under her arm, leaned closer as they proceeded. 'You will have the First Wizard's divided attention. There will be other people talking to him at the same time. Don't be distracted. He will be listening to you as he also listens to or talks to others. Just ignore the others who are speaking and ask what you have come to ask. He will hear you.'

Abby was dumbfounded. 'While he's talking to other people?'

'Yes.' Abby felt the hand squeeze her arm ever so slightly. 'Try to be calm, and not to judge by what has come before you.'

The killing. That was what she meant. That a man had come to speak to the First Wizard, and he had been killed for it. She was simply supposed to put that from her thoughts? When she glanced down, she saw that she was walking through a trail of blood. She didn't see the headless body anywhere.

Her bracelet tingled so that she looked down at it. The hand under her arm halted her. When Abby looked up, she saw a confusing knot of people before her. Some rushed in from the sides as others rushed away. Some flailed their arms as they spoke with great conviction. So many were talking that Abby could scarcely understand a word of it. At the same time, others were leaning in, nearly whispering. She felt as if she were confronting a human beehive.

Abby's attention was snagged by a form in white to the side. The instant she saw the long fall of hair and the violet eyes looking right at her, Abby went rigid. A small cry escaped her throat as she fell to her knees and bowed over until her back protested. She trembled and shuddered, fearing the worst.

In the instant before she dropped to her knees, she had seen that the elegant, satiny, white dress was cut square at the neck, the same as the black dresses had been. The long flag of hair was unmistakable. Abby had never seen the woman before, but without doubt knew who she was. There could be no mistaking this woman. Only one of them wore the white dress.

It was the Mother Confessor herself.

She heard muttering above her, but feared to listen, lest it was death being summoned.

'Rise, my child,' came a clear voice.

Abby recognized it as the formal response of the Mother Confessor to one of her people. It took a moment for Abby to realize it represented no threat, but simple acknowledgement. She stared at a smear of blood on the floor as she debated what to do next. Her mother had never instructed her as to how to conduct herself should she ever meet the Mother Confessor. As far as she knew, no one from Coney Crossing had ever seen the Mother Confessor, much less met her. Then again, none of them had ever seen a wizard, either.

Overhead, the sorceress whispered a growl. 'Rise.'

Abby scurried to her feet, but kept her eyes to the floor, even though the smear of blood was making her sick. She could smell it, like a fresh butchering of one of their animals. From the long trail, it looked as if the body had been dragged away to one of the doors in the back of the room.

The sorceress spoke calmly into the chaos. 'Wizard Zorander, this is Abigail, born of Helsa. She wishes a word with you. Abigail, this is First Wizard Zeddicus Zu'l Zorander.'

Abby dared to cautiously lift her gaze. Hazel eyes gazed back.

To each side before her were knots of people: big, forbidding officers – some of them looked as if they might be generals; several old men in robes, some simple and some ornate; several middle-aged men, some in robes and some in livery; three women – sorceresses all; a variety of other men and women; and the Mother Confessor.

The man at the centre of the turmoil, the man with the hazel eyes, was not what Abby had been expecting. She had expected some grizzled, gruff old man. This man was young – perhaps as young as she. Lean but sinewy, he wore the simplest of robes, hardly better made than Abby's burlap sack – the mark of his high office.

Abby had not anticipated this sort of man in such an office as that of First Wizard. She remembered what her mother had told her – not to trust what your eyes told you where wizards were concerned.

All about, people spoke to him, argued at him, a few even shouted, but the wizard was silent as he looked into her eyes. His face was pleasing enough to look upon, gentle in appearance, even though his wavy brown hair looked ungovernable, but his eyes . . . Abby had never seen the likes of those eyes. They seemed to see all, to know all, to understand all. At the same time they were bloodshot and weary-looking, as if sleep eluded him. They had, too, the slightest glaze of distress. Even so, he was calm at the centre of the storm. For that moment that his attention was on her, it was as if no one else were in the room.

The lock of hair Abby had seen around the noble's finger was now held wrapped around the First Wizard's finger. He brushed it to his lips before lowering his arm.

'I am told you are the daughter of a sorceress.' His voice was placid water flowing through the tumult raging all about. 'Are you gifted, child?'

'No, sir . . .'

Even as she answered, he was turning to another who had just finished speaking. 'I told you, if you do, we chance losing them. Send word that I want him to cut south.'

The tall officer to whom the wizard spoke threw his hands up. 'But he said they've reliable scouting information that the D'Harans went east on him.'

'That's not the point,' the wizard said. 'I want that pass to the south sealed. That's where their main force went; they have gifted among them. They are the ones we must kill.'

The tall officer was saluting with a fist to his heart as the wizard turned to an old sorceress. 'Yes, that's right, three invocations before attempting the transposition. I found the reference last night.'

The old sorceress departed to be replaced by a man jabbering in a foreign tongue as he opened a scroll and held it up for the wizard to see. The wizard squinted towards it, reading a moment before waving the man away, while giving orders in the same foreign language.

The wizard turned to Abby. 'You're a skip?'

Abby felt her face heat and her ears burn. 'Yes, Wizard Zorander.'

'Nothing to be ashamed of, child,' he said while the Mother Confessor herself was whispering confidentially in his ear.

But it *was* something to be ashamed of. The gift hadn't passed on to her from her mother – it had skipped her.

The people of Coney Crossing had depended on Abby's mother. She helped with those who were ill or hurt. She advised people on matters of community and those of family. For some she arranged marriages. For some she meted out discipline. For some she bestowed favours available only through magic. She was a sorceress; she protected the people of Coney Crossing.

She was revered openly. By some, she was feared and loathed privately.

She was revered for the good she did for the people of Coney Crossing. By some, she had been feared and loathed because she had the gift – because she wielded magic. Others wanted nothing so much as to live their lives without any magic about.

Abby had no magic and couldn't help with illness or injury or shapeless fears. She dearly wished she could, but she couldn't. When Abby had asked her mother why she would abide all the thankless resentment, her mother told her that helping was its own reward and you should not expect gratitude for it. She said that if you went through life expecting gratitude for the help you provided, you might end up leading a miserable life.

When her mother was alive, Abby had been shunned in subtle ways; after her mother died, the shunning became more overt. It had been expected by the people of Coney Crossing that she would serve as her mother had served. People didn't understand about the gift, how it often wasn't passed on to an offspring; instead they thought Abby selfish.

The wizard was explaining something to a sorceress about the casting of a spell. When he finished, his gaze swept past Abby on its way to someone else. She needed his help, now.

'What is it you wanted to ask me, Abigail?'

Abby's fingers tightened on the sack. 'It's about my home of Coney Crossing.' She paused while the wizard pointed in a book being held out to him. He rolled his hand at her, gesturing for her to go on as a man was explaining an intricacy to do with inverting a duplex spell. 'There's terrible trouble there,' Abby said. 'D'Haran troops came through the Crossing . . .'

The First Wizard turned to an older man with a long white beard. By his simple robes, Abby guessed him as a wizard, too.

'I'm telling you, Thomas, it can be done,' Wizard Zorander insisted. 'I'm not saying I agree with the council, I'm just telling you what I found and their unanimous decision that it be done. I'm not claiming to understand the details of just how it works, but I've studied it; it can be done. As I told the council, I can activate it. I have yet to decide if I agree with them that I should.'

The man, Thomas, wiped a hand across his face. 'You mean what I heard is true, then? That you really do think it's possible? Are you out of your mind, Zorander?'

'I found it in a book in the First Wizard's private enclave. A book from before the war with the Old World. I've seen it with my own eyes. I've cast a whole series of verification webs to test it.' He turned his attention to Abby. 'Yes, that would be Anargo's legion. Coney Crossing is in Pendisan Reach.'

'That's right,' Abby said. 'And so then this D'Haran army swept through there and –'

'Pendisan Reach refused to join with the rest of the Midlands under central command to resist the invasion from D'Hara. Standing by their sovereignty, they chose to fight the enemy in their own way. They have to live with the consequences of their actions.'

The old man was tugging on his beard. 'Still, do you know if it's real? All proven out? I mean, that book would have to be thousands of years old. It might have been conjecture. Verification webs don't always confirm the entire structure of such a thing.'

'I know that as well as you, Thomas, but I'm telling you, it's real,' Wizard Zorander said. His voice lowered to a whisper. 'The spirits preserve us, it's genuine.'

Abby's heart was pounding. She wanted to tell him her story, but she couldn't seem to get a word in. He had to help her. It was the only way.

An army officer rushed in from one of the back doors. He pushed his way into the crowd around the First Wizard.

'Wizard Zorander! I've just got word! When we unleashed the horns you sent, they worked! Urdland's force turned tail!'

Several voices fell silent. Others didn't.

'At least three thousand years old,' the First Wizard said to the man with the beard. He put a hand on the newly-arrived officer's shoulder and leaned close. 'Tell General Brainard to hold short at the Kern River. Don't burn the bridges, but hold them. Tell him to split his men. Leave half to keep Urdland's force from changing their mind; hopefully they won't be able to replace their field wizard. Have Brainard take the rest of his men north to help cut Anargo's escape route; that's where our concern lies, but we may still need the bridges to go after Urdland.'

One of the other officers, an older man looking possibly to be a general himself, went red in the face. 'Halt at the river? When the horns have done their job, and we have them on the run?

But why! We can take them down before they have a chance to regroup and join up with another force to come back at us!'

Hazel eyes turned towards the man. 'And do you know what waits over the border? How many men will die if Panis Rahl has something waiting that the horns can't turn away? How many innocent lives has it already cost us? How many of our men will die to bleed them on their own land – land we don't know as they do?'

'And how many of our people will die if we don't eliminate their ability to come back at us another day! We must pursue them. Panis Rahl will never rest. He'll be working to conjure up something else to gut us all in our sleep. We must hunt them down and kill every last one!'

'I'm working on that,' the First Wizard said cryptically.

The old man twisted his beard and made a sarcastic face. 'Yes, he thinks he can unleash the underworld itself on them.'

Several officers, two of the sorceresses, and a couple of the men in robes paused to stare in open disbelief.

The sorceress who had brought Abby to the audience leaned close. 'You wanted to talk to the First Wizard. Talk. If you have lost your nerve, then I will see you out.'

Abby wet her lips. She didn't know how she could talk into the middle of such a roundabout conversation, but she knew she must, so she just started back in.

'Sir, I don't know anything about what my homeland of Pendisan Reach has done. I know little of the king. I don't know anything about the council, or the war, or any of it. I'm from a small place, and I only know that the people there are in grave trouble. Our defenders were overrun by the enemy. There is an army of Midlands men who drive towards the D'Harans.'

She felt foolish talking to a man who was carrying on a half-dozen conversations all at once. Mostly, though, she felt anger and frustration. Those people were going to die if she couldn't convince him to help.

'How many D'Harans?' the wizard asked.

Abby opened her mouth, but an officer spoke in her place. 'We're not sure how many are left in Anargo's legion. They may be wounded, but they're an enraged wounded bull. Now they're in sight of their homeland. They can only come back at us, or escape us. We've got Sanderson sweeping down from the north and Mardale cutting up from the southwest. Anargo made a mistake going into the Crossing; in there he must fight us or run for home. We have to finish them. This may be our only chance.'

The First Wizard drew a finger and thumb down his smooth jaw. 'Still, we aren't sure of their numbers. The scouts were dependable, but they never returned. We can only assume they're dead. And why would Anargo do such a thing?'

'Well,' the officer said, 'it's the shortest escape route back to D'Hara.'

The First Wizard turned to a sorceress to answer a question she had just finished. 'I can't see how we can afford it. Tell them I said no. I'll not cast that kind of web for them and I'll not give them the means to it for no more offered than a "maybe".'

The sorceress nodded before rushing off.

Abby knew that a web was the spell cast by a sorceress. Apparently the spell cast by a wizard was called the same.

'Well, if such a thing is possible,' the bearded man was saying, 'then I'd like to see your exegesis of the text. A three-thousand-year-old book is a lot of risk. We've no clue as to how the wizards of that time could do most of what they did.'

The First Wizard, for the first time, cast a hot glare towards the man. 'Thomas, do you want to see exactly what I'm talking about? The spell-form?'

Some of the people had fallen silent at the tone in his voice. The First Wizard threw open his arms, urging everyone back out of his way. The Mother Confessor stayed close behind his left shoulder. The sorceress beside Abby pulled her back a step.

The First Wizard motioned. A man snatched a small sack off the table and handed it to him. Abby noticed that some of the sand on the tables wasn't simply spilled, but had been used to draw symbols. Abby's mother had occasionally drawn spells with sand, but mostly used a variety of other things, from ground bone to dried herbs. Abby's mother had used sand for practice; spells, real spells, had to be drawn in proper order and without error.

The First Wizard squatted down and took a handful of sand from the sack. He drew on the floor by letting the sand drizzle from the side of his fist.

Wizard Zorander's hand moved with practised precision. His arm swept around, drawing a circle. He returned for a handful of sand and drew an inner circle. It appeared he was drawing a Grace.

Abby's mother had always drawn the square second; everything in order inward and then the rays back out. Wizard Zorander drew the eight-pointed star inside the smaller circle. He drew the lines radiating outward, through both circles, but left one absent.

He had yet to draw the square, representing the boundary between worlds. He was the First Wizard, so Abby guessed that it wasn't improper to do it in a different order than a sorceress in a little place like Coney Crossing. But several of the men Abby took as wizards, and the two sorceresses behind him, were turning grave glances to one another.

Wizard Zorander laid down the lines of sand for two sides of the square. He scooped up more sand from the sack and began the last two sides.

Instead of a straight line, he drew an arc that dipped well into the edge of the inner circle – the one representing the world of life. The arc, instead of ending at the outer circle, crossed it. He drew the last side, likewise arced, so that it too crossed into the inner circle. He brought the line to meet the other where the ray from the Light was missing. Unlike the other three points of the square, this last point ended outside the larger circle – in the world of the dead.

People gasped. A hush fell over the room for a moment before worried whispers spread among those gifted.

Wizard Zorander rose. 'Satisfied, Thomas?'

Thomas's face had gone as white as his beard. 'The Creator preserve us.' His eyes turned to Wizard Zorander. 'The council doesn't truly understand this. It would be madness to unleash it.'

Wizard Zorander ignored him and turned towards Abby. 'How many D'Harans did you see?'

'Three years past, the locust swarms came. The hills of the Crossing were brown with them. I think I saw more D'Harans than I saw locusts.'

Wizard Zorander grunted his discontent. He looked down at the Grace he had drawn. 'Panis Rahl won't give up. How long, Thomas? How long until he finds something new to conjure and sends Anargo back on us?' His gaze swept among the people around him. 'How many years have we thought we would be annihilated by the invading horde from D'Hara? How many of our people have been killed by Rahl's magic? How many thousands have died of the fevers he sent? How many thousands have blistered and bled to death from the touch of the shadow people he conjured? How many villages, towns, and cities has he wiped from existence?'

When no one spoke, Wizard Zorander went on.

'It has taken us years to come back from the brink. The war has finally turned; the enemy is running. We now have three choices. The first choice is to let him run for home and hope he never comes back to again visit us with his brutality. I think it would only be a matter of time until he tried again. That leaves two realistic options. We can either pursue him into his lair and kill him for good at the cost of tens, perhaps hundreds of thousands of our men – or I can end it.'

Those gifted among the crowd cast uneasy glances to the Grace drawn on the floor.

'We still have other magic,' another wizard said. 'We can use it to the same effect without unleashing such a cataclysm.'

'Wizard Zorander is right,' another said, 'and so is the council. The enemy has earned this fate. We must set it upon them.'

The room fell again to arguing. As it did, Wizard Zorander looked into Abby's eyes. It was a clear instruction to finish her supplication.

'My people – the people in Coney Crossing – have been taken by the D'Harans. They have others, too, who they've captured.

They have a sorceress holding the captives with a spell. Please, Wizard Zorander, you must help me.

'When I was hiding, I heard the sorceress talking to their officers. The D'Harans plan to use the captives as shields. They will use the captives to blunt the deadly magic you send against them, or to blunt the spears and arrows the Midlands army sends against them. If they decide to turn and attack, they plan to drive the captives ahead. They called it "dulling the enemies' weapons on their own women and children".'

No one looked at her. They were all once again engaged in their mass talking and arguing. It was as if the lives of all those people were beneath their consideration.

Tears stung at Abby's eyes. 'Either way all those innocent people will die. Please, Wizard Zorander, we must have your help, otherwise they'll all die.'

He looked her way briefly. 'There is nothing we can do for them.'

Abby panted, trying to hold back the tears. 'My father was captured, along with others of my kin. My husband is among the captives. My daughter is among them. She is not yet five. If you send magic, they will be killed. If you attack, they will be killed. You must rescue them, or hold the attack.'

He looked genuinely saddened. 'I'm sorry. I can't help them. May the good spirits watch over them and take their souls to the Light.' He began turning away.

'No!' Abby screamed. Some of the people fell silent. Others only glanced her way as they went on. 'My child! You can't!' She thrust a hand into the sack. 'I have a bone –'

'Doesn't everyone,' he grumbled, cutting her off. 'I can't help you.'

'But you must!'

'We would have to abandon our cause. We must take the D'Haran force down – one way or another. Innocent though those people are, they are in the way. I can't allow the D'Harans to succeed in such a scheme or it would encourage its widespread use, and then even more innocents would die. The enemy must be shown that it will not deter us from our course.'

'NO!' Abby wailed. 'She's only a child! You're condemning my baby to death! There are other children! What kind of monster are you?'

No one but the wizard was even listening to her any more as they all went on with their talking.

The First Wizard's voice cut through the din and fell on her ears as clearly as the knell of death. 'I am a man who must make choices such as this one. I must deny your petition.'

Abby screamed with the agony of failure. She wasn't even to be allowed to show him.

'But it's a debt!' she cried. 'A solemn debt!'

'And it cannot be paid now.'

Abby screamed hysterically. The sorceress began pulling her away. Abby broke from the woman and ran out of the room. She staggered down the stone steps, unable to see through the tears.

At the bottom of the steps she buckled to the floor in helpless sobbing. He wouldn't help her. He wouldn't help a helpless child. Her daughter was going to die.

Abby, convulsing in sobs, felt a hand on her shoulder. Gentle arms pulled her closer. Tender fingers brushed back her hair as she wept into a woman's lap. Another person's hand touched her back and she felt the warm comfort of magic seeping into her.

'He's killing my daughter,' she cried. 'I hate him.'

'It's all right, Abigail,' the voice above said. 'It's all right to weep for such a pain as this.'

Abby wiped at her eyes, but couldn't stop the tears. The sorceress was there, beside her, at the bottom of the steps.

Abby looked up at the woman in whose arms she lay. It was the Mother Confessor herself. She could do her worst, for all Abby cared. What did it matter, what did any of it matter, now?

'He's a monster,' she sobbed. 'He is truly named. He is the ill wind of death. This time it's my baby he's killing, not the enemy.'

'I understand why you feel that way, Abigail,' the Mother Confessor said, 'but it is not true.'

'How can you say that! My daughter has not yet had a chance to live, and he will kill her! My husband will die. My father, too, but he has had a chance to live a life. My baby hasn't!'

She fell to hysterical wailing again, and the Mother Confessor once again drew her into comforting arms. Comfort was not what Abby wanted.

'You have just the one child?' the sorceress asked.

Abby nodded as she sucked a breath. 'I had another, a boy, but he died at birth. The midwife said I will have no more. My little Jana is all I will ever have.' The wild agony of it ripped through her. 'And he will kill her. Just as he killed that man before me. Wizard Zorander is a monster. May the good spirits strike him dead!'

With a poignant expression, the sorceress smoothed Abby's hair back from her forehead 'You don't understand. You see only a part of it. You don't mean what you say.'

But she did. 'If you had –'

'Delora understands,' the Mother Confessor said, gesturing towards the sorceress. 'She has a daughter of ten years, and a son, too.'

Abby peered up at the sorceress. She gave Abby a sympathetic smile and a nod to confirm the truth of it.

'I, too, have a daughter,' the Mother Confessor said. 'She is twelve. Delora and I both understand your pain. So does the First Wizard.'

Abby's fists tightened. 'He couldn't! He's hardly more than a boy himself, and he wants to kill my baby. He is the wind of death and that's all he cares about – killing people!'

The Mother Confessor patted the stone step beside her. 'Abigail, sit up here beside me. Let me tell you about the man in there.'

Still weeping, Abby pushed herself up and slid on to the step. The Mother Confessor was older by maybe twelve or fourteen years, and pleasant-looking, with those violet eyes. Her mass of long hair reached her waist. She had a warm smile. It had never occurred to Abby to think of a Confessor as a woman, but that was what she saw now. She didn't fear this woman as she had before; nothing she did could be worse than what already had been done.

'I sometimes minded Zeddicus when he was but a toddler and I was still coming into womanhood.' The Mother Confessor gazed off with a wistful smile. 'I swatted his bottom when he misbehaved, and later twisted his ear to make him sit at a lesson. He was mischief on two legs, driven not by guile but by curiosity. He grew into a fine man.

'For a long time, when the war with D'Hara started, Wizard Zorander wouldn't help us. He didn't want to fight, to hurt people. But in the end, when Panis Rahl, the leader of D'Hara, started using magic to slaughter our people, Zedd knew that the only hope to save more lives in the end was to fight.

'Zeddicus Zu'l Zorander may look young to you, as he did to many of us, but he is a special wizard, born of a wizard and a sorceress. Zedd was a prodigy. Even those other wizards in there, some of them his teachers, don't always understand how he is able to unravel some of the enigmas in the books or how he uses his gift to bring so much power to bear, but we do understand that he has heart. He uses his heart, as well as his head. He was named First Wizard for all these things and more.'

'Yes,' Abby said, 'he is very talented at being the wind of death.'

The Mother Confessor smiled a small smile. She tapped her chest. 'Among ourselves, those of us who really know him call him the trickster. The trickster is the name he has truly earned. We named him the wind of death for others to hear, so as to strike terror into the hearts of the enemy. Some people on our side take that name to heart. Perhaps, since your mother was gifted, you can understand how people sometimes unreasonably fear those with magic?'

'And sometimes,' Abby argued, 'those with magic really are monsters who care nothing for the life they destroy.'

The Mother Confessor appraised Abby's eyes a moment, and then held up a cautionary finger. 'In confidence, I am going to tell you about Zeddicus Zu'l Zorander. If you ever repeat this story, I will never forgive you for betraying my confidence.'

'I won't, but I don't see –'

'Just listen.'

After Abby remained silent the Mother Confessor began. 'Zedd married Erilyn. She was a wonderful woman. We all loved her very much, but not as much as did he. They had a daughter.'

Abby's curiosity got the best of her. 'How old is she?'

'About the age of your daughter,' Delora said.

Abby swallowed. 'I see.'

'When Zedd became First Wizard, things were grim. Panis Rahl had conjured the shadow people.'

'I'm from Coney Crossing, I've never heard of such a thing.'

'Well, the war had been bad enough, but then Panis Rahl taught his wizards to conjure shadow people.' The Mother Confessor sighed at the anguish of retelling the story. 'They are so called because they are like shadows in the air. They have no precise shape or form. They are not living, but created out of magic. Weapons have no more effect on them than they would have on smoke.

'You can't hide from the shadow people. They drift towards you across fields, or through the woods. They find you.

'When they touch someone, the person's whole body blisters and swells until their flesh splits open. They die in screaming agony. Not even the gift can heal one touched by a shadow person.

'As the enemy attacked, their wizards would send the shadow people out ahead. In the beginning whole battalions of our brave young soldiers were found killed to a man. We saw no hope. It was our darkest hour.'

'And Wizard Zorander was able to stop them?' Abby asked.

The Mother Confessor nodded. 'He studied the problem and then conjured battle horns. Their magic swept the shadow people away like smoke in the wind. The magic coming from the horns also traced its way back through the spell, to seek out the one who cast it, and kill them. The horns aren't foolproof, though, and Zedd must constantly alter their magic to keep up with the way the enemy changes their conjuring.

'Panis Rahl summoned other magic, too: fevers and sickness,

wasting illnesses, fogs that caused blindness – all sorts of horrors. Zedd worked day and night, and managed to counter them all. While Panis Rahl's magic was being checked, our troops were once again able to fight on even terms. Because of Wizard Zorander, the tide of battle turned.'

'Well, that much of it is good, but –'

The Mother Confessor again lifted her finger, commanding silence. Abby held her tongue as the woman lowered her hand and went on.

'Panis Rahl was enraged at what Zedd had done. He tried and failed to kill him, so he instead sent a quad to kill Erilyn.'

'A quad? What's a quad?'

'A quad,' the sorceress answered, 'is a unit of four special assassins sent with the protection of a spell from the one who sent them: Panis Rahl. It is not only their assignment to kill the victim, but to make it unimaginably torturous and brutal.'

Abby swallowed. 'And did they . . . murder his wife?'

The Mother Confessor leaned closer. 'Worse. They left her, her legs and arms all broken, to be found still alive.'

'Alive?' Abby whispered. 'Why would they leave her alive, if it was their mission to kill her?'

'So that Zedd would find her all broken and bleeding and in inconceivable agony. She was able only to whisper his name in love.' The Mother Confessor leaned even closer. Abby could feel the breath of the woman's whispered words against her own face. 'When he used his gift to try to heal her, it activated the worm spell.'

Abby had to force herself to blink. 'Worm spell . . . ?'

'No wizard would have been able to detect it.' The Mother Confessor clawed her fingers and, in front of Abby's stomach, spread her hands outward, in a tearing gesture. 'The spell ripped her insides apart. Because he had used his loving touch of magic, she died in screaming pain as he knelt helpless beside her.'

Wincing, Abby touched her own stomach, almost feeling the wound. 'That's terrible.'

The Mother Confessor's violet eyes held an iron look. 'The

quad also took their daughter. Their daughter, who had seen everything those men had done to her mother.'

Abby felt tears burning her eyes again. 'They did that to his daughter, too?'

'No,' the Mother Confessor said. 'They hold her captive.'

'Then she still lives? There is still hope?'

The Mother Confessor's satiny white dress rustled softly as she leaned back against the white marble balustrade and nested her hands in her lap. 'Zedd went after the quad. He found them, but his daughter had been given to others, and they passed her on to yet others, and so on, so they had no idea who had her, or where she might be.'

Abby looked to the sorceress and back to the Mother Confessor. 'What did Wizard Zorander do to the quad?'

'No less than I myself would have done.' The Mother Confessor stared back through a mask of cold rage. 'He made them regret ever being born. For a very long time he made them regret it.'

Abby shrank back. 'I see.'

As the Mother Confessor drew a calming breath, the sorceress took up the story. 'As we speak, Wizard Zorander uses a spell that none of us understands; it holds Panis Rahl at his palace in D'Hara. It helps blunt the magic Rahl is able to conjure against us, and enables our men to drive his troops back whence they came.

'But Panis Rahl is consumed with wrath for the man who has thwarted his conquest of the Midlands. Hardly a week passes that an attempt is not made on Wizard Zorander's life. Rahl sends dangerous and vile people of all sorts. Even the Mord-Sith.'

Abby's breath caught. That was a word she had heard. 'What are Mord-Sith?'

The sorceress smoothed back her glossy black hair as she glared with a venomous expression. 'Mord-Sith are women who, along with their red leather uniform, wear a single long braid as the mark of their profession. They are trained in the torture and killing of those with the gift. If a gifted person tries to use their magic against a Mord-Sith, she is able to capture their magic and use it against them. There is no escaping a Mord-Sith.'

'But surely, a person as strong in the gift as Wizard Zorander –'

'Even he would be lost if he tried to use magic against a Mord-Sith,' the Mother Confessor said. 'A Mord-Sith can be defeated with common weapons – but not with magic. Only the magic of a Confessor works against them. I have killed two.

'In part because of the brutal nature of the training of Mord-Sith, they have been outlawed for as long as anyone knows, but in D'Hara the ghastly tradition of taking young women to be indoctrinated as Mord-Sith continues to this day. D'Hara is a distant and secretive land. We don't know much about it, except what we have learned through unfortunate experience.

'Mord-Sith have captured several of our wizards and sorceresses. Once captured, they cannot kill themselves, nor can they escape. Before they die, they give over everything they know. Panis Rahl knows of our plans.

'We, too, have managed to get our hands on several high-ranking D'Harans, and through the touch of Confessors, we know the extent of how we have been compromised. Time works against us.'

Abby wiped the palms of her hands on her thighs. 'And that man who was killed just before I went in to see the First Wizard, he couldn't have been an assassin; the two with him were allowed to leave.'

'No, he was not an assassin.' The Mother Confessor folded her hands. 'I believe Panis Rahl knows of the spell Wizard Zorander discovered, that it has the potential to obliterate all of D'Hara. Panis Rahl is desperate to rid himself of Wizard Zorander.'

The Mother Confessor's violet eyes seemed to glisten with a keen intellect. Abby looked away and picked at a stray thread on her sack. 'But I don't see what this has to do with denying me help to save my daughter. He has a daughter. Wouldn't he do anything to get her back? Wouldn't he do whatever he must to have his daughter back and safe?'

The Mother Confessor's head lowered and she stroked her fingers over her brow, as if trying to rub at a grievous ache.

'The man who came before you was a messenger. His message had been passed through many hands so that it could not be traced back to its source.'

Abby felt cold goose bumps running up her arms. 'What was the message?'

'The lock of hair he brought was from Zedd's daughter. Panis Rahl offered the life of Zedd's daughter if Zedd would surrender himself to Panis Rahl to be executed.'

Abby clutched at her sack. 'But wouldn't a father who loved his daughter do even this to save her life?'

'At what cost?' the Mother Confessor whispered. 'At the cost of the lives of all those who will die without his help?

'He couldn't do such a selfish thing, even to save the life of one he loves more than any other. Before he denied your daughter help, he had just refused the offer, thus sentencing his own innocent daughter to death.'

Abby felt her hopes again tumbling into blackness. The thought of Jana's terror, of her being hurt, made Abby dizzy and sick. Tears began running down her cheeks again.

'But I'm not asking him to sacrifice everyone else to save her.'

The sorceress gently touched Abby's shoulder. 'He believes that sparing those people harm would mean letting the D'Harans escape to kill more people in the end.'

Abby snatched desperately for a solution. 'But I have a bone.'

The sorceress sighed. 'Abigail, half the people who come to see a wizard bring a bone. Hucksters convince supplicants that they are true bones. Desperate people, just like you, buy them.'

'Most of them come seeking a wizard to somehow give them a life free of magic,' the Mother Confessor said. 'Most people fear magic, but I'm afraid that with the way it's been used by D'Hara, they now want nothing so much as to never again see magic. An ironic reason to buy a bone, and doubly ironic that they buy sham bones, thinking they have magic, in order to petition to be free of magic.'

Abby blinked. 'But I bought no bone. This is a debt true. On my mother's deathbed she told me of it. She said it was Wizard Zorander himself bound in it.'

The sorceress squinted her scepticism. 'Abigail, true debts of this nature are exceedingly rare. Perhaps it was a bone she had and you only thought . . .'

Abby held her sack open for the sorceress to see. The sorceress glanced in and fell silent. The Mother Confessor looked in the sack for herself.

'I know what my mother told me,' Abby insisted. 'She also told me that if there was any doubt, he had but to test it, then he would know it true, for the debt was passed down to him from his father.'

The sorceress stroked the beads at her throat. 'He could test it. If it is true, he would know. Still, solemn debt though it may be, that doesn't mean that the debt must be paid now.'

Abby leaned boldly towards the sorceress. 'My mother said it is a debt true, and that it had to be paid. Please, Delora, you know the nature of such things. I was so confused when I met with him, with all those people shouting. I foolishly failed to press my case by asking that he test it.' She turned and clutched the Mother Confessor's arm. 'Please, help me? Tell him what I have and ask that he test it?'

The Mother Confessor considered behind a blank expression. At last she spoke. 'This involves a debt bound in magic. Such a thing must be considered seriously. I will speak to Wizard Zorander on your behalf and request that you be given a private audience.'

Abby squeezed her eyes shut as tears sprang anew. 'Thank you.' She put her face in both hands and began to weep with relief at the flame of hope rekindled.

The Mother Confessor gripped Abby's shoulders. 'I said I will try. He may deny my request.'

The sorceress snorted a humourless laugh. 'Not likely. I will twist his ear, too. But Abigail, that does not mean that we can convince him to help you – bone or no bone.'

Abby wiped her cheek. 'I understand. Thank you both. Thank you both for understanding.'

With a thumb, the sorceress wiped a tear from Abby's chin. 'It is said that the daughter of a sorceress is a daughter to all sorceresses.'

The Mother Confessor stood and smoothed her white dress. 'Delora, perhaps you could take Abigail to a rooming house for women travellers. She should get some rest. Do you have money, child?'

'Yes, Mother Confessor.'

'Good. Delora will take you to a room for the night. Return to the Keep just before sunrise. We will meet you and let you know if we were able to convince Zedd to test your bone.'

'I will pray to the good spirits that Wizard Zorander will see me and help my daughter.' Abby felt sudden shame at her own words. 'And I will pray, too, for his daughter.'

The Mother Confessor cupped Abby's cheek. 'Pray for all of us, child. Pray that Wizard Zorander unleashes the magic against D'Hara, before it is too late for all the children of the Midlands – old and young alike.'

On their walk down to the city, Delora kept the conversation from Abby's worries and hopes, and what magic might contribute to either. In some ways, talking with the sorceress was reminiscent of talking with her mother. Sorceresses evaded talk of magic with one not gifted, daughter or not. Abby got the feeling that it was as uncomfortable for them as it was for Abby when Jana asked how a mother came to have a child in her tummy.

Even though it was late, the streets were teeming with people. Worried gossip of the war floated to Abby's ears from every direction. At one corner a knot of women murmured tearfully of menfolk gone for months with no word of their fate.

Delora took Abby down a market street and had her buy a small loaf of bread with meats and olives baked right inside. Abby wasn't really hungry. The sorceress made her promise that she would eat. Not wanting to do anything to cause disfavour, Abby promised.

The rooming house was up a side-street among tightly packed

buildings. The racket of the market carried up the narrow street and flittered around buildings and through tiny courtyards with the ease of a chickadee through a dense wood. Abby wondered how people could stand to live so close together and with nothing to see but other houses and people. She wondered, too, how she was going to be able to sleep with all the strange sounds and noise, but then, sleep had rarely come since she had left home, despite the dead-quiet nights in the countryside.

The sorceress bid Abby a good night, putting her in the hands of a sullen-looking woman of few words who led her to a room at the end of a long hall and left her to her night's rest, after collecting a silver coin. Abby sat on the edge of the bed and, by the light of a single lamp sitting on a shelf by the bed, eyed the small room as she nibbled at the loaf of bread. The meat inside was tough and stringy, but had an agreeable flavour, spiced with salt and garlic.

Without a window, the room wasn't as noisy as Abby had feared it might be. The door had no bolt, but the woman who kept the house had said in a mumble for her not to fret, that no men were allowed in the establishment. Abby set the bread aside and, at a basin atop a simple stand two strides across the room, washed her face. She was surprised at how dirty it left the water.

She twisted the lever stem on the lamp, lowering the wick as far as it would go without snuffing the flame; she didn't like sleeping in the dark in a strange place. Lying in bed, staring up at the water-stained ceiling, she prayed earnestly to the good spirits, despite knowing that they would ignore a request such as she made. She closed her eyes and prayed for Wizard Zorander's daughter, too. Her prayers were fragmented by intruding fears that felt as if they clawed her insides raw.

She didn't know how long she had lain in the bed, wishing for sleep to take her, wishing for morning to come, when the door slowly squeaked open. A shadow climbed the far wall.

Abby froze, eyes wide, breath held tight, as she watched a crouched figure move towards the bed. It wasn't the woman of the house. She would be taller. Abby's fingers tightened on the scratchy blanket, thinking that maybe she could throw it over the intruder and then run for the door.

'Don't be alarmed, dearie. I've just come to see if you had success up at the Keep.'

Abby gulped air and sat up in the bed. 'Mariska?' It was the old woman who had waited with her in the line all day. 'You frightened the wits out of me!'

The small flame from the lamp reflected in a sharp shimmer in the woman's eye as she surveyed Abby's face. 'Worse things to fear than your own safety.'

'What do you mean?'

Mariska smiled. It was not a reassuring smile. 'Did you get what you wanted?'

'I saw the First Wizard, if that's what you mean.'

'And what did he say, dearie?'

Abby swung her feet down off the bed. 'That's my business.'

The sly smile widened. 'Oh, no, dearie, it's our business.'

'What do you mean by that?'

'Answer the question. You've not much time left. Your family has not much time left.'

Abby shot to her feet. 'How do you –'

The old woman seized Abby's wrist and twisted until Abby was forced to sit. 'What say the First Wizard?'

'He said he couldn't help me. Please, that hurts. Let me go.'

'Oh, dearie, that's too bad, it is. Too bad for your little Jana.'

'How . . . how do you know about her? I never –'

'So, Wizard Zorander denied your petition. Such sad news.' She clicked her tongue. 'Poor, unfortunate, little Jana. You were warned. You knew the price of failure.'

She released Abby's wrist and turned away. Abby's mind raced in hot panic as the woman shuffled towards the door.

'No! Please! I'm to see him again, tomorrow. At sunrise.'

Mariska peered back over her shoulder. 'Why? Why would he agree to see you again, after he has denied you? Lying will buy your daughter no more time. It will buy her nothing.'

'It's true. I swear it on my mother's soul. I talked to the sorceress, the one who took us in. I talked to her and the

Mother Confessor, after Wizard Zorander denied my petition. They agreed to convince him to give me a private audience.'

Her brow bunched. 'Why would they do this?'

Abby pointed to her sack sitting on the end of the bed. 'I showed them what I brought.'

With one gnarled finger, Mariska lifted open the sack. She looked for a moment and then glided closer to Abby.

'You have yet to show this to Wizard Zorander?'

'That's right. They will get me an audience with him. I'm sure of it. Tomorrow, he will see me.'

From her bulky waistband, Mariska drew a knife. She waved it slowly back and forth before Abby's face. 'We grow weary of waiting for you.'

Abby licked her lips. 'But I –'

'In the morning I leave for Coney Crossing. I leave to see your frightened little Jana.' Her hand slid behind Abby's neck. Fingers like oak roots gripped Abby's hair, holding her head fast. 'If you bring him right behind me, she will go free, as you were promised.'

Abby couldn't nod. 'I will. I swear. I'll convince him. He is bound by a debt.'

Mariska put the point of the knife so close to Abby's eye that it brushed her eyelashes. Abby feared to blink.

'Arrive late, and I will stab my knife in little Jana's eye. Stab it through. I will leave her the other so that she can watch as I cut out her father's heart, just so that she will know how much it will hurt when I do her. Do you understand, dearie?'

Abby could only whine that she did, as tears streamed down her cheeks.

'There's a good girl,' Mariska whispered from so close that Abby was forced to breathe the spicy stink of the woman's sausage dinner. 'If we even suspect any tricks, they will all die.'

'No tricks. I'll hurry. I'll bring him.'

Mariska kissed Abby's forehead. 'You're a good mother.' She released Abby's hair. 'Jana loves you. She cries for you day and night.'

After Mariska closed the door, Abby curled into a trembling ball in the bed and wept against her knuckles.

Delora leaned closer as they marched across the broad rampart. 'Are you sure you're all right, Abigail?'

Wind snatched at her hair, flicking it across her face. Brushing it from her eyes, Abby looked out at the sprawl of the city below beginning to coalesce out of the gloom. She had been saying a silent prayer to her mother's spirit.

'Yes. I just had a bad night. I couldn't sleep.'

The Mother Confessor's shoulder pressed against Abby's from the other side. 'We understand. At least he agreed to see you. Take heart in that. He's a good man, he really is.'

'Thank you,' Abby whispered in shame. 'Thank you both for helping me.'

The people waiting along the rampart – wizards, sorceresses, officers, and others – all momentarily fell silent and bowed towards the Mother Confessor as the three women passed. Among several people she recognized from the day before, Abby saw the wizard Thomas, grumbling to himself and looking hugely impatient and vexed as he shuffled through a handful of papers covered in what Abby recognized as magical symbols.

At the end of the rampart they came to the stone face of a round turret. A steep roof overhead protruded down low above a round-topped door. The sorceress rapped on the door and opened it without waiting for a reply. She caught the twitch of Abby's brow.

'He rarely hears the knock,' she explained in a hushed tone.

The stone room was small, but had a cosy feel to it. A round window to the right overlooked the city below and another on the opposite side looked up on soaring walls of the Keep, the distant highest ones glowing pink in the first faint rays of dawn. An elaborate iron candelabrum held a small army of candles that provided a warm glow to the room.

Wizard Zorander, his unruly wavy brown hair hanging down around his face as he leaned on his hands, was absorbed in studying a book lying open on the table. The three women came to a halt.

'Wizard Zorander,' the sorceress announced, 'we bring Abigail, born of Helsa.'

'Bags, woman,' the wizard grouched without looking up, 'I heard your knock, as I always do.'

'Don't you curse at me, Zeddicus Zu'l Zorander,' Delora grumbled back.

He ignored the sorceress, rubbing his smooth chin as he considered the book before him. 'Welcome, Abigail.'

Abby's fingers fumbled at the sack. But then she remembered herself and curtsied. 'Thank you for seeing me, Wizard Zorander. It is of vital importance that I have your help. As I've already told you, the lives of innocent children are at stake.'

Wizard Zorander finally peered up. After appraising her a long moment he straightened. 'Where does the line lie?'

Abby glanced to the sorceress on one side of her and then the Mother Confessor on the other side. Neither looked back.

'Excuse me, Wizard Zorander? The line?'

The wizard's brow drew down. 'You imply a higher value to a life because of a young age. The line, my dear child, across which the value of life becomes petty. Where is the line?'

'But a child –'

He held up a cautionary finger. 'Do not think to play on my emotions by plying me with the value of the life of a child, as if a higher value can be placed on life because of age. When is life worth less? Where is the line? At what age? Who decides?

'All life is of value. Dead is dead, no matter the age. Don't think to produce a suspension of my reason with a callous, calculated twisting of emotion, like some slippery officeholder stirring the passions of a mindless mob.'

Abby was struck speechless by such an admonition. The wizard turned his attention to the Mother Confessor.

'Speaking of bureaucrats, what did the council have to say for themselves?'

The Mother Confessor clasped her hands and sighed. 'I told

them your words. Simply put, they didn't care. They want it done.'

He grunted his discontent. 'Do they, now?' His hazel eyes turned to Abby. 'Seems the council doesn't care about the lives of even children, when the children are D'Haran.' He wiped a hand across his tired-looking eyes. 'I can't say I don't comprehend their reasoning, or that I disagree with them, but dear spirits, they are not the ones to do it. It is not by their hand. It will be by mine.'

'I understand, Zedd,' the Mother Confessor murmured.

Once again he seemed to notice Abby standing before him. He considered her as if pondering some profound notion. It made her fidget. He held out his hand and waggled his fingers. 'Let me see it, then.'

Abby stepped closer to the table as she reached in her sack. 'If you cannot be persuaded to help innocent people, then maybe this will mean something more to you.'

She drew her mother's skull from the sack and placed it in the wizard's upturned palm. 'It is a debt of bones. I declare it due.'

One eyebrow lifted. 'It is customary to bring only a tiny fragment of bone, child.'

Abby felt her face flush. 'I didn't know,' she stammered. 'I wanted to be sure there was enough to test . . . to be sure you would believe me.'

He smoothed a gentle hand over the top of the skull. 'A piece smaller than a grain of sand is enough.' He watched Abby's eyes. 'Didn't your mother tell you?'

Abby shook her head. 'She said only that it was a debt passed to you from your father. She said the debt must be paid if it was called due.'

'Indeed it must,' he whispered.

Even as he spoke, his hand was gliding back and forth over the skull. The bone was dull and stained by the dirt from which Abby had pulled it, not at all the pristine white she had fancied it would be. It had horrified her to have to uncover her mother's bones, but the alternative horrified her more.

Beneath the wizard's fingers, the bone of the skull began to glow with soft amber light. Abby's breathing nearly stilled when the air hummed, as if the spirits themselves whispered to the wizard. The sorceress fussed with the beads at her neck. The Mother Confessor chewed her lower lip. Abby prayed.

Wizard Zorander set the skull on the table and turned his back on them. The amber glow faded away.

When he said nothing, Abby spoke into the thick silence. 'Well? Are you satisfied? Did your test prove it a debt true?'

'Oh yes,' he said quietly without turning towards them. 'It is a debt of bones true, bound by the magic invoked until the debt is paid.'

Abby's fingers worried at the frayed edge of her sack. 'I told you. My mother wouldn't have lied to me. She told me that if not paid while she was alive, it became a debt of bones upon her death.'

The wizard slowly rounded to face her. 'And did she tell you anything of the engendering of the debt?'

'No.' Abby cast a furtive, sidelong glance at Delora before going on. 'Sorceresses hold secrets close, and reveal only that which serves their purposes.'

With a slight, fleeting smile, he grunted his concurrence.

'She said only that it was your father and she who were bound in it, and that until paid it would continue to pass on to the descendants of each.'

'Your mother spoke the truth. But that does not mean that it must be paid now.'

'It is a solemn debt of bones.' Abby's frustration and fear erupted with venom. 'I declare it due! You will yield to the obligation!'

Both the sorceress and the Mother Confessor gazed off at the walls, uneasy at a woman, an ungifted woman, raising her voice to the First Wizard himself. Abby suddenly wondered if she might be struck dead for such insolence. But if he didn't help her, it wouldn't matter.

The Mother Confessor diverted the possible results of Abby's outburst with a question. 'Zedd, did your reading tell you of the nature of the engendering of the debt?'

'Indeed it did,' he said. 'My father, too, told me of a debt. My test has proven to me that this is the one of which he spoke, and that the woman standing before me carries the other half of the link.'

'So, what was the engendering?' the sorceress asked.

He turned his palms up. 'It seems to have slipped my mind. I'm sorry; I find myself to be more forgetful than usual of late.'

Delora sniffed. 'And you dare to call sorceresses taciturn?'

Wizard Zorander silently considered her a moment and then turned a squint on the Mother Confessor. 'The council wants it done, do they?' He smiled a sly smile. 'Then it shall be done.'

The Mother Confessor cocked her head. 'Zedd . . . are you sure about this?'

'About what?' Abby asked. 'Are you going to honour the debt or not?'

The wizard shrugged. 'You have declared the debt due.' He plucked a small book from the table and slipped it into a pocket in his robe. 'Who am I to argue?'

'Dear spirits,' the Mother Confessor whispered to herself. 'Zedd, just because the council –'

'I am just a wizard,' he said, cutting her off, 'serving the wants and wishes of the people.'

'But if you travel to this place you would be exposing yourself to needless danger.'

'I must be near the border – or it will claim parts of the Midlands, too. Coney Crossing is as good a place as any other to ignite the conflagration.'

Beside herself with relief, Abby was hardly hearing anything else he said. 'Thank you, Wizard Zorander. Thank you.'

He strode around the table and gripped her shoulder with sticklike fingers of surprising strength.

'We are bound, you and I, in a debt of bones. Our life paths have intersected.' His smile looked at once sad and sincere. His powerful fingers closed around her wrist, around her bracelet, and he put her mother's skull in her hands. 'Please, Abby, call me Zedd.'

Near tears, she nodded. 'Thank you, Zedd.'

Outside, in the early light, they were accosted by the waiting crowd. Wizard Thomas, waving his papers, shoved his way through.

'Zorander! I've been studying these elements you've provided. I have to talk to you.'

'Talk, then,' the First Wizard said as he marched by. The crowd followed in his wake.

'This is madness.'

'I never said it wasn't.'

Wizard Thomas shook the papers as if for proof. 'You can't do this, Zorander!'

'The council has decided that it is to be done. The war must be ended while we have the upper hand and before Panis Rahl comes up with something we won't be able to counter.'

'No, I mean I've studied this thing, and you won't be able to do it. We don't understand the power those wizards wielded. I've looked over the elements you've shown me. Even trying to invoke such a thing will create intense heat.'

Zedd halted and put his face close to Thomas. He lifted his eyebrows in mock surprise. 'Really, Thomas? Do you think? Igniting a light spell that will rip the fabric of the world of life might cause an instability in the elements of the web field?'

Thomas charged after as Zedd stormed off. 'Zorander! You won't be able to control it! If you were able to invoke it – and I'm not saying I believe you can – you would breach the Grace. The invocation uses heat. The breach feeds it. You won't be able to control the cascade. No one can do such a thing!'

'I can do it,' the First Wizard muttered.

Thomas shook the fists of papers in a fury. 'Zorander, your arrogance will be the end of us all! Once parted, the veil will be rent and all life will be consumed. I demand to see the book in which you found this spell. I demand to see it myself. The whole thing, not just parts of it!'

The First Wizard paused and lifted a finger. 'Thomas, if you were meant to see the book, then you would be First Wizard and have access to the First Wizard's private enclave. But you are not, and you don't.'

Thomas's face glowed scarlet above his white beard. 'This is a foolhardy act of desperation!'

Wizard Zorander flicked the finger. The papers flew from the old wizard's hand and swirled up into a whirlwind, there to ignite, flaring into ashes that lifted away on the wind.

'Sometimes, Thomas, all that is left to you is an act of desperation. I am First Wizard, and I will do as I must. That is the end of it. I will hear no more.' He turned and snatched the sleeve of an officer. 'Alert the lancers. Gather all the cavalry available. We ride for Pendisan Reach at once.'

The man thumped a quick salute to his chest before dashing off. Another officer, older and looking to be of much higher rank, cleared his throat.

'Wizard Zorander, may I know of your plan?'

'It is Anargo,' the First Wizard said, 'who is the right hand of Panis Rahl, and in conjunction with Rahl conjures death to stalk us. Quite simply put, I intend to send death back at them.'

'By leading the lancers into Pendisan Reach?'

'Yes. Anargo holds at Coney Crossing. We have General Brainard driving north towards Pendisan Reach, General Sanderson sweeping south to join with him, and Mardale charging up from the southwest. We will go in there with the lancers and whoever of the rest of them is able to join with us.'

'Anargo is no fool. We don't know how many other wizards and gifted he has with him, but we know what they're capable of. They've bled us time and time again. At last we have dealt them a blow.' The officer chose his words carefully. 'Why do you think they wait? Why wouldn't they simply slip back into D'Hara?'

Zedd rested a hand on the crenellated wall and gazed out on the dawn, out on the city below.

'Anargo relishes the game. He performs it with high drama; he wants us to think them wounded. Pendisan Reach is the only terrain in all those mountains that an army can get through with any speed. Coney Crossing provides a wide field for battle, but not wide enough to let us manoeuvre easily, or flank them. He is trying to bait us in.'

The officer didn't seem surprised. 'But why?'

Zedd looked back over his shoulder at the officer. 'Obviously, he believes that in such terrain he can defeat us. I believe otherwise. He knows that we can't allow the menace to remain there, and he knows our plans. He thinks to draw me in, kill me, and end the threat I alone hold over them.'

'So . . .' the officer reasoned aloud, 'you are saying that for Anargo, it is worth the risk.'

Zedd stared out once more at the city below the Wizard's Keep. 'If Anargo is right, he could win it all at Coney Crossing. When he has finished me, he will turn his gifted loose, slaughter the bulk of our forces all in one place, and then, virtually unopposed, cut out the heart of the Midlands: Aydindril.

'Anargo plans that before the snow flies, he will have killed me, annihilated our joint forces, have the people of the Midlands in chains, and be able to hand the whip to Panis Rahl.'

The officer stared, dumbfounded. 'And you plan to do as Anargo is hoping and go in there to face him?'

Zedd shrugged. 'What choice have I?'

'And do you at least know how Anargo plans to kill you, so that we might take precautions? Take countermeasures?'

'I'm afraid not.' Vexed, he waved his hand, dismissing the matter. He turned to Abby. 'The lancers have swift horses. We will ride hard. We will be to your home soon – we will be there in time – and then we'll see to our business.'

Abby only nodded. She couldn't put into words the relief of her petition granted, nor could she express the shame she felt to have her prayer answered. But most of all, she couldn't utter a word of her horror at what she was doing, for she knew the D'Harans' plan.

Flies swarmed around dried scraps of viscera, all that was left of Abby's prized bearded pigs. Apparently, even the breeding stock, which Abby's parents had given her as a wedding gift, had been slaughtered and taken.

Abby's parents, too, had chosen Abby's husband. Abby had never met him before: he came from the town of Lynford where her mother and father bought the pigs. Abby had been beside herself with anxiety over who her parents would choose for her husband. She had hoped for a man who would be of good cheer – a man to bring a smile to the difficulties of life.

When she first saw Philip, she thought he must be the most serious man in all the world. His young face looked to her as if it had never once smiled. That first night after meeting him, she had cried herself to sleep over thoughts of sharing her life with so solemn a man. She thought her life caught up on the sharp tines of grim fate.

Abby came to find that Philip was a hardworking man who looked out at life through a great grin. That first day she had seen him, she only later learned, he had been putting on his most sober face so that his new family would not think him a slacker unworthy of their daughter. In a short time, Abby had come to know that Philip was a man upon whom she could depend. By the time Jana had been born, she had come to love him.

Now Philip, and so many others, depended upon her.

Abby brushed her hands clean after putting her mother's bones to rest once more. The fences Jana had watched Philip so often mend, she saw, were all broken down. Coming back around the house, she noticed that barn doors were missing. Anything an animal or human could eat was gone. Abby could not recall having ever seen her home looking so barren.

It didn't matter, she told herself. It didn't matter, if only Jana would be returned to her. Fences could be mended. Pigs could be replaced, somehow, someday. Jana could never be replaced.

'Abby,' Zedd asked as he peered around at the ruins of her home, 'how is it that you weren't taken, when your husband and daughter and everyone else were?'

Abby stepped through the broken doorway, thinking that her home had never looked so small. Before she had gone to Aydindril, to the Wizard's Keep, her home had seemed as big as anything she could imagine. Here, Philip had laughed and filled the simple room with his comfort and conversation. With charcoal he had drawn animals on the stone hearth for Jana.

Abby pointed. 'Under that door is the root cellar. That's where I was when I heard the things I told you about.'

Zedd ran the toe of his boot across the knothole used as a finger-hold to lift the hatch. 'They were taking your husband, and your daughter, and you stayed down there? While your daughter was screaming for you, you didn't run up to help her?'

Abby summoned her voice. 'I knew that if I came up, they would have me, too. I knew that the only chance my family had was if I waited and then went for help. My mother always told me that even a sorceress was no more than a fool if she acted like one. She always told me to think things through, first.'

'Wise advice.' Zedd set down a ladle that had been bent and holed. He rested a gentle hand on her shoulder. 'It would have been hard to leave your daughter crying for you, and do the wise thing.'

Abby could only manage a whisper. 'You speak the spirits' own truth.' She pointed through the window on the side wall. 'That way – across the Coney River – lies town. They took Jana and Philip with them as they went on to take all the people from town. They had others, too, that they had already captured. The army set up camp in the hills beyond.'

Zedd stood at the window, gazing out at the distant hills. 'Soon, I hope, this war will be ended. Dear spirits, let it end.'

Remembering the Mother Confessor's admonition not to repeat the story she told, Abby never asked about the wizard's daughter or murdered wife. When on their swift journey back to Coney Crossing she spoke of her love for Jana, it must have broken his heart to think of his own daughter in the brutal hands of the enemy, knowing that he had left her to death lest many more die.

Zedd pushed open the bedroom door. 'And back here?' he asked as he put his head into the room beyond.

Abby looked up from her thoughts. 'The bedroom. In the rear is a door back to the garden and the barn.'

Though he never once mentioned his dead wife or missing

daughter, Abby's knowledge of them ate away at her like a swelling spring river ate at a hole in the ice.

Zedd stepped back in from the bedroom as Delora came silently slipping in through the front doorway. 'As Abigail said, the town across the river has been sacked,' the sorceress reported. 'From the looks of it, the people were all taken.'

Zedd brushed back his wavy hair. 'How close is the river?'

Abby gestured out the window. Night was falling. 'Just there. A walk of five minutes.'

In the valley, on its way to join the Kern, the Coney River slowed and spread wide, so that it became shallow enough to cross easily. There was no bridge; the road simply led to the river's edge and took up again on the other side. Though the river was near to a quarter-mile across in most of the valley, it was in no place much more than knee-deep. Only in the spring melt was it occasionally treacherous to cross. The town of Coney Crossing was two miles beyond, up on the rise of hills, safe from spring floods, as was the knoll where Abby's farmyard stood.

Zedd took Delora by the elbow. 'Ride back and tell everyone to hold station. If anything goes wrong . . . well, if anything goes wrong, then they must attack. Anargo's legion must be stopped, even if they have to go into D'Hara after them.'

Delora did not look pleased. 'Before we left, the Mother Confessor made me promise that I would be sure that you were not left alone. She told me to see to it that gifted were always near if you needed them.'

Abby, too, had heard the Mother Confessor issue the orders. Looking back at the Keep as they had crossed the stone bridge, Abby had seen the Mother Confessor up on a high rampart, watching them leave. The Mother Confessor had helped when Abby had feared all was lost. She wondered what would become of the woman.

Then she remembered she didn't have to wonder. She knew.

The wizard ignored what the sorceress had said. 'As soon as I help Abby, I'll send her back, too. I don't want anyone near when I unleash the spell.'

Delora gripped his collar and pulled him close. She looked as if she might be about to give him a heated scolding. Instead she drew him into an embrace.

'Please, Zedd,' she whispered, 'don't leave us without you as First Wizard.'

Zedd smoothed back her dark hair. 'And abandon you all to Thomas?' He smirked. 'Never.'

The dust from Delora's horse drifted away into the gathering darkness as Zedd and Abby descended the slope towards the river. Abby led him along the path through the tall grasses and rushes, explaining that the path would offer them better concealment than the road. Abby was thankful that he didn't argue for the road.

Her eyes darted from the deep shadows on one side to the shadows on the other as they were swallowed into the brush. Her pulse raced. She flinched whenever a twig snapped underfoot.

It happened as she feared it would, as she knew it would.

A figure enfolded in a long hooded cloak darted out of nowhere, knocking Abby aside. She saw the flash of a blade as Zedd flipped the attacker into the brush. He squatted, putting a hand back on Abby's shoulder as she lay in the grass panting.

'Stay down,' he whispered urgently.

Light gathered at his fingers. He was conjuring magic. That was what they wanted him to do.

Tears welled, burning her eyes. She snatched his sleeve. 'Zedd, don't use magic.' She could hardly speak past the tightening pain in her chest. 'Don't –'

The figure sprang again from the gloom of the bushes. Zedd threw up a hand. The night lit with a flash of hot light that struck the cloaked figure.

Rather than the assailant going down, it was Zedd who cried out and crumpled to the ground. Whatever he had thought to do to the attacker, it had been turned back on him, and he was in the grip of the most terrible anguish, preventing him from rising, or speaking. That was why they had wanted him to conjure magic: so they could capture him.

The figure standing over the wizard glowered at Abby. 'Your part here is finished. Go.'

Abby scuttled into the grass. The woman pushed the hood back, and cast off her cloak. In the near darkness, Abby could see the woman's long braid and red leather uniform. It was one of the women Abby had been told about, the women used to capture those with magic: the Mord-Sith.

The Mord-Sith watched with satisfaction as the wizard at her feet writhed in choking pain. 'Well, well. Looks like the First Wizard himself has just made a very big mistake.'

The belts and straps of her red leather uniform creaked as she leaned down towards him, grinning at his agony. 'I have been given the whole night to make you regret ever having lifted a finger to resist us. In the morning I'm to allow you to watch as our forces annihilate your people. Afterwards, I am to take you to Lord Rahl himself, the man who ordered the death of your wife, so you can beg him to order me to kill you, too.' She kicked him. 'So you can beg Lord Rahl for your death, as you watch your daughter die before your eyes.'

Zedd could only scream in horror and pain.

On her hands and knees, Abby crabbed her way farther back into the weeds and rushes. She wiped at her eyes, trying to see. She was horrified to witness what was being done to the man who had agreed to help her for no more reason than a debt to her mother. By contrast, these people had coerced her service by holding hostage the life of her child.

As she backed away, Abby saw the knife the Mord-Sith had dropped when Zedd had thrown her into the weeds. The knife was a pretext, used to provoke him to act; it was magic that was the true weapon. The Mord-Sith had used his own magic against him – used it to cripple and capture him, and now used it to hurt him.

It was the price demanded. Abby had complied. She had no choice.

But what toll was she imposing on others?

How could she save her daughter's life at the cost of so many others? Would Jana grow up to be a slave to people who would do this? With a mother who would allow it? Jana would grow up to learn to bow to Panis Rahl and his minions, to submit to evil, or worse, grow up to become a willing party to the scourge, never tasting liberty or knowing the value of honour.

With dreadful finality, everything seemed to fall to ruin in Abby's mind.

She snatched up the knife. Zedd was wailing in pain as the Mord-Sith bent, doing some foul thing to him. Before she had time to lose her resolve, Abby was moving towards the woman's back.

Abby had butchered animals. She told herself that this was no different. These were not people, but animals. She lifted the knife.

A hand clamped over her mouth. Another seized her wrist.

Abby moaned against the hand, against her failure to stop this madness when she had had the chance. A mouth close to her ear urged her to hush.

Struggling against the figure in a hooded cloak that held her, Abby turned her head as much as she could, and in the last of the daylight saw violet eyes looking back. For a moment she couldn't make sense of it, couldn't make sense of how the woman could be there when Abby had seen her remain behind. But it truly was her.

Abby stilled. The Mother Confessor released her and, with a quick hand signal, urged her back. Abby didn't question; she scurried back into the rushes as the Mother Confessor reached out towards the woman in red leather. The Mord-Sith was bent over, intent on her grisly business with the screaming wizard.

In the distance, bugs chirped and clicked. Frogs called with insistent croaks. Not far away the river sloshed and burbled as it always did – a familiar, comforting sound of home.

And then there came a sudden, violent concussion to the air. Thunder without sound. It drove the wind from Abby's lungs. The wallop nearly knocked her senseless, making every joint in her body burn in sharp pain.

There was no flash of light – just that pure and flawless jolt to the air. The world seemed to stop in its terrible splendour.

Grass flattened as if in a wind radiating out in a ring from the

Mord-Sith and the Mother Confessor. Abby's senses returned as the pain in her joints thankfully melted away.

Abby had never seen it done before, and had never expected to see it in the whole of her life, but she knew without doubt that she had just witnessed a Confessor unleashing her power. From what Abby's mother had told her, it was the destruction of a person's mind so complete that it left only numb devotion to the Confessor. She had but to ask and they would confess any truth, no matter the crime they had previously attempted to conceal or deny.

'Mistress,' the Mord-Sith moaned in piteous lamentation.

Abby, first staggered by the shock of the soundless thunder of the Mother Confessor's power, and now stunned by the abject anguish of the woman crumpled on the ground, felt a hand grip her arm. It was the wizard.

With the back of his other hand he wiped blood from his mouth. He laboured to get his breath. 'Leave her to it.'

'Zedd . . . I . . . I'm so sorry. I tried to tell you not to use magic, but I didn't call loud enough for you to hear.'

He managed to smile through obvious pain. 'I heard you.'

'But why then did you use your gift?'

'I thought that in the end, you would not be the kind of person to do such a terrible thing, and that you would show your true heart.' He pulled her away from the cries. 'We used you. We wanted them to think they had succeeded.'

'You knew what I was going to do? You knew I was to bring you to them so that they could capture you?'

'I had a good idea. From the first there seemed more to you than you presented. You are not very talented at being a spy and a traitor. Since we arrived here you've been watching the shadows and jumping at the chirp of every bug.'

The Mother Confessor rushed up. 'Zedd, are you all right?'

He put a hand on her shoulder. 'I'll be fine.' His eyes still held the glaze of terror. 'Thank you for not being late. For a moment, I feared . . .'

'I know.' The Mother Confessor offered a quick smile. 'Let us hope your trick was worth it. You have until dawn. She said they expect her to torture you all night before bringing you to them in the morning. Their scouts alerted Anargo to our troops' arrival.'

Back in the rushes the Mord-Sith was screaming as though she were being flayed alive.

Shivers ran through Abby's shoulders. 'They'll hear her and know what's happened.'

'Even if they could hear at this distance, they will think it is Zedd, being tortured by her.' The Mother Confessor took the knife from Abby's hand. 'I am glad that you rewarded my faith and in the end chose not to join with them.'

Abby wiped her palms on her skirts, shamed by all she had done, by what she had intended to do. She was beginning to shake. 'Are you going to kill her?'

The Mother Confessor, despite looking bone-weary after having touched the Mord-Sith, still had iron resolve in her eyes. 'A Mord-Sith is different from anyone else. She does not recover from the touch of a Confessor. She would suffer in profound agony until she dies, sometime before morning.' She glanced back towards the cries. 'She has told us what we need to know, and Zedd must have his power back. It is the merciful thing to do.'

'It also buys me time to do what I must do.' Zedd's fingers turned Abby's face towards him, away from the shrieks. 'And time to get Jana back. You will have until morning.'

'I will have until morning? What do you mean?'

'I'll explain. But we must hurry if you are to have enough time. Now, take off your clothes.'

Abby was running out of time.

She moved through the D'Haran camp, holding herself stiff and tall, trying not to look frantic, even though that was how she felt. All night long she had been doing as the wizard had instructed: acting haughty. To anyone who noticed her, she directed disdain. To anyone who looked her way, thinking to speak to her, she growled.

Not that many, though, so much as dared to catch the attention of what appeared to be a red-leather-clad Mord-Sith. Zedd had told her, too, to keep the Mord-Sith's weapon in her fist. It looked like nothing more than a small red leather rod. How it worked, Abby had no idea – the wizard had said only that it involved magic, and she wouldn't be able to call it to her aid – but it did have an effect on those who saw it in her hand: it made them melt back into the darkness, away from the light of the campfires, away from Abby.

Those who were awake, anyway. Although most people in the camp were sleeping, there was no shortage of alert guards. Zedd had cut the long braid from the Mord-Sith who had attacked him, and tied it into Abby's hair. In the dark, the mismatch of colour wasn't obvious. When the guards looked at Abby they saw a Mord-Sith, and quickly turned their attention elsewhere.

By the apprehension on people's faces when they saw her coming, Abby knew she must look fearsome. They didn't know how her heart pounded. She was thankful for the mantle of night so that the D'Harans couldn't see her knees trembling. She had seen only two real Mord-Sith, both sleeping, and she had kept far away from them, as Zedd had warned her. Real Mord-Sith were not likely to be fooled so easily.

Zedd had given her until dawn. Time was running out. He had told her that if she wasn't back in time, she would die.

Abby was thankful she knew the lay of the land, or long since she would have become lost among the confusion of tents, campfires, wagons, horses, and mules. Everywhere pikes and lances were stacked upright in circles with their points leaning together. Men – farriers, fletchers, blacksmiths and craftsmen of all sorts – worked through the night.

The air was thick with woodsmoke and rang with the sound of metal being shaped and sharpened and wood being worked for everything from bows to wagons. Abby didn't know how people could sleep through the noise, but sleep they did.

Shortly the immense camp would wake to a new day – a day of battle, a day the soldiers went to work doing what they did best. They were getting a good night's sleep so they would be rested for the killing of the Midlands army. From what she had heard, D'Haran soldiers were very good at their job.

Abby had searched relentlessly, but she had been unable to find her father, her husband, or her daughter. She had no intention of giving up. She had resigned herself to the knowledge that if she didn't find them, she would die with them.

She had found captives tied together and staked to trees, or the ground, to keep them from running. Many more were chained. Some she recognized, but many more she didn't. Most were kept in groups and under guard.

Abby never once saw a guard asleep at his post. When they looked her way, she acted as if she were looking for someone, and she wasn't going to go easy on them when she found them. Zedd had told her that her safety, and the safety of her family, depended on her playing the part convincingly. Abby thought about these people hurting her daughter, and it wasn't hard to act angry.

But she was running out of time. She couldn't find them, and she knew that Zedd would not wait. Too much was at stake; she understood that, now. She was coming to appreciate that the wizard and the Mother Confessor were trying to stop a war; that they were people resolved to the dreadful task of weighing the lives of a few against the lives of many.

Abby lifted another tent-flap, and saw soldiers sleeping. She squatted and looked at the faces of prisoners tied to wagons. They stared back with hollow expressions. She bent to gaze at the faces of children pressed together in nightmares. She couldn't find Jana. The huge camp sprawled across the hilly countryside; there were a thousand places she could be.

As she marched along a crooked line of tents, she scratched at her wrist. Only when she went farther did she notice that it was the bracelet warming that made her wrist itch. It warmed yet more as she proceeded, but then the warmth began fading. Her brow twitched. Out of curiosity, she turned and went back the way she had come.

Where a pathway between tents turned off, her bracelet tingled again with warmth. Abby paused a moment, looking off into the darkness. The sky was just beginning to colour with light. She took the path between the tents, following until the bracelet cooled, then backtracked to where it warmed again and took a new direction where it warmed yet more.

Abby's mother had given her the bracelet, telling her to wear it always, and that someday it would be of value. Abby wondered if somehow the bracelet had magic that would help her find her daughter. With dawn nearing, this seemed the only chance she had left. She hurried onward, wending where the warmth from the bracelet directed.

The bracelet led her to an expanse of snoring soldiers. There were no prisoners in sight. Guards patrolled the men in bedrolls and blankets. There was one tent set among the big men – for an officer, she guessed.

Not knowing what else to do, Abby strode among the sleeping men. Near the tent, the bracelet sent tingling heat up her arm.

Abby saw that sentries hung around the small tent like flies around meat. The canvas sides glowed softly, probably from a candle inside. Off to the side, she noticed a sleeping form different from the men. As she got closer, she saw that it was a woman: Mariska.

The old woman breathed with a little raspy whistle as she slept. Abby stood paralysed. Guards looked up at her.

Needing to do something before they asked any questions, Abby scowled at them and marched towards the tent. She tried not to make any noise; the guards might think she was a Mord-Sith, but Mariska would not long be fooled. A glare from Abby turned the guards' eyes to the dark countryside.

Her heart pounding nearly out of control, Abby gripped the tent-flap. She knew Jana would be inside. She told herself that she must not cry out when she saw her daughter. She reminded herself that she must put a hand over Jana's mouth before she could cry out with joy, lest they be caught before they had a chance to escape.

The bracelet was so hot it felt as if it would blister her skin. Abby ducked into the low tent.

A trembling little girl huddled in a tattered wool cloak sat in blankets on the ground. She stared up with big eyes that blinked with the terror of what might come next. Abby felt a stab of anguish. It was not Jana.

They stared at each other, this little girl and Abby. The child's face was lit clearly by the candle set to the side, as Abby's must be. In those big grey eyes that looked to have beheld unimaginable terrors, the little girl seemed to reach a judgement.

Her arms stretched up in supplication.

Instinctively, Abby fell to her knees and scooped up the little girl, hugging her small trembling body. The girl's spindly arms came out from the tattered cloak and wrapped around Abby's neck, holding on for dear life.

'Help me? Please?' the child whimpered in Abby's ear.

Before she had picked her up she had seen the face in the candlelight. There was no doubt in Abby's mind. It was Zedd's daughter.

'I've come to help you,' Abby comforted. 'Zedd sent me.'

The child moaned expectantly.

Abby held the girl out at arm's length. 'I'll take you to your father, but you mustn't let these people know I'm rescuing you. Can you play along with me? Can you pretend that you're my prisoner, so that I can get you away?'

Near tears, the girl nodded. She had the same wavy hair as Zedd, and the same eyes, although they were an arresting grey, not hazel.

'Good,' Abby whispered, cupping a chilly cheek, almost lost in those grey eyes. 'Trust me, then, and I will get you away.'

'I trust you,' came the small voice.

Abby snatched up a rope lying nearby and looped it around the girl's neck. 'I'll try not to hurt you, but I must make them think you are my prisoner.'

The girl cast a worried look at the rope, as if she knew the rope well, and then nodded that she would go along.

Abby stood, once outside the tent, and by the rope pulled the child out after her. The guards looked her way. Abby started out.

One of them scowled as he stepped close. 'What's going on?'

Abby stomped to a halt and lifted the red leather rod, pointing it at the guard's nose. 'She has been summoned. And who are you to question? Get out of my way or I'll have you gutted and cleaned for my breakfast!'

The man paled and hurriedly stepped aside. Before he had time to reconsider, Abby charged off, the girl in tow at the end of the rope, dragging her heels, making it look real.

No one followed. Abby wanted to run, but she couldn't. She wanted to carry the girl, but she couldn't. It had to look as if a Mord-Sith was taking a prisoner away.

Rather than take the shortest route back to Zedd, Abby followed the hills upriver to a place where the trees offered concealment almost to the water's edge. Zedd had told her where to cross, and warned her not to return by a different way; he had set traps of magic to prevent the D'Harans from charging down from the hills to stop whatever it was he was going to do.

Closer to the river she saw, downstream a way, a bank of fog hanging close to the ground. Zedd had emphatically warned her not to go near any fog. She suspected it a poison cloud of some sort that he had conjured.

The sound of the water told her she was close to the river. The pink sky provided enough light to finally see it when she reached the edge of the trees. Although she could see the massive camp on the hills in the distance behind her, she saw no one following.

Abby took the rope from the child's neck. The girl watched her with those big round eyes. Abby lifted her and held her tight.

'Hold on, and keep quiet.'

Pressing the girl's head to her shoulder, Abby ran for the river.

There was light, but it was not the dawn. They had crossed the frigid water and made the other side when she first noticed it. Even as she ran along the bank of the river, before she could see the source of the light, Abby knew that magic was being called there that was unlike any magic she had ever seen before. A sound, low and thin, whined up the river towards her. A smell, as if the air itself had been burned, hung along the riverbank.

The little girl clung to Abby, tears running down her face, afraid to speak – afraid, it seemed, to hope that she had at last been rescued, as if asking a question might somehow make it all vanish like a dream upon waking. Abby felt tears coursing down her own cheeks.

When she rounded a bend in the river, she spotted the wizard. He stood in the centre of the river, on a rock that Abby had never before seen. The rock was just large enough to clear the surface of the water by a few inches, making it almost appear as if the wizard stood on the surface of the water.

Before him as he faced towards distant D'Hara, shapes, dark and wavering, floated in the air. They curled around, as if confiding in him, conversing, warning, tempting him with floating arms and reaching fingers that wreathed like smoke.

Animate light twisted up around the wizard. Colours both dark and wondrous glimmered about him, cavorting with the shadowy forms undulating through the air. It was at once the most enchanting and the most frightening thing Abby had ever seen. No magic her mother conjured had ever seemed . . . aware.

But the most frightening thing by far was what hovered in the air before the wizard. It appeared to be a molten sphere, so hot it glowed from within, its surface a crackling of fluid dross. An arm of water from the river magically turned skyward in a fountain spray, and poured down over the rotating silvery mass.

The water hissed and steamed as it hit the sphere, leaving behind clouds of white vapour to drift away in the gentle dawn wind. The molten form blackened at the touch of the water cascading over it, and yet the intense inner heat melted the glassy surface again as fast as the water cooled it, making the whole thing bubble and boil in mid-air, a pulsing sinister menace.

Transfixed, Abby let the child slip to the silty ground.

The little girl's arms stretched out. 'Papa.'

He was too far away to hear her, but he heard.

Zedd turned, at once larger than life in the midst of magic Abby could see but not begin to fathom, yet at the same time small with the frailty of human need. Tears filled his eyes as he gazed at his daughter standing beside Abby. This man who seemed to be consulting with spirits looked as if for the first time he were seeing a true apparition.

Zedd leaped off the rock and charged through the water. When he reached her and took her up in the safety of his arms, she began to wail at last with the contained terror released.

'There, there, dear one,' Zedd comforted. 'Papa is here now.'

'Oh, Papa,' she cried against his neck, 'they hurt Mama. They were wicked. They hurt her so . . .'

He hushed her tenderly. 'I know, dear one. I know.'

For the first time, Abby saw the sorceress and the Mother Confessor standing off to the side, watching. They, too, shed tears at what they were seeing. Though Abby was glad for the wizard and his daughter, the sight only intensified the pain in her chest at what she had lost. She was choked with tears.

'There, there, dear one,' Zedd was cooing. 'You're safe, now. Papa won't let anything happen to you. You're safe now.'

Zedd turned to Abby. By the time he had smiled his tearful appreciation, the child was asleep.

'A little spell,' he explained when Abby's brow twitched with surprise. 'She needs to rest. I need to finish what I am doing.'

He put his daughter in Abby's arms. 'Abby, would you take her up to your house where she can sleep until I'm finished here? Please, put her in bed and cover her up to keep her warm. She will sleep for now.'

Thinking about her own daughter in the hands of the brutes across the river, Abby could only nod before turning to the task. She was happy for Zedd, and even felt pride at having rescued his little girl, but as she ran for her home, she was near to dying with grief over her failure to recover her own family.

Abby settled the dead weight of the sleeping child into her bed. She drew the curtain across the small window in her bedroom, and unable to resist, smoothed back silky hair and pressed a kiss to the soft brow before leaving the girl to her blessed rest.

With the child safe at last and asleep, Abby raced back down the knoll to the river. She thought to ask Zedd to give her just a little more time so she could return to look for her own daughter. Fear for Jana had her heart pounding wildly. He owed her a debt, and had not yet seen it through.

Wringing her hands, Abby came to a panting halt at the water's edge. She watched the wizard up on his rock in the river, light and shadow coursing up around him. She had been around magic enough to have the sense to fear approaching him. She could hear his chanted words; though they were words she had never heard before, she recognized the idiosyncratic cadence of words spoken in a spell, words calling together frightful forces.

On the ground beside her was the strange Grace she had seen him draw before, the one that breached the worlds of life and death. The Grace was drawn with a sparkling, pure white sand that stood out in stark relief against the dark silt. Abby shuddered even to look upon it, much less contemplate its meaning. Around the Grace, carefully drawn with the same sparkling white sand, were geometric forms of magical invocations.

Abby lowered her fists, about to call out to the wizard, when Delora leaned close. Abby flinched in surprise.

'Not now, Abigail,' the sorceress murmured. 'Don't disturb him in the middle of this part.'

Reluctantly, Abby heeded the sorceress's words. The Mother Confessor was there, too. Abby chewed her bottom lip as she watched the wizard throw up his arms. Sparkles of coloured light curled up along twisting shafts of shadows. 'But I must. I haven't been able to find my family. He must help me. He must save them. It's a debt of bones that must be satisfied.'

The other two women shared a look. 'Abby,' the Mother Confessor said, 'he gave you a chance, gave you time. He tried. He did his best, but he has everyone else to think of, now.'

The Mother Confessor took up Abby's hand, and the sorceress put an arm around Abby's shoulders as she stood weeping on the riverbank. It wasn't supposed to end this way, not after all she had been through, not after all she had done. Despair crushed her.

The wizard, his arms raised, called forth more light, more

shadows, more magic. The river roiled around him. The hissing thing in the air grew as it slowly slumped closer to the water. Shafts of light shot from the hot, rotating, bloom of power.

The sun was rising over the hills behind the D'Harans. This part of the river wasn't as wide as elsewhere, and Abby could see the activity in the trees beyond. Men moved about, but the fog hanging on the far bank kept them wary, kept them in the trees.

Also across the river, at the edge of the tree-covered hills, another wizard had appeared to conjure magic. He too stood atop a rock as his arms launched sparkling light up into the air. Abby thought that the strong morning sun might outshine the conjured illuminations, but it didn't.

Abby could stand it no longer. 'Zedd!' she called out across the river. 'Zedd! Please, you promised! I found your daughter! What about mine? Please don't do this until she is safe!'

Zedd turned and looked at her as if from a great distance, as if from another world. Arms of dark forms caressed him. Fingers of dark smoke dragged along his jaw, urging his attention back to them, but he gazed instead at Abby.

'I'm so sorry.' Despite the distance, Abby could clearly hear his whispered words. 'I gave you time to try to find them. I can spare no more, or countless other mothers will weep for their children – mothers still living, and mothers in the spirit world.'

Abby cried out in an anguished wail as he turned back to the ensorcellment. The two women tried to comfort her, but Abby was not to be comforted in her grief.

Thunder rolled through the hills. A clacking clamour from the spell around Zedd rose to echo up and down the valley. Shafts of intense light shot upward. It was a disorienting sight, light shining up into sunlight.

Across the river, the counter to Zedd's magic seemed to spring forth. Arms of light twisted like smoke, lowering to tangle with the light radiating up around Zedd. The fog along the riverbank diffused suddenly.

In answer, Zedd spread his arms wide. The glowing, tumbling furnace of molten light thundered. The water sluicing over it roared as it boiled and steamed. The air wailed as if in protest.

Behind the wizard across the river, the D'Haran soldiers were pouring out of the trees, driving their prisoners before them. People cried out in terror. They quailed at the wizard's magic, only to be driven onward by the spears and swords at their backs.

Abby saw several who refused to move fall to the blades. At the mortal cries, the rest rushed onward, like sheep before wolves.

If whatever Zedd was doing failed, the army of the Midlands would then charge into this valley to confront the enemy. The prisoners would be caught in the middle.

A figure worked its way up along the opposite bank, dragging a child behind. Abby's flesh flashed icy cold with sudden frigid sweat. It was Mariska. Abby shot a quick glance back over her shoulder. It was impossible. She squinted across the river.

'Nooo!' Zedd called out.

It was Zedd's little girl that Mariska had by the hair.

Somehow, Mariska had followed and found the child sleeping in Abby's home. With no one there to watch over her as she slept, Mariska had stolen the child back.

Mariska held the child out before herself, for Zedd to see. 'Cease and surrender, Zorander, or she dies!'

Abby tore away from the arms holding her and charged into the water. She struggled to run against the current, to reach the wizard. Part way there, he turned to stare into her eyes.

Abby froze. 'I'm sorry.' Her own voice sounded to her like a plea before death. 'I thought she was safe.'

Zedd nodded in resignation. It was out of his hands. He turned back to the enemy. His arms lifted to his sides. His fingers spread, as if commanding all to stop – magic and men alike.

'Let the prisoners go!' Zedd called across the water to the enemy wizard. 'Let them go, Anargo, and I'll give you all your lives!'

Anargo's laugh rang out over the water.

'Surrender,' Mariska hissed, 'or she dies.'

The old woman pulled out the knife she kept in the wrap

around her waist. She pressed the blade to the child's throat. The girl was screaming in terror, her arms reaching to her father, her little fingers clawing the air.

Abby struggled ahead into the water. She called out, begging Mariska to let Zedd's daughter go free. The woman paid no more heed to Abby than to Zedd.

'Last chance!' Mariska called.

'You heard her,' Anargo growled out across the water. 'Surrender now or she will die.'

'You know I can't put myself above my people!' Zedd called back. 'This is between us, Anargo! Let them all go!'

Anargo's laugh echoed up and down the river. 'You are a fool, Zorander! You had your chance!' His expression twisted to rage. 'Kill her!' he screamed to Mariska.

Fists at his side, Zedd shrieked. The sound seemed to split the morning with its fury.

Mariska lifted the squealing child by her hair. Abby gasped in disbelief as the woman sliced the little girl's throat.

The child flailed. Blood spurted across Mariska's gnarly fingers as she viciously sawed the blade back and forth. She gave a final, mighty yank of the knife. The blood-soaked body dropped in a limp heap. Abby felt vomit welling up in the back of her throat. The silty dirt of the riverbank turned a wet red.

Mariska held the severed head high with a howl of victory. Strings of flesh and blood swung beneath it. The mouth hung in a slack, silent cry.

Abby threw her arms around Zedd's legs. 'Dear spirits, I'm sorry! Oh, Zedd, forgive me!'

She wailed in anguish, unable to gather her senses at witnessing a sight so grisly.

'And now, child,' Zedd asked in a hoarse voice from above, 'what would you have me do? Would you have me let them win, to save your daughter from what they have done to mine? Tell me, child, what should I do?'

Abby couldn't beg for the life of her family at a cost of such people rampaging unchecked across the land. Her sickened heart wouldn't allow it. How could she sacrifice the lives and peace of everyone else just so her loved ones would live?

She would be no better than Mariska, killing innocent children.

'Kill them all!' Abby screamed up at the wizard. She threw her arm out, pointing at Mariska and the hateful wizard Anargo. 'Kill the bastards! Kill them all!'

Zedd's arms flung upward. The morning cracked with a peal of thunder. As if he had loosed it, the molten mass before him plunged into the water. The ground shook with a jolt. A huge geyser of water exploded forth. The air itself quaked. All around the most dreadful rumbling whipped the water into froth.

Abby, squatted down with the water to her waist, felt numb not only from the cold, but also from the cold knowledge that she'd been forsaken by the good spirits she had always thought would watch over her. Zedd turned and snatched her arm, dragging her up on the rock with him.

It was another world.

The shapes around them called to her, too. They reached out, bridging the distance between life and death. Searing pain, frightful joy, profound peace, spread through her at their touch. Light moved up through her body, filling her like air filled her lungs, and exploded in showers of sparks in her mind's eye. The thick howl of the magic was deafening.

Green light ripped through the water. Across the river, Anargo had been thrown to the ground. The rock atop which he had stood had shattered into needle-like shards. The soldiers called out in fright as the air all about danced with swirling smoke and sparks of light.

'Run!' Mariska screamed. 'While you have the chance! Run for your lives!' Already she was racing towards the hills. 'Leave the prisoners to die! Save yourselves! Run!'

The mood across the river suddenly galvanized with a single determination. The D'Harans dropped their weapons. They cast aside the ropes and chains holding the prisoners. They kicked up dirt as they turned and ran. In a single instant, the whole of an army that had a moment before stood grimly facing them, were all, as if of a single fright, running for their lives.

From the corner of her eye, Abby saw the Mother Confessor and the sorceress struggling to run into the water. Although the water was hardly above their knees, it bogged them down in their rush nearly as much as would mud.

Abby watched it all as if in a dream. She floated in the light surrounding her. Pain and rapture were one within her. Light and dark, sound and silence, joy and sorrow, all were one, everything and nothing together in a cauldron of raging magic.

Across the river, the D'Haran army had vanished into the woods. Dust rose above the trees, marking their horses, wagons, and footfalls racing away, while at the riverbank, the Mother Confessor and the sorceress were shoving people into the water, screaming at them, though Abby didn't hear the words, so absorbed was she by the strange harmonious trills twisting her thoughts into visions of dancing colour overlaying what her eyes were trying to tell her.

She thought briefly that surely she was dying. She thought briefly that it didn't matter. And then her mind was swimming again in the cold colour and hot light, the drumming music of magic and worlds meshing. The wizard's embrace made her feel as if she were being held in her mother's arms again. Maybe she was.

Abby was aware of the people reaching the Midlands side of the river and running ahead of the Mother Confessor and sorceress. They vanished into the rushes and then Abby saw them far away, beyond the tall grass, running uphill, away from the sublime sorcery erupting from the river.

The world thundered around her. A subterranean thump brought sharp pain deep in her chest. A whine, like steel being shredded, tore through the morning air. All around the water danced and quaked.

Hot steam felt as if it would scald Abby's legs. The air went white with it. The noise hurt her ears so much that she squeezed her eyes shut. She saw the same thing with her eyes closed as she saw with them open – shadowy shapes swirling through the green air. Everything was going crazy in her mind, making no sense. Green fury tore at her body and soul.

Abby felt pain, as if something inside her tore asunder. She gasped and opened her eyes. A horrific wall of green fire was receding away from them, towards the far side of the river. Founts of water lashed upward, like a thunderstorm in reverse. Lightning laced together above the surface of the river.

As the conflagration reached the far bank, the ground beneath it rent apart. Shafts of violet light shot up from the ripping wounds in the earth, like the blood of another realm.

Worse, though, than any of it, were the howls. Howls of the dead, Abby was sure. It felt as if her own soul moaned in sympathy with the agony of cries filling the air. From the receding green wall of glimmering fire, the shapes twisted and turned, calling, begging, trying to escape the world of the dead.

She understood now that that was what the wall of green fire was – death, come to life.

The wizard had breached the boundary between worlds.

Abby had no idea how much time passed; in the grip of the strange light in which she swam there seemed to be no time, any more than there was anything solid. There was nothing familiar about any of the sensations upon which to hang understanding.

It seemed to Abby that the wall of green fire had halted its advance in the trees on the far hillside. The trees over which it had passed, and those she could see embraced by the shimmering curtain, had blackened and shrivelled at the profound touch of death itself. Even the grass over which the grim presence had passed looked to have been baked black and crisp by a high summer sun.

As Abby watched the wall, it dulled. As she stared, it seemed to waver in and out of her vision, sometimes a glimmering green gloss, like molten glass, and sometimes no more than a pale hint, like a fog just now passed from the air.

To each side, it was spreading, a wall of death raging across the world of life.

Abby realized she heard the river again, the comfortable, common, sloshing, lapping, burbling sounds that she lived her life hearing but most of the time didn't notice.

Zedd hopped down from the rock. He took her hand and helped her down. Abby gripped his hand tightly to brace against the dizzying sensations swimming through her head.

Zedd snapped his fingers, and the rock upon which they had just stood leaped into the air, causing her to gasp in fright. In an instant so brief that she doubted she had seen it, Zedd caught the rock. It had become a small stone, smaller than an egg. He winked at her as he slipped it into a pocket. She thought the wink the oddest thing she could imagine, odder even than the boulder, now a stone in his pocket.

On the bank, the Mother Confessor and the sorceress waited. They took her arms, helping her out of the water.

The sorceress looked grim. 'Zedd, why isn't it moving?'

It sounded to Abby more like an accusation than a question. Either way, Zedd ignored it.

'Zedd,' Abby mumbled, 'I'm so sorry. It's my fault. I shouldn't have left her alone. I should have stayed. I'm so sorry.'

The wizard, hardly hearing her words, was looking off to the wall of death on the other side of the river. He brought his clawed fingers up past his chest, calling something forth from within himself.

With a sudden thump to the air, fire erupted between his hands. He held it out as he would hold an offering. Abby threw an arm up in front of her face at the heat.

Zedd lifted the roiling ball of liquid fire. It grew between his hands, tumbling and turning, roaring and hissing with rage.

The three women backed away. Abby had heard of such fire. She had once heard her mother name it in a hushed tone: wizard's fire. Even then, not seeing or knowing its like, those whispered words forming a picture in Abby's mind as her mother recounted it, had sent a chill through Abby. Wizard's fire was the bane of life, called forth to scourge an enemy. This could be nothing else.

'For killing my love, my Erilyn, the mother of our daughter, and all the other innocent loved ones of innocent people,' Zedd whispered, 'I send you, Panis Rahl, the gift of death.'

The wizard opened his arms outward. The liquid blue and yellow fire, bidden by its master, tumbled forward, gathering speed, roaring away towards D'Hara. As it crossed the river, it grew like angry lightning blooming forth, wailing with wrathful fury, reflecting in glimmering points from the water in thousands of bright sparkles.

The wizard's fire shot across the growing wall of green, just catching the upper edge. At the contact, green flame flared forth, some of it tearing away, caught up behind the wizard's fire, trailing after like smoke behind flame. The deadly mix howled towards the horizon. Everyone stood transfixed, watching, until all trace of it had vanished in the distance.

When Zedd, pale and drawn, turned back to them, Abby clutched his robes. 'Zedd, I'm so sorry. I shouldn't –'

He put his fingers to her lips to silence her. 'There is someone waiting for you.'

He tilted his head. She turned. Back by the rushes, Philip stood holding Jana's hand. Abby gasped with a jolt of giddy joy. Philip grinned his familiar grin. At his other side, her father smiled and nodded his approval to her.

Arms reaching, Abby ran to them. Jana's face wrinkled. She backed against Philip. Abby fell to her knees before her.

'It's Mama,' Philip said to Jana. 'She just has herself some new clothes.'

Abby realized Jana was frightened by the red leather outfit she was wearing. Abby grinned through her tears.

'Mama!' Jana cried at seeing the smile.

Abby threw her arms around her daughter. She laughed and hugged Jana so hard the child squeaked in protest. Abby felt Philip's hand on her shoulder in loving greeting. Abby stood and threw an arm around him, tears choking her voice. Her father put a comforting hand to her back while she squeezed Jana's hand.

Zedd, Delora, and the Mother Confessor gathered them and herded them up the hill towards the people waiting at the top.

Soldiers, mostly officers, some that Abby recognized, a few other people from Aydindril, and the wizard Thomas waited with the freed prisoners. Among the people liberated were those of Coney Crossing; people who held Abby, the daughter of a sorceress, in no favour. But they were her people, the people from her home, the people she had wanted saved.

Zedd rested a hand on Abby's shoulder. Abby was shocked to see that his wavy brown hair was now partly snow-white. She knew without a looking-glass that hers had undergone the same transformation in the place beyond the world of life, where, for a time, they had been.

'This is Abigail, born of Helsa,' the wizard called out to the people gathered. 'She is the one who went to Aydindril to seek my help. Though she does not have magic, it is because of her that you people are all free. She cared enough to beg for your lives.'

Abby, with Philip's arm around her waist and Jana's hand in hers, looked from the wizard to the sorceress, and then to the Mother Confessor. The Mother Confessor smiled. Abby thought it a cold-hearted thing to do in view of the fact that Zedd's daughter had been murdered before their eyes not long before. She whispered as much.

The Mother Confessor's smile widened. 'Don't you remember?' she asked as she leaned close. 'Don't you remember what I told you we call him?'

Abby, confused by everything that had happened, couldn't imagine what the Mother Confessor was talking about. When she admitted she didn't, the Mother Confessor and the sorceress shepherded her onward, past the grave where Abby had reburied her mother's skull upon her return, and into the house.

With a hand, the Mother Confessor eased back the door to Abby's bedroom. There, on the bed where Abby had placed her, was Zedd's daughter, still sleeping. Abby stared in disbelief.

'The trickster,' the Mother Confessor said. 'I told you that was our name for him.'

'And not a very flattering one,' Zedd grumbled as he stepped up behind them.

'But . . . how?' Abby pressed her fingers to her temples. 'I don't understand.'

Zedd gestured. Abby saw, for the first time, the body lying just beyond the door out the back. It was Mariska.

'When you showed me the room when we first came here,' Zedd told her, 'I laid a few traps for those intent on harm. That woman was killed by those traps because she came here intent on taking my daughter from where she slept.'

'You mean it was all an illusion?' Abby was dumbfounded. 'Why would you do such a cruel thing? How could you?'

'I am the object of vengeance,' the wizard explained. 'I didn't want my daughter to pay the price her mother has already paid. Since my spell killed the woman as she tried to harm my daughter, I was able to use a vision of her to accomplish the deception. The enemy knew the woman, and that she acted for Anargo. I used what they expected to see to convince them and to frighten them into running and leaving the prisoners.

'I cast the death spell so that everyone would think they saw my daughter being killed. This way, the enemy thinks my daughter dead, and will have no reason to hunt her or ever again try to harm her. I did it to protect her from the unforeseen.'

The sorceress scowled at him. 'If it were any but you, Zeddicus, and for any reason but the reason you had, I'd see you brought up on charges for casting such a web as a death spell.' She broke into a grin. 'Well done, First Wizard.'

Outside, the officers all wanted to know what was happening.

'No battle today,' Zedd told them. 'I've just ended the war.'

They cheered with genuine joy. Had Zedd not been the First Wizard, Abby suspected they would have hoisted him on their shoulders. It seemed that there was no one more glad for peace than those whose job it was to fight for it.

Wizard Thomas, looking more humble than Abby had ever seen him, cleared his throat. 'Zorander, I . . . I . . . I simply can't believe what my own eyes have seen.' His face finally took on its familiar scowl. 'But we have people already in near revolt over magic. When news of this spreads, it is only going to make it worse. The demands for relief from magic grow every day and you have fed the fury. With this, we're liable to have revolt on our hands.'

'I still want to know why it isn't moving,' Delora growled from behind. 'I want to know why it's just sitting there, all green and still.'

Zedd ignored her and directed his attention to the old wizard. 'Thomas, I have a job for you.'

He motioned several officers and officials from Aydindril forward, and passed a finger before all their faces, his own turning grim and determined. 'I have a job for all of you. The people have reason to fear magic. Today we have seen magic deadly and dangerous. I can understand those fears.

'In appreciation of these fears, I shall grant their wish.'

'What!' Thomas scoffed. 'You can't end magic, Zorander! Not even you can accomplish such a paradox.'

'Not end it,' Zedd said. 'But give them a place without it. I want you to organize an official delegation large enough to travel all the Midlands with the offer. All those who would quit a world with magic are to move to the lands to the west. There they shall set up new lives free of any magic. I shall ensure that magic cannot intrude on their peace.'

Thomas threw up his hands. 'How can you make such a promise!'

Zedd's arm lifted to point off behind him, to the wall of green fire growing towards the sky. 'I shall call up a second wall of death, through which none can pass. On the other side it shall be a place free of magic. There, people will be free to live their lives without magic.

'I want you all to see that the word is passed through the land. People have until spring to emigrate to the lands west. Thomas, you will warrant that none with magic make the journey. We have books we can use to ensure that we purge a place of any with a trace of magic. We can assure that there will be no magic there.

'In the spring, when all who wish have gone to their new

homeland, I will seal them off from magic. In one fell swoop, I will satisfy the large majority of the petitions that come to us; they will have lives without magic. May the good spirits watch over them, and may they not come to regret their wish granted.'

Thomas pointed heatedly at the thing Zedd had brought into the world. 'But what about that thing? What if people go wandering into it in the dark? They will be walking into death.'

'Not only in the dark,' Zedd said. 'Once it has stabilized it will be hard to see at all. We will have to set up guards to keep people away. We will have to set aside land near the boundary and have men guard the area to keep people out.'

'Men?' Abby asked. 'You mean you will have to start a corps of boundary wardens?'

'Yes,' Zedd said, his eyebrows lifting, 'that's a good name for them. Boundary wardens.'

Silence settled over those leaning in to hear the wizard's words. The mood had changed and was now serious with the grim matter at hand. Abby couldn't imagine a place without magic, but she knew how vehemently some wished it.

Thomas finally nodded. 'Zedd, this time I think you've got it right. Sometimes, we must serve the people by not serving them.' The others mumbled their agreement, though, like Abby, it seemed to them a bleak solution.

Zedd straightened. 'Then it is decided.'

He turned and announced to the crowd the end of the war, and the division to come in which those who had petitioned for years would finally have their petition granted; for those who wished it, a land outside the Midlands, without magic, would be created.

While everyone was chattering about such a mysterious and exotic thing as a land without magic, or cheering and celebrating the end of the war, Abby whispered to Jana to wait with her father a moment. She kissed her daughter and then took the opportunity to pull Zedd aside.

'Zedd, may I speak with you? I have a question.'

Zedd smiled and took her by the elbow, urging Abby into her small home. 'I'd like to check on my daughter. Come along.'

Abby cast caution to the winds and took the Mother Confessor's hand in one of hers, Delora's in the other, and pulled them in with her. They had a right to hear this, too.

'Zedd,' Abby asked once they were away from the crowd in her yard, 'may I please know the debt your father owed my mother?'

Zedd lifted an eyebrow. 'My father owed your mother no debt.'

Abby frowned. 'But it was a debt of bones, passed down from your father to you, and from my mother to me.'

'Oh, it was a debt all right, but not owed to your mother, but by your mother.'

'What?' Abby asked in stunned confusion. 'What do you mean?'

Zedd smiled. 'When your mother was giving birth to you, she was in trouble. You both were dying in the labour. My father used magic to save her. Helsa begged him to save you, too. In order to keep you in the world of the living and out of the Keeper's grasp, without thought to his own safety, he worked far beyond the endurance anyone would expect of a wizard.

'Your mother was a sorceress, and understood the extent of what was involved in saving your life. In appreciation of what my father had done, she swore a debt to him. When she died, the debt passed to you.'

Abby, eyes wide, tried to reconcile the whole thing in her mind. Her mother had never told her the nature of the debt.

'But . . . but you mean that it is I who owe the debt to you? You mean that the debt of bones is my burden?'

Zedd pushed open the door to the room where his daughter slept, smiling as he looked in. 'The debt is paid, Abby. The bracelet your mother gave you had magic, linking you to the debt. Thank you for my daughter's life.'

Abby glanced to the Mother Confessor. Trickster indeed. 'But why would you help me, if it was really not a debt of bones you owed me? If it was really a debt I owed you?'

Zedd shrugged. 'We reap a reward merely in the act of helping others. We never know how, or if, that reward will come back to us. Helping is the reward; none other is needed nor better.'

Abby watched the beautiful little girl sleeping in the room beyond. 'I am thankful to the good spirits that I could help keep such a life in this world. I may not have the gift, but I can foresee that she will go on to be a person of import, not only for you, but for others.'

Zedd smiled idly as he watched his daughter sleeping. 'I think you may have the gift of prophecy, my dear, for she is already a person who has played a part in bringing a war to an end, and in so doing, saved the lives of countless people.'

The sorceress pointed out the window. 'I still want to know why that thing isn't moving. It was supposed to pass over D'Hara and purge it of all life, to kill them all for what they have done.' Her scowl deepened. 'Why is it just sitting there?'

Zedd folded his hands. 'It ended the war. That is enough. The wall is a part of the underworld itself, the world of the dead. Their army will not be able to cross it and make war on us for as long as such a boundary stands.'

'And how long will that be?'

Zedd shrugged. 'Nothing remains for ever. For now, there will be peace. The killing is ended.'

The sorceress did not look to be satisfied. 'But they were trying to kill us all!'

'Well, now they can't. Delora, there are those in D'Hara who are innocent, too. Just because Panis Rahl wished to conquer and subjugate us, that does not mean that all the D'Haran people are evil. Many good people in D'Hara have suffered under harsh rule. How could I kill everyone there, including all the people who have caused no harm, and themselves wish only to live their lives in peace?'

Delora wiped a hand across her face. 'Zeddicus, sometimes I don't know about you. Sometimes, you make a lousy wind of death.'

The Mother Confessor stood staring out the window, towards D'Hara. Her violet eyes turned back to the wizard.

'There will be those over there who will be your foes for life because of this, Zedd. You have made bitter enemies with this. You have left them alive.'

'Enemies,' the wizard said, 'are the price of honour.'

Tales
of Alvin
Maker

ORSON SCOTT
CARD

TALES
OF ALVIN
MAKER

ORSON SCOTT
CARD

The Tales of Alvin Maker:
Book One: *Seventh Son* (1987)
Book Two: *Red Prophet* (1988)
Book Three: *Prentice Alvin* (1989)
Book Four: *Alvin Journeyman* (1996)
Book Five: *Master Alvin* (1998)

In the Tales of Alvin Maker series, an alternate-history view of an America that never was, Orson Scott Card postulated what the world might have been like if the Revolutionary War had never happened, and if folk magic actually worked.

America is divided into several provinces, with the Spanish and French still having a strong presence in the New World. The emerging scientific revolution in Europe has led many people with 'talent', that is, magical ability, to emigrate to North America, bringing their prevailing magic with them. The books chronicle the life of Alvin, the seventh son of a seventh son – a fact that marks him right away as a person of great power. It is Alvin's ultimate destiny to become a Maker, an adept being of a kind that has not existed for a thousand years. However, there exists an Unmaker for every Maker – a being of great supernatural evil – who is Alvin's adversary, and strives to use Alvin's brother Calvin against him.

During the course of his adventures, Alvin explores the world around him and encounters such problems as slavery and the continued enmity between the settlers and the Native Americans who control the western half of the continent. The series appears to be heading towards an ultimate confrontation between Alvin and the Unmaker, with the fate of the entire continent, perhaps even the world, hinging on the outcome.

◆

GRINNING MAN

BY ORSON SCOTT CARD

The first time Alvin Maker run across the grinning man was in the steep woody hills of eastern Kenituck. Alvin was walking along with his ward, the boy Arthur Stuart, talking either deep philosophy or the best way for travellers to cook beans, I can't bring to mind now which, when they come upon a clearing where a man was squatting on his haunches looking up into a tree. Apart from the unnatural grin upon his face, there wasn't all that much remarkable about him, for that time and place. Dressed in buckskin, a cap made of coonhide on his head, a musket lying in the grass ready to hand – plenty of men of such youth and roughness walked the game trails of the unsettled forest in those days.

Though come to think of it, eastern Kenituck wasn't all that unsettled by then, and most men gave up buckskin for cotton during summer, less they was too poor to get them none. So maybe it *was* partly his appearance that made Alvin stop up short and look at the fellow. Arthur Stuart, of course, he did what he saw Alvin do, till he had some good reason to do otherwise, so he stopped at the meadow's edge too, and fell silent too, and watched.

The grinning man had his gaze locked on the middle branches of a scruffy old pine that was getting somewhat choked out by slower-growing flat-leaf trees. But it wasn't no tree he was grinning at. No sir, it was the bear.

There's bears and there's bears, as everyone knows. Some little old brown bears are about as dangerous as a dog – which means if you beat it with a stick you deserve what you get, but otherwise it'll leave you alone. But some black bears and some grizzlies, they have a kind of bristle to the hair on their backs, a kind of spikiness like a porcupine that tells you they're just spoiling for a fight, hoping you'll say a cross word so's they can take a swipe at your head and suck your lunch back up through your neck. Like a likkered-up river man.

This was that kind of bear. A little old, maybe, but as spiky as they come, and it wasn't up that tree 'cause it was afraid, it was up there for honey, which it had plenty of, along with bees that were now so tired of trying to sting through that matted fur that they were mostly dead, all stung out. There was no shortage of buzzing, though, like a choir of folks as don't know the words to the hymn so they just hum, only the bees was none too certain of the tune, neither.

But there sat that man, grinning at the bear. And there sat the bear, looking down at him with its teeth showing.

Alvin and Arthur stood watching for many a minute while nothing in the tableau changed. The man squatted on the ground, grinning up; the bear squatted on a branch, grinning down. Neither one showed the slightest sign that he knew Alvin and Arthur was even there.

So it was Alvin broke the silence. 'I don't know who started the ugly contest, but I know who's going to win.'

Without breaking his grin, through clenched teeth the man said, 'Excuse me for not shaking your hands but I'm a-busy grinning this bear.'

Alvin nodded wisely – it certainly seemed to be a truthful statement. 'And from the look of it,' says Alvin, 'that bear thinks he's grinning you, too.'

'Let him think what he thinks,' said the grinning man. 'He's coming down from that tree.'

Arthur Stuart, being young, was impressed. 'You can do that just by grinning?'

'Just hope I never turn my grin on *you*,' said the man. 'I'd hate to have to pay your master the purchase price of such a clever blackamoor as you.'

It was a common mistake, to take Arthur Stuart for a slave. He was half-Black, wasn't he? And south of the Hio was all slave country then, where a Black man either was, or used to be, or sure as shooting was bound to become somebody's property. In those parts, for safety's sake, Alvin didn't bother correcting the assumption. Let folks think Arthur Stuart already had an owner, so folks didn't get their hearts set on volunteering for the task.

'That must be a pretty strong grin,' said Alvin Maker. 'My name's Alvin. I'm a journeyman blacksmith.'

'Ain't much call for a smith in these parts. Plenty of better land farther west, more settlers, you ought to try it.' The fellow was still talking through his grin.

'I might,' said Alvin. 'What's your name?'

'Hold still now,' says the grinning man. 'Stay right where you are. He's a-coming down.'

The bear yawned, then clambered down the trunk and rested on all fours, his head swinging back and forth, keeping time to whatever music it is that bears hear. The fur around his mouth was shiny with honey and dotted with dead bees. Whatever the bear was thinking, after a while he was done, whereupon he stood on his hind legs like a man, his paws high, his mouth open like a baby showing its mama it swallowed its food.

The grinning man rose up on *his* hind legs, then, and spread *his* arms, just like the bear, and opened his mouth to show a fine set of teeth for a human, but it wasn't no great shakes compared to bear's teeth. Still, the bear seemed convinced. It bent back down to the ground and ambled away without complaint into the brush.

'That's my tree now,' said the grinning man.

'Ain't much of a tree,' said Alvin.

'Honey's about all et up,' added Arthur Stuart.

'My tree and all the land round about,' said the grinning man.

'And what you plan to do with it? You don't look to be a farmer.'

'I plan to sleep here,' said the grinning man. 'And my intention was to sleep without no bear coming along to disturb my slumber. So I had to tell him who was boss.'

'And that's all you do with that knack of yours?' asked Arthur Stuart. 'Make bears get out of the way?'

'I sleep under bearskin in winter,' said the grinning man. 'So when I grin a bear, it stays grinned till I done what I'm doing.'

'Don't it worry you that someday you'll meet your match?' asked Alvin mildly.

'I got no match, friend. My grin is the prince of grins. The king of grins.'

'The emperor of grins,' said Arthur Stuart. 'The Napoleon of grins!'

The irony in Arthur's voice was apparently not subtle enough to escape the grinning man. 'Your boy got him a mouth.'

'Helps me pass the time,' said Alvin. 'Well, now you done us the favour of running off that bear, I reckon this is a good place for us to stop and build us a canoe.'

Arthur Stuart looked at him like he was crazy. 'What do we need a canoe for?'

'Being a lazy man,' said Alvin, 'I mean to use it to go downstream.'

'Don't matter to me,' said the grinning man. 'Float it, sink it, wear it on your head or swallow it for supper, you ain't building nothing right here.' The grin was still on his face.

'Look at that, Arthur,' said Alvin. 'This fellow hasn't even told us his name, and he's a-grinning *us*.'

'Ain't going to work,' said Arthur Stuart. 'We been grinned at by politicians, preachers, witchers, and lawyers, and you ain't got teeth enough to scare us.'

With that, the grinning man brought his musket to bear right on Alvin's heart. 'I reckon I'll stop grinning then,' he said.

'I think this ain't canoe-building country,' said Alvin. 'Let's move along, Arthur.'

'Not so fast,' said the grinning man. 'I think maybe I'd be doing all my neighbours a favour if I kept you from ever moving away from this spot.'

'First off,' said Alvin, 'you got no neighbours.'

'All mankind is my neighbour,' said the grinning man. 'Jesus said so.'

'I recall he specified Samaritans,' said Alvin, 'and Samaritans got no call to fret about me.'

'What I see is a man carrying a poke that he hides from my view.'

That was true, for in that sack was Alvin's golden plough, and he always tried to keep it halfway hid behind him so folks wouldn't get troubled if they happened to see it move by itself, which it was prone to do from time to time. Now, though, to answer the challenge, Alvin moved the sack around in front of him.

'I got nothing to hide from a man with a gun,' said Alvin.

'A man with a poke,' said the grinning man, 'who *says* he's a blacksmith but his only companion is a boy too scrawny and stubby to be learning his trade. But the boy is just the right size to skinny his way through an attic window or the eaves of a loose-made house. So I says to myself, this here's a second-storey man, who lifts his boy up with those big strong arms so he can sneak into houses from above and open the door to the thief. So shooting you down right now would be a favour to the world.'

Arthur Stuart snorted. 'Burglars don't get much trade in the woods.'

'I never said you-all looked smart,' said the grinning man.

'Best point your gun at somebody else now,' said Arthur Stuart quietly. 'Iffen you want to keep the use of it.'

The grinning man's answer was to pull the trigger. A spurt of flame shot out as the barrel of the gun exploded, splaying into iron strips like the end of a worn-out broom. The musket ball rolled slowly down the barrel and plopped out into the grass.

'Look what you done to my gun,' said the grinning man.

'Wasn't me as pulled the trigger,' said Alvin. 'And you was warned.'

'How come you still grinning?' asked Arthur Stuart.

'I'm just a cheerful sort of fellow,' said the grinning man, drawing his big old knife.

'Do you like that knife?' asked Arthur Stuart.

'Got it from my friend Jim Bowie,' said the grinning man. 'It's took the hide off six bears and I can't count how many beavers.'

'Take a look at the barrel of your musket,' said Arthur Stuart, 'and then look at the blade of that knife you like so proud, and think real hard.'

The grinning man looked at the gun barrel and then at the blade. 'Well?' asked the man.

'Keep thinking,' said Arthur Stuart. 'It'll come to you.'

'You let him talk to White men like that?'

'A man as fires a musket at me,' said Alvin, 'I reckon Arthur Stuart here can talk to him any old how he wants.'

The grinning man thought that over for a minute, and then, though no one would have thought it possible, he grinned even wider, put away his knife, and stuck out his hand. 'You got some knack,' he said to Alvin.

Alvin reached out and shook the man's hand. Arthur Stuart knew what was going to happen next, because he'd seen it before. Even though Alvin was announced as a blacksmith and any man with eyes could see the strength of his arms and hands, this grinning man just had to brace foot to foot against him and try to pull him down.

Not that Alvin minded a little sport. He let the grinning man work himself up into quite a temper of pulling and tugging and twisting and wrenching. It would have looked like quite a contest, except that Alvin could've been fixing to nap, he looked so relaxed.

Finally Alvin got interested. He squished down hard and the grinning man yelped and dropped to his knees and began to beg Alvin to give him back his hand. 'Not that I'll ever have the use of it again,' said the grinning man, 'but I'd at least like to have it so I got a place to store my second glove.'

'I got no plan to keep your hand,' said Alvin.

'I know, but it crossed my mind you might be planning to leave it here in the meadow and send me somewheres else,' said the grinning man.

'Don't you ever stop grinning?' asked Alvin.

'Don't dare try,' said the grinning man. 'Bad stuff happens to me when I don't smile.'

'You'd be doing a whole lot better if you'd've frowned at me but kept your musket pointed at the ground and your hands in your pockets,' said Alvin.

'You got my fingers squished down to one, and my thumb's about to pop off,' said the grinning man. 'I'm willing to say uncle.'

'Willing is one thing. Doing's another.'

'Uncle,' said the grinning man.

'Nope, that won't do,' said Alvin. 'I need two things from you.'

'I got no money and if you take my traps I'm a dead man.'

'What I want is your name, and permission to build a canoe here,' said Alvin.

'My name, if it don't become "One-handed Davy", is Crockett, in memory of my daddy,' said the grinning man. 'And I reckon I was wrong about this tree. It's your tree. Me and that bear, we're both far from home and got a ways to travel before nightfall.'

'You're welcome to stay,' said Alvin. 'Room for all here.'

'Not for me,' said Davy Crockett. 'My hand, should I get it back, is going to be mighty swoll up, and I don't think there's room enough for it in this clearing.'

'I'll be sorry to see you go,' said Alvin. 'A new friend is a precious commodity in these parts.' He let go. Tears came to Davy's eyes as he gingerly felt the sore palm and fingers, testing to see if any of them was about to drop off.

'Pleased to meet you, Mr Journeyman Smith,' said Davy. 'You too, boy.' He nodded cheerfully, grinning like an innkeeper. 'I reckon you couldn't possibly be no burglar. Nor could you possibly be the famous Prentice Smith what stole a golden plough from his master and run off with the plough in a poke.'

'I never stole nothing in my life,' said Alvin. 'But now you ain't got a gun, what's in my poke ain't none of your business.'

'I'm pleased to grant you full title to this land,' said Davy, 'and all the rights to minerals under the ground, and all the rights to rain and sunlight on top of it, plus the lumber and all hides and skins.'

'You a lawyer?' asked Arthur Stuart suspiciously.

Instead of answering, Davy turned tail and slunk out of the

clearing just like that bear done, and in the same direction. He kept on slinking, too, though he probably wanted to run; but running would have made his hand bounce and that would hurt too much.

'I think we'll never see *him* again,' said Arthur Stuart.

'I think we will,' said Alvin.

'Why's that?'

''Cause I changed him deep inside, to be a little more like the bear. And I changed that bear to be a little bit more like Davy.'

'You shouldn't go messing with people's insides like that,' said Arthur Stuart.

'The Devil makes me do it,' said Alvin.

'You don't believe in the Devil.'

'Do so,' said Alvin. 'I just don't think he looks the way folks say he does.'

'Oh? What does he look like then?' demanded the boy.

'Me,' said Alvin. 'Only smarter.'

Alvin and Arthur set to work making them a dugout canoe. They cut down a tree just the right size – two inches wider than Alvin's hips – and set to burning one surface of it, then chipping out the ash and burning it deeper. It was slow, hot work, and the more they did of it, the more puzzled Arthur Stuart got.

'I reckon you know your business,' he says to Alvin, 'but we don't need no canoe.'

'*Any* canoe,' says Alvin. 'Miss Larner'd be right peeved to hear you talking like that.'

'First place,' says Arthur Stuart, 'you learned from Tenskwa-Tawa how to run like a Red man through the forest, faster than any canoe can float, and with a lot less work than this.'

'Don't feel like running,' said Alvin.

'Second place,' Arthur Stuart continued, 'water works against you every chance it gets. The way Miss Larner tells it, water near killed you sixteen times before you was ten.'

'It wasn't the water, it was the Unmaker, and these days he's about give up on using water against me. He mostly tries to kill me now by making me listen to fools with questions.'

'Third,' says Arthur Stuart, 'in case you're keeping count, we're supposed to be meeting up with Mike Fink and Verily Cooper, and making this canoe ain't going to help us get there on time.'

'Those are two boys as need to learn patience,' says Alvin calmly.

'Fourth,' says Arthur Stuart, who was getting more and more peevish with every answer Alvin gave, '*fourth* and final reason, you're a *maker*, dagnabbit, you could just think this tree hollow and float it over to the water light as a feather, so even if you had a reason to make this canoe, which you don't, and a safe place to float it, which you don't, you sure don't have to put me through this work to make it by hand!'

'You working too hard?' asked Alvin.

'Harder than is needed is always too hard,' said Arthur.

'Needed by whom and for what?' asked Alvin. 'You're right that I'm not making this canoe because we need to float down the river, and I'm not making it because it'll hurry up our travel.'

'Then why? Or have you give up altogether on doing things for reasons?'

'I'm not making a canoe at all,' says Alvin.

There knelt Arthur Stuart, up to his elbows in a hollowed-out log, scraping ash. 'This sure ain't a house!'

'Oh, *you're* making a canoe,' said Alvin. 'And we'll float in that canoe down that river over there. But *I'm* not making a canoe.'

Arthur Stuart kept working while he thought this over. After a few minutes he said, 'I know what you're making.'

'Do you?'

'You're making *me* do what you want.'

'Close.'

'You're making me make this tree into something, but you're also using this tree to make me into something.'

'And what would I be trying to make *you* into?'

'Well, I think *you* think you're making me into a maker,' said Arthur Stuart. 'But all you're making me into is a *canoe*-maker, which ain't the same thing as being an all-around all-purpose maker like yourself.'

'Got to start somewhere.'

'*You* didn't,' says Arthur. 'You was born knowing how to make stuff.'

'I was born with a knack,' says Alvin. 'But I wasn't born knowing how to use it, or when, or why. I learned to love making for its own sake. I learned to love the feel of the wood and the stone under my hands, and from that I learned to see inside it, to feel how it felt, to know how it worked, what held it together, and how to help it come apart in just the right way.'

'But I'm not learning any of that,' says Arthur.

'Yet.'

'No sir,' says Arthur Stuart. 'I'm not seeing inside nothing, I'm not feeling inside nothing except how my back aches and my whole body's pouring off sweat and I'm getting more and more annoyed at being made to labour on a job you could do with a wink of your eye.'

'Well, that's something,' says Alvin. 'At least you're learning to see inside yourself.'

Arthur Stuart fumed a little more, chipping away burnt wood as he did. 'Someday I'm going to get fed up with your smugness,' he says to Alvin, 'and I won't follow you any more.'

Alvin shook his head. 'Arthur Stuart, I tried to get you not to follow me this time, if you'll recall.'

'Is *that* what this is about? You're punishing me for following you when you told me not to?'

'You said you wanted to learn everything about being a maker,' says Alvin. 'And when I try to teach you, all I get is pissing and moaning.'

'You also get work from me,' says Arthur. 'I never stopped working the whole time we talked.'

'That's true,' says Alvin.

'And here's something you didn't consider,' says Arthur Stuart. 'All the time we're making a canoe, we're also *un*making a tree.'

Alvin nodded. 'That's how it's done. You never make something out of nothing. You always make it out of something else. When it becomes the new thing, it ceases to be what it was before.'

'So every time you do a making, you do an unmaking, too,' says Arthur Stuart.

'Which is why the Unmaker always knows where I am and what I'm doing,' says Alvin. 'Because along with doing my work, I'm also doing a little bit of his.'

That didn't sound right or true to Arthur Stuart, but he couldn't figure out an argument to answer it, and while he was trying to think one up, they kept on a-burning and a-chipping and lo and behold, they had them a canoe. They dragged it to the stream and put it in and got inside it and it tipped them right over. Spilled them into the water three times, till Alvin finally gave up and used his knack to feel the balance of the thing and then reshape it just enough that it had a good balance to it.

Arthur Stuart had to laugh at him then. 'What lesson am I supposed to learn from *this*? How to make a *bad* canoe?'

'Shut up and row,' said Alvin.

'We're going downstream,' said Arthur Stuart, 'and I don't have to row. Besides which all I've got is this stick, which is no kind of paddle.'

'Then use it to keep us from running into the bank,' said Alvin, 'which we're about to do thanks to your babbling.'

Arthur Stuart fended the canoe away from the bank of the stream, and they kept on floating down until they joined a larger stream, and a larger, and then a river. All the time, Arthur kept coming back to the things Alvin said to him, and what he was trying to teach, and as usual Arthur Stuart despaired of learning it. And yet he couldn't help but think he had learned *something*, even if he had no idea at present what the thing he learned might be.

Because folks build towns on rivers, when you float down a river you're likely as not to come upon a town, which they did one morning with mist still on the river and sleep still in their eyes. It wasn't much of a town, but then it wasn't much of a river, and they weren't in much of a boat. They put in to shore and dragged the canoe on to the bank, and Alvin shouldered his poke with the plough inside and they trudged on into town just as folks was getting up and about their day.

First thing they looked for was a roadhouse, but the town was too small and too new. Only a dozen houses, and the road so little travelled that grass was growing from one front door to the next. But that didn't mean there was no hope of breakfast. If there's light in the sky, somebody's up, getting a start on the day's work. Passing one house with a barn out back, they heard the ping-ping-ping of a cow getting milked into a tin pail. At another house, a woman was coming in with the night's eggs from a chicken coop. That looked promising.

'Got anything for a traveller?' asked Alvin.

The woman looked them up and down. Without a word she walked on into her house.

'If you wasn't so ugly,' said Arthur Stuart, 'she would have asked us in.'

'Whereas looking at you is like seeing an angel,' said Alvin.

They heard the front door of the house opening.

'Maybe she was just hurrying in to cook them eggs for us,' said Arthur Stuart.

But it wasn't the woman who came out. It was a man, looking like he hadn't had much time to fasten his clothing. In fact, his trousers were kind of droopy, and they might have started laying bets on how quick they'd drop to the porch if he hadn't been aiming a pretty capable-looking blunderbuss at them.

'Move along,' the man said.

'We're moving,' said Alvin. He hoisted his poke to his back and started walking across in front of the house. The barrel of the shotgun followed them. Sure enough, just as they were about even with the front door, the trousers dropped. The man looked embarrassed and angry. The barrel of the blunderbuss dipped. The loose birdshot rolled out of the barrel, dozens of tiny lead balls hitting the porch like rain. The man looked confused now.

'Got to be careful loading up a big-barrel gun like that,' Alvin said. 'I always wrap the shot in paper so it don't do that.'

The man glared at him. 'I did.'

'Why, I know you did,' said Alvin.

But there sat the shot on the porch, a silent refutation. Nevertheless, Alvin was telling the simple truth. The paper was still in the barrel, as a matter of fact, but Alvin had persuaded it to break open at the front, freeing the shot.

'Your pants is down,' said Arthur Stuart.

'Move along,' said the man. His face was turning red. His wife was watching from the doorway behind him.

'Well, you know, we was already planning to,' said Alvin, 'but as long as you can't quite kill us, for the moment at least, can I ask you a couple of questions?'

'No,' said the man. He set down the gun and pulled up his trousers.

'First off, I'd like to know the name of this town. I reckon it must be called "Friendly" or "Welcome".'

'It ain't.'

'Well, that's two down,' said Alvin. 'We got to keep guessing, or you think you can just tell us like one fellow to another?'

'How about "Pantsdown Landing"?' murmured Arthur Stuart.

'This here is Westville, Kenituck,' said the man. 'Now move along.'

'My second question is, seeing as how you folks don't have enough to share with a stranger, is there somebody who's prospering a bit more and might have something to spare for travellers as have a bit of silver to pay for it?'

'Nobody here got a meal for the likes of you,' said the man.

'I can see why this road got grass growing on it,' said Alvin. 'But your graveyard must be full of strangers as died of hunger hoping for breakfast here.'

On his knees picking up loose shot, the man didn't answer, but his wife stuck her head out the door and proved she had a voice after all. 'We're as hospitable as anybody else, except to known burglars and thieving prentices.'

Arthur Stuart let out a low whistle. 'What you want to bet Davy Crockett came this way?' he said softly.

'I never stole a thing in my life,' said Alvin.

'What you got in that poke, then?' demanded the woman.

'I wish I could say it was the head of the last man who pointed a gun at me, but unfortunately I left it attached to his neck, so he could come here and tell lies about me.'

'So you're ashamed to show the golden plough you stole?'

'I'm a blacksmith, ma'am,' said Alvin, 'and I got my tools here. You're welcome to look, if you want.'

He turned to address the other folks who were gathering, out on their porches or into the street, a couple of them armed.

'I don't know what you folks heard tell,' said Alvin, setting down his poke, 'but you're welcome to look at my tools.' He drew open the mouth of the poke and let the sides drop so his hammer, tongs, bellows, and nails lay exposed in the street. Not a sign of a plough.

Everyone looked closely, as if taking inventory.

'Well, maybe you ain't the one we heared tell of,' said the woman.

'No, ma'am, I'm the exact one, if it was a certain trapper in a coonskin cap named Davy Crockett who was telling the tale.'

'So you confess to being that Prentice Smith who stole the plough? And a burglar?'

'No, ma'am, I just confess to being a fellow as got himself on the wrong side of a trapper who talks a man harm behind his back.' He gathered up his bag over the tools and drew the mouth closed. 'Now, if you-all want to turn me away, go ahead, but don't go thinking you turned away a thief, because it ain't so. You pointed a gun at me and turned me away without a bite to eat for me or this hungry boy, without so much as a trial or a scrap of evidence, just on the word of a traveller who was as much a stranger here as me.'

The accusation made them all sheepish. One old woman, though, wasn't having any of it. 'We know Davy, I reckon,' she said. 'It's you we never set eyes on.'

'And never will again, I promise you,' said Alvin. 'You can bet I'll tell this tale wherever I travel – Westville, Kenituck, where a stranger can't get a bite to eat, and a man is guilty before he even hears the accusation.'

'If there's no truth to it,' said the old woman, 'how did you know it was Davy Crockett a-telling the tale?'

The others nodded and murmured as if this were a telling point.

''Cause Davy Crockett accused me of it to my face,' said Alvin, 'and he's the only one who ever looked at me and my boy and thought of burglaring. I'll tell you what I told him. If we're burglars, why ain't we in a big city with plenty of fine houses to rob? A burglar could starve to death, trying to find something to steal in a town as poor as this one.'

'We ain't poor,' said the man on the porch.

'You got no food to spare,' said Alvin. 'And there ain't a house here with a door that even locks.'

'See?' cried the old woman. 'He's already checked our doors to see how easy they'll be to break into!'

Alvin shook his head. 'Some folks see sin in sparrows and wickedness in willow trees.' He took Arthur Stuart by the shoulder and turned to head back out of town the way they came.

'Hold, stranger!' cried a man behind them. They turned to see a large man on horseback approaching slowly along the road. The people parted to make way for him.

'Quick, Arthur,' Alvin murmured. 'Who do you reckon this is?'

'The miller,' said Arthur Stuart.

'Good morning to you, Mr Miller!' cried Alvin in greeting.

'How did you know my trade?' asked the miller.

'The boy here guessed,' said Alvin.

The miller rode nearer, and turned his gaze to Arthur Stuart. 'And how did you guess such a thing?'

'You spoke with authority,' said Arthur Stuart, 'and you're riding a horse, and people made way for you. In a town this size, that makes you the miller.'

'And in a bigger town?' asked the miller.

'You'd be a lawyer or a politician,' said Arthur Stuart.

'The boy's a clever one,' said the miller.

'No, he just runs on at the mouth,' said Alvin. 'I used to beat him but I plumb gave out the last time. Only thing I've found that shuts him up is a mouthful of food, preferably pancakes, but we'd settle for eggs, boiled, scrambled, poached, or fried.'

The miller laughed. 'Come along to my house, not three rods beyond the commons and down the road towards the river.'

'You know,' said Alvin, 'my father's a miller.'

The miller cocked his head. 'Then how does it happen you don't follow his trade?'

'I'm well down the list of eight boys,' said Alvin. 'Can't all be millers, so I got put out to a smith. I've got a ready hand with mill equipment, though, in case you'll let me help you to earn our breakfast.'

'Come along and we'll see how much you know,' said the miller. 'As for these folks, never mind them. If some wanderer came through and told them the sun was made of butter, you'd see them all trying to spread it on their bread.' His mirth at this remark was not widely appreciated among the others, but that didn't faze him. 'I've got a shoeing shed, too, so if you ain't above a little ferrier work, I reckon there's horses to be shod.'

Alvin nodded his agreement.

'Well, go on up to the house and wait for me,' said the miller. 'I won't be long. I come to pick up my laundry.' He looked at the woman that Alvin had first spoken to. Immediately she ducked back inside the house to fetch the clothes the miller had come for.

On the road to the mill, once they were out of sight of the villagers, Alvin began to chuckle.

'What's so funny?' asked Arthur Stuart.

'That fellow with his pants around his ankles and birdshot dribbling out of his blunderbuss.'

'I don't like that miller,' said Arthur Stuart.

'Well, he's giving us breakfast, so I reckon he can't be all bad.'

'He's just showing up the town folks,' said Arthur Stuart.

'Well, excuse me, but I don't think that'll change the flavour of the pancakes.'

'I don't like his voice.'

That made Alvin perk up and pay attention. Voices were

part of Arthur Stuart's knack. 'Something wrong with the way he talks?'

'There's a meanness in him,' said Arthur Stuart.

'May well be,' said Alvin. 'But his meanness is better than hunting for nuts and berries again, or taking another squirrel out of the trees.'

'Or another fish.' Arthur made a face.

'Millers get a name for meanness sometimes,' Alvin said. 'People need their grain milled, all right, but they always think the miller takes too much. So millers are used to having folks accuse them. Maybe that's what you heard in his voice.'

'Maybe,' said Arthur Stuart. Then he changed the subject. 'How'd you hide the plough when you opened your poke?'

'I kind of opened up a hole in the ground under the poke,' said Alvin, 'and the plough sank down out of sight.'

'You going to teach me how to do things like *that*?'

'I'll do my best to teach,' said Alvin, 'if you do your best to learn.'

'What about making shot spill out of a gun that's pointed at you?'

'My knack opened the paper, but his own trousers, that's what made the barrel dip and spill out the shot.'

'And you didn't make his trousers fall?'

'If he'd pulled up his suspenders, his pants would've stayed up just fine,' said Alvin.

'It's all unmaking though, isn't it?' said Arthur Stuart. 'Spilling shot, dropping trousers, making them folks feel guilty for not taking you in.'

'So I should've let them drive us away without breakfast?'

'I've skipped breakfasts before.'

'Well, aren't you the prissy one,' said Alvin. 'Why are you suddenly so critical of the way I do things?'

'You're the one made me dig out a canoe with my own hands,' said Arthur Stuart. 'To teach me making. So I keep looking to see how much making *you* do. And all I see is how you unmake things.'

Alvin took that a little hard. Didn't get mad, but he was kind of thoughtful and didn't speak much the rest of the way to the miller's house.

So nearly a week later, there's Alvin working in a mill for the first time since he left his father's place in Vigor Church and set out to be a prentice smith in Hatrack River. At first he was happy, running his hands over the machinery, analysing how the gears all meshed. Arthur Stuart, watching him, could see how each bit of machinery he touched ran a little smoother – a little less friction, a little tighter fit – so more and more of the power from the water flowing over the wheel made it to the rolling millstone. It ground faster and smoother, less inclined to bind and jerk. Rack Miller, for that was his name, also noticed, but since he hadn't been watching Alvin work, he assumed that he'd done something with tools and lubricants. 'A good can of oil and a keen eye do wonders for machinery,' said Rack, and Alvin had to agree.

But after those first few days, Alvin's happiness faded, for he began to see what Arthur Stuart had noticed from the beginning: Rack was one of the reasons why millers had a bad name. It was pretty subtle. Folks would bring in a sack of corn to be ground into meal, and Rack would cast it in handfuls on to the millstone, then brush the corn flour into a tray and back into the same sack they brought it in. That's how all millers did it. No one bothered with weighing before and after, because everyone knew there was always some corn flour lost on the millstone.

What made Rack's practice a little different was the geese he kept. They had free rein in the millhouse, the yard, the millrace, and – some folks said – Rack's own house at night. Rack called them his daughters, though this was a perverse kind of thing to say, seeing as how only a few laying geese and a gander or two ever lasted out the winter. What Arthur Stuart saw at once, and Alvin finally noticed when he got over his love scene with the machinery, was how those geese were fed. It was expected that a few kernels of corn would drop; couldn't be helped. But Rack always took the sack and held it, not by the top, but by the shank of the sack, so kernels of corn dribbled out the whole way to the millstone. The geese were on that corn like – well, like geese on corn. And then he'd take big sloppy handfuls of corn to throw on to the millstone. A powerful lot of kernels hit the side of the stone instead of the top, and of course they dropped and ended up in the straw on the floor, where the geese would have them up in a second.

'Sometimes as much as a quarter of the corn,' Alvin told Arthur Stuart.

'You counted the kernels? Or are you weighing corn in your head now?' asked Arthur.

'I can tell. Never less than a tenth.'

'I reckon he figures he ain't stealing, it's the geese doing it,' said Arthur Stuart.

'Miller's supposed to keep his tithe of the ground corn, not double or triple it or more in gooseflesh.'

'I don't reckon it'll do much good for me to point out to you that this ain't none of our business,' said Arthur Stuart.

'I'm the adult here, not you,' said Alvin.

'You keep saying that, but the things you do, I keep wondering,' said Arthur Stuart. 'I'm not the one gallivanting all over creation while my pregnant wife is resting up to have the baby back in Hatrack River. I'm not the one keeps getting himself throwed in jail or guns pointed at him.'

'You're telling me that when I see a thief I got to keep my mouth shut?'

'You think these folks are going to thank you?'

'They might.'

'Put their miller in jail? Where they going to get their corn ground then?'

'They don't put the *mill* in jail.'

'Oh, you going to stay here, then? You going to run this mill for them, till you taught the whole works to a prentice? How about me? You can bet they'll love paying their miller's tithe to a free half-Black prentice. What are you *thinking*?'

Well, that was always the question, wasn't it? Nobody ever knew, really, what Alvin was thinking. When he talked, he pretty much told the truth, he wasn't much of a one for fooling folks.

But he also knew how to keep his mouth shut so you didn't know what was in his head. Arthur Stuart knew, though. He might've been just a boy, though more like a near-man these days, height coming on him kind of quick, his hands and feet getting big even faster than his legs and arms was getting long, but Arthur Stuart was an expert, he was a bona fide certified scholar on one subject, and that was Alvin, journeyman blacksmith, itinerant all-purpose dowser and doodlebug, and secret maker of golden ploughs and reshaper of the universe. He knew Alvin had him a plan for putting a stop to this thievery without putting anybody in jail.

Alvin picked his time. It was a morning getting on towards harvest time, when folks was clearing out a lot of last year's corn to make room for the new. So a lot of folks, from town and the nearby farms, was queued up to have their grain ground. And Rack Miller, he was downright exuberant in sharing that corn with the geese. But as he was handing the sack of corn flour to the customer, less about a quarter of its weight in goosefodder, Alvin scoops up a fine fat gosling and hands it to the customer right along with the grain.

The customer and Rack just looks at him like he's crazy, but Alvin pretends not to notice Rack's consternation at all. It's the customer he talks to. 'Why, Rack Miller told me it was bothering him how much corn these geese've been getting, so this year he was giving out his goslings, one to each regular customer, as long as they last, to make up for it. I think that shows Rack to be a man of real honour, don't you?'

Well, it showed *something*, but what could Rack say after that? He just grinned through clenched teeth and watched as Alvin gave away gosling after gosling, making the same explanation, so everybody, wide-eyed and happy as clams, gave profuse thanks to the provider of their Christmas feast about four months off. Them geese would be monsters by then, they were already so big and fat.

Of course, Arthur Stuart noticed how, as soon as Rack saw how things was going, suddenly he started holding the sacks by the top, and taking smaller handfuls, so most of the time not a kernel fell to the ground. Why, that fellow had just learned himself a marvellous species of efficiency, returning corn to the customer diminished by nought but the true miller's tithe. It was plain enough that Rack Miller wasn't about to feed no corn to geese that somebody else was going to be feasting on that winter!

And when the day's work ended, with every last gosling gone, and only two ganders and five layers left, Rack faced Alvin square on and said, 'I won't have no liar working for me.'

'Liar?' asked Alvin.

'Telling them fools I meant to give them goslings!'

'Well, when I first said it, it wasn't true *yet*, but the minute you didn't raise your voice to argue with me, it became true, didn't it?' Alvin grinned, looking for all the world like Davy Crockett grinning him a bear.

'Don't chop no logic with me,' said Rack. 'You know what you was doing.'

'I sure do,' said Alvin. 'I was making your customers happy with you for the first time since you come here, and making an honest man out of you in the meantime.'

'I already *was* an honest man,' said Rack. 'I never took but what I was entitled to, living in a godforsaken place like this.'

'Begging your pardon, my friend, but God ain't forsaken this place, though now and then a soul around here might have forsaken *Him*.'

'I'm done with your help,' said Rack icily. 'I think it's time for you to move on.'

'But I haven't even looked at the machinery you use for weighing the corn wagons,' said Alvin. Rack hadn't been in a hurry for Alvin to check them over – the heavy scales out front was only used at harvest time, when farmers brought in whatever corn they meant to sell. They'd roll the wagons on to the scales, and through a series of levers the scale would be balanced with much lighter weights. Then the wagon would be rolled back on empty and weighed, and the difference between the two weights was the weight of the corn. Later on the buyers would come, roll on their empty wagons and weigh them, then load them up and weigh them again. It was a clever bit of machinery, a scale like that, and it was only natural that Alvin wanted to get his hands on it.

But Rack wasn't having none of it. 'My scales is my business, stranger,' he says to Alvin.

'I've et at your table and slept in your house,' says Alvin. 'How am I a stranger?'

'Man who gives away my geese, he's a stranger here for ever.'

'Well, then, I'll be gone from here.' Still smiling, Alvin turned to his young ward. 'Let's be on our way, Arthur Stuart.'

'No sir,' says Rack Miller. 'You owe me for thirty-six meals these last six days. I didn't notice this Black boy eating one whit less than you. So you owe me in service.'

'I gave you due service,' says Alvin. 'You said yourself that your machinery was working smooth.'

'You didn't do nought but what I could have done myself with an oilcan.'

'But the fact is I did it, and you didn't, and that was worth our keep. The boy's worked, too, sweeping and fixing and cleaning and hefting.'

'I want six days' labour out of your boy. Harvest is upon us, and I need an extra pair of hands and a sturdy back. I've seen he's a good worker and he'll do.'

'Then take three days' service from me *and* the boy. I won't give away any more geese.'

'I don't have any more geese to give, except the layers. Anyway I don't want no miller's son, I just want the boy's labour.'

'Then we'll pay you in silver money.'

'What good is silver money here? Ain't nothing to spend it on. Nearest city of any size is Carthage, across the Hio, and hardly anybody goes there.'

'I don't use Arthur Stuart to discharge my debts. He's not my –'

Well, long before those words got to Alvin's lips, Arthur Stuart knew what he was about to do – he was going to declare that Arthur wasn't his slave. And that would be about as foolish a thing as Alvin could do. So Arthur Stuart spoke right up before the words could get away. 'I'm happy to work off the debt,' he says. 'Except I don't think it's possible. In six days I'll eat eighteen more meals and then I'll owe another three days, and in those three days I'll eat nine meals and I'll owe a day and a half, and at that rate I reckon I'll never pay off that debt.'

'Ah yes,' says Alvin. 'Zeno's paradox.'

'And you told me there was never any practical use for that "bit of philosophical balderdash", as I recall you saying,' says Arthur Stuart. It was an argument from the days they both studied with Miss Larner, before she became Mrs Alvin Smith.

'What the Sam Hill you boys talking about?' asked Rack Miller.

Alvin tried to explain. 'Each day that Arthur Stuart works for you, he'll build up half again the debt that he pays off by his labour. So he only covers half the distance towards freedom. Half and half and half again, only he never quite gets to the goal.'

'I don't get it,' says Rack. 'What's the joke?'

By this point, though, Arthur Stuart had another idea in mind. Mad as Rack Miller was about the goslings, if he truly needed help at harvest time he'd keep Alvin on for it, unless there was some other reason for getting rid of him. There was something Rack Miller planned to do that he didn't want Alvin to see. What he didn't reckon on was that this half-Black 'servant' boy was every bit smart enough to figure it out himself. 'I'd like to stay and see how we solve the paradox,' says Arthur Stuart.

Alvin looks at him real close. 'Arthur, I got to go see a man about a bear.'

Well, that tore Arthur Stuart's resolve a bit. If Alvin was looking for Davy Crockett, to settle things, there might be scenes that Arthur wanted to see. At the same time, there was a mystery here at the millhouse, too, and with Alvin gone Arthur Stuart had a good chance at solving it all by himself. The one temptation was greater than the other. 'Good luck,' said Arthur Stuart. 'I'll miss you.'

Alvin sighed. 'I don't plan to leave you here at the tender mercy of a man with a peculiar fondness for geese.'

'What does *that* mean?' Rack said, growing more and more certain that they were making fun of him underneath all their talk.

'Why, you call them your daughters and then cook them and eat them,' says Alvin. 'What woman would ever marry you? She wouldn't dare leave you alone with the children!'

'Get out of my millhouse!' Rack bellowed.

'Come on, Arthur Stuart,' said Alvin.

'I *want* to stay,' Arthur Stuart insisted. 'It can't be no worse than the time you left me with that schoolmaster.' (Which is another story, not to be told right here.)

Alvin looked at Arthur Stuart real steady. He was no Torch, like his wife. He couldn't look into Arthur's heartfire and see a blame thing. But somehow he saw something that let him make up his mind the way Arthur Stuart wanted him to. 'I'll go for now. I'll be back, though, in six days, and I'll have an accounting with you. You don't raise a hand or a stick against this boy, and you feed him and treat him proper.'

'What do you think I am?' asked Rack.

'A man who gets what he wants,' said Alvin.

'I'm glad you recognize that about me,' said Rack.

'Everybody knows that about you,' said Alvin. 'It's just that you aren't too good at picking what you ought to be wanting.' With another grin, Alvin tipped his hat and left Arthur Stuart.

Well, Rack was as good as his word. He worked Arthur Stuart hard, getting ready for the harvest. A late summer rain delayed the corn in the field, but they put the time to good account, and Arthur was given plenty to eat and a good night's rest, though it was the millhouse loft he slept in now, and not the house; he had only been allowed inside as Alvin's personal servant, and with Alvin gone, there was no excuse for a half-Black boy sleeping in the house.

What Arthur noticed was that all the customers were in good cheer when they came to the millhouse for whatever business they had, especially during the rain when there wasn't no field work to be done. The story of the goslings had spread far and wide, and folks pretty much believed that it really had been Rack's idea, and not Alvin's doing at all. So instead of being polite but distant, the way folks usually was with a miller, they gave him hail-fellow-well-met and he heard the kind of jokes and gossip that folks shared with their friends. It was a new experience for Rack, and Arthur Stuart could see that this change was one Rack Miller didn't mind.

Then, the last day before Alvin was due to return, the harvest started up, and farmers from miles around began to bring in their corn wagons. They'd line up in the morning, and the first would pull his wagon on to the scale. The farmer would unhitch the horses and Rack would weigh the whole wagon. Then they'd hitch up the horses, pull the wagon to the dock, the waiting farmers would help unload the corn sacks – of course they helped, it meant they'd be home all the sooner themselves – and then back the wagon on to the scale and weigh it again, empty. Rack would figure the difference between the two weighings, and that difference was how many pounds of corn the farmer got credit for.

Arthur Stuart went over the figures in his head, and Rack wasn't cheating them with his arithmetic. He looked carefully to see if Rack was doing something like standing on the scale when the empty wagon was being weighed, but no such thing.

Then, in the dark of that night, he remembered something one of the farmers grumbled as they were backing an empty wagon on to the scale. 'Why didn't he build this scale right at the loading dock, so we could unload the wagon and reweigh it without having to move the durn thing?' Arthur Stuart didn't know the mechanism of it, but he thought back over the day and remembered that another time a farmer had asked if he could get his full wagon weighed while the previous farmer's wagon was being unloaded. Rack glared at the man. 'You want to do things your way, go build your own mill.'

Yes sir, the only thing Rack cared about was that every wagon get two weighings, right in a row. And the same system would work just as well in reverse when the buyers came with their empty wagons to haul corn east for the big cities. Weigh the empty, load it, and weigh it again. When Alvin got back, Arthur Stuart would be ready with the mystery mostly solved.

Meanwhile, Alvin was off in the woods, looking for Davy

Crockett, that grinning man who was singlehandedly responsible for getting two separate guns pointed at Alvin's heart. But it wasn't vengeance that was on Alvin's mind. It was rescue.

For he knew what he'd done to Davy and the bear, and kept track of their heartfires. He couldn't see into heartfires the way Margaret could, but he could see the heartfires themselves, and keep track of who was who. In fact, knowing that no gun could shoot him and no jail could hold him, Alvin had deliberately come to the town of Westville because he knew Davy Crockett had come through that town, the bear not far behind him, though Davy wouldn't know that, not at the time.

He knew it now, though. What Alvin saw back in Rack's millhouse was that Davy and the bear had met again, and this time it might come out a little different. For Alvin had found the place deep in the particles of the body where knacks were given, and he had taken the bear's best knack and given as much to Davy, and Davy's best knack and given the same to the bear. They were evenly matched now, and Alvin figured he had some responsibility to see to it that nobody got hurt. After all, it was partly Alvin's fault that Davy didn't have a gun to defend himself. Mostly it was Davy's fault for pointing it at him, but Alvin hadn't had to wreck the gun the way he did, making the barrel blow apart.

Running lightly through the woods, leaping a stream or two, and stopping to eat from a fine patch of wild strawberries on a riverbank, Alvin got to the place well before nightfall, so he had plenty of time to reconnoitre. There they were in the clearing, just as Alvin expected, Davy and the bear, not five feet apart, both of them a-grinning, staring each other down, neither one budging. That bear was all spiky, but he couldn't get past Davy's grin; and Davy matched the bear's single-minded tenacity, oblivious to pain, so even though his butt was already sore and he was about out of his mind with sleepiness, he didn't break his grin.

Just as the sun set, Alvin stepped out into the clearing behind the bear. 'Met your match, Davy?' he asked.

Davy didn't have an ounce of attention to spare for chat. He just kept grinning.

'I think this bear don't mean to be your winter coat this year,' said Alvin.

Davy just grinned.

'In fact,' said Alvin, 'I reckon the first one of you to fall asleep, that's who the loser is. And bears store up so much sleep in the winter, they just flat out don't need as much come summertime.'

Grin.

'So there you are barely keeping your eyelids up, and there's the bear just happy as can be, grinning at you out of sincere love and devotion.'

Grin. With maybe a little more desperation around the eyes.

'But here's the thing, Davy,' said Alvin. 'Bears is better than people, mostly. You got your bad bears, sometimes, and your good people, but on average, I'd trust a bear to do what he thinks is right before I'd trust a human. So now what you got to wonder is, what does that bear think will be the right thing to do with you, once he's grinned you down?'

Grin grin grin.

'Bears don't need no coats of human skin. They do need to pile on the fat for winter, but they don't generally eat meat for that. Lots of fish, but you ain't a swimmer and the bear knows that. Besides, that bear don't think of you as meat, or he wouldn't be grinning you. He thinks of you as a rival. He thinks of you as his equal. What *will* he do? Don't you kind of wonder? Don't you have some speck of curiosity that just wants to know the answer to that question?'

The light was dimming now, so it was hard to see much more of either Davy or the bear than their white, white teeth. And their eyes.

'You've already stayed up one whole night,' said Alvin. 'Can you do it again? I don't think so. I think pretty soon you're going to understand the mercy of bears.'

Only now, in his last desperate moments before succumbing to sleep, did Davy dare to speak. 'Help me,' he said.

'And how would I do that?' asked Alvin.

'Kill that bear.'

Alvin walked up quietly behind the bear and gently rested his hand on the bear's shoulder. 'Why would I do that? This bear never pointed no gun at me.'

'I'm a dead man,' Davy whispered. The grin faded from his face. He bowed his head, then toppled forward, curled up on the ground, and waited to be killed.

But it didn't happen. The bear came up, nosed him, snuffled him all over, rolled him back and forth a little, all the time ignoring the little whimpering sounds Davy was making. Then the bear lay down beside the man, flung one arm over him, and dozed right off to sleep.

Unbelieving, Davy lay there, terrified yet hopeful again. If he could just stay awake a little longer.

Either the bear was a light sleeper in the summertime, or Davy made his move too soon, but no sooner did his hand slide towards the knife at his waist than the bear was wide awake, slapping more or less playfully at Davy's hand.

'Time for sleep,' said Alvin. 'You've earned it, the bear's earned it, and come morning you'll find things look a lot better.'

'What's going to happen to me?' asked Davy.

'Don't you think that's kind of up to the bear?'

'You're controlling him somehow,' said Davy. 'This is all your doing.'

'He's controlling himself,' said Alvin, careful not to deny the second charge, seeing how it was true. 'And he's controlling you. Because that's what grinning is all about – deciding who is master. Well, that bear is master here, and I reckon tomorrow we'll find out what bears do with domesticated humans.'

Davy started to murmur a prayer.

The bear laid a heavy paw on Davy's mouth.

'Prayers are done,' intoned Alvin. 'Gone the sun. Shadows creep. Go to sleep.'

That's how it came about that when Alvin returned to Westville, he did it with two friends along – Davy Crockett and a big old grizzly bear. Oh, folks was alarmed when that bear come into town, and ran for their guns, but the bear just grinned at them and they didn't shoot. And when the bear gave Davy a little poke, why, he'd step forward and say a few words. 'My friend here doesn't have much command of the American language,' said Davy, 'but he'd just as soon you put that gun away and didn't go pointing it at him. Also, he'd be glad of a bowl of corn mush or a plate of corn bread, if you've got any to spare.'

Why, that bear plumb ate his way through Westville, setting down to banquets without raising a paw except to poke at Davy Crockett, and folks didn't even mind it, it was such a sight to see a man serve gruel and corn bread to a bear. And that wasn't all, either. Davy Crockett spent a good little while picking burrs out of the bear's fur, especially in the rumpal area, and singing to the bear whenever it crooned in a high-pitched tone. Davy sang pert near every song that he ever heard, even if he only heard it once, or didn't hear the whole thing, for there's nothing to bring back the memory of tunes and lyrics like having an eleven-foot bear poking you and whining to get you to sing, and when he flat out couldn't remember, why, he made it something up, and since the bear wasn't altogether particular, the song was almost always good enough.

As for Alvin, he'd every now and then pipe up and ask Davy to mention whether it was true that Alvin was a burglar and a plough-stealing prentice, and each time Davy said no, it wasn't true, that was just a made-up lie because Davy was mad at Alvin and wanted to get even. And whenever Davy told the truth like that, the bear rumbled its approval and stroked Davy's back with his big old paw, which Davy was just barely brave enough to endure without wetting himself much.

Only when they'd gone all through the town and some of the outlying houses did this parade come to the millhouse, where the horses naturally complained a little at the presence of a bear. But Alvin spoke to each of them and put them at ease, while the bear curled up and took him a nap, his belly being full of corn in various forms. Davy didn't go far, though, for the bear kept sniffing, even in his sleep, to make sure Davy was close by.

Davy was putting the best face on things, though. He had his pride.

'A man does things for a friend, and this here bear's my friend,' said Davy. 'I'm done with trapping, as you can guess, so I'm looking for a line of work that can help my friend get ready for the winter. What I mean is, I got to earn some corn, and I hope some of you have jobs for me to do. The bear just watches, I promise, he's no danger to your livestock.'

Well, they heard him out, of course, because one tends to listen for a while at least to a man who's somehow got himself hooked up as a servant to a grizzly bear. But there wasn't a chance in hell that they were going to let no bear anywhere near their pigsties, nor their chicken coops, especially not when the bear clearly showed no disposition to earn its food honestly. If it would beg, they figured, it would steal, and they'd have none of it.

Meanwhile, as the bear napped and Davy talked to the farmers, Alvin and Arthur had their reunion, with Arthur Stuart telling him what he'd figured out. 'Some mechanism in the scale makes it weigh light when the wagon's full, and heavy when it's empty, so the farmers get short weight. But then, without changing a thing, it'll weigh light on the buyers' empty wagons, and heavy when they're full, so Rack gets extra weight when he's selling the same corn.'

Alvin nodded. 'You find out if this theory is actually true?'

'The only time he ain't watching me is in the dark, and in the dark I can't sneak down and see a thing. I'm not crazy enough to risk getting myself caught sneaking around the machinery in the dark, anyway.'

'Glad to know you got a brain.'

'Says the man who keeps getting himself put in jail.'

Alvin made a face at him, but in the meantime he was sending out his doodlebug to probe the machinery of the scale underground. Sure enough, there was a ratchet that engaged on one weighing, causing the levering to shift a little, making short weight; and on the next weighing, the ratchet would disengage and the levers would move back, giving long weight.

No wonder Rack didn't want Alvin looking over the machinery of the scale.

The solution, as Alvin saw it, was simple enough. He told Arthur Stuart to stand near the scale but not to step on it. Rack wrote down the weight of the empty wagon, and while it was being pulled off the scale, he stood there calculating the difference. The moment the wagon was clear of the scale, Alvin rounded on Arthur Stuart, speaking loud enough for all to hear.

'Fool boy! What were you doing! Didn't you see you was standing on that scale?'

'I wasn't!' Arthur Stuart cried.

'I don't think he was,' said a farmer. 'I worried about that, he was so close, so I looked.'

'And I say I saw him stand on it,' said Alvin. 'This farmer shouldn't be out the cost of a boy's weight in corn, I think!'

'I'm sure the boy didn't stand on the scale,' Rack said, looking up from his calculation.

'Well, there's a simple enough test,' said Alvin. 'Let's get that empty wagon back on to the scale.'

Now Rack grew alarmed. 'Tell you what,' he said to the farmer, 'I'll just *give* you credit for the boy's weight.'

'Is this scale sensitive enough to weigh the boy?' asked Alvin.

'Well, I don't know,' said Rack. 'Let's just estimate.'

'No!' cried Alvin. 'This farmer doesn't want any more than his fair credit, and it's not right for him to receive any less. Haul the wagon back on and let's weigh it again.'

Rack was about to protest again, when Alvin said, 'Unless there's something wrong with the scale. There wouldn't be something wrong with the scale, now, would there?'

Rack got a sick look on his face. He couldn't very well confess. 'Nothing wrong with the scale,' he said gruffly.

'Then let's weigh this wagon and see if my boy's weight made any difference.'

Well, you guessed it. As soon as the wagon was back on the scale, it showed near a hundred pounds lighter than it did the first time. The other witnesses were flummoxed. 'Could have sworn the boy never stepped on that scale,' said one. And another said, 'I don't know as I would have guessed that boy to weigh a hundred pounds.'

'Heavy bones,' says Alvin.

'No sir, it's my brain that weighs heavy,' said Arthur Stuart, winning a round of laughter.

And Rack, trying to put a good face on it, pipes up, 'No, it's the food he's been eating at my table – that's fifteen pounds of it right there!'

In the meantime, though, the farmer's credit was being adjusted by a hundred pounds.

And the next wagon to come on the scale was a full one, while the scale was set to read heavy. In vain did Rack try to beg off early – Alvin simply offered to keep on weighing for him, with the farmers as witnesses so he wrote down everything square. 'You don't want any of these men to have to wait an extra day to sell you their market grain, do you?' Alvin said. 'Let's weigh it all!'

And weigh it all they did, thirty wagons before the day was done, and the farmers was all remarking to each other about what a good corn year it was, the kernels heavier than usual. Arthur Stuart did hear one man start to grumble that his wagon seemed to be lighter this year than in any previous year, but Arthur immediately spoke up loud enough for all to hear. 'It don't matter if the scale is weighing light or heavy – it's the difference between the full weight and the empty weight that matters, and as long as it's the same scale, it's going to be correct.' The farmers thought that over and it sounded right to them, while Rack couldn't very well explain.

Arthur Stuart figured it all out in his head and he realized that Alvin hadn't exactly set things to rights. On the contrary, this year Rack was getting cheated royally, recording credits for these farmers that were considerably more than the amount of corn they actually brought in. He could bear such losses for one day; and by tomorrow, Alvin and Arthur both knew, Rack meant to have the scale back in its regular pattern – light for the full wagons, heavy for the empty ones.

Still, Alvin and Arthur cheerfully bade Rack farewell, not even commenting on the eagerness he showed to be rid of them.

That night, Rack Miller's lantern bobbed across the yard between his house and the mill. He closed the mill door behind him and headed for the trapdoor leading down to the scale mechanism. But to his surprise, there was something lying on top of that trapdoor. A bear. And nestled in to sleep with the bear wrapped around him was Davy Crockett.

'I hope you don't mind,' said Davy, 'but this here bear took it into his head to sleep right here, and I'm not inclined to argue with him.'

'Well, he can't, so that's that,' said the miller.

'You tell him,' said Davy. 'He just don't pay no heed to my advice.'

The miller argued and shouted, but the bear paid no mind. Rack got him a long stick and poked at the bear, but the bear just opened one eye, slapped the stick out of Rack's hand, then took it in his mouth and crunched it up like a cracker. Rack Miller proposed to bring a gun out, but Davy drew his knife then. 'You'll have to kill me along with the bear,' he said, ''cause if you harm him, I'll carve you up like a Christmas goose.'

'I'll be glad to oblige you,' said Rack.

'But then you'll have to explain how I came to be dead. If you manage to kill the bear with one shot, that is. Sometimes these bears can take a half dozen balls into their bodies and still swipe a man's head clean off and then go fishing for the afternoon. Lots of fat, lots of muscle. And how's your aim, anyway?'

So it was that next morning, the scale still weighed opposite to Rack's intent, and so it went day after day until the harvest was over. Every day the bear and his servant ate their corn mush and corn bread and drank their corn likker and lay around in the shade, with onlookers gathering and lingering to see the marvel. The result was that witnesses were around all day and not far off at night. And it went on just the same when the buyers started showing up to haul away the corn.

Stories about the bear who had tamed a man brought more

than just onlookers, too. More farmers than usual came to Rack Miller to sell their corn, so they could see the sight; and more buyers went out of their way to come to buy, so there was maybe half again as much business as usual. At the end of the whole harvest season, there was Rack Miller with a ledger book showing a huge loss. He wouldn't be paid enough by the buyers to come close to making good on what he owed the farmers. He was ruined.

He went through a few jugs of corn likker and took some long walks, but by late October he'd given up all hope. One time his despair led him to point a pistol at his head and fire, but the powder for some reason wouldn't ignite, and when Rack tried to hang himself he couldn't tie a knot that didn't slip. Since he couldn't even succeed at killing himself, he finally gave up even that project and took off in the dead of night, abandoning mill and ledger and all. Well, he didn't mean to abandon it – he meant to burn it. But the fires he started kept blowing out, so that was yet another project he failed at. In the end, he left with the clothes on his back and two geese tucked under his arms, and they honked so much he turned them loose before he was out of town.

When it was clear Rack wasn't just off on a holiday, the town's citizens and some of the more prominent farmers from round about met in Rack Miller's abandoned house and went over his ledger. What they learned there told them clear enough that Rack Miller was unlikely to return. They divided up the losses evenly among the farmers, and it turned out that nobody lost a thing. Oh, the farmers got paid less than Rack Miller's ledger showed, but they'd get a good deal more than they had in previous years, so it was still a good year for them. And when they got to inspecting the property, they found the ratchet mechanism in the scale and the picture was crystal-clear.

All in all, they decided, they were well rid of Rack Miller, and a few folks had suspicions that it was that Alvin Smith and his half-Black boy who'd turned the tables on this cheating miller. They even tried to find out where he might be, to offer him the mill in gratitude. Someone had heard tell he came from Vigor Church up in Wobbish, and a letter there did bring results – a letter in reply, from Alvin's father. 'My boy thought you might make such an offer, and he asked me to give you a better suggestion. He says that since a man done such a bad job as miller, maybe you'd be better off with a bear, especially if the bear has him a manservant who can keep the books.'

At first they laughed off the suggestion, but after a while they began to like it, and when they proposed it to Davy and the bear, they cottoned to it, too. The bear got him all the corn he wanted without ever lifting a finger, except to perform a little for folks at harvest time, and in the winter he could sleep in a warm dry place. The years he mated, the place was a little crowded with bearflesh, but the cubs were no trouble and the mama bears, though a little suspicious, were mostly tolerant, especially because Davy was still a match for any of *them*, and could grin them into docility when the need arose.

As for Davy, he kept true books, and fixed the scale so it didn't ratchet anymore, giving honest weight every time. As time went on, he was so well-liked that folks talked about running him for mayor of Westville. He refused, of course, since he wasn't his own man. But he allowed as how, if they elected the bear, he'd be glad to serve as the bear's secretary and interpreter, and that's what they did. After a year or two of having a bear as mayor, they up and changed the name to Bearsville, and the town prospered. Years later, when Kenituck joined the United States of America, it's not hard to guess who got elected to Congress from that part of the state, which is how it happened that for seven terms of Congress a bear put its hand on the Bible right along with the other Congressmen, and then proceeded to sleep through every session it attended, while its clerk, one Davy Crockett, cast all its votes for it and gave all its speeches, every one of which ended with the sentence, 'Or at least that's how it looks to one old grizzly bear.'

Majipoor

ROBERT SILVERBERG

Majipoor

ROBERT SILVERBERG

Lord Valentine's Castle (1980)
Majipoor Chronicles (1981)
Valentine Pontifex (1983)
The Mountains of Majipoor (1995)
Sorcerers of Majipoor (1997)
Lord Prestimion (1999)

The giant world of Majipoor, with a diameter at least ten times as great as that of our own planet, was settled in the distant past by colonists from Earth, who made a place for themselves amidst the Piurivars, the intelligent native beings, whom the intruders from Earth called Shapeshifters or Metamorphs because of their ability to alter their bodily forms. Majipoor is an extraordinarily beautiful planet, with a largely benign climate, and is a place of astonishing zoological, botanical, and geographical wonders. Everything on Majipoor is large-scale – fantastic, marvellous.

Over the course of thousands of years friction between the human colonists and the Piurivars eventually led to a lengthy war and the defeat of the natives, who were penned up in huge reservations in remote regions of the planet. During those years, also, species from various other worlds came to settle on Majipoor – the tiny gnomish Vroons, the great shaggy four-armed Skandars, the two-headed Su-Suheris race, and several more. Some of these – notably the Vroons and the Su-Suheris – were gifted with extrasensory mental powers that permitted them to practise various forms of wizardry. But throughout the thousands of years of Majipoor history the humans remained the dominant species. They flourished and expanded and eventually the human population of Majipoor came to number in the billions, mainly occupying huge and distinctive cities of ten to twenty million people.

The governmental system that evolved over those years was a kind of non-hereditary dual monarchy. The senior ruler, known as the Pontifex, selects his own junior ruler, the Coronal, when he comes to power. Technically the Coronal is regarded as the adoptive son of the Pontifex, and upon the death of the Pontifex takes his place on the senior throne, naming a new Coronal as his own successor. Both of these rulers make their homes on Alhanroel, the largest and most populous of Majipoor's three continents. The imperial residence of the Pontifex is in the lowest level of a vast subterranean city called the Labyrinth, from which he emerges only at rare intervals. The Coronal, by contrast, lives in an enormous castle at the summit of Castle Mount, a thirty-mile-high peak whose atmosphere is maintained in an eternal springtime by elaborate machinery. From time to time the Coronal descends from the opulence of the Castle to travel across the face of the world in a Grand Processional, an event designed to remind Majipoor of the might and power of its rulers. Such a journey, which in Majipoor's vast distances could take several years, invariably brings the Coronal to Zimroel, the second continent, a place of gigantic cities interspersed among tremendous rivers and great unspoiled forests. More rarely he goes to the torrid third continent in the south, Suvrael, largely a wasteland of Sahara-like deserts.

Two other functionaries became part of the Majipoor governmental system later on. The development of a method of world-wide telepathic communication made possible nightly sendings of oracular advice and occasional therapeutic counsel, which became the responsibility of the mother of the incumbent Coronal, under the title of Lady of the Isle of Sleep. Her headquarters are situated on an island of continental size midway between Alhanroel and Zimroel. Later, a second telepathic authority, the King of Dreams, was set in place. He employs more powerful telepathic equipment in order to monitor and chastise criminals and other citizens whose behaviour deviates from accepted

Majipoor norms. This office is the hereditary property of the Barjazid family of Suvrael.

The first of the Majipoor novels, *Lord Valentine's Castle*, tells of a conspiracy that succeeds in overthrowing the legitimate Coronal, Lord Valentine, and replacing him with an impostor. Valentine, stripped of all his memories, is set loose in Zimroel to live the life of a wandering juggler, but gradually regains an awareness of his true role and launches a successful campaign to reclaim his throne. In the sequel, *Valentine Pontifex*, the now mature Valentine, a pacifist at heart, must deal with an uprising among the Metamorphs, who are determined to drive the hated human conquerors from their world at last. Valentine defeats them and restores peace with the help of the giant maritime beasts known as sea-dragons, whose intelligent powers were not previously suspected on Majipoor.

The story collection *Majipoor Chronicles* depicts scenes from many eras and social levels of Majipoor life, providing detailed insight into a number of aspects of the giant world not described in the novels. The short novel *The Mountains of Majipoor*, set five hundred years after Valentine's reign, carries the saga into the icy northlands, where a separate barbaric civilization has long endured. And the most recent of the Majipoor books, *Sorcerers of Majipoor*, begins a new trilogy set a thousand years prior to Valentine's time, in which the powers of sorcery and magic have become rife on Majipoor. The Coronal Lord Prestimion, after being displaced from his throne by the usurping son of the former Coronal with the assistance of mages and warlocks, leads his faction to victory in a civil war in which he too makes use of necromantic powers. The sequel, *Lord Prestimion*, shows him struggling to deal with the day-by-day problems of kingship in a world that has been immensely altered by the wizardry employed at the climax of the war.

The story presented here offers an episode from a period late in Valentine's reign as Pontifex, when the war against the Metamorphs has been over for some years but the process of reconciliation is still incomplete.

◆

THE SEVENTH SHRINE

BY ROBERT SILVERBERG

One last steep ridge of the rough, boulder-strewn road lay between the royal party and the descent into Velalisier Plain. Valentine, who was leading the way, rode up over it and came to a halt, looking down with amazement into the valley. The land that lay before him seemed to have undergone a bewildering transformation since his last visit. 'Look there,' the Pontifex said, bemused. 'This place is always full of surprises, and here is ours.'

The broad shallow bowl of the arid plain spread out below them. From this vantage point, a little way east of the entrance to the archaeological site, they should easily have been able to see a huge field of sand-swept ruins. There had been a mighty city here once, that notorious Shapeshifter city where, in ancient times, so much dark history had been enacted, such monstrous sacrilege and blasphemy. But – surely it was just an illusion? – the sprawling zone of fallen buildings at the centre of the plain was almost completely hidden now by a wondrous rippling body of water, pale pink along its rim and pearly grey at its middle: a great lake where no lake ever had been.

Evidently the other members of the royal party saw it too. But did they understand that it was simply a trick? Some fleeting combination of sunlight and dusty haze and the stifling midday heat must have created a momentary mirage above dead Velalisier, so that it seemed as if a sizable lagoon, of all improbable things, had sprung up in the midst of this harsh desert to engulf the dead city.

It began just a short distance beyond their vantage point and extended as far as the distant grey-blue wall of great stone monoliths that marked the city's western boundary. Nothing of Velalisier could be seen. None of the shattered and time-worn temples and palaces and basilicas, nor the red basalt blocks of the arena, the great expanses of blue stone that had been the sacrificial platforms, the tents of the archaeologists who had been at work here at Valentine's behest since late last year. Only the six steep and narrow pyramids that were the tallest surviving structures of the prehistoric Metamorph capital were visible – their tips, at least, jutting out of the grey heart of the ostensible lake like a line of daggers fixed point-upward in its depths.

'Magic,' murmured Tunigorn, the oldest of Valentine's boyhood friends, who held the post now of Minister of External Affairs at the Pontifical court. He drew a holy symbol in the air. Tunigorn had grown very superstitious, here in his later years.

'I think not,' said Valentine, smiling. 'Just an oddity of the light, I'd say.'

And, just as though the Pontifex had conjured it up with some counter-magic of his own, a lusty gust of wind came up from the north and swiftly peeled the haze away. The lake went with it, vanishing like the phantom it had been. Valentine and his companions found themselves now beneath a bare and merciless iron-blue sky, gazing down at the true Velalisier – that immense dreary field of stony rubble, that barren and incoherent tumble of dun-coloured fragments and drab threadbare shards lying in gritty beds of wind-strewn sand, which was all that remained of the abandoned Metamorph metropolis of long ago.

'Well, now,' said Tunigorn, 'perhaps you were right, majesty. Magic or no, though, I liked it better the other way. It was a pretty lake, and these are ugly stones.'

'There's nothing here to like at all, one way or another,' said Duke Nascimonte of Ebersinul. He had come all the way from his great estate on the far side of the Labyrinth to take part in this expedition. 'This is a sorry place and always has been. If I were Pontifex in your stead, your majesty, I'd throw a dam across the River Glayge and send a raging torrent this way, that would bury this accursed city and its whole history of abominations under two miles of water for all time to come.'

Some part of Valentine could almost see the merit of that. It was easy enough to believe that the sombre spells of antiquity still hovered here, that this was a territory where ominous enchantments held sway.

But of course Valentine could hardly take Nascimonte's suggestion seriously. 'Drown the Metamorphs' sacred city, yes! By all means, let's do that,' he said lightly. 'Very fine diplomacy, Nascimonte. What a splendid way of furthering harmony between the races that would be!'

Nascimonte, a lean and hard-bitten man of eighty years, with keen sapphire eyes that blazed like fiery gems in his broad furrowed forehead, said pleasantly, 'Your words tell us what we already know, majesty: that it's just as well for the world that you are Pontifex, not I. I lack your benign and merciful nature – especially, I must say, when it comes to the filthy Shapeshifters. I know you love them and would bring them up out of their degradation. But to me, Valentine, they are vermin and nothing but vermin. Dangerous vermin at that.'

'Hush,' said Valentine. He was still smiling, but he let a little annoyance show as well. 'The Rebellion's long over. It's high time we put these old hatreds to rest for ever.'

Nascimonte's only response was a shrug.

Valentine turned away, looking again towards the ruins. Greater mysteries than that mirage awaited them down there. An event as grim and terrible as anything out of Velalisier's doleful past had lately occurred in this city of long-dead stones: a murder, no less.

Violent death at another's hands was no common thing on Majipoor. It was to investigate that murder that Valentine and his friends had journeyed to ancient Valalisier this day.

'Come,' he said. 'Let's be on our way.'

He spurred his mount forward, and the others followed him down the stony road into the haunted city.

The ruins appeared much less dismal at close range than they had on either of Valentine's previous two visits. This winter's rains must have been heavier than usual, for wildflowers were blooming everywhere amidst the dark, dingy waste of ashen dunes and overturned building-blocks. They dappled the grey gloominess with startling little bursts of yellow and red and blue and white that were almost musical in their emphatic effect. A host of fragile bright-winged kelebekkos flitted about amongst the blossoms, sipping at their nectar, and multitudes of tiny gnat-like ferushas moved about in thick swarms, forming broad misty patches in the air that glistened like silvery dust.

But more was happening here than the unfolding of flowers and the dancing of insects. As he made his descent into Velalisier, Valentine's imagination began to teem suddenly with strangenesses, fantasies, marvels. It seemed to him that inexplicable flickers of sorcery and wonder were arising just beyond the periphery of his vision. Sprites and visitations, singing wordlessly to him of Majipoor's infinite past, drifted upward from the broken edge-tilted slabs and capered temptingly about him, leaping to and fro over the porous, limy soil of the site's surface with frantic energy. A subtle shimmer of delicate jade-green iridescence that had not been apparent at a distance rose above everything, tinting the air: some effect of the hot noontime light striking a luminescent mineral in the rocks, he supposed. It was a wondrous sight all the same, whatever its cause.

These unexpected touches of beauty lifted the Pontifex's mood. Which, ever since the news had reached him the week before of the savage and perplexing death of the distinguished Metamorph archaeologist Huukaminaan amidst these very ruins, had been uncharacteristically bleak. Valentine had had such high hopes for the work that was being done here to uncover and restore the old Shapeshifter capital; and this murder had stained everything.

The tents of his archaeologists came into view now, lofty ones gaily woven from broad strips of green, maroon, and scarlet cloth, billowing atop a low sandy plateau in the distance. Some of the excavators themselves, he saw, were riding towards him down the long rock-ribbed avenues on fat plodding mounts:

about half a dozen of them, with chief archaeologist Magadone Sambisa at the head of the group.

'Majesty,' she said, dismounting, making the elaborate sign of respect that one would make before a Pontifex. 'Welcome to Velalisier.'

Valentine hardly recognized her. It was only about a year since Magadone Sambisa had come before him in his chambers at the Labyrinth. He remembered a dynamic, confident, bright-eyed woman, sturdy and strapping, with rounded cheeks florid with life and vigour and glossy cascades of curling red hair tumbling down her back. She seemed oddly diminished now, haggard with fatigue, her shoulders slumped, her eyes dull and sunken, her face sallow and newly-lined and no longer full. That great mass of hair had lost its sheen and bounce. He let his amazement show, only for an instant, but long enough for her to see it. She pulled herself upright immediately, trying, it seemed, to project some of her former vigour.

Valentine had intended to introduce her to Duke Nascimonte and Prince Mirigant and the rest of the visiting group. But before he could do it, Tunigorn came officially forward to handle the task.

There had been a time when citizens of Majipoor could not have any sort of direct conversation with the Pontifex. They were required then to channel all intercourse through the court official known as the High Spokesman. Valentine had quickly abolished that custom, and many another stifling bit of imperial etiquette. But Tunigorn, by nature conservative, had never been comfortable with those changes. He did whatever he could to preserve the traditional aura of sanctity in which Pontifexes once had been swathed. Valentine found that amusing and charming and only occasionally irritating.

The welcoming party included none of the Metamorph archae-ologists connected with the expedition. Magadone Sambisa had brought just five human archaeologists and a Ghayrog with her. That seemed odd, to have left the Metamorphs elsewhere. Tunigorn formally repeated the archaeologists' names to Valen-tine, getting nearly every one garbled in the process. Then, and only then, did he step back and allow the Pontifex to have a word with her.

'The excavations,' he said. 'Tell me, have they been going well?'

'Quite well, majesty. Splendidly, in fact, until – *until* –' She made a despairing gesture: grief, shock, incomprehension, helplessness, all in a single poignant movement of her head and hands.

The murder must have been like a death in the family for her, for all of them here. A sudden and horrifying loss.

'*Until*, yes. I understand.'

Valentine questioned her gently but firmly. Had there, he asked, been any important new developments in the investigation? Any clues discovered? Claims of responsibility for the killing? Were there any suspects at all? Had the archaeological party received any threats of further attacks?

But there was nothing new at all. Huukaminaan's murder had been an isolated event, a sudden, jarring, and unfathomable intrusion into the serene progress of work at the site. The slain Metamorph's body had been turned over to his own people for interment, she told him, and a shudder that she made an ineffectual effort to hide ran through the entire upper half of her body as she said it. The excavators were attempting now to put aside their distress over the killing and get on with their tasks.

The whole subject was plainly an uncomfortable one for her. She escaped from it as quickly as she could. 'You must be tired from your journey, your majesty. Shall I show you to your quarters?'

Three new tents had been erected to house the Pontifex and his entourage. They had to pass through the excavation zone itself to reach them. Valentine was pleased to see how much progress had been made in clearing away the clusters of pernicious little ropy-stemmed weeds and tangles of woody vines that for so many centuries had been patiently at work pulling the blocks of stone one from another.

Along the way Magadone Sambisa poured forth voluminous

streams of information about the city's most conspicuous features as though Valentine were a tourist and she his guide. Over here, the broken but still awesome aqueduct. There, the substantial jagged-sided oval bowl of the arena. And there, the grand ceremonial boulevard, paved with sleek greenish flagstones.

Shapeshifter glyphs were visible on those flagstones even after the lapse of twenty thousand years, mysterious swirling symbols, carved deep into the stone. Not even the Shapeshifters themselves were able to decipher them now.

The rush of archaeological and mythological minutiae came gushing from her with scarcely a pause for breath. There was a certain frantic, even desperate, quality about it all, a sign of the uneasiness she must feel in the presence of the Pontifex of Majipoor. Valentine was accustomed enough to that sort of thing. But this was not his first visit to Velalisier and he was already familiar with much of what she was telling him. And she looked so weary, so depleted, that it troubled him to see her expending her energy in such needless outpourings.

But she would not stop. They were passing, now, a huge and very dilapidated edifice of grey stone that appeared ready to fall down if anyone should sneeze in its vicinity. 'This is called the Palace of the Final King,' she said. 'Probably an erroneous name, but that's what the Piurivars call it, and for lack of a better one we do too.'

Valentine noted her careful use of the Metamorphs' own name for themselves. *Piurivars*, yes. University people tended to be very formal about that, always referring to the aboriginal folk of Majipoor that way, never speaking of them as Metamorphs or Shapeshifters, as ordinary people tended to do. He would try to remember that.

As they came to the ruins of the royal palace she offered a disquisition on the legend of the mythical Final King of Piurivar antiquity, he who had presided over the atrocious act of defilement that had brought about the Metamorphs' ancient abandonment of their city. It was a story with which all of them were familiar. Who did not know that dreadful tale?

But they listened politely as she told of how, those many thousands of years ago, long before the first human settlers had come to live on Majipoor, the Metamorphs of Velalisier had in some fit of blind madness hauled two living sea-dragons from the ocean: intelligent beings of mighty size and extraordinary mental powers, whom the Metamorphs themselves had thought of as gods. Had dumped them down on these platforms, had cut them to pieces with long knives, had burned their flesh on a pyre before the Seventh Pyramid as a crazed offering to some even greater gods in whom the King and his subjects had come to believe.

When the simple folk of the outlying provinces heard of that orgy of horrendous massacre, so the legend ran, they rushed upon Velalisier and demolished the temple at which the sacrificial offering had been made. They put to death the Final King and wrecked his palace, and drove the wicked citizens of the city forth into the wilderness, and smashed its aqueduct and put dams across the rivers that had supplied it with water, so that Velalisier would be thenceforth a deserted and accursed place, abandoned through all eternity to the lizards and spiders and jakkaboles of the fields.

Valentine and his companions moved on in silence when Magadone Sambisa was done with her narrative. The six sharply tapering pyramids that were Velalisier's best-known monuments came now into view, the nearest rising just beyond the courtyard of the Final King's palace, the other five set close together in a straight line stretching to the east. 'There was a seventh, once,' Magadone Sambisa said. 'But the Piurivars themselves destroyed it just before they left here for the last time. Nothing was left but scattered rubble. We were about to start work there early last week, but that was when – when –' She faltered and looked away.

'Yes,' said Valentine softly. 'Of course.'

The road now took them between the two colossal platforms fashioned from gigantic slabs of blue stone that were known to the modern-day Metamorphs as the Tables of the Gods. Even though they were abutted by the accumulated debris of two hundred centuries, they still rose nearly ten feet above the surrounding plain, and the area of their flat-topped surfaces would have been great enough to hold hundreds of people at a time.

In a low sepulchral tone Magadone Sambisa said, 'Do you know what these are, your majesty?'

Valentine nodded. 'The sacrificial altars, yes. Where the Defilement was carried out.'

Magadone Sambisa said, 'Indeed. It was also at this site that the murder of Huukaminaan happened. I could show you the place. It would take only a moment.'

She indicated a staircase a little way down the road, made of big square blocks of the same blue stone as the platforms themselves. It gave access to the top of the western platform. Magadone Sambisa dismounted and scrambled swiftly up. She paused on the highest step to extend a hand to Valentine as though the Pontifex might be having difficulty in making the ascent, which was not the case. He was still almost as agile as he had been in his younger days. But he reached for her hand for courtesy's sake, just as she – deciding, maybe, that it would be impermissible for a commoner to make contact with the flesh of a Pontifex – began to pull it anxiously back. Valentine, grinning, leaned forward and took the hand anyway, and levered himself upwards.

Old Nascimonte came bounding swiftly up just behind him, followed by Valentine's cousin and close counsellor, Prince Mirigant, who had the little Vroonish wizard Autifon Deliamber riding on his shoulder. Tunigorn remained below. Evidently this place of ancient sacrilege and infamous slaughter was not for him.

The surface of the altar, roughened by time and pockmarked everywhere by clumps of scruffy weeds and incrustations of red and green lichen, stretched on and on before them, a stupendous expanse. It was hard to imagine how even a great multitude of Shapeshifters, those slender and seemingly boneless people, could ever have hauled so many tremendous blocks of stone into place.

Magadone Sambisa pointed to a marker of yellow tape in the form of a six-pointed star that was affixed to the stone a dozen feet or so away. 'We found him here,' she said. 'Some of him, at any rate. And some here.' There was another marker off to the left, about twenty feet farther on. 'And here.' A third star of yellow tape.

'They dismembered him?' Valentine said, appalled.

'Indeed. You can see the bloodstains all about.' She hesitated for an instant. Valentine noticed that she was trembling now. 'All of him was here except his head. We discovered that far away, over in the ruins of the Seventh Pyramid.'

'They know no shame,' said Nascimonte vehemently. 'They are worse than beasts. We should have eradicated them all.'

'Who do you mean?' asked Valentine.

'You know who I mean, majesty. You know quite well.'

'So you think this was Shapeshifter work, this crime?'

'Oh, no, majesty, no!' Nascimonte said, colouring the words with heavy scorn. 'Why would I think such a thing? One of our own archaeologists must have done it, no doubt. Out of professional jealousy, let's say, because the dead Shapeshifter had come upon on some important discovery, maybe, and our own people wanted to take credit for it. Is that what you think, Valentine? Do you believe any human being would be capable of this sort of loathsome butchery?'

'That's what we're here to discover, my friend,' said Valentine amiably. 'We are not quite ready for arriving at conclusions, I think.'

Magadone Sambisa's eyes were bulging from her head, as though Nascimonte's audacity in upbraiding a Pontifex to his face was a spectacle beyond her capacity to absorb. 'Perhaps we should continue on to your tents now,' she said.

It felt very odd, Valentine thought, as they rode on down the rubble-bordered roadway that led to the place of encampment, to be here in this forlorn and eerie zone of age-old ruins once again. But at least he was not in the Labyrinth. So far as he was concerned, any place at all was better than the Labyrinth.

This was his third visit to Velalisier. The first had been long ago when he had been Coronal, in the strange time of his brief overthrow by the usurper Dominin Barjazid. He had stopped off here with his little handful of supporters – Carabella, Nascimonte, Sleet, Ermanar, Deliamber, and the rest – during the course of his northward march to Castle Mount, where he was to reclaim his throne from the false Coronal in the War of Restoration.

Valentine had still been a young man, then. But he was young no longer. He had been Pontifex of Majipoor, senior monarch of the realm, for nine years now, following upon the fourteen of his service as Coronal Lord. There were a few strands of white in his golden hair, and though he still had an athlete's trim body and easy grace he was starting to feel the first twinges of the advancing years.

He had vowed, that first time at Velalisier, to have the weeds and vines that were strangling the ruins cleared away, and to send in archaeologists to excavate and restore the old toppled buildings. And he had intended to allow the Metamorph leaders to play a role in that work, if they were willing. That was part of his plan for giving those once-despised and persecuted natives of the planet a more significant place in Majipoori life; for he knew that Metamorphs everywhere were smouldering with barely contained wrath, and could no longer be shunted into the remote reservations where his predecessors had forced them to live.

Valentine had kept that vow. And had come back to Velalisier years later to see what progress the archaeologists had made.

But the Metamorphs, bitterly resenting Valentine's intrusion into their holy precincts, had shunned the enterprise entirely. That was something he had not expected.

He was soon to learn that although the Shapeshifters were eager to see Velalisier rebuilt, they meant to do the job themselves – after they had driven the human settlers and all other offworld intruders from Majipoor and taken control of their planet once more. A Shapeshifter uprising, secretly planned for many years, erupted just a few years after Valentine had regained the throne. The first group of archaeologists that Valentine had sent to Velalisier could achieve nothing more at the site than some preliminary clearing and mapping before the War of the Rebellion broke out; and then all work there had had to be halted indefinitely.

The war had ended with victory for Valentine's forces. In designing the peace that followed it he had taken care to alleviate as many of the grievances of the Metamorphs as he could. The Danipiur – that was the title of their queen – was brought into the government as a full Power of the Realm, placing her on an even footing with the Pontifex and the Coronal. Valentine had, by then, himself moved on from the Coronal's throne to that of the Pontifex. And now he had revived the idea of restoring the ruins of Velalisier once more; but he had made certain that it would be with the full cooperation of the Metamorphs, and that Metamorph archaeologists would work side by side with the scholars from the venerable University of Arkilon in the north to whom he had assigned the task.

In the year just past great things had been done towards rescuing the ruins from the oblivion that had been encroaching on them for so long. But he could take little joy in any of that. The ghastly death that had befallen the senior Metamorph archaeologist atop this ancient altar argued that sinister forces still ran deep in this place. The harmony that he thought his reign had brought to the world might be far shallower than he suspected.

Twilight was coming on by the time Valentine was settled in his tent. By a custom that even he was reluctant to set aside, he would stay in it alone, since his consort Carabella had remained behind in the Labyrinth on this trip. Indeed, she had tried very strongly to keep him from going himself. Tunigorn, Mirigant, Nascimonte, and the Vroon would share the second tent; the third was occupied by the security forces that had accompanied the Pontifex to Velalisier.

He stepped out into the gathering dusk. A sprinkling of early stars had begun to sparkle overhead, and the Great Moon's bright glint could be seen close to the horizon. The air was parched and crisp, with a brittle quality to it, as though it could be torn in one's hands like dry paper and crumbled to dust between one's fingers. There was a strange stillness in it, an eerie hush.

But at least he was out of doors, here, gazing up at actual stars, and the air he breathed here, dry as it was, was *real* air, not the manufactured stuff of the Pontifical city. Valentine was grateful for that.

By rights he had no business being out and abroad in the world at all.

As Pontifex, his place was in the Labyrinth, hidden away in his secret imperial lair deep underground beneath all those coiling levels of subterranean settlement, shielded always from the view of ordinary mortals. The Coronal, the junior king who lived in the lofty castle of forty thousand rooms atop the great heaven-piercing peak that was Castle Mount, was meant to be the active figure of governance, the visible representative of royal majesty on Majipoor. But Valentine loathed the dank Labyrinth where his lofty rank obliged him to dwell. He relished every opportunity he could manufacture to escape from it.

And in fact this one had been thrust unavoidably upon him. The killing of Huukaminaan was serious business, requiring an enquiry on the highest levels; and the Coronal Lord Hissune was many months' journey away just now, touring the distant continent of Zimroel. And so the Pontifex was here in the Coronal's stead.

'You love the sight of the open sky, don't you?' said Duke Nascimonte, emerging from the tent across the way and limping over to stand by Valentine's side. A certain tenderness underlay the harshness of his rasping voice. 'Ah, I understand, old friend. I do indeed.'

'I see the stars so infrequently, Nascimonte, in the place where I must live.'

The duke chuckled. '*Must* live! The most powerful man in the world, and yet he's a prisoner! How ironic that is! How sad!'

'I knew from the moment I became Coronal that I'd have to live in the Labyrinth eventually,' Valentine said. 'I've tried to make my peace with that. But it was never my plan to be Coronal in the first place, you know. If Voriax had lived –'

'Ah, yes, Voriax.' Valentine's brother, the elder son of the High Counsellor Damiandane: the one who had been reared from childhood to occupy the throne of Majipoor. Nascimonte gave Valentine a close look. 'It was a Metamorph, was it not, who struck him down in the forest? That has been proven now?'

Uncomfortably Valentine said, 'What does it matter now who killed him? He died. And the throne came to me, because I was our father's other son. A crown I had never dreamed of wearing. Everyone knew that Voriax was the one who was destined for it.'

'But he had a darker destiny also. Poor Voriax!'

Poor Voriax, yes. Struck down by a bolt out of nowhere while hunting in the forest eight years into his reign as Coronal, a bolt from the bow of some Metamorph assassin skulking in the trees. By accepting his dead brother's crown, Valentine had doomed himself inevitably to descend into the Labyrinth some day, when the old Pontifex died and it became the Coronal's turn to succeed to the greater title, and to the cheerless obligation of underground residence that went with it.

'As you say, it was the decision of fate,' Valentine replied, 'and now I am Pontifex. Well, so be it, Nascimonte. But I won't hide down there in the darkness all the time. I can't.'

'And why should you? The Pontifex can do as he pleases.'

'Yes. Yes. But only within our law and custom.'

'You shape law and custom to suit yourself, Valentine. You always have.'

Valentine understood what Nascimonte was saying. He had never been a conventional monarch. For much of the time during his exile from power in the period of the usurpation he had wandered the world earning a humble living as an itinerant juggler, kept from awareness of his true rank by the amnesia that the usurping faction had induced in him. Those years had transformed him irreversibly; and after his restoration to the royal heights of Castle Mount he had comported himself in a way that few Coronals ever had before – mingling openly with the populace, spreading a cheerful gospel of peace and love even as the Shapeshifters were making ready to launch their long-cherished campaign of war against the conquerors who had taken their world from them.

And then, when the events of that war made Valentine's succession to the Pontificate unavoidable, he had held back as long as possible before relinquishing the upper world to his protégé Lord Hissune, the new Coronal, and descending into the subterranean city that was so alien to his sunny nature.

In his nine years as Pontifex he had found every excuse to emerge from it. No Pontifex in memory had come forth from the Labyrinth more than once a decade or so, and then only to attend high rites at the castle of the Coronal; but Valentine popped out as often as he could, riding hither and thither through the land as though he were still obliged to undertake the formal grand processionals across the countryside that a Coronal must make. Lord Hissune had been very patient with him on each of those occasions, though Valentine had no doubt that the young Coronal was annoyed by the senior monarch's insistence on coming up into public view so frequently.

'I change what I think needs changing,' Valentine said. 'But I owe it to Lord Hissune to keep myself out of sight as much as possible.'

'Well, here you are above ground today, at any rate!'

'It seems that I am. This is one time, though, when I would gladly have forgone the chance to come forth. But with Hissune off in Zimroel –'

'Yes. Clearly you had no choice. You had to lead this investigation yourself.' They fell silent. 'A nasty mess, this murder,' Nascimonte said, after a time. 'Pfaugh! Pieces of the poor bastard strewn all over the altar like that!'

'Pieces of the government's Metamorph policy, too, I think,' said the Pontifex, with a rueful grin.

'You think there's something political in this, Valentine?'

'Who knows? But I fear the worst.'

'You, the eternal optimist!'

'It would be more accurate to call me a realist, Nascimonte. A realist.'

The old duke laughed. 'As you prefer, majesty.' There was another pause, a longer one than before. Then Nascimonte said, more quietly now, 'Valentine, I need to ask your forgiveness for an earlier fault. I spoke too harshly, this afternoon, when I talked of the Shapeshifters as vermin who should be exterminated. You know I don't truly believe that. I'm an old man. Sometimes I speak so bluntly that I amaze even myself.'

Valentine nodded, but made no other reply.

'And telling you so dogmatically that it had to be one of his fellow Shapeshifters who killed him, too. As you said, it's out of line for us to be jumping to conclusions that way. We haven't even started to collect evidence yet. At this point we have no justification for assuming –'

'On the contrary. We have *every* reason to assume it, Nascimonte.'

The duke stared at Valentine in bewilderment. 'Majesty!'

'Let's not play games, old friend. There's no one here right now but you and me. In privacy we're free to speak unvarnished truths, are we not? And you said it truly enough this afternoon. I did tell you then that we mustn't jump to conclusions, yes, but sometimes a conclusion is so obvious that it comes jumping right at *us*. There's no rational reason why one of the human archaeologists – or one of the Ghayrogs, for that matter – would have murdered one of his colleagues. I don't see why anyone else would have done it, either. Murder is such a very rare crime, Nascimonte. We can hardly even begin to understand the motivations of someone who'd be capable of doing it. But someone did.'

'Yes.'

'Well, and which race's motivations are hardest for us to understand, eh? To my way of thinking the killer almost certainly would have to be a Shapeshifter – either a member of the archaeological team, or one who came in from outside for the particular purpose of carrying out the assassination.'

'So one might assume. But what possible purpose could a Shapeshifter have for killing one of his own kind?'

'I can't imagine. Which is why we're here as investigators,' said Valentine. 'And I have a nasty feeling that I'm not going to like the answer when we find it.'

At dinner that night in the archaeologists' open-air mess hall, under a clear black sky ablaze now with swirling streams of brilliant stars that cast cold dazzling light on the mysterious humps and mounds of the surrounding ruins, Valentine made the acquaintance of Magadone Sambisa's entire scientific team. There were seventeen in all: six other humans, two Ghayrogs, eight Metamorphs. They seemed, every one of them, to be gentle, studious creatures. Not by the greatest leap of the imagination could Valentine picture any of these people slaying and dismembering their venerable colleague Huukaminaan.

'Are these the only persons who have access to the archaeological zone?' he asked Magadone Sambisa.

'There are the day-labourers also, of course.'

'Ah. And where are they just now?'

'They have a village of their own, over beyond the last pyramid. They go to it at sundown and don't come back until the start of work the next day.'

'I see. How many are there altogether? A great many?'

Magadone Sambisa looked across the table towards a pale and long-faced Metamorph with strongly inward-sloping eyes. He was her site supervisor, Kaastisiik by name, responsible for each day's deployment of diggers. 'What would you say? About a hundred?'

'One hundred twelve,' said Kaastisiik, and clamped his little slit of a mouth in a way that demonstrated great regard for his own precision.

'Mostly Piurivar?' Valentine asked.

'Entirely Piurivar,' said Magadone Sambisa. 'We thought it was best to use only native workers, considering that we're not only excavating the city but to some extent rebuilding it. They don't appear to have any problem with the presence of non-Piurivar archaeologists, but having humans taking part in the actual reconstruction work would very likely be offensive to them.'

'You hired them all locally, did you?'

'There are no settlements of any kind in the immediate vicinity of the ruins, your majesty. Nor are there many Piurivars living anywhere in the surrounding province. We had to bring them in from great distances. A good many from Piurifayne itself, in fact.'

Valentine raised an eyebrow at that. From *Piurifayne*?

Piurifayne was a province of far-off Zimroel, an almost unthinkable distance away on the other side of the Inner Sea. Eight thousand years before, the great conqueror Lord Stiamot – he who had ended for all time the Piurivars' hope of remaining independent on their own world – had driven those Metamorphs who had survived his war against them into Piurifayne's humid jungles and had penned them up in a reservation there. Though the old restrictions had long since been lifted and Metamorphs now were permitted to settle wherever they pleased, more of them still lived in Piurifayne than anywhere else; and it was in the subtropical glades of Piurifayne that the revolutionary Faraataa had founded the underground movement that had sent the War of the Rebellion forth upon peaceful Majipoor like a river of seething lava.

Tunigorn said, 'You've questioned them all, naturally? Established their comings and goings at the time of the murder?'

Magadone Sambisa seemed taken aback. 'You mean, treat them as though they were suspects in the killing?'

'They *are* suspects in the killing,' said Tunigorn.

'They are simple diggers and haulers of burdens, nothing more, Prince Tunigorn. There are no murderers among them, that much I know. They *revered* Dr Huukaminaan. They regarded him as a guardian of their past – almost a sacred figure. It's inconceivable that any one of them could have carried out such a dreadful and hideous crime. Inconceivable!'

'In this very place some twenty thousand years ago,' Duke Nascimonte said, looking upwards as if he were speaking only to the air, 'the King of the Shapeshifters, as you yourself reminded us earlier today, caused two enormous sea-dragons to be butchered alive atop those huge stone platforms back there. It was clear from your words this afternoon that the Shapeshifters of those days must have regarded sea-dragons with even more reverence than you say your labourers had for Dr Huukaminaan. They called them "water-kings", am I not right, and gave them names, and thought of them as holy elder brothers, and addressed prayers to them? Yet the bloody sacrifice took place here in Velalisier even so, the thing that to this very day the Shapeshifters themselves speak of as the Defilement. Is this not true? Permit me to suggest, then, that if the King of the Shapeshifters could have done such a thing back then, it isn't all that inconceivable that one of your own hired Metamorphs here could have found some reason to perpetrate a similar atrocity last week upon the unfortunate Dr Huukaminaan on the very same altar.'

Magadone Sambisa appeared stunned, as though Nascimonte had struck her in the face. For a moment she could make no reply. Then she said hoarsely, 'How can you use an ancient myth, a fantastic legend, to cast suspicion on a group of harmless, innocent –'

'Ah, so it's a myth and a legend when you want to protect these harmless and innocent diggers and haulers of yours, and absolute historical truth when you want us to shiver with rapture over the significance of these piles of old jumbled stones?'

'Please,' Valentine said, glaring at Nascimonte. '*Please.*' To Magadone Sambisa he said, 'What time of day did the murder take place?'

'Late at night. Past midnight, it must have been.'

'I was the last to see Dr Huukaminaan,' said one of the Metamorph archaeologists, a frail-looking Piurivar whose skin had an elegant emerald hue. Vo-Siimifon was his name; Magadone Sambisa had introduced him as an authority on ancient Piurivar script. 'We sat up late in our tent, he and I, discussing an inscription that had been found the day before. The lettering was extremely minute; Dr Huukaminaan complained of a headache, and said finally that he was going out for a walk. I went to sleep. Dr Huukaminaan did not return.'

'It's a long way,' Mirigant observed, 'from here to the sacrificial platforms. *Quite* a long way. It would take at least half an hour to walk there, I'd guess. Perhaps more, for someone his age. He was an old man, I understand.'

'But if someone happened to encounter him just outside the camp, though,' Tunigorn suggested, 'and *forced* him to go all the way down to the platform area –'

Valentine said, 'Is a guard posted here at the encampment at night?'

'No. There seemed to be no purpose in doing that.'

'And the dig site itself? It's not fenced off, or protected in any way?'

'No.'

'Then anyone at all could have left the day-labourers' village as soon as it grew dark,' Valentine said, 'and waited out there in the road for Dr Huukaminaan to come out.' He glanced toward Vo-Siimifon. 'Was Dr Huukaminaan in the habit of taking a walk before bedtime?'

'Not that I recall.'

'And if he *had* chosen to go out late at night for some reason, would he have been likely to take so long a walk?'

'He was quite a robust man, for his age,' said the Piurivar. 'But even so that would have been an unusual distance to go just for a stroll before bedtime.'

'Yes. So it would seem.' Valentine turned again to Magadone Sambisa. 'It'll be necessary, I'm afraid, for us to question your labourers. And each member of your expedition, too. You understand that at this point we can't arbitrarily rule anyone out.'

Her eyes flashed. 'Am I under suspicion too, your majesty?'

'At this point,' said Valentine, 'nobody here is under suspicion. And everyone is. Unless you want me to believe that Dr Huukaminaan committed suicide by dismembering himself and distributing parts of himself all over the top of that platform.'

The night had been cool, but the sun sprang into the morning sky with incredible swiftness. Almost at once, early as it was in the day, the air began to throb with desert warmth. It was necessary to get a quick start at the site, Magadone Sambisa had told them, since by midday the intense heat would make work very difficult.

Valentine was ready for her when she called for him soon after dawn. At her request he would be accompanied only by some members of his security detachment, not by any of his fellow lords. Tunigorn grumbled about this, as did Mirigant. But she said – and would not yield on the point – that she preferred that the Pontifex alone come with her today, and after he had seen what she had to show him he could make his own decisions about sharing the information with the others.

She was taking him to the Seventh Pyramid. Or what was left of it, rather, for nothing now remained except the truncated base, a square structure about twenty feet long on each side and five or six feet high, constructed from the same reddish basalt from which the great arena and some of the other public buildings had been made. East of that stump the fragments of the pyramid's upper section, smallish broken blocks of the same reddish stone, lay strewn in the most random way across a wide area. It was as though some angry colossus had contemptuously given the western face of the pyramid one furious slap with the back of his ponderous hand and sent it flying into a thousand pieces. On the side of the stump away from the debris Valentine could make out the pointed summit of the still-intact Sixth Pyramid about five hundred feet away, rising above a copse of little contorted trees, and beyond it were the other five, running onward one after another to the edge of the royal palace itself.

'According to Piurivar lore,' Magadone Sambisa said, 'the people of Velalisier held a great festival every thousand years, and constructed a pyramid to commemorate each one. So far as we've been able to confirm by examining and dating the six undamaged ones, that's correct. This one, we know, was the last in the series. If we can believe the legend –' and she gave Valentine a meaningful look '– it was built to mark the very festival at which the Defilement took place. And had just been completed when the city was invaded and destroyed by those who had come here to punish its inhabitants for what they had done.'

She beckoned to him, leading him around towards the northern side of the shattered pyramid. They walked perhaps fifty feet onward from the stump. Then she halted. The ground had been carefully cut away here. Valentine saw a rectangular opening just large enough for a man to enter, and the beginning of a passageway leading underground and heading back towards the foundations of the pyramid.

A star-shaped marker of bright yellow tape was fastened to a good-sized boulder just to the left of the excavation.

'That's where you found the head, is it?' he asked.

'Not there. Below.' She pointed into the opening. 'Will you follow me, your majesty?'

Six members of Valentine's security force had gone with Valentine to the pyramid site that morning: the giant warrior-woman Lisamon Hultin, his personal bodyguard, who had accompanied him on all his travels since his juggling days; two shaggy hulking Skandars; a couple of Pontifical officials whom he had inherited from his predecessor's staff; and even a Metamorph, one Aarisiim, who had defected to Valentine's forces from the service of the arch-rebel Faraataa in the final hours of the War of the Rebellion and had been with the Pontifex ever since. All six stepped forward now as if they meant to go down into the excavation with him, though the Skandars and Lisamon Hultin were plainly too big to fit into the entrance. But Magadone Sambisa shook her head fiercely; and Valentine, smiling, signalled to them all to wait for him above.

The archaeologist, lighting a hand-torch, entered the opening in the ground. The descent was steep, via a series of precisely chiselled earthen steps that took them downwards nine or ten feet. Then, abruptly, the subterranean passageway levelled off. Here there was a flagstone floor made of broad slabs hewn from some glossy green rock. Magadone Sambisa flashed her light at one and Valentine saw that the slabs bore carved glyphs, runes of some kind, reminiscent of those he had seen in the paving of the grand ceremonial boulevard that ran past the royal palace.

'This is our great discovery,' she said. 'There are shrines, previously unknown and unsuspected, under each of the seven pyramids. We were working near the Third Pyramid about six months ago, trying to stabilize its foundation, when we stumbled on the first one. It had been plundered, very probably in antiquity. But it was an exciting find all the same, and immediately we went looking for similar shrines beneath the other five intact pyramids. And found them: also plundered. For the time being we didn't bother to go digging for the shrine of the Seventh Pyramid. We assumed that there was no hope of finding anything interesting there, that it must have been looted at the time the pyramid was destroyed. But then Huukaminaan and I decided that we might as well check it out too, and we put down this trench that we've been walking through. Within a day or so we reached this flagstone paving. Come.'

They went deeper in, entering a carefully constructed tunnel just about wide enough for four people to stand in it abreast. Its walls were fashioned of thin slabs of black stone laid sideways like so many stacked books, leading upward to a vaulted roof of the same stone that tapered into a series of pointed arches. The craftsmanship was very fine, and distinctly archaic in appearance. The air in the tunnel was hot and musty and dry, ancient air, lifeless air. It had a stale, dead taste in Valentine's nostrils.

'We call this kind of underground vault a processional hypogeum,' Magadone Sambisa explained. 'Probably it was used by priests carrying offerings to the shrine of the pyramid.'

Her torch cast a spreading circlet of pallid light that allowed Valentine to perceive a wall of finely-dressed white stone blocking the path just ahead of them. 'Is that the foundation of the pyramid we're looking at?' he asked.

'No. What we see here is the wall of the shrine, nestling against the pyramid's base. The pyramid itself is on the far side of it. The other shrines were located right up against their pyramids in the same way. The difference is that all the others had been smashed open. This one has apparently never been breached.'

Valentine whistled softly. 'And what do you think is inside it?'

'We don't have any idea. We were putting off opening it, waiting for Lord Hissune to return from his processional in

Zimroel, so that you and he could be on hand when we broke through the wall. But then – the murder –'

'Yes,' Valentine said soberly. And, after a moment: 'How strange that the destroyers of the city demolished the Seventh Pyramid so thoroughly, but left the shrine beneath it intact! You'd think they would have made a clean sweep of the place.'

'Perhaps there was something walled up in the shrine that they didn't want to go near, eh? It's a thought, anyway. We may never know the truth, even after we open it. *If* we open it.'

'If?'

'There may be problems about that, majesty. Political problems, I mean. We need to discuss them. But this isn't the moment for that.'

Valentine nodded. He indicated a row of small indented apertures, perhaps nine inches deep and about a foot high, that had been chiselled in the wall some eighteen inches above ground level. 'Were those for putting offerings in?'

'Exactly.' Magadone Sambisa flashed the torch across the row from right to left. 'We found microscopic traces of dried flowers in several of them, and potsherds and coloured pebbles in others – you can still see them there, actually. And some animal remains.' She hesitated. 'And then, in the alcove on the far left –'

The torch came to rest on a star of yellow tape attached to the shallow alcove's back wall.

Valentine gasped in shock. '*There?*'

'Huukaminaan's head, yes. Placed very neatly in the centre of the alcove, facing outward. An offering of some sort, I suppose.'

'To whom? To what?'

The archaeologist shrugged and shook her head.

Then, abruptly, she said, 'We should go back up now, your majesty. The air down here isn't good to spend a lot of time in. I simply wanted you to see where the shrine was situated. And where we found the missing part of Dr Huukaminaan's body.'

Later in the day, with Nascimonte and Tunigorn and the rest now joining him, Magadone Sambisa showed Valentine the site of the expedition's other significant discovery: the bizarre cemetery, previously unsuspected, where the ancient inhabitants of Velalisier had buried their dead. Or, more precisely, had buried certain fragments of their dead.

'There doesn't appear to be a complete body anywhere in the whole graveyard. In every interment we've opened, what we've found is mere tiny bits – a finger here, an ear there, a lip, a toe. Or some internal organ, even. Each item carefully embalmed, and placed in a beautiful stone casket and buried beneath one of these gravestones. The part for the whole: a kind of metaphorical burial.'

Valentine stared in wonder and astonishment.

The twenty-thousand-year-old Metamorph cemetery was one of the strangest sights he had seen in all his years of exploring the myriad wondrous strangenesses that Majipoor had to offer.

It covered an area hardly more than a hundred feet long and sixty feet wide, off in a lonely zone of dunes and weeds a short way beyond the end of one of the north–south flagstone boulevards. In that small plot of land there might have been ten thousand graves, all jammed together. A small stela of brown sandstone, a hand's-width broad and about fifteen inches high, jutted upward from each of the grave plots. And each of them crowded in upon the ones adjacent to it in a higgledy-piggledy fashion so that the cemetery was a dense agglomeration of slender close-set gravestones, tilting this way and that in a manner that utterly befuddled the eye.

At one time every stone must have lovingly been set in a vertical position above the casket containing the bit of the departed that had been chosen for interment here. But the Metamorphs of Velalisier had evidently gone on jamming more and more burials into this little funereal zone over the course of centuries, until each grave overlapped the next in the most chaotic manner. Dozens of them were packed into every square yard of terrain.

As the headstones continued to be crammed one against another without heed for the damage that each new burial was doing to the tombs already in place, the older ones were pushed out of perpendicular by their new neighbours. The slender stones all leaned precariously one way and another, looking the way a forest might after some monstrous storm had passed through, or after the ground beneath it had been bent and buckled by the force of some terrible earthquake. They all stood at crazy angles now, no two slanting in the same direction.

On each of these narrow headstones a single elegant glyph was carved precisely one-third of the way from the top, an intricately patterned whorl of the sort found in other zones of the city. No symbol seemed like any other one. Did they represent the names of the deceased? Prayers to some long-forgotten god?

'We hadn't any idea that this was here,' Magadone Sambisa said. 'This is the first burial site that's ever been discovered in Velalisier.'

'I'll testify to that,' Nascimonte said, with a great jovial wink. 'I did a little digging here myself, you know, long ago. Tomb-hunting, looking for buried treasure that I might be able to sell somewhere, during the time I was forced from my land in the reign of the false Lord Valentine and living like a bandit in this desert. But not a single grave did any of us come upon then. Not one.'

'Nor did we detect any, though we tried,' said Magadone Sambisa. 'When we found this place it was only by sheer luck. It was hidden deep under the dunes, ten, twelve, twenty feet below the surface of the sand. No one suspected it was here. But one day last winter a terrific whirlwind swept across the valley and hovered right up over this part of the city for half an hour, and by the time it was done whirling the whole dune had been picked up and tossed elsewhere and this amazing collection of gravestones lay exposed. Here. Look.'

She knelt and brushed a thin coating of sand away from the base of a gravestone just in front of her. In moments the upper lid of a small box made of polished grey stone came into view. She pried it free and set it to one side.

Tunigorn made a sound of disgust. Valentine, peering down, saw a thing like a curling scrap of dark leather lying within the box.

'They're all like this,' said Magadone Sambisa. 'Symbolic burial, taking up a minimum of space. An efficient system, considering what a huge population Velalisier must have had in its prime. One tiny bit of the dead person's body buried here, preserved so artfully that it's still in pretty good condition even after all these thousands of years. The rest of it exposed on the hills outside town, for all we know, to be consumed by natural processes of decay. A Piurivar corpse would decay very swiftly. We'd find no traces, after all this time.'

'How does that compare with present-day Shapeshifter burial practices?' Mirigant asked.

Magadone Sambisa looked at him oddly. 'We know next to nothing about present-day Piurivar burial practices. They're a pretty secretive race, you know. They've never chosen to tell us anything about such things and evidently we've been too polite to ask, because there's hardly a thing on record about it. Hardly a thing.'

'You have Shapeshifter scientists on your own staff,' Tunigorn said. 'Surely it wouldn't be impolite to consult your own associates about something like that. What's the point of training Shapeshifters to be archaeologists if you're going to be too sensitive of their feelings to make any use of their knowledge of their own people's ways?'

'As a matter of fact,' said Magadone Sambisa, 'I did discuss this find with Dr Huukaminaan not long after it was uncovered. The layout of the place, the density of the burials, seemed pretty startling to him. But he didn't seem at all surprised by the concept of burial of body parts instead of entire bodies. He gave me to understand what had been done here wasn't all that different in some aspects from things the Piurivars still do today. There wasn't time just then for him to go into further details, though, and we both let the subject slip. And now – now –'

Once more she displayed that look of stunned helplessness, of futility and confusion in the face of violent death, that came over her whenever the topic of the murder of Huukaminaan arose.

Not all that different in some aspects from things the Piurivars still do today, Valentine repeated silently.

He considered the way Huukaminaan's body had been cut apart, the sundered pieces left in various places atop the sacrificial platform, the head carried down into the tunnel beneath the Seventh Pyramid and carefully laid to rest in one of the alcoves of the underground shrine.

There was something implacably alien about that grisly act of dismemberment that brought Valentine once again to the conclusion, mystifying and distasteful but seemingly inescapable, that had been facing him since his arrival here. *The murderer of the Metamorph archaeologist must have been a Metamorph himself.* As Nascimonte had suggested earlier, there seemed to be a ritual aspect to the butchery that had all the hallmarks of Metamorph work.

But still it made no sense. Valentine had difficulty believing that the old man could have been killed by one of his own people.

'What was Huukaminaan like?' he asked Magadone Sambisa. 'I never met him, you know. Was he contentious? Cantankerous?'

'Not in the slightest. A sweet, gentle person. A brilliant scholar. There was no one, Piurivar or human, who didn't love and admire him.'

'There must have been one person, at least,' said Nascimonte wryly.

Perhaps Nascimonte's theory was worth exploring. Valentine said, 'Could there have been some sort of bitter professional disagreement? A dispute over the credit for a discovery, a battle over some piece of theory?'

Magadone Sambisa stared at the Pontifex as though he had gone out of his mind. 'Do you think we kill each other over such things, your majesty?'

'It was a foolish suggestion,' Valentine said, with a smile. 'Well, then,' he went on, 'suppose Huukaminaan had come into possession of some valuable artefact in the course of his work here, some priceless treasure that would fetch a huge sum in the antiquities market. Might that not have been sufficient cause for murdering him?'

Again the incredulous stare. 'The artefacts we find here, majesty, are of the nature of simple sandstone statuettes, and bricks bearing inscriptions, not golden tiaras and emeralds the size of gihorna eggs. Everything worth looting was looted a long, long time ago. And we would no more dream of trying to make a private sale of the little things that we find here than we would – would – than, well, than we would of murdering each other. Our finds are divided equally between the university museum in Arkilon and the Piurivar treasury at Ilirivoyne. In any case – no, no, it's not even worth discussing. The idea's completely absurd.' Instantly her cheeks turned flame-red. 'Forgive me, majesty, I meant no disrespect.'

Valentine brushed the apology aside. 'What I'm doing, you see, is groping for some plausible explanation of the crime. A place to begin our investigation, at least.'

'I'll give you one, Valentine,' Tunigorn said suddenly. His normally open and genial face was tightly drawn in a splenetic scowl that brought his heavy eyebrows together into a single dark line. 'The basic thing that we need to keep in mind all the time is that there's a curse on this place. You know that, Valentine. A *curse*. The Shapeshifters themselves put the dark word on the city, the Divine knows how many thousands of years ago, when they smashed it up to punish those who had chopped up those two sea-dragons. They intended the place to be shunned for ever. Only ghosts have lived here ever since. By sending these archaeologists of yours in here, Valentine, you're disturbing those ghosts. Making them angry. And so they're striking back. Killing old Huukaminaan was the first step. There'll be more, mark my words!'

'And you think, do you, that ghosts are capable of cutting someone into five or six pieces and scattering the parts far and wide?'

Tunigorn was not amused. 'I don't know what sorts of things ghosts may or may not be capable of doing,' he said staunchly. 'I'm just telling you what has crossed my mind.'

'Thank you, my good old friend,' said Valentine pleasantly. 'We'll give the thought the examination it deserves.' And to Magadone Sambisa he said, 'I must tell you what has crossed *my* mind, based on what you've shown me today, here and at the pyramid shrine. Which is that the killing of Huukaminaan strikes me as a ritual murder, and the ritual involved is some kind of Piurivar ritual. I don't say that that's what it was; I just say that it certainly looks that way.'

'And if it does?'

'Then we have our starting point. It's time now to move to the next phase of our work, I think. Please have the kindness to call your entire group of Piurivar archaeologists together this afternoon. I want to speak with them.'

'One by one, or all together?'

'All of them together at first,' said Valentine. 'After that, we'll see.'

But Magadone Sambisa's people were scattered all over the huge archaeological zone, each one involved with some special project, and she begged Valentine not to have them called in until the working day was over. It would take so long to reach them all, she said, that the worst of the heat would have descended by the time they began their return to camp, and they would be compelled to trek across the ruins in the full blaze of noon, instead of settling in some dark cavern to await the cooler hours that lay ahead. Meet with them at sundown, she implored him. Let them finish their day's tasks.

That seemed only reasonable. He said that he would.

But Valentine himself was unable to sit patiently by until dusk. The murder had jarred him deeply. It was one more symptom of the strange new darkness that had come over the world in his lifetime. Huge as it was, Majipoor had long been a peaceful place where there was comfort and plenty for all, and crime of any sort was an extraordinary rarity. But, even so, just in this present generation there had been the assassination of the Coronal Lord Voriax, and then the diabolically contrived usurpation that had pushed Voriax's successor – Valentine – from his throne for a time.

The Metamorphs, everyone knew now, had been behind both of those dire acts.

And after Valentine's recovery of the throne had come the War of the Rebellion, organized by the embittered Metamorph Faraataa, bringing with it plagues, famines, riots, a worldwide panic, great destruction everywhere. Valentine had ended that uprising, finally, by reaching out himself to take Faraataa's life – a deed that the gentle Valentine had regarded with horror, but which he had carried out all the same, because it had to be done.

Now, in this new era of worldwide peace and harmony that Valentine, reigning as Pontifex, had inaugurated, an admirable and beloved old Metamorph scholar had been murdered in the most brutal way. Murdered here in the holy city of the Metamorphs themselves, while he was in the midst of archaeological work that Valentine had instituted as one way of demonstrating the newfound respect of the human people of Majipoor for the aboriginal people they had displaced. And there was every indication, at least at this point, that the murderer was himself a Metamorph.

But that seemed insane.

Perhaps Tunigorn was right, that all of this was merely the working out of some ancient curse. That was a hard thing for Valentine to swallow. He had little belief in such things as curses. And yet – yet –

Restlessly he stalked the ruined city all through the worst heat of the day, heedless of the discomfort, pulling his hapless companions along. The sun's great golden-green eye stared unrelentingly down. Heat-shimmers danced in the air. The leathery-leaved little shrubs that grew all over the ruins seemed to fold in upon themselves to hide from those torrid blasts of light. Even the innumerable skittering lizards that infested these rocks grew reticent as the temperature climbed.

'I would almost think we had been transported to Suvrael,' said Tunigorn, panting in the heat as he dutifully laboured along beside the Pontifex. 'This is the climate of the miserable southland, not of our pleasant Alhanroel.'

Nascimonte gave him a sardonic squinting smirk. 'Just one more example of the malevolence of the Shapeshifters, my lord Tunigorn. In the days when the city was alive there were green forests all about this place, and the air was cool and mild. But then the river was turned aside, and the forests died, and nothing was left here but the bare rock that you see, which soaks up the heat of noon and holds it like a sponge. Ask the archaeologist lady, if you don't believe me. This province was deliberately turned into a desert, for the sake of punishing those who had committed great sins in it.'

'All the more reason for us to be somewhere else,' Tunigorn muttered. 'But no, no, this is our place, here with Valentine, now and ever.'

Valentine scarcely paid attention to what they were saying. He wandered aimlessly onward, down one weedy byway and another, past fallen columns and shattered façades, past the empty shells of what might once have been shops and taverns, past the ghostly outlines marking the foundations of vanished dwellings that must once have been palatial in their grandeur. Nothing was labelled, and Magadone Sambisa was not with him, now, to bend his ear with endless disquisitions about the former identities of these places. They were bits and pieces of lost Velalisier, that was all he knew: skeletonic remnants of this ancient metropolis.

It was easy enough, even for him, to imagine this place as the lair of ancient phantoms. A glassy glimmer of light shining out of some tumbled mass of broken columns – odd scratchy sounds that might have been those of creatures crawling about where no creatures could be seen – the occasional hiss and slither of shifting sand, sand that moved, so it would appear, of its own volition –

'Every time I visit these ruins,' he said to Mirigant, who was walking closest to him now, 'I'm astounded by the antiquity of it all. The weight of history that presses down on it.'

'History that no one remembers,' Mirigant said.

'But its weight remains.'

'Not our history, though.'

Valentine shot his cousin a scornful look. 'So you may believe. But it's Majipoor's history, and what is that if not ours?'

Mirigant shrugged and made no answer.

Was there any meaning, Valentine wondered, in what he had just said? Or was the heat addling his brain?

He pondered it. Into his mind there came, with a force almost like that of an explosion, a vision of the totality of vast Majipoor. Its great continents and overwhelming rivers and immense shining seas, its dense moist jungles and great deserts, its forests of towering trees and mountains rich with strange and wonderful creatures, its multitude of sprawling cities with their populations of many millions. His soul was flooded with an overload of sensation, the perfume of a thousand kinds of flowers, the aromas of a thousand spices, the savoury tang of a thousand wondrous meats, the bouquet of a thousand wines. It was a world of infinite richness and variety, this Majipoor of his.

And by a fluke of descent and his brother's bad luck he had come first to be Coronal and now Pontifex of that world. Twenty billion people hailed him as their emperor. His face was on the coinage; the world resounded with his praises; his name would be inscribed for ever on the roster of monarchs in the House of Records, an imperishable part of the history of this world.

But once there had been a time when there were no Pontifexes and Coronals here. When such wondrous cities as Ni-Moya and Alaisor and the fifty great urban centres of Castle Mount did not exist. And in that time before human settlement had begun on Majipoor, this city of Velalisier already was.

What right did he have to appropriate this city, already thousands of years dead and desolate when the first colonists arrived from space, into the flow of human history here? In truth there was a discontinuity so deep between *their* Majipoor and *our* Majipoor, he thought, that it might never be bridged.

In any case he could not rid himself of the feeling that this place's great legion of ghosts, in whom he did not even believe, were lurking all around him, and that their fury was still unappeased. Somehow he would have to deal with that fury, which had broken out now, so it seemed, in the form of a terrible act that had cost the life of a studious and inoffensive old man. The logic that infused every aspect of Valentine's soul balked at any comprehension of such a thing. But his own fate, he knew, and perhaps the fate of the world, might depend on his finding a solution to the mystery that had exploded here.

'You will pardon me, good majesty,' said Tunigorn, breaking in on Valentine's broodings just as a new maze of ruined streets opened out before them. 'But if I take another step in this heat, I will fall down gibbering like a madman. My very brain is melting.'

'Why, then, Tunigorn, you should certainly seek refuge quickly, and cool it off! You can ill afford to damage what's left of it, can you, old friend?' Valentine pointed in the direction of the camp. 'Go back. Go. But I will continue, I think.'

He was not sure why. But something drove him grimly forward across this immense bedraggled sprawl of sand-choked sun-blasted ruins, seeking he knew not what. One by one his other companions dropped away from him, with this apology or that, until only the indefatigable Lisamon Hultin remained. The giantess was ever-faithful. She had protected him from the dangers of Mazadone Forest in the days before his restoration to the Coronal's throne. She had been his guardian in the belly of the sea-dragon that had swallowed them both in the sea off Piliplok, that time when they were shipwrecked sailing from Zimroel to Alhanroel, and she had cut him free and carried him up to safety. She would not leave him now. Indeed she seemed willing to walk on and on with him through the day and the night and the day that followed as well, if that was what he required of her.

But eventually even Valentine had had enough. The sun had long since moved beyond its noon height. Sharp-edged pools of shadow, rose and purple and deepest obsidian, were beginning to reach out all about him. He was feeling a little light-headed now, his head swimming a little and his vision wavering from the prolonged strain of coping with the unyielding glare of that blazing sun, and each street of tumbled-down buildings had come to look exactly like its predecessor. It was time to go back. Whatever penance he had been imposing on himself by such an exhausting journey through this dominion of death and destruction must surely have been fulfilled by now. He leaned on Lisamon Hultin's arm now and again as they made their way towards the tents of the encampment.

Magadone Sambisa had assembled her eight Metamorph archaeologists. Valentine, having bathed and rested and had a little to eat, met with them just after sundown in his own tent, accompanied only by the little Vroon, Autifon Deliamber. He wanted to form his opinions of the Metamorphs undistracted by the presence of Nascimonte and the rest; but Deliamber had certain Vroonish wizardly skills that Valentine prized highly, and the small many-tentacled being might well be able to perceive things with those huge and keen golden eyes of his that would elude Valentine's own human vision.

The Shapeshifters sat in a semicircle with Valentine facing them and the tiny wizened old Vroon at his left hand. The Pontifex ran his glance down the group, from the site-boss Kaastisiik at one end to the palaeographer Vo-Siimifon on the other. They looked back at him calmly, almost indifferently, these seven rubbery-faced slope-eyed Piurivars, as he told them of the things he had seen this day, the cemetery and the shattered pyramid and the shrine beneath it, and the alcove where Huukaminaam's severed head had been so carefully placed by his murderer.

'There was, wouldn't you say, a certain formal aspect to the murder?' Valentine said. 'The cutting of the body into pieces? The carrying of the head down to the shrine, the placement in the alcove of offerings?' His gaze fastened on Thiuurinen, the ceramics expert, a lithe, diminutive Metamorph woman with lovely jade-green skin. 'What's your reading on that?' he asked her.

Her expression was wholly impassive. 'As a ceramicist I have no opinion at all.'

'I don't want your opinion as a ceramicist, just as a member of the expedition. A colleague of Dr Huukaminaan's. Does it seem to you that putting the head there meant that some kind of offering was being made?'

'It is only conjecture that those alcoves were places of offering,' said Thiuurinen primly. 'I am not in a position to speculate.'

Nor would she. Nor would any of them. Not Kaastisiik, not Vo-Siimifon, not the stratigrapher Pamikuuk, not Hieekraad, the custodian of material artefacts, nor Driismiil, the architectural specialist, nor Klelliin, the authority on Piurivar palaeotechnology, nor Viitaal-Twuu, the specialist in metallurgy.

Politely, mildly, firmly, unshakably, they brushed aside Valentine's hypotheses about ritual murder. Was the gruesome dismemberment of Dr Huukaminaan a hearkening-back to the funeral practices of ancient Velalisier? Was the placing of his head in that alcove likely to have been any kind of propitiation of some supernatural being? Was there anything in Piurivar tradition that might countenance killing someone in that particular fashion? They could not say. They would not say. Nor, when he enquired as to whether their late colleague might have had an enemy here at the site, did they provide him with any information.

And they merely gave him the Piurivar equivalent of a shrug when he wondered out loud whether there could have been some struggle over the discovery of a valuable artefact that might have led to Huukaminaan's murder; or even a quarrel of a more abstract kind, a fierce disagreement over the findings or goals of the expedition. Nobody showed any sign of outrage at his implication that one of them might have killed old Huukaminaan over such a matter. They behaved as though the whole notion of doing such a thing were beyond their comprehension, a concept too alien even to consider.

During the course of the interview Valentine took the opportunity to aim at least one direct question at each of them. But the result was always the same. They were unhelpful without seeming particularly evasive. They were unforthcoming without appearing unusually sly or secretive. There was nothing overtly suspicious about their refusal to cooperate. They seemed to be precisely what they claimed to be: scientists, studious scholars, devoted to uncovering the buried mysteries of their race's remote past, who knew nothing at all about the mystery that had erupted right here in their midst. He did not feel himself to be in the presence of murderers here.

And yet – and yet –

They were Shapeshifters. He was the Pontifex, the emperor of the race that had conquered them, the successor across eight thousand years of the half-legendary soldier-king Lord Stiamot who had deprived them of their independence for all time. Mild and scholarly though they might be, these eight Piurivars before him surely could not help but feel anger, on some level of their souls, towards their human masters. They had no reason to cooperate with him. They would not see themselves under any obligation to tell him the truth. And – was this only his innate and inescapable racial prejudices speaking, Valentine wondered? – intuition told him to take nothing at face value among these people. Could he really trust the impression of apparent innocence that they gave? Was it possible ever for a human to read the things that lay hidden behind a Metamorph's cool impenetrable features?

'What do you think?' he asked Deliamber, when the eight Shapeshifters had gone. 'Murderers or not?'

'Probably not,' the Vroon replied. 'Not these. Too soft, too citified. But they were holding something back. I'm certain of that.'

'You felt it too, then?'

'Beyond any doubt. What I sensed, your majesty – do you know what the Vroon word *hsirthiir* means?'

'Not really.'

'It isn't easy to translate. But it has to do with questioning someone who doesn't intend to tell you any lies but isn't necessarily going to tell you the truth, either, unless you know exactly how to call it forth. You pick up a powerful perception that there's an important layer of meaning hidden somewhere beneath the surface of what you're being told, but that you won't be allowed to elicit that hidden meaning unless you ask precisely the right question to unlock it. Which means, essentially, that you already have to know the information that you're looking for before you can ask the question that would reveal it. It's a very frustrating sensation, *hsirthiir*: almost painful, in fact. It is like hitting one's beak against a stone wall. I felt myself placed in a state of *hsirthiir* just now. Evidently so did you, your majesty.'

'Evidently I did,' said Valentine.

There was one more visit to make, though. It had been a long day and a terrible weariness was coming over Valentine now. But he felt some inner need to cover all the basic territory in a single sweep; and so, once darkness had fallen, he asked Magadone Sambisa to conduct him to the village of the Metamorph labourers.

She was unhappy about that. 'We don't usually like to intrude on them after they've finished their day's work and gone back there, your majesty.'

'You don't usually have murders here, either. Or visits from the Pontifex. I'd rather speak with them tonight than disrupt tomorrow's digging, if you don't mind.'

Deliamber accompanied him once again. At her own insistence, so did Lisamon Hultin. Tunigorn was too tired to go – his hike through the ruins at midday had done him in – and Mirigant was feeling feverish from a touch of sunstroke; but formidable old Duke Nascimonte readily agreed to ride with the Pontifex, despite his great age. The final member of the party was Aarisiim, the Metamorph member of Valentine's security staff, whom Valentine brought with him not so much for protection – Lisamon Hultin would look after that – as for the *hsirthiir* problem.

Aarisiim, turncoat though he once had been, seemed to Valentine to be as trustworthy as any Piurivar was likely to be: he had risked his own life to betray his master Faraataa to Valentine in the time of the Rebellion, when he had felt that Faraataa had gone beyond all decency by threatening to slay the Metamorph queen. He could be helpful now, perhaps, detecting things that eluded even Deliamber's powerful perceptions.

The labourers' village was a gaggle of meagre wickerwork huts outside the central sector of the dig. In its flimsy makeshift look it reminded Valentine of Ilirivoyne, the Shapeshifter capital in the jungle of Zimroel, which he had visited so many years before. But this place was even sadder and more disheartening than Ilirivoyne. There, at least, the Metamorphs had had an abundance of tall straight saplings and jungle vines with which to build their ramshackle huts, whereas the only construction materials available to them here were the gnarled and twisted desert shrubs that dotted the Velalisier plain. And so their huts were miserable little things, dismally warped and contorted.

They had had advance word, somehow, that the Pontifex was coming. Valentine found them arrayed in groups of eight or ten in front of their shacks, clearly waiting for his arrival. They were a pitiful starved-looking bunch, gaunt and shabby and ragged, very different from the urbane and cultivated Metamorphs of Magadone Sambisa's archaeological team. Valentine wondered where they found the strength to do the digging that was required of them in this inhospitable climate.

As the Pontifex came into view they shuffled forward to meet him, quickly surrounding him and the rest of his party in a way that caused Lisamon Hultin to hiss sharply and put her hand to the hilt of her vibration-sword.

But they did not appear to mean any harm. They clustered excitedly around him and to his amazement offered homage in the most obsequious way, jostling among themselves for a chance to kiss the hem of his tunic, kneeling in the sand before him, even prostrating themselves. 'No,' Valentine cried, dismayed. 'This isn't necessary. It isn't right.' Already Magadone Sambisa was ordering them brusquely to get back, and Lisamon Hultin and Nascimonte were shoving the ones closest to Valentine away from him. The giantess was doing it calmly, unhurriedly, efficiently, but Nascimonte was prodding them more truculently, with real detestation apparent in his fiery eyes.

Others came pressing forward as fast as the first wave retreated, though, pushing in upon him in frantic determination.

So eager were these weary toil-worn people to show their obeisance to the Pontifex, in fact, that he could not help regarding their enthusiasm as blatantly false, an ostentatious overdoing of whatever might have been appropriate. How likely was it, he wondered, that any group of Piurivars, however lowly and simple, would feel great unalloyed joy at the sight of the Pontifex of Majipoor? Or would, of their own accord, stage such a spontaneous demonstration of delight?

Some, men and women both, were even allowing themselves to mimic the forms of the visitors by way of compliment, so that half a dozen blurry distorted Valentines stood before him, and a couple of Nascimontes, and a grotesque half-sized imitation of Lisamon Hultin. Valentine had experienced that peculiar kind of honour before, in his Ilirivoyne visit, and he had found it disturbing and even chilling then. It distressed him again now. Let them shift shapes if they wished – they had that capacity, to use as they pleased – but there was something almost sinister about this appropriation of the visages of their visitors.

And the jostling began to grow even wilder and more frenzied. Despite himself Valentine started to feel some alarm. There were more than a hundred villagers, and the visitors numbered only a handful. There could be real trouble if things got out of control.

Then in the midst of the hubbub a powerful voice called out, 'Back! Back!' And at once the whole ragged band of Shapeshifters shrank away from Valentine as though they had been struck by whips. There was a sudden stillness and silence. Out of the now motionless throng there stepped a tall Metamorph of unusually muscular and powerful build. He made a deep gesticulation and announced, in a dark rumbling tone quite unlike that of any Metamorph voice Valentine had ever heard before, 'I am Vathiimeraak, the foreman of these workers. I beg you to feel welcome here among us, Pontifex. We are your servants.'

But there was nothing servile about him. He was plainly a man of presence and authority. Briskly he apologized for the uncouth behaviour of his people, explaining that they were simple peasants astounded by the presence of a Power of the Realm among them, and this was merely their way of showing respect.

'I know this man,' murmured Aarisiim into Valentine's left ear.

But there was no opportunity just then to find out more; for Vathiimeraak, turning away, made a signal with one upraised hand and instantly the scene became one of confusion and noise once again. The villagers went running off in a dozen different directions, some returning almost at once with platters of sausages and bowls of wine for their guests, others hauling lop-sided tables and benches from the huts. Platoons of them came crowding in once more on Valentine and his companions, this time urging them to sample the delicacies they had to offer.

'They're giving us their own dinners!' Magadone Sambisa protested. And she ordered Vathiimeraak to call off the feast. But the foreman replied smoothly that it would offend the villagers to refuse their hospitality, and in the end there was no help for it: they must sit down at table and partake of all that the villagers brought for them.

'If you will, majesty,' said Nascimonte, as Valentine reached for a bowl of wine. The duke took it from him and sipped it first; and only after a moment did he return it. He insisted also on tasting Valentine's sausages for him, and the scraps of boiled vegetables that went with them.

It had not occurred to Valentine that the villagers would try to poison him. But he allowed old Nascimonte to enact his charming little rite of medieval chivalry without objection. He was too fond of the old man to want to spoil his gesture.

Vathiimeraak said, when the feasting had gone on for some time, 'You are here, your majesty, about the death of Dr Huukaminaam, I assume?'

The foreman's bluntness was startling. 'Could it not be,' Valentine said good-humouredly, 'that I just wanted to observe the progress being made at the excavations?'

Vathiimeraak would have none of that. 'I will do whatever

you may require of me in your search for the murderer,' he said, rapping the table sharply to underscore his words. For an instant the outlines of his broad, heavy-jowled face rippled and wavered as if he were on the verge of undergoing an involuntary metamorphosis. Among the Piurivar, Valentine knew, that was a sign of being swept by some powerful emotion. 'I had the greatest respect for Dr Huukaminaam. It was a privilege to work beside him. I often dug for him myself, when I felt the site was too delicate to entrust to less skilful hands. He thought that that was improper, at first, that the foreman should dig, but I said, No, no, Dr Huukaminaam, I beg you to allow me this glory, and he understood, and permitted me. How may I help you to find the perpetrator of this dreadful crime?'

He seemed so solemn and straightforward and open that Valentine could not help but find himself immediately on guard. Vathiimeraak's strong, booming voice and formal choice of phrase had an overly theatrical quality. His elaborate sincerity seemed much like the extreme effusiveness of the villagers' demonstration, all that kneeling and kissing of his hem: unconvincing because it was so excessive.

You are too suspicious of these people, he told himself. This man is simply speaking as he thinks a Pontifex should be spoken to. And in any case I think he can be useful.

He said, 'How much do you know of how the murder was committed?'

Vathiimeraak responded without hesitation, as if he had been holding a well-rehearsed reply in readiness. 'I know that it happened late at night, the week before this, somewhere between the Hour of the Gihorna and the Hour of the Jackal. A person or persons lured Dr Huukaminaam from his tent and led him to the Tables of the Gods, where he was killed and cut into pieces. We found the various segments of his body the next morning atop the western platform, all but his head. Which we discovered later that day in one of the alcoves along the base of the Shrine of the Downfall.'

Pretty much the standard account, Valentine thought. Except for one small detail.

'The Shrine of the Downfall? I haven't heard that term before.'

'The shrine of the Seventh Pyramid is what I mean,' said Vathiimeraak. 'The unopened shrine that Dr Magadone Sambisa found. The name that I used is what we call it among ourselves. You notice that I do not say she "discovered" it. We have always known that it was there, adjacent to the broken pyramid. But no one ever asked us, and so we never spoke of it.'

Valentine glanced across at Deliamber, who nodded ever so minutely. *Hsirthiir* again, yes.

Something was not quite right, though. Valentine said, 'Dr Magadone Sambisa told me that she and Dr Huukaminaan came upon the seventh shrine jointly, I think. She indicated that he was just as surprised at finding it there as she had been. Are you claiming that you knew of its existence, but he didn't?'

'There is no Piurivar who does not know of the existence of the Shrine of the Downfall,' said Vathiimeraak stolidly. 'It was sealed at the time of the Defilement and contains, we believe, evidence of the Defilement itself. If Dr Magadone Sambisa formed the impression that Dr Huukaminaan was unaware that it was there, that was an incorrect impression.' Once again the edges of the foreman's face flickered and wavered. He looked worriedly toward Magadone Sambisa and said, 'I mean no offence in contradicting you, Dr Magadone Sambisa.'

'None taken,' she said, a little stiffly. 'But if Huukaminaan knew of the shrine before the day we found it, he never said a thing about it to me.'

'Perhaps he had hoped it would not be found,' Vathiimeraak replied.

This brought a show of barely concealed consternation from Magadone Sambisa; and Valentine himself sensed that there was something here that needed to be followed up. But they were drifting away from the main issue.

'What I need you to do,' said Valentine to the foreman, 'is to determine the whereabouts of every single one of your people during the hours when the murder was committed.' He saw Vathiimeraak's reaction beginning to take form, and added quickly, 'I'm not suggesting that we believe at this point that anyone from the village killed Dr Huukaminaan. No one at all is under suspicion at this point. But we do need to account for everybody who was present in or around the excavation zone that night.'

'I will do what I can to find out.'

'Your help will be invaluable, I know,' Valentine said.

'You will also want to enlist the aid of our khivanivod,' Vathiimeraak said. 'He is not among us tonight. He has gone off on a spiritual retreat into the farthest zone of the city to pray for the purification of the soul of the killer of Dr Huukaminaan, whoever that may be. I will send him to you when he returns.'

Another little surprise.

A khivanivod was a Piurivar holy man, something midway between a priest and a wizard. They were relatively uncommon in modern Metamorph life, and it was remarkable that there should be one in residence at this scruffy out-of-the-way village. Unless, of course, the high religious leaders of the Piurivars had decided that it was best to install one at Velalisier for the duration of the dig, to ensure that everything was done with the proper respect for the holy places. It was odd that Magadone Sambisa hadn't mentioned to him that a khivanivod was present here.

'Yes,' said Valentine, a little uneasily. 'Send him to me, yes. By all means.'

As they rode away from the labourers' village Nascimonte said, 'Well, Valentine, I'm pained to confess that I find myself once again forced to question your judgement.'

'You do suffer much pain on my behalf,' said Valentine, with a twinkling smile. 'Tell me, Nascimonte: where have I gone amiss this time?'

'You enlisted that man Vathiimeraak as your ally in the investigation. You treated him, in fact, as though he were a trusted constable of police.'

'He seems steady enough to me. And the villagers are terrified of him. What harm is there in asking him to question them for us? If we interrogate them ourselves, they'll just shut up like clams – or at best they'll tell us all kinds of fantastic stories. Whereas Vathiimeraak might just be able to bully the truth out of them. Some useful fraction of it, anyway.'

'Not if he's the murderer himself,' said Nascimonte.

'Ah, is that it? You've solved the crime, my friend? Vathiimeraak did it?'

'That could very well be.'

'Explain, if you will, then.'

Nascimonte gestured to Aarisiim. 'Tell him.'

The Metamorph said, 'Majesty, I remarked to you when I first saw Vathiimeraak that I thought I knew that man from somewhere. And indeed I do, though it took me a little while more to place him. He is a kinsman of the rebel Faraataa. In the days when I was with Faraataa in Piurifayne, this Vathiimeraak was often by our side.'

That was unexpected. But Valentine kept his reaction to himself. Calmly he said, 'Does that matter? What of our amnesty, Aarisiim? All rebels who agreed to keep the peace after the collapse of Faraataa's campaign have been forgiven and restored to full civil rights. I should hardly need to remind you, of all people, of that.'

'It doesn't mean they all turned into good citizens overnight, does it, Valentine?' Nascimonte demanded. 'Surely it's possible that this Vathiimeraak, a man of Faraataa's own blood, still harbours powerful feelings of –'

Valentine looked towards Magadone Sambisa. 'Did you know he was related to Faraataa when you hired him as foreman?'

She seemed embarrassed. 'No, majesty, I certainly did not. But I was aware that he had been in the Rebellion and had accepted the amnesty. And he came with the highest recommendation. We're supposed to believe that the amnesty has some meaning, doesn't it? That the Rebellion's over and done with, that those who took part in it and repented deserve to be allowed –'

'And has he truly repented, do you think?' Nascimonte asked. 'Can anyone know, really? I say he's a fraud from top to toe. That big booming voice! That high-flown style of speaking! Those expressions of profound reverence for the Pontifex! Phoney, every bit of it. And as for killing Huukaminaan, just look at him! Do you think it could have been easy to cut the poor man up in pieces that way? But Vathiimeraak's built like a bull-bidlak. In that village of thin flimsy folk he stands out the way a dwikka tree would in a flat meadow.'

'Because he has the strength for the crime doesn't yet prove that he's guilty of it,' said Valentine in some annoyance. 'And this other business, of his being related to Faraataa – what possible motive does that give him for slaughtering that harmless old Piurivar archaeologist? No, Nascimonte. No. No. No. You and Tunigorn between you, I know, would take about five minutes to decree that the man should be locked away for life in the Sangamor vaults that lie deep under the Castle. But we need a little evidence before we proclaim anyone a murderer.' To Magadone Sambisa he said, 'What about this khivanivod, now? Why weren't we told that there's a khivanivod living in this village?'

'He's been away since the day after the murder, your majesty,' she said, looking at Valentine apprehensively. 'To be perfectly truthful, I forgot all about him.'

'What kind of person is he? Describe him for me.'

A shrug. 'Old. Dirty. A miserable superstition-monger, like all these tribal shamans. What can I say? I dislike having him around. But it's the price we pay for permission to dig here, I suppose.'

'Has he caused any trouble for you?'

'A little. Constantly sniffing into things, worrying that we'll commit some sort of sacrilege. *Sacrilege*, in a city that the Piurivars themselves destroyed and put a curse on! What possible harm could we do here, after what they've already inflicted on it?'

'This was their capital,' said Valentine. 'They were free to do with it as they pleased. That doesn't mean they're glad to have us come in here and root around in its ruins. But has he actually tried to halt any part of your work, this khivanivod?'

'He objects to our unsealing the Shrine of the Downfall.'

'Ah. You did say there was some political problem about that. He's filed a formal protest, has he?' The understanding by which Valentine had negotiated the right to send archaeologists into Velalisier included a veto power for the Piurivars over any aspect of the work that was not to their liking.

'So far he's simply told us he doesn't want us to open the shrine,' said Magadone Sambisa. 'He and I and Dr Huukaminaam were supposed to have a meeting about it last week and try to work out a compromise, although what kind of middle ground there can be between opening the shrine and *not* opening it is hard for me to imagine. In any event the meeting never happened, for obvious tragic reasons. Now that you're here, perhaps you'll adjudicate the dispute for us when Torkkinuuminaad gets back from wherever he's gone off to.'

'Torkinuuminaad?' Valentine said. 'Is that the khivanivod's name?'

'Torkinuuminaad, yes.'

'These jawbreaking Shapeshifter names,' Nascimonte said grumpily. 'Torkkinuuminaad! Vathiimeraak! Huukaminaan!' He glowered at Aarisiim. 'By the Divine, fellow, was it absolutely necessary for you people to give yourself names that are so utterly impossible to pronounce, when you could just as easily have –'

'The system is very logical,' Aarisiim replied serenely. 'The doubling of the vowels in the first part of a name implies –'

'Save this discussion for some other time, if you will,' said Valentine, making a chopping gesture with his hand. To Magadone Sambisa he said, 'Just out of curiosity, what was the khivanivod's relationship with Dr Huukaminaan like? Difficult? Tense? Did he think it was sacrilegious to pull the weeds off these ruins and set some of the buildings upright again?'

'Not at all,' Magadone Sambisa said. 'They worked hand in glove. They had the highest respect for each other, though the Divine only knows why Dr Huukaminaan tolerated that filthy old savage for half a minute. Why? Are you suggesting that *Torkkinuuminaad* could have been the murderer?'

'Is that so unlikely? You haven't had a single good thing to say about him yourself.'

'He's an irritating nuisance and in the matter of the shrine, at least, he's certainly made himself a serious obstacle to our work. But a murderer? Even I wouldn't go that far, your majesty. Anyone could see that he and Huukaminaan had great affection for each other.'

'We should question him, all the same,' said Nascimonte.

'Indeed,' said Valentine. 'Tomorrow, I want messengers sent out through the archaeological zone in search of him. He's somewhere around the ruins, right? Let's find him and bring him in. If that interrupts his spiritual retreat, so be it. Tell him that the Pontifex commands his presence.'

'I'll see to it,' said Magadone Sambisa.

'The Pontifex is very tired, now,' said Valentine. 'The Pontifex is going to go to sleep.'

Alone in his grand royal tent at last after the interminable exertions of the busy day, he found himself missing Carabella with surprising intensity: that small and sinewy woman who had shared his destiny almost from the beginning of the strange time when he had found himself at Pidruid, at the other continent's edge, bereft of all memory, all knowledge of self. It was she, loving him only for himself, all unknowing that he was in fact a Coronal in baffled exile from his true identity, who had helped him join the juggling troupe of Zalzan Kavol; and gradually their lives had merged; and when he had commenced his astounding return to the heights of power she had followed him to the summit of the world.

He wished she were with him now. To sit beside him, to talk with him as they always talked before bedtime. To go over with him the twisting ramifications of all that had been set before him this day. To help him make sense out of the tangled mysteries this dead city posed for him. And simply to *be* with him.

But Carabella had not followed him here to Velalisier. It was a foolish waste of his time, she had argued, for him to go in person to investigate this murder. Send Tunigorn; send Mirigant; send Sleet; send any one of a number of high Pontifical officials. But why go yourself?

'Because I must,' Valentine had replied. 'Because I've made myself responsible for integrating the Metamorphs into the life of this world. The excavations at Velalisier are an essential part of that enterprise. And the murder of the old archaeologist leads me to think that conspirators are trying to interfere with those excavations.'

'This is very far-fetched,' said Carabella, then.

'And if it is, so be it. But you know how I long for a chance to free myself of the Labyrinth, if only for a week or two. So I will go to Velalisier.'

'And I will not. I loathe that place, Valentine. It's a horrid place of death and destruction. I've seen it twice, and its charm isn't growing on me. If you go, you'll go without me.'

'I mean to go, Carabella.'

'Go, then. If you must.' And she kissed him on the tip of the nose, for they were not in the custom of quarrelling, or even of disagreeing greatly. But when he went, it was indeed without her. She was in their royal chambers in the Labyrinth tonight, and he was here, in his grand but solitary tent, in this parched and broken city of ancient ghosts.

They came to him that night in his dreams, those ghosts.

They came to him with such intensity that he thought he was having a sending – a lucid and purposeful direct communication in the form of a dream.

But this was like no sending he had ever had. Hardly had he closed his eyes but he found himself wandering in his sleep among the cracked and splintered buildings of dead Velalisier. Eerie ghost-light, mystery-light, came dancing up out of every shattered stone. The city glowed lime-green and lemon-yellow, pulsating with inner luminescence. Glowing faces, ghost-faces, grinned mockingly at him out of the air. The sun itself swirled and leaped in wild loops across the sky.

A dark hole leading into the ground lay open before him, and unquestioningly he entered it, descending a long flight of massive lichen-encrusted stone steps with archaic twining runes carved in them. Every movement was arduous for him. Though he was going steadily lower, the effort was like that of climbing. Struggling all the way, he made his way ever deeper, but he felt constantly as though he were travelling upwards against a powerful pull, ascending some inverted pyramid, not a slender one like those above ground in this city, but one of unthinkable mass and diameter. He imagined himself to be fighting his way up the side of a mountain; but it was a mountain that pointed downwards, deep into the world's bowels. And the path was carrying him down, he knew, into some labyrinth far more frightful than the one in which he dwelled in daily life.

The whirling ghost-faces flashed dizzyingly by him and went spinning away. Cackling laughter floated backwards to him out of the darkness. The air was moist and hot and rank. The pull of gravity was oppressive. As he descended, travelling through level after endless level, momentary flares of dizzying yellow light showed him caverns twisting away from him on all sides, radiating outwards at incomprehensible angles that were both concave and convex.

And now there was sudden numbing brightness. The throbbing fire of an underground sun streamed upward towards him from the depths ahead, a harsh, menacing glare.

Valentine found himself drawn helplessly towards that terrible light; and then, without perceptible transition, he was no longer underground at all, but out in the vastness of Velalisier Plain, standing atop one of the great platforms of blue stone known as the Tables of the Gods.

There was a long knife in his hand, a curving scimitar that flashed like lightning in the brilliance of the noon sun.

And as he looked out across the plain he saw a mighty procession coming towards him from the east, from the direction of the distant sea: thousands of people, hundreds of thousands, like an army of ants on the march. No, two armies; for the marchers were divided into two great parallel columns. Valentine could see, at the end of each column far off near the horizon, two enormous wooden wagons mounted on titanic wheels. Great hawsers were fastened to them, and the marchers, with mighty groaning tugs, were hauling the wagons slowly forward, a foot or two with each pull, into the centre of the city.

Atop each of the wagons a colossal water-king lay trussed, a sea-dragon of monstrous size. The great creatures were glaring furiously at their captors but were unable, even with a sea-dragon's prodigious strength, to free themselves from their bonds, strain as they might. And with each tug on the hawsers the wagons bearing them carried them closer to the twin platforms called the Tables of the Gods.

The place of the sacrifice.

The place where the terrible madness of the Defilement was to happen. Where Valentine the Pontifex of Majipoor waited with the long gleaming blade in his hand.

'Majesty? Majesty?'

Valentine blinked and came groggily awake. A Shapeshifter stood above him, extremely tall and greatly attenuated of form, his eyes so sharply slanted and narrowed that it seemed at first glance that he had none at all. Valentine began to jump up in alarm; and then, recognizing the intruder after a moment as Aarisiim, he relaxed.

'You cried out,' the Metamorph said. 'I was on my way to you to tell you some strange news I have learned, and when I was outside your tent I heard your voice. Are you all right, your majesty?'

'A dream, only. A very nasty dream.' Which still lingered disagreeably at the edges of his mind. Valentine shivered and tried to shake himself free of its grasp. 'What time is it, Aarisiim?'

'The Hour of the Haigus, majesty.'

Past the middle of the night, that was. Well along towards dawn.

Valentine forced himself the rest of the way into wakefulness. Eyes fully open now, he stared up into the practically featureless face. 'There's news, you say? What news?'

The Metamorph's colour deepened from pale green to a rich chartreuse, and his eye-slits fluttered swiftly three or four times. 'I have had a conversation this night with one of the archaeologists, the woman Hieekraad, she who keeps the records of the discovered artefacts. The foreman of the diggers brought her to me, the man Vathiimeraak, from the village. He and this Hieekraad are lovers, it seems.'

Valentine stirred impatiently. 'Get to the point, Aarisiim.'

'I approach it, sir. The woman Hieekraad, it seems, has revealed things to the man Vathiimeraak about the excavations that a mere foreman might otherwise not have known. He has told those things to me this evening.'

'Well?'

'They have been lying to us, majesty – all the archaeologists, the whole pack of them, deliberately concealing something important. Something *quite* important, a major discovery. Vathiimeraak, when he learned from this Hieekraad that we had been deceived in this way, made the woman come with him to me, and compelled her to reveal the whole story to me.'

'Go on.'

'It was this,' said Aarisiim. He paused a moment, swaying a little as though he were about to plunge into a fathomless abyss. 'Dr Huukaminaan, two weeks before he died, uncovered a burial site that had never been detected before. This was in an otherwise desolate region out at the western edge of the city. Magadone Sambisa was with him. It was a post-abandonment site, dating from the historic era. From a time not long after Lord Stiamot, actually.'

'But how could that be?' said Valentine, frowning. 'Completely aside from the little matter that there was a curse on this place and no Piurivar would have dared to set foot in it after it was destroyed, there weren't any Piurivars living on this continent at that time anyway. Stiamot had sent them all into the reservations on Zimroel. You know that very well, Aarisiim. Something's wrong here.'

'This was not a Piurivar burial, your majesty.'

'What?'

'It was the tomb of a human,' Aarisiim said. 'The tomb of a *Pontifex*, according to the woman Hieekraad.'

Valentine would not have been more surprised if Aarisiim had set off an explosive charge. 'A Pontifex?' he repeated numbly. 'The tomb of a Pontifex, here in Velalisier?'

'So did this Hieekraad say. A definite identification. The symbols on the wall of the tomb – the Labyrinth sign, and other things of that sort – the ceremonial objects found lying next to the body – inscriptions – everything indicated that this was a Pontifex's grave, thousands of years old. So she said; and I think she was telling the truth. Vathiimeraak was standing over her, scowling, as she spoke. She was too frightened of him to have uttered any falsehoods just then.'

Valentine rose and paced fiercely about the tent. 'By the Divine, Aarisiim! If this is true, it's something that should have been brought to my attention as soon as it came to light. Or at least mentioned to me upon my arrival here. The tomb of some ancient Pontifex, and they hide it from me? Unbelievable. Unbelievable!'

'It was Magadone Sambisa herself who ordered that all news of the discovery was to be suppressed. There would be no public announcement whatever. Not even the diggers were told what had been uncovered. It was to be a secret known to the archaeologists of the dig, only.'

'This according to Hieekraad also?'

'Yes, majesty. She said that Magadone Sambisa gave those orders the very day the tomb was found. This Hieekraad furthermore told me that Dr Huukaminaam disagreed strenuously with Magadone Sambisa's decision, that indeed they had a major quarrel over it. But in the end he gave in. And when the murder happened, and word came that you were going to visit Velalisier, Magadone Sambisa called a meeting of the staff and reiterated that nothing was to be said to you about it. Everyone involved with the dig was specifically told to keep all knowledge of it from you.'

'Absolutely incredible,' Valentine muttered.

Earnestly Aarisiim said, 'You must protect the woman Hieekraad, majesty, as you investigate this thing. She will be in great trouble if Magadone Sambisa learns that she's the one who let the story of the tomb get out.'

'Hieekraad's not the only one who's going to be in trouble,' Valentine said. He slipped from his nightclothes and started to dress.

'One more thing, majesty. The khivanivod – Torkkinuuminaad? He's at the tomb site right now. That's where he went to make his prayer retreat. I have this information from the foreman Vathiimeraak.'

'Splendid,' Valentine said. His head was whirling. 'The village khivanivod mumbling Piurivar prayers in the tomb of a Pontifex! Beautiful! Wonderful! Get me Magadone Sambisa, right away, Aarisiim.'

'Majesty, the hour is very early, and –'

'Did you hear me, Aarisiim?'

'Majesty,' said the Shapeshifter, more subserviently this time. He bowed deeply. And went out to fetch Magadone Sambisa.

'An ancient Pontifex's tomb, Magadone Sambisa, and no announcement is made? An ancient Pontifex's tomb, and when the current Pontifex comes to inspect your dig, you go out of your way to keep him from learning about it? This is all extremely difficult for me to believe, let me assure you.'

Dawn was still an hour away. Magadone Sambisa, called from her bed for this interview, looked even paler and more haggard than she had yesterday, and now there might have been a glint of fear in her eyes as well. But for all that, she still was capable of summoning some of the unrelenting strength that had propelled her to the forefront of her profession: there was even a steely touch of defiance in her voice as she said, 'Who told you about this tomb, your majesty?'

Valentine ignored the sally. 'It was at your order, was it, that the story was suppressed?'

'Yes.'

'Over Dr Huukaminaan's strong objections, so I understand.'

Now fury flashed across her features. 'They've told you every-thing, haven't they? Who was it? Who?'

'Let me remind you, lady, that I am the one asking the questions here. It's true, then, that Huukaminaan disagreed with you about concealing the discovery?'

'Yes.' In a very small voice.

'Why was that?'

'He saw it as a crime against the truth,' Magadone Sambisa said, still speaking very quietly now. 'You have to understand, majesty, that Dr Huukaminaan was utterly dedicated to his work. Which was, as it is for us all, the recovery of the lost aspects of our past through rigorous application of formal archaeological disciplines. He was totally committed to this, a true and pure scientist.'

'Whereas you are not committed quite so totally?'

Magadone Sambisa reddened and glanced shamefacedly to one side. 'I admit that my actions may make it seem that way. But sometimes even the pursuit of truth has to give way, at least for a time, before tactical realities. Surely you, a Pontifex, would not deny that. And I had reasons, reasons that seemed valid enough to me, for not wanting to let news of this tomb reach the public. Dr Huukaminaan didn't agree with my position; and he and I battled long and hard over it. It was the only occasion in our time as co-leaders of this expedition that we disagreed over anything.'

'And finally it became necessary, then, for you to have him murdered? Because he yielded to you only grudgingly, and you weren't sure he really would keep quiet?'

'*Majesty!*' It was a cry of almost inexpressible shock.

'A motive for the killing can be seen there. Isn't that so?'

She looked stunned. She waved her arms helplessly about, the palms of her hands turned outward in appeal. A long moment passed before she could bring herself to speak. But she had recovered much of her composure when she did.

'Majesty, what you have just suggested is greatly offensive to me. I am guilty of hiding the tomb discovery, yes. But I swear to you that I had nothing to do with Dr Huukaminaan's death.

I can't possibly tell you how much I admired that man. We had our professional differences, but . . .' She shook her head. She looked drained. Very quietly she said, 'I didn't kill him. I have no idea who did.'

Valentine chose to accept that, for now. It was hard for him to believe that she was merely play-acting her distress.

'Very well, Magadone Sambisa. But now tell me why you decided to conceal the finding of that tomb.'

'I would have to tell you, first, an old Piurivar legend, a tale out of their mythology, one that I heard from the khivanivod Torkinuuminaad on the day that we found the tomb.'

'Must you?'

'I must, yes.'

Valentine sighed. 'Go ahead, then.'

Magadone Sambisa moistened her lips and drew a deep breath.

'There once was a Pontifex, so the story goes,' she said, 'who lived in the years soon after the conquest of the Piurivars by Lord Stiamot. This Pontifex had fought in the War of the Conquest himself when he was a young man, and had had charge over a camp of Piurivar prisoners, and had listened to some of their campfire tales. Among which was the story of the Defilement at Velalisier – the sacrifice by the Final King of the two sea-dragons, and the destruction of the city that followed it. They told him also of the broken Seventh Pyramid, and of the shrine beneath it, the Shrine of the Downfall, as they called it. In which, they said, certain artefacts dating from the day of the Defilement had been buried – artefacts that would, when properly used, grant their wielder godlike power over all the forces of space and time. This story stayed with him, and many years later when he had become Pontifex he came to Velalisier with the intention of locating the shrine of the Seventh Pyramid, the Shrine of the Downfall, and opening it.'

'For the purpose of bringing forth these magical artefacts, and using them to gain godlike power over the forces of space and time?'

'Exactly,' said Magadone Sambisa.

'I think I see where this is heading.'

'Perhaps you do, majesty. We are told that he went to the site of the shattered pyramid. He drove a tunnel into the ground; he came upon the stone passageway that leads to the wall of the shrine. He found the wall and made preparations for breaking through it.'

'But the seventh shrine, you told me, is intact. Since the time of the abandonment of the city no one has ever entered it. Or so you believe.'

'No one ever has. I'm sure of that.'

'This Pontifex, then . . . ?'

'Was just at the moment of breaching the shrine wall when a Piurivar who had hidden himself in the tunnel overnight rose up out of the darkness and put a sword through his heart.'

'Wait a moment,' said Valentine. Exasperation began to stir in him. 'A Piurivar popped out of nowhere and killed him, you say? A *Piurivar*? I've just gone through this same thing with Aarisiim. Not only weren't there any Piurivars anywhere in Alhanroel at that time, because Stiamot had locked them all up in reservations over in Zimroel, but there was supposed to be a curse on this place that would have prevented members of their race from going near it.'

'Except for the guardians of the shrine, who were exempted from the curse,' said Magadone Sambisa.

'Guardians?' Valentine said. 'What guardians? I've never heard anything about Piurivar guardians here.'

'Nor had I, until Torkinuuminaad told me this story. But at the time of the city's destruction and abandonment, evidently, a decision was made to post a small band of watchmen here, so that nobody would be able to break into the seventh shrine and gain access to whatever's in there. And that guard force remained on duty here throughout the centuries. There were still guardians here when the Pontifex came to loot the shrine. One of them tucked himself away in the tunnel and killed the Pontifex just as he was about to chop through the wall.'

'And his people buried him *here*? Why in the world would they do that?'

Magadone Sambisa smiled. 'To hush things up, of course.

Consider, majesty: a Pontifex comes to Velalisier in search of forbidden mystical knowledge, and is assassinated by a Piurivar who has been sneaking around undetected in the supposedly abandoned city. If word of that got around, it would make everyone look bad.'

'I suppose that it would.'

'The Pontifical officials certainly wouldn't have wanted to let it be known that their master had been struck down right under their noses. Nor would they be eager to advertise the story of the secret shrine, which might lead others to come here looking for it too. And surely they'd never want anyone to know that the Pontifex had died at the hand of a Piurivar, something that could reopen all the wounds of the War of the Conquest and perhaps touch off some very nasty reprisals.'

'And so they covered everything up,' said Valentine.

'Exactly. They dug a tomb off in a remote corner of the ruins and buried the Pontifex in it with some sort of appropriate ritual, and went back to the Labyrinth with the news that his majesty had very suddenly been stricken down at the ruins by an unknown disease and it had seemed unwise to bring his body back from Velalisier for the usual kind of state funeral. Ghorban, was his name. There's an inscription in the tomb that names him. Ghorban Pontifex, three Pontifexes after Stiamot. He really existed. I did research in the House of Records. You'll see him listed there.'

'I'm not familiar with the name.'

'No. He's not exactly one of the famous ones. But who can remember them all, anyway? Hundreds and hundreds of them, across all those thousands of years. Ghorban was Pontifex only a short while, and the only event of any importance that occurred during his reign was something that was carefully obliterated from the records. I'm speaking of his visit to Velalisier.'

Valentine nodded. He had paused by the great screen outside the Labyrinth's House of Records often enough, and many times had stared at that long list of his predecessors, marvelling at the names of all-but-forgotten monarchs, Meyk and Spurifon and Heslaine and Kandibal and dozens more. Who must have been great men in their day, but their day was thousands of years in the past. No doubt there was a Ghorban on the list, if Magadone Sambisa said there had been: who had reigned in regal grandeur for a time as the Coronal Lord Ghorban atop Castle Mount, and then had succeeded to the Pontificate in the fulness of his years, and for some reason had paid a visit to this accursed city of Velalisier, where he died, and was buried, and fell into oblivion.

'A curious tale,' Valentine said. 'But what is there in it that would have made you want to suppress the discovery of this Ghorban's tomb?'

'The same thing that made those ancient Pontifical officials suppress the real circumstances of his death,' replied Magadone Sambisa. 'You surely know that most ordinary people already are sufficiently afraid of this city. The horrible story of the Defilement, the curse, all the talk of ghosts lurking in the ruins, the general spookiness of the place – well, you know what people are like, your majesty. How timid they can be in the face of the unknown. And I was afraid that if the Ghorban story came out – the secret shrine, the search for mysterious magical lore by some obscure ancient Pontifex, the murder of that Pontifex by a Piurivar – there'd be such public revulsion against the whole idea of excavating Velalisier that the dig would be shut down. I didn't want that to happen. That's all it was, your majesty. I was trying to preserve my own job, I suppose. Nothing more than that.'

It was a humiliating confession. Her tone, which had been vigorous enough during the telling of the tale, now was flat, weary, almost lifeless. To Valentine it had the sound of complete sincerity.

'And Dr Huukaminaam didn't agree with you that revealing the discovery of the tomb could be a threat to the continuation of your work here?'

'He saw the risk. He didn't care. For him the truth came first and foremost, always. If public opinion forced the dig to be shut down, and nobody worked here again for fifty or a hundred or five hundred years, that was all right with him. His integrity wouldn't permit hiding a startling piece of history like that, not for any reason. So we had a big battle and finally I pushed him into giving in. You've seen how stubborn I can be. But I didn't kill him. If I had wanted to kill anybody, it wouldn't have been Dr Huukaminaam. It would have been the khivanivod, who actually *does* want the dig shut down.'

'He does? You said he and Huukaminaam worked hand in glove.'

'In general, yes. As I told you yesterday, there was one area where he and Huukaminaan diverged: the issue of opening the shrine. Huukaminaan and I, you know, were planning to open it as soon as we could arrange for you and Lord Hissune to be present at the work. But the khivanivod was passionately opposed. The rest of our work here was acceptable to him, but not that. The Shrine of the Downfall, he kept saying, is the holy of holies, the most sacred Piurivar place.'

'He might just have a point there,' Valentine said.

'You also don't think we should look inside that shrine?'

'I think that there are certain important Piurivar leaders who might very much not want that to happen.'

'But the Danipiur herself has given us permission to work here! Not only that, but she and all the rest of the Piurivar leaders understand that we've come here to restore the city – that we hope to undo as much as we can of the harm that thousands of years of neglect have caused. They have no quarrel with that. But just to be completely certain that our work would give no offence to the Piurivar community, we all agreed that the expedition would consist of equal numbers of Piurivar and non-Piurivar archaeologists, and that Dr Huukaminaam and I would share the leadership on a co-equal basis.'

'Although you turned out to be somewhat more co-equal than he was when there happened to be a significant disagreement between the two of you, didn't you?'

'In that one instance of the Ghorban tomb, yes,' said Magadone Sambisa, looking just a little out of countenance. 'But only that one. He and I were in complete agreement at all times on everything else. On the issue of opening the shrine, for example.'

'A decision which the khivanivod then vetoed.'

'The khivanivod has no power to veto anything, majesty. The understanding we had was that any Piurivar who objected to some aspect of our work on religious grounds could appeal to the Danipiur, who would then adjudicate the matter in consultation with you and Lord Hissune.'

'Yes. I wrote that decree myself, actually.'

Valentine closed his eyes a moment and pressed the tips of his fingers against them. He should have realized, he told himself, that problems like these would inevitably crop up. This city had too much tragic history. Terrible things had happened here. The mysterious aura of Piurivar sorcery still hovered over the place, thousands of years after its destruction.

He had hoped to dispel some of that aura by sending in these scientists. Instead he had only enmeshed himself in its dark folds.

After a time he looked up and said, 'I understand from Aarisiim that where your khivanivod has gone to make his spiritual retreat is in fact the Ghorban tomb that you've taken such pains to hide from me, and that he's there at this very moment. Is that true?'

'I believe it is.'

The Pontifex walked to the tent entrance and peered outside. The first bronze streaks of the desert dawn were arching across the great vault of the sky.

'Last night,' he said, 'I asked you to send messengers out looking for him, and you said that you would. You didn't, of course, tell me that you knew where he was. But since you do know, get your messengers moving. I want to speak with him first thing this morning.'

'And if he refuses to come, your majesty?'

'Then have him brought.'

The khivanivod Torkinuuminaad was every bit as disagreeable as Magadone Sambisa had led Valentine to expect, although the fact that it had been necessary for Valentine's security people to threaten to drag him bodily from the Ghorban tomb must not have improved his temper. Lisamon Hultin was the one who had ordered him out of there, heedless of his threats and curses. Piurivar witcheries and spells held little dread for her, and she let him know that if he didn't go to Valentine more or less willingly on his own two feet, she would carry him to the Pontifex herself.

The Shapeshifter shaman was an ancient, emaciated man, naked but for some wisps of dried grass around his waist and a nasty-looking amulet, fashioned of interwoven insect legs and other such things, that dangled from a frayed cord about his neck. He was so old that his green skin had faded to a faint grey, and his slitted eyes, bright with rage, glared balefully at Valentine out of sagging folds of rubbery skin.

Valentine began on a conciliatory note. 'I ask your pardon for interrupting your meditations. But certain urgent matters must be dealt with before I return to the Labyrinth, and your presence was needed for that.'

Torkkinuuminaad said nothing.

Valentine proceeded regardless. 'For one thing, a serious crime has been committed in the archaeological zone. The killing of Dr Huukaminaam is an offence not only against justice but against knowledge itself. I'm here to see that the murderer is identified and punished.'

'What does this have to do with me?' asked the khivanivod, glowering sullenly. 'If there has been a murder, you should find the murderer and punish him, yes, if that is what you feel you must do. But why must a servant of the Gods That Are be compelled by force to break off his sacred communion like this? Because the Pontifex of Majipoor commands it?' Torkinuuminaad laughed harshly. 'The Pontifex! Why should the commands of the Pontifex mean anything to me? I serve only the Gods That Are.'

'You also serve the Danipiur,' said Valentine in a calm, quiet tone. 'And the Danipiur and I are colleagues in the government of Majipoor.' He indicated Magadone Sambisa and the other archaeologists, both human and Metamorph, who stood nearby. 'These people are at work in Velalisier this day because the

Danipiur has granted her permission for them to be here. You yourself are here at the Danipiur's request, I believe. To serve as spiritual counsellor for those of your people who are involved in the work.'

'I am here because the Gods That Are require me to be here, and for no other reason.'

'Be that as it may, your Pontifex stands before you, and he has questions to ask you, and you will answer.'

The shaman's only response was a sour glare.

'A shrine has been discovered near the ruins of the Seventh Pyramid,' Valentine went on. 'I understand that the late Dr Huukaminaam intended to open that shrine. You had strong objections to that, am I correct?'

'You are.'

'Objections on what grounds?'

'That the shrine is a sacred place not to be disturbed by profane hands.'

'How can there be a sacred place,' asked Valentine, 'in a city that had a curse pronounced on it?'

'The shrine is sacred nevertheless,' the khivanivod said obdurately.

'Even though no one knows what may be inside it?'

'*I* know what is inside it,' said the khivanivod.

'You? How?'

'I am the guardian of the shrine. The knowledge is handed down from guardian to guardian.'

Valentine felt a chill travelling along his spine. 'Ah,' he said. 'The guardian. Of the shrine.' He was silent a moment. 'As the officially designated successor, I suppose, of the guardian who murdered a Pontifex here once thousands of years ago. The place where you were found praying just now, so I've been told, was the tomb of that very Pontifex. Is that so?'

'It is.'

'In that case,' said Valentine, allowing a little smile to appear at the corners of his mouth, 'I need to ask my guards to keep very careful watch on you. Because the next thing I'm going to do, my friend, is to instruct Magadone Sambisa and her people to proceed at once with the opening of the seventh shrine. And I see now that that might place me in some danger at your hands.'

Torkinuuminaad looked astounded. Abruptly the Metamorph shaman began to go through a whole repertoire of violent changes of form, contracting and elongating wildly, the borders of his body blurring and recomposing with bewildering speed.

But the archaeologists too, both the human ones and the two Ghayrogs and the little tight-knit group of Shapeshifters, were staring at Valentine as though he had just said something beyond all comprehension. Even Tunigorn and Mirigant and Nascimonte were flabbergasted. Tunigorn turned to Mirigant and said something, to which Mirigant replied only with a shrug, and Nascimonte, standing near them, shrugged also in complete bafflement.

Magadone Sambisa said in hoarse choking tones, 'Majesty? Do you mean that? I thought you said only a little while ago that the best thing would be to leave the shrine unopened!'

'I said that? I?' Valentine shook his head. 'Oh, no. No. How long will it take you to get started on the job?'

'Why – let me see . . .' He heard her murmur, 'The recording devices, the lighting equipment, the masonry drills . . .' She grew quiet, as if counting additional things off in her mind. Then she said, 'We could be ready to begin in half an hour.'

'Good. Let's get going, then.'

'No! This will not be!' cried Torkinuuminaad, a wild screech of rage.

'It will,' said Valentine. 'And you'll be there to watch it. As will I.' He beckoned toward Lisamon Hultin. 'Speak with him, Lisamon. Tell him in a persuasive way that it'll be much better for him if he remains calm.'

Magadone Sambisa said, wonderingly, 'Are you serious about all this, Pontifex?'

'Oh, yes. Yes. Very serious indeed.'

The day seemed a hundred hours long.

Opening any sealed site for the first time would ordinarily have been a painstaking process. But this one was so important, so freighted with symbolic significance, so potentially explosive in its political implications, that every task was done with triple care.

Valentine waited at surface level during the early stages of the work. What they were doing down there had all been explained to him – running cables for illumination and ventilating pipes for the excavators; carefully checking with sonic probes to make sure that opening the shrine wall would not cause the ceiling of the vault to collapse; sonic testing of the interior of the shrine itself to see if there was anything important immediately behind the wall that might be imperilled by the drilling operation.

All that took hours. Finally they were ready to start cutting into the wall.

'Would you like to watch, majesty?' Magadone Sambisa asked.

Despite the ventilation equipment, Valentine found it hard work to breathe inside the tunnel. The air had been hot and stale enough on his earlier visit; but now, with all these people crowded into it, it was thin, feeble stuff, and he had to strain his lungs to keep from growing dizzy.

The close-packed archaeologists parted ranks to let him come forward. Bright lights cast a brilliant glare on the white stone façade of the shrine. Five people were gathered there, three Piurivars, two humans. The actual drilling seemed to be the responsibility of the burly foreman Vathiimeraak. Kaastisiik, the Piurivar archaeologist who was the site boss, was assisting. Just behind them was Driismiil, the Piurivar architectural expert, and a human woman named Shimrayne Gelvoin, who also was an architect, evidently. Magadone Sambisa stood to the rear, quietly issuing orders.

They were peeling the wall back stone by stone. Already an area of the façade perhaps three feet square had been cleared just above the row of offering-alcoves. Behind it lay rough brickwork, no more than one course thick. Vathiimeraak, muttering to himself in Piurivar as he worked, now was chiselling away at one of the bricks. It came loose in a crumbling mass, revealing an inner wall made of the same fine black stone slabs as the tunnel wall itself.

A long pause, now, while the several layers of the wall were measured and photographed. Then Vathiimeraak resumed the inward probing. Valentine was at the edge of queasiness in this foul, acrid atmosphere, but he forced it back.

Vathiimeraak cut deeper, halting to allow Kaastisiik to remove some broken pieces of the black stone. The two architects came forward and inspected the opening, conferring first with each other, then with Magadone Sambisa; and then Vathiimeraak stepped towards the breach once again with his drilling tool.

'We need a torch,' Magadone Sambisa said suddenly. 'Give me a torch, someone!'

A hand-torch was passed up the line from the crowd in the rear of the tunnel. Magadone Sambisa thrust it into the opening, peered, gasped.

'Majesty? Majesty, would you come and look?'

By that single shaft of light Valentine made out a large rectangular room, which appeared to be completely empty except for a large square block of dark stone. It was very much like the glossy block of black opal, streaked with veins of scarlet ruby, from which the glorious Confalume Throne at the castle of the Coronal had been carved.

There were things lying on that block. But what they were was impossible to tell at this distance.

'How long will it take to make an opening big enough for someone to enter the room?' Valentine asked.

'Three hours, maybe.'

'Do it in two. I'll wait aboveground. You call me when the opening is made. Be certain that no one enters it before me.'

'You have my word, majesty.'

Even the dry desert air was a delight after an hour or so of breathing the dank stuff below. Valentine could see by the lengthening shadows creeping across the deep sockets of the distant dunes that the afternoon was well along. Tunigorn, Mirigant, and Nascimonte were pacing about amidst the rubble of the fallen pyramid. The Vroon Deliamber stood a little distance apart.

'Well?' Tunigorn asked.

'They've got a little bit of the wall open. There's something inside, but we don't know what, yet.'

'Treasure?' Tunigorn asked, with a lascivious grin. 'Mounds of emeralds and diamonds and jade?'

'Yes,' said Valentine. 'All that and more. Treasure. An enormous treasure, Tunigorn.' He chuckled and turned away. 'Do you have any wine with you, Nascimonte?'

'As ever, my friend. A fine Muldemar vintage.'

He handed his flask to the Pontifex, who drank deep, not pausing to savour the bouquet at all, guzzling as though the wine were water.

The shadows deepened. One of the lesser moons crept into the margin of the sky.

'Majesty? Would you come below?'

It was the archaeologist Vo-Siimifon. Valentine followed him into the tunnel.

The opening in the wall was large enough now to admit one person. Magadone Sambisa, her hand trembling, handed Valentine the torch.

'I must ask you, your majesty, to touch nothing, to make no disturbance whatever. We will not deny you the privilege of first entry, but you must bear in mind that this is a scientific enterprise. We have to record everything just as we find it before anything, however trivial, can be moved.'

'I understand,' said Valentine.

He stepped carefully over the section of the wall below the opening and clambered in.

The shrine's floor was of some smooth glistening stone, perhaps rosy quartz. A fine layer of dust covered it. No one has walked across this floor for twenty thousand years, Valentine thought. No human foot has ever come in contact with it at all.

He approached the broad block of black stone in the centre of the room and turned the torch full on it. Yes, a single dark mass of ruby-streaked opal, just like the Confalume Throne. Atop it, with only the faintest tracery of dust concealing its brilliance, lay a flat sheet of gold, engraved with intricate Piurivar glyphs and inlaid with cabochons of what looked like beryl and carnelian and lapis lazuli. Two long, slender objects that could have been daggers carved from some white stone lay precisely in the centre of the gold sheet, side by side.

Valentine felt a tremor of the deepest awe. He knew what those two things were.

'Majesty? Majesty?' Magadone Sambisa called. 'Tell us what you see! Tell us, please!'

But Valentine did not reply. It was as though Magadone Sambisa had not spoken. He was deep in memory, travelling back eight years to the climactic hour of the War of the Rebellion.

He had, in that hour, held in his hand a dagger-like thing much like these two, and had felt the strange coolness of it, a coolness that gave a hint of a fiery core within, and had heard a complex far-off music emanating from it into his mind, a turbulent rush of dizzying sound.

It had been the tooth of a sea-dragon that he had been grasping then. Some mystery within that tooth had placed his mind in communion with the mind of the mighty water-king Maazmoorn, a dragon of the distant Inner Sea. And with the aid of the mind of Maazmoorn had Valentine Pontifex reached across the world to strike down the unrepentant rebel Faraataa and bring that sorry uprising to an end.

Whose teeth were these, now?

He thought he knew. This was the Shrine of the Downfall, the Place of the Defilement. Not far from here, long ago, two water-kings had been brought from the sea to be sacrificed on platforms of blue stone. That was no myth. It had actually happened. Valentine had no doubt of that, for the sea-dragon Maazmoorn had shown it to him with the full communion of his mind, in a manner that admitted of no question. He knew their names, even: one was the water-king Niznorn and the other the water-king Domsitor. Was this tooth here Niznorn's, and this one Domsitor's?

Twenty thousand years.

'Majesty? Majesty?'

'One moment,' Valentine said, speaking as though from half-way around the world.

He picked up the left-hand tooth. Grasped it tightly. Hissed as its fiery chill stung the palm of his hand. Closed his eyes, allowed his mind to be pervaded by its magic. Felt his spirit beginning to soar outward and outward and outward, towards some waiting dragon of the sea – Maazmoorn again, for all he could know, or perhaps some other one of the giants who swam in those waters out there – while all the time he heard the sounding bells, the tolling music of that sea-dragon's mind.

And was granted a vision of the ancient sacrifice of the two water-kings, the event known as the Defilement.

He already knew, from Maazmoorn in that meeting of minds years ago, that the traditional name was a misnomer. There had been no defilement whatever. It had been a voluntary sacrifice; it had been the formal acceptance by the sea-dragons of the power of That Which Is, which is the highest of all the forces of the universe.

The water-kings had given themselves gladly to those Piurivars of long-ago Velalisier to be slain. The slayers themselves had understood what they were doing, perhaps, but the simple Piurivars of the outlying provinces had not; and so those simpler Piurivars had called it a Defilement, and had put the Final King of Velalisier to death and smashed the Seventh Pyramid and then had wrecked all the rest of this great capital, and had laid a curse on the city for ever. But the shrine of these teeth they had not dared to touch.

Valentine, holding the tooth, beheld the sacrifice once more. Not with the bound sea-dragons writhing in fury as they were brought to the knife, the way he had seen it in his nightmare of the previous night. No. He saw it now as a serene and holy ceremony, a benign yielding up of the living flesh. And as the knives flashed, as the great sea-creatures died, as their dark flesh was carried to the pyres for burning, a resounding wave of triumphant harmony went rolling out to the boundaries of the universe.

He put the tooth down and picked up the other one. Grasped. Felt. Surrendered himself to its power.

This time the music was more discordant. The vision that

came to him was that of some unknown man of middle years, garbed in a rich costume of antique design, clothing befitting a Pontifex. He was moving cautiously by the smoky light of a flickering torch down the very passageway outside this room where Magadone Sambisa and her archaeologists now clustered. Valentine watched that Pontifex of long ago approaching the white unsullied wall of the shrine. Saw him press the flat of his hand against it, pushing as though he hoped to penetrate it by his own strength alone. Turning from it, then, beckoning to workmen with picks and spades, indicating that they should start hacking their way through it.

And a figure uncoiling out of the darkness, a Shapeshifter, long and lean and grim-faced, taking one great step forward and in a swift unstoppable lunge driving a knife upward and inward beneath the heart of the man in the brocaded Pontifical robes –

'Majesty, I beg you!'

Magadone Sambisa's voice, ripe with anguish.

'Yes,' said Valentine, in the distant tone of one who has been lost in a dream. 'I'm coming.'

He had had enough visions, for the moment. He set the torch down on the floor, aiming it towards the opening in the wall to light his way. Carefully he picked up the two dragon teeth – letting them rest easily on the palms of his hands, taking care not to touch them so tightly as to activate their powers, for he did not want now to open his mind to them – and made his way back out of the shrine.

Magadone Sambisa stared at him in horror. 'I asked you, your majesty, not to touch the objects in the vault, not to cause any disturbance to –'

'Yes. I know that. You will pardon me for what I have done.'

It was not a request.

The archaeologists melted back out of his way as he strode through their midst, heading for the exit to the upper world. Every eye was turned to the things that rested on Valentine's upturned hands.

'Bring the khivanivod to me here,' he said quietly to Aarisiim.

The light of day was nearly gone now, and the ruins were taking on the greater mysteriousness that came over them by night, when moonlight's cool gleam danced across the shattered city's ancient stones.

The Shapeshifter went rushing away. Valentine had not wanted the khivanivod anywhere near the shrine while the opening of the wall was taking place; and so, over his violent objections, Torkkinuuminaad had been bundled off to the archaeologists' headquarters in the custody of some of Valentine's security people. The two immense woolly Skandars brought him forth now, holding him by the arms.

Anger and hatred were bubbling up from the shaman like black gas rising from a churning marsh. And, staring into that jagged green wedge of a face, Valentine had a powerful sense of the ancient magic of this world, of mysteries reaching towards him out of the timeless misty Majipoor dawn, when Shapeshifters had moved alone and unhindered through this great planet of marvels and splendours.

The Pontifex held the two sea-dragon teeth aloft.

'Do you know what these are, Torkkinuuminaad?'

The rubbery eye-folds drew back. The narrow eyes were yellow with rage. 'You have committed the most terrible of all sacrileges, and you will die in the most terrible of agonies.'

'So you do know what they are, eh?'

'They are the holiest of holies! You must return them to the shrine at once!'

'Why did you have Dr Huukaminaan killed, Torkkinuuminaad?'

The khivanivod's only answer was an even more furiously defiant glare.

He would kill me with his magic, if he could, thought Valentine. And why not? I know what I represent to Torkkinuuminaad. For I am Majipoor's emperor and therefore I am Majipoor itself, and if one thrust would send us all to our doom he would strike that thrust.

Yes. Valentine was in his own person the embodiment of the Enemy: of those who had come out of the sky and taken the world away from the Piurivars, who had built their own gigantic sprawling cities over virgin forests and glades, had intruded themselves by the billions into the fragile fabric of the Piurivars' trembling web of life. And so Torkkinuuminaad would kill him, if he could, and by killing the Pontifex kill, by the symbolism of magic, all of human-dominated Majipoor.

But magic can be fought with magic, Valentine thought.

'Yes, look at me,' he told the shaman. 'Look right into my eyes, Torkkinuuminaad.'

And let his fingers close tightly about the two talismans he had taken from the shrine.

The double force of the teeth struck into Valentine with a staggering impact as he closed the mental circuit. He felt the full range of the sensations all at once, not simply doubled, but multiplied many times over. He held himself upright nevertheless; he focused his concentration with the keenest intensity; he aimed his mind directly at that of the khivanivod.

Looked. Entered. Penetrated the khivanivod's memories and quickly found what he was seeking.

Midnight darkness. A sliver of moonlight. The sky ablaze with stars. The billowing tent of the archaeologists. Someone coming out of it, a Piurivar, very thin, moving with the caution of age.

Dr Huukaminaam, surely.

A slender figure stands in the road, waiting: another Metamorph, also old, just as gaunt, raggedly and strangely dressed.

The khivanivod, that one is. Viewing himself in his own mind's eye.

Shadowy figures moving about behind him, five, six, seven of them. Shapeshifters all. Villagers, from the looks of them. The old archaeologist does not appear to see them. He speaks with the khivanivod; the shaman gestures, points. There is a discussion of some sort. Dr Huukaminaam shakes his head. More pointing. More discussion. Gestures of agreement. Everything seems to be resolved.

As Valentine watches, the khivanivod and Huukaminaam start off together down the road that leads to the heart of the ruins.

The villagers, now, emerging from the shadows that have concealed them. Surrounding the old man; seizing him; covering his mouth to keep him from crying out. The khivanivod approaches him.

The khivanivod has a knife.

Valentine did not need to see the rest of the scene. Did not *want* to see that monstrous ceremony of dismemberment at the stone platform, nor the weird ritual afterward in the excavation leading to the Shrine of the Downfall, the placing of the dead man's head in that alcove.

He released his grasp on the two sea-dragon teeth and set them down with great care beside him on the ground.

'Now,' he said to the khivanivod, whose expression had changed from one of barely controllable wrath to one that might almost have been resignation. 'There's no need for further pretending here, I think. Why did you kill Dr Huukaminaan?'

'Because he would have opened the shrine.' The khivanivod's tone was completely flat, no emotion in it at all.

'Yes. Of course. But Magadone Sambisa also was in favour of opening it. Why not kill her instead?'

'He was one of us, and a traitor,' said Torkinuuminaad. 'She did not matter. And he was more dangerous to our cause. We know that she might have been prevented from opening the shrine, if we objected strongly enough. But nothing would stop him.'

'The shrine was opened anyway, though,' Valentine said.

'Yes, but only because you came here. Otherwise the excavations would have been closed down. The outcry over Huukaminaan's death would demonstrate to the whole world that the curse of this place still had power. You came, and you opened the shrine; but the curse will strike you just as it struck the Pontifex Ghorban long ago.'

'There is no curse,' Valentine said calmly. 'This is a city that has seen much tragedy, but there is no curse, only misunderstanding piled on misunderstanding.'

'The Defilement –'

'There was no Defilement either, only a sacrifice. The destruction of the city by the people of the provinces was a vast mistake.'

'So you understand our history better than we do, Pontifex?'

'Yes,' said Valentine. 'Yes. I do.' He turned away from the shaman and said, glancing towards the village foreman, 'Vathiimeraak, there are murderers living in your settlement. I know who they are. Go to the village now and announce to everyone that if the guilty ones will come forward and confess their crime, they'll be pardoned after they undergo a full cleansing of their souls.'

Turning next to Lisamon Hultin, he said, 'As for the khivanivod, I want him handed over to the Danipiur's officials to be tried in her own courts. This falls within her area of responsibility. And then –'

'Majesty!' someone called. 'Beware!'

Valentine swung around. The Skandar guards had stepped back from the khivanivod and were staring at their own trembling hands as though they had been burned in a fiery furnace. Torkinuuminaad, freed of their grasp, thrust his face up into Valentine's. His expression was one of diabolical intensity.

'Pontifex!' he whispered. 'Look at me, Pontifex! Look at me!'

Taken by surprise, Valentine had no way of defending himself. Already a strange numbness had come over him. Torkinuuminaad was shifting shape, now, running through a series of grotesque changes at a frenzied rate, so that he appeared to have a dozen arms and legs at once, and half a dozen bodies; and he was casting some sort of spell. Valentine was caught in it like a moth in a spider's cunningly woven strands. The air seemed thick and blurred before him, and a wind had come up out of nowhere. Valentine stood perplexed, trying to force his gaze away from the khivanivod's fiery eyes, but he could not. Nor could he find the strength to reach down and seize hold of the two dragon teeth that lay at his feet. He stood as though frozen, muddled, dazed, tottering. There was a burning sensation in his breast and it was a struggle simply to draw breath.

There seemed to be phantoms all around him.

A dozen Shapeshifters – a hundred, a thousand –

Grimacing faces. Glowering eyes. Teeth; claws; knives. A horde of wildly cavorting assassins surrounded him, dancing, bobbing, gyrating, hissing, mocking him, calling his name derisively –

He was lost in a whirlwind of ancient sorceries.

'Lisamon?' Valentine cried, baffled. 'Deliamber? Help me – help –' But he was not sure that the words had actually escaped his lips.

Then he saw that his guardians had indeed perceived his danger. Deliamber, the first to react, came rushing forward, flinging his own many tentacles up hastily in a counter-spell, a set of gesticulations and thrusts of mental force intended to neutralize whatever was emanating from Torkkinuuminaad. And then, as the little Vroon began to wrap the Piurivar shaman in his web of Vroonish wizardry, Vathiimeraak advanced on Torkkinuuminaad from the opposite side, boldly seizing the shaman in complete indifference to his spells, forcing him down to the ground, bending him until his forehead was pressing against the soil at Valentine's feet.

Valentine felt the grip of the shaman's wizardry beginning to ebb, then easing further, finally losing its last remaining hold on his soul. The contact between Torkkinuuminaad's mind and his gave way with an almost audible snap.

Vathiimeraak released the khivanivod and stepped back. Lisamon Hultin now came to the shaman's side and stood menacingly over him. But the episode was over. The shaman remained where he was, absolutely still now, staring at the ground, scowling bitterly in defeat.

'Thank you,' Valentine said simply to Deliamber and Vathiimeraak. And, with a dismissive gesture: 'Take him away.'

Lisamon Hultin threw Torkkinuuminaad over her shoulder like a sack of calimbots and went striding off down the road.

A long stunned silence followed. Magadone Sambisa broke it, finally. In a hushed voice she said, 'Your majesty, are you all right?'

He answered only with a nod.

'And the excavations,' she said anxiously, after another moment. 'What will happen to them? Will they continue?'

'Why not?' Valentine replied. 'There's still much work to be done.' He took a step or two away from her. He touched his hands to his chest, to his throat. He could still almost feel the pressure of those relentless invisible hands.

Magadone Sambisa was not finished with him, though.

'And these?' she asked, indicating the sea-dragon teeth. She spoke more aggressively now, taking charge of things once again, beginning to recover her vigour and poise. 'If I may have them now, majesty –'

Angrily Valentine said, 'Take them, yes. But put them back in the shrine. And then seal up the hole you made today.'

The archaeologist stared at him as though he had turned into a Piurivar himself. With a note of undisguised asperity in her voice she said, 'What, your majesty? What? Dr Huukaminaan died for those teeth! Finding that shrine was the pinnacle of his work. If we seal it up now –'

'Dr Huukaminaan was the perfect scientist,' Valentine said, not troubling to conceal his great weariness now. 'His love of the truth cost him his life. Your own love of truth, I think, is less than perfect, and therefore you will obey me in this.'

'I beg you, majesty –'

'No. Enough begging. I don't pretend to be a scientist at all, but I understand my own responsibilities. Some things should remain buried. These teeth are not things for us to handle and study and put on display at a museum. The shrine is a holy place to the Piurivars, even if they don't understand its own holiness. It's a sad business for us all that it ever was uncovered. The dig itself can continue, in other parts of the city. But put these back. Seal that shrine and stay away from it. Understood?'

She looked at him numbly, and nodded.

'Good. Good.'

The full descent of darkness was settling upon the desert now. Valentine could feel the myriad ghosts of Velalisier hovering around him. It seemed that bony fingers were plucking at his tunic, that eerie whispering voices were murmuring perilous magics in his ears.

Most heartily he yearned to be quit of these ruins. He had had all he cared to have of them for one lifetime.

To Tunigorn he said, 'Come, old friend, give the orders, make things ready for our immediate departure.'

'Now, Valentine? At this late hour?'

'Now, Tunigorn. Now.' He smiled. 'Do you know, this place has made the Labyrinth seem almost appealing to me! I feel a great desire to return to its familiar comforts. Come: get everything organized for leaving. We've been here quite long enough.'

Earthsea

URSULA K. LE GUIN

EARTHSEA

URSULA K. LE GUIN

A Wizard of Earthsea (1968)
The Tombs of Atuan (1971)
The Farthest Shore (1972)
Tehanu: The Last Book of Earthsea (1990)

The island world of Earthsea is inhabited by human beings and by dragons. The dragons are aloof and dangerous creatures, whose native tongue is the Language of the Making. Some events and stories (in *Tehanu*) suggest that there was a time when dragons and human beings were all one kind, but they have long been divided and unfriendly. Among the human beings, magic is a gift with which some people are born, but which must also be learned as an art or science. Essential to the practice of magic is learning at least some words of the Language of the Making, in which things are given their true names. By learning the true name, the witch or wizard gains power over the thing or the person. Power, of course, may be used for good or for ill.

A Wizard of Earthsea opens on Gont Island. Ged, a young peasant boy with a great gift of magic, goes to the School for Wizards on Roke Island. There, attempting to prove his superiority to another boy, he brings a shadow-being from the realm of the dead into the world of the living. This shadow hunts him through the islands, driving him always towards danger and evil. At last, guided by his old teacher Ogion, he turns on it, and pursues it on a desperate course that leads him out of the world across the barrier of death. There Ged and his shadow, confronting each other, find that they are one; and thus Ged's being is healed and made whole.

The Tombs of Atuan is set on one of the four islands of the Kargish people, whose language and customs are different from those of the Archipelagans. A child named Tenar is taken from her parents, renamed Arha, 'the Eaten One', and trained as the High Priestess of the Tombs, an ancient desert sanctuary in Atuan, where only women and eunuchs may come. When she is near the end of her training, she comes upon a stranger, a man, in the underground Labyrinth, the heart of the sacred place. This is Ged, now a powerful wizard, seeking the missing half of the Ring of Erreth-Akbe, on which is engraved the broken Rune of Peace. The young priestess's duty is to kill him. Talking with her prisoner, she begins to see that she herself is a prisoner in the Tombs, bound by a meaningless and cruel ritual. Ged gives her back her true name, Tenar. As he has freed her, she frees him: she leads him out of the Labyrinth, and the two escape with the reunited Ring of Peace. Tenar is honoured in Havnor, the City of the Kings of Earthsea, but Ged will take her to live and study with his old master Ogion, on Gont.

In *The Farthest Shore*, Ged, now Archmage of Roke and the most powerful man in the Archipelago, goes with young Arren, Prince of Enlad, on a quest to find why magic seems to be losing its power. After strange adventures far in the south, they are led to the dragons' islands; and on Selidor, the westernmost of them all, their quest takes them into the realm of death, the dry land of darkness. There they find the wizard Cob, who, desiring immortality for himself, has breached the wall between life and death. Ged takes Cob's power from him and closes the wound in the world, but it takes all his own power to do so. Arren, who will inherit the throne of Earthsea, empty for five centuries, leads him back into life. The dragon Kalessin carries them both to Roke, where Ged salutes Arren as king; then Kalessin bears him home to Gont Island.

Tehanu, though written seventeen years after *The Farthest Shore*, takes up the story where it ended. Tenar of the Tombs did not stay with Ogion but married a farmer, Flint, had two children, and has lived these thirty years as a farm woman. Dying, Ogion sends for her. She stays on at the old mage's house after his death. With her is her adopted daughter. This girl, Therru, who was raped and burned and left for dead by the men who travelled with her mother, is a silent child full of fear and uncomprehended power. The dragon brings Ged to Gont. Worn out and ill, having lost all his powers of magic, Ged is full of shame, and hides even from Arren, who comes seeking him. Aspen, a disciple of Cob, brews evil magic on Gont; Handy, one of the men who abused the child Therru, keeps hanging around. The young king takes Tenar back to her husband's farm. There Handy and the others try to get at Tenar and the child; Ged comes in time to help her fight them off. That winter Ged stays with Tenar at the farm, and though he has lost his power as a mage, he finds at last his power as a sexual human being. In the spring, Aspen lures Ged and Tenar back to Ogion's house, and since they cannot work magic they have no defence against him. He humiliates them and is about to kill them. Now the disfigured, powerless child Therru finds her true name, Tehanu, and her own power. She summons the dragon Kalessin in the dragons' speech, the Language of the Making. The dragon destroys Aspen, and greets Therru as a daughter. She will live with Ged and Tenar now, but will live with the dragons later: 'I give you my child,' Kalessin says to Ged, 'as you will give me yours.'

$\blacklozenge$

Dragonfly

BY URSULA K. LE GUIN

1. Iria

Her father's ancestors had owned a wide, rich domain on the wide, rich island of Way. Claiming no title or court privilege in the days of the kings, through all the dark years after Maharion fell they held their land and people with firm hands, putting their gains back into the land, upholding some sort of justice, and fighting off petty tyrants. As order and peace returned to the Archipelago under the sway of the wise men of Roke, for a while yet the family and their farms and villages prospered. That prosperity and the beauty of the meadows and upland pastures and oak-crowned hills made the domain a byword, so that people said, 'as fat as a cow of Iria', or, 'as lucky as an Irian'. The masters and many tenants of the domain added its name to their own, calling themselves Irian. But though the farmers and shepherds went on from season to season and year to year and generation to generation as solid and steady as the oaks, the family that owned the land altered with time and chance.

A quarrel between brothers over their inheritance divided them. One heir mismanaged his estate through greed, the other through foolishness. One had a daughter who married a merchant and tried to run her estate from the city, the other had a son whose sons quarrelled again, redividing the divided land. By the time the girl called Dragonfly was born, the domain of Iria, though still one of the loveliest regions of hill and field and meadow in all Earthsea, was a battleground of feuds and litigations. Farmlands went to weeds, farmsteads went unroofed, milking sheds stood unused, and shepherds followed their flocks over the mountain to better pastures. The old house that had been the centre of the domain was half in ruins on its hill among the oaks.

Its owner was one of four men who called themselves Master of Iria. The other three called him Master of Old Iria. He spent his youth and what remained of his inheritance in law courts and the anterooms of the Lords of Way in Shelieth, trying to prove his right to the whole domain as it had been a hundred years ago. He came back unsuccessful and embittered and spent his age drinking the hard red wine from his last vineyard and walking his boundaries with a troop of ill-treated, underfed dogs to keep interlopers off his land.

He had married while he was in Shelieth, a woman no one at Iria knew anything about, for she came from some other island, it was said, somewhere in the west, and she never came to Iria, for she died in childbirth there in the city. When he came home he had a three-year-old daughter with him. He turned her over to the housekeeper and forgot about her. When he was drunk sometimes he remembered her. If he could find her, he made her stand by his chair or sit on his knees and listen to all the wrongs that had been done to him and to the house of Iria. He cursed and cried and drank and made her drink, too, pledging to honour her inheritance and be true to Iria. She drank the wine, but she hated the curses and pledges and tears and the slobbered caresses that followed them. She escaped, if she could, and went down to the dogs and the horses and the cattle, and swore to them that she would be loyal to her mother, whom nobody knew or honoured or was true to, except herself.

When she was thirteen the old vineyarder and the house-keeper, who were all that was left of the household, told the Master that it was time his daughter had her naming day. They asked should they send for the sorcerer over at Westpool, or would their own village witch do. The Master of Iria fell into a screaming rage. 'A village witch? A hex-hag to give Irian's daughter her true name? Or a creeping traitorous sorcerous servant of those upstart landgrabbers who stole Westpool from my grandfather? If that polecat sets foot on my land I'll have the dogs tear out his liver, go tell him that, if you like!' And so on. Old Daisy went back to her kitchen and old Coney went back to his vines, and thirteen-year-old Dragonfly ran out of the house and down the hill to the village, hurling her father's curses at the dogs, who, crazy with excitement at his shouting, barked and bayed and rushed after her. 'Get back, you black-hearted bitch!' she yelled. 'Home, you crawling traitor!' And the dogs fell silent and went sidling back to the house with their tails down.

Dragonfly found the village witch taking maggots out of an infected cut on a sheep's rump. The witch's use-name was Rose, like a great many women of Way and other islands of the Hardic Archipelago. People who have a secret name that holds their power the way a diamond holds light may well like their public name to be ordinary, common, like other people's names.

Rose was muttering a rote spell, but it was her hands and her little short sharp knife that did most of the work. The ewe bore the digging knife patiently, her opaque, amber, slotted eyes gazing into silence; only she stamped her small left front foot now and then, and sighed. Dragonfly peered close at Rose's work. Rose brought out a maggot, dropped it, spat on it, and probed again. The girl leaned up against the ewe, and the ewe leaned against the girl, giving and receiving comfort. Rose extracted, dropped, and spat on the last maggot, and said, 'Just hand me that bucket now.' She bathed the sore with salt water. The ewe sighed deeply and suddenly walked out of the yard, heading for home. She had had enough of medicine. 'Bucky!' Rose shouted. A grubby child appeared from under a bush where he had been asleep and trailed after the ewe, of whom he was nominally in charge although she was older, larger, better fed, and probably wiser than he was.

'They said you should give me my name,' said Dragonfly. 'Father fell to raging. So that's that.'

The witch said nothing. She knew the girl was right. Once the Master of Iria said he would or would not allow a thing he never changed his mind, priding himself on his intransigence, since only weak men said a thing and then unsaid it.

'Why can't I give myself my own true name?' Dragonfly asked, while Rose washed the knife and her hands in the salt water.

'Can't be done.'

'Why not? Why does it have to be a witch or a sorcerer? What do you *do*?'

'Well,' Rose said, and dumped out the salt water on the bare dirt of the small front yard of her house, which, like most witches' houses, stood somewhat apart from the village. 'Well,' she said, straightening up and looking about vaguely as if for an answer, or a ewe, or a towel. 'You have to know something about the power, see,' she said at last, and looked at Dragonfly with one eye. Her other eye looked a little off to the side. Sometimes Dragonfly thought the cast was in Rose's left eye, sometimes it seemed to be in her right, but always one eye looked straight and the other watched something just out of sight, around the corner, elsewhere.

'Which power?'

'The one,' Rose said. As suddenly as the ewe had walked off, she went into her house. Dragonfly followed her, but only to the door. Nobody entered a witch's house uninvited.

'You said I had it,' the girl said into the reeking gloom of the one-roomed hut.

'I said you have a strength in you, a great one,' the witch said from the darkness. 'And you know it too. What you are to do I don't know, nor do you. That's to find. But there's no such power as to name yourself.'

'Why not? What's more yourself than your own true name?'

A long silence.

The witch emerged with a soapstone drop-spindle and a ball of greasy wool. She sat down on the bench beside her door and set the spindle turning. She had spun a yard of grey-brown yarn before she answered.

'My name's myself. True. But what's a name, then? It's what another calls me. If there was no other, only me, what would I want a name for?'

'But,' said Dragonfly and stopped, caught by the argument. After a while she said, 'So a name has to be a gift?'

Rose nodded.

'Give me my name, Rose,' the girl said.

'Your dad says not.'

'I say to.'

'He's the Master here.'

'He can keep me poor and stupid and worthless, but he can't keep me nameless!'

The witch sighed, like the ewe, uneasy and constrained.

'Tonight,' Dragonfly said. 'At our spring, under Iria Hill. What he doesn't know won't hurt him.' Her voice was half-coaxing, half-savage.

'You ought to have your proper name day, your feast and dancing, like any young 'un,' the witch said. 'It's at daybreak a name should be given. And then there ought to be music and feasting and all. Not sneaking about at night and no one knowing . . .'

'I'll know. How do you know what name to say, Rose? Does the water tell you?'

The witch shook her iron-grey head once. 'I can't tell you.' Her 'can't' did not mean 'won't'. Dragonfly waited. 'It's the power, like I said. It comes just so.' Rose stopped her spinning and looked up with one eye at a cloud in the west; the other looked a little northward of the sky. 'You're there in the water, together, you and the child. You take away the child-name. People may go on using that name for a use-name, but it's not her name, nor ever was. So now she's not a child, and she has no name. So then you wait. You open your mind up, like. Like opening the doors of a house to the wind. So it comes. Your tongue speaks it, the name. Your breath makes it. You give it to that child, the breath, the name. You can't think of it. You let it come to you. It must come through you to her it belongs to. That's the power, the way it works. It's all like that. It's not a thing you do. You have to know how to let it do. That's all the mastery.'

'Mages can do more than that,' the girl said.

'Nobody can do more than that,' said Rose.

Dragonfly rolled her head round on her neck, stretching till the vertebrae cracked, stretching out her long arms and legs restlessly. 'Will you?' she said.

Rose nodded once.

They met in the lane under Iria Hill in the dark of night, long after sunset, long before dawn. Rose made a dim glow of werelight so that they could find their way through the marshy ground around the spring without falling in a sinkhole among the reeds. In the cold darkness under a few stars and the black curve of the hill, they stripped and waded into the shallow water, their feet sinking deep in velvet mud. The witch touched the girl's hand, saying, 'I take your name, child. You are no child. You have no name.'

It was utterly still.

In a whisper the witch said, 'Woman, be named. You are Irian.'

For a moment longer they held still; then the night wind blew across their naked shoulders, and shivering, they waded out, dried themselves as well as they could, struggled barefoot and wretched through the sharp-edged reeds and tangling roots, and found their way back to the lane. And there Dragonfly spoke in a ragged, raging whisper: 'How could you name me that!'

The witch said nothing.

'It isn't right. It isn't my true name! I thought my name would make me be me. But this makes it worse. You got it wrong. You're only a witch. You did it wrong. It's *his* name. He can have it. He's so proud of it, his stupid domain, his stupid grandfather. I don't want it. I won't have it. It isn't me. I still don't know who I am. I'm not Irian!' She fell silent abruptly, having spoken the name.

The witch still said nothing. They walked along in the darkness side by side. At last, in a placating, frightened voice, Rose said, 'It came so . . .'

'If you ever tell it to anyone I'll kill you,' Dragonfly said.

At that, the witch stopped walking. She hissed like a cat. '*Tell* anyone?'

Dragonfly stopped too. She said after a moment, 'I'm sorry. But I feel like – I feel like you betrayed me.'

'I spoke your true name. It's not what I thought it would be. And I don't feel easy about it. As if I'd left something unfinished. But it is your name. If it betrays you, then that's the truth of it.' Rose hesitated and then spoke less angrily, more coldly: 'If you want the power to betray me, Irian, I'll give you that. My name is Etaudis.'

The wind had come up again. They were both shivering, their teeth chattering. They stood face to face in the black lane, hardly able to see where the other was. Dragonfly put out her groping hand and met the witch's hand. They put their arms round each other in a fierce, long embrace. Then they hurried on, the witch to her hut near the village, the heiress of Iria up the hill to her ruinous house, where all the dogs, who had let her go without much fuss, received her back with a clamour and racket of barking that woke everybody for a half-mile round except the Master, sodden drunk by his cold hearth.

2. Ivory

The Master of Iria of Westpool, Birch, didn't own the old house, but he did own the central and richest lands of the old domain. His father, more interested in vines and orchards than in quarrels with his relatives, had left Birch a thriving property. Birch hired men to manage the farms and wineries and cooperage and cartage and all, while he enjoyed his wealth. He married the timid daughter of the younger brother of the Lord of Wayfirth, and took infinite pleasure in thinking that his daughters were of noble blood. The fashion of the time among the nobility was to have a wizard in their service, a genuine wizard with a staff and a grey cloak, trained on the Isle of the Wise, and so the Master of Iria of Westpool got himself a wizard from Roke. He was surprised how easy it was to get one, if you paid the price.

The young man, called Ivory, did not actually have his staff and cloak yet; he explained that he was to be made wizard when he went back to Roke. The Masters had sent him out in the world to gain experience, for all the classes in the School cannot give a man the experience he needs to be a wizard. Birch looked a little dubious at this, and Ivory reassured him that his training on Roke had equipped him with every kind of magic that could be needed in Iria of Westpool on Way. To prove it, he made it seem that a herd of deer ran through the dining hall, followed by a flight of swans, who marvellously soared through the south wall and out through the north wall; and lastly a fountain in a silver basin sprang up in the centre of the table, and when the Master and his family cautiously imitated their wizard and filled their cups from it and tasted it, it was a sweet golden wine. 'Wine of the Andrades,' said the young man with a modest, complacent smile. By then the wife and daughters were entirely won over. And Birch thought the young man was worth his fee, although his own silent preference was for the dry red Fanian of his own vineyards, which got you drunk if you drank enough, while this yellow stuff was just honeywater.

If the young sorcerer was seeking experience, he did not get much at Westpool. Whenever Birch had guests from Kembermouth or from neighbouring domains, the herd of deer, the swans, and the fountain of golden wine made their appearance. He also worked up some very pretty fireworks for warm spring evenings. But if the managers of the orchards and vineyards came to the Master to ask if his wizard might put a spell of increase on the pears this year or maybe charm the black rot off the Fanian vines on the south hill, Birch said, 'A wizard of Roke doesn't lower himself to such stuff. Go tell the village sorcerer to earn his keep!' And when the youngest daughter came down with a wasting cough, Birch's wife dared not trouble the wise young man about it, but sent humbly to Rose of Old Iria, asking her to come in by the back door and maybe make a poultice or sing a chant to bring the girl back to health. Ivory never noticed that the girl was ailing, nor the pear trees, nor the vines. He kept himself to himself, as a man of craft and learning should. He spent his days riding about the countryside on the pretty black mare that his employer had given him for his use when he made it clear that he had not come from Roke to trudge about on foot in the mud and dust of country byways.

On his rides, he sometimes passed an old house on a hill among great oaks. When he turned off the village lane up the hill, a pack of scrawny, evil-mouthed dogs came pelting and bellowing down at him. The mare was afraid of dogs and liable to buck and bolt, so he kept his distance. But he had an eye for beauty, and liked to look at the old house dreaming away in the dappled light of the early summer afternoons.

He asked Birch about the place. 'That's Iria,' Birch said – 'Old Iria, I mean to say. I own the house by rights. But after a century of feuds and fights over it, my granddad let the place go to settle the quarrel. Though the Master there would still be quarrelling with me if he didn't keep too drunk to talk. Haven't seen the old man for years. He had a daughter, I think.'

'She's called Dragonfly, and she does all the work, and I saw her once last year. She's tall, and as beautiful as a flowering tree,' said the youngest daughter, Rose, who was busy crowding a lifetime of keen observation into the fourteen years that were all she was going to have for it. She broke off, coughing. Her mother shot an anguished, yearning glance at the wizard. Surely he would hear that cough, this time? He smiled at young Rose, and the mother's heart lifted. Surely he wouldn't smile so if Rose's cough was anything serious?

'Nothing to do with us, that lot at the old place,' Birch said, displeased. The tactful Ivory asked no more. But he wanted to see the girl as beautiful as a flowering tree. He rode past Old Iria regularly. He tried stopping in the village at the foot of the hill to ask questions, but there was nowhere to stop and nobody would answer questions. A wall-eyed witch took one look at him and scuttled into her hut. If he went up to the house he would have to face the pack of hellhounds and probably a drunk old man. But it was worth the chance, he thought; he was bored out of his wits with the dull life at Westpool, and was never slow to take a risk. He rode up the hill till the dogs were yelling around him in a frenzy, snapping at the mare's legs. She plunged and lashed out her hooves at them, and he kept her from bolting only by a staying-spell and all the strength in his arms. The dogs were leaping and snapping at his own legs now, and he was about to let the mare have her head when somebody came among the dogs shouting curses and beating them back with a strap. When he got the lathered, gasping mare to stand still, he saw the girl as beautiful as a flowering tree. She was very tall, very sweaty, with big hands and feet and mouth and nose and eyes, and a head of wild dusty hair. She was yelling, 'Down! Back to the house, you carrion, you vile sons of bitches!' to the whining, cowering dogs.

Ivory clapped his hand to his right leg. A dog's tooth had ripped his breeches at the calf, and a trickle of blood came through.

'Is she hurt?' the woman said. 'Oh, the traitorous vermin!' She was stroking down the mare's right foreleg. Her hands came away covered with blood-streaked horse sweat. 'There, there,' she said. 'The brave girl, the brave heart.' The mare put her head down and shivered all over with relief. 'What did you keep her standing there in the middle of the dogs for?' the woman demanded furiously. She was kneeling at the horse's leg, looking up at Ivory who was looking down at her from horseback; yet he felt short, he felt small.

She did not wait for an answer. 'I'll walk her up,' she said, standing up, and put out her hand for the reins. Ivory saw that he was supposed to dismount. He did so, asking, 'Is it very bad?' and peering at the horse's leg, seeing only bright, bloody foam.

'Come on then, my love,' the young woman said, not to him. The mare followed her trustfully. They set off up the rough path round the hillside to an old stone and brick stableyard, empty of horses, inhabited only by nesting swallows that swooped about over the roofs calling their quick gossip.

'Keep her quiet,' said the young woman, and left him holding the mare's reins in this deserted place. She returned after some time lugging a heavy bucket, and set to sponging off the mare's leg. 'Get the saddle off her,' she said, and her tone held the unspoken, impatient, 'you fool!' Ivory obeyed, half-annoyed by this crude giantess and half-intrigued. She did not put him in mind of a flowering tree at all, but she was in fact beautiful, in a large, fierce way. The mare submitted to her absolutely. When she said, 'Move your foot!' the mare moved her foot. The woman wiped her down all over, put the saddle blanket back on her, and made sure she was standing in the sun. 'She'll be all right,' she said. 'There's a gash, but if you'll wash it with warm salt water four or five times a day, it'll heal clean. I'm sorry.' She said the last honestly, though grudgingly, as if she still wondered how he could have let his mare stand there to be assaulted, and she looked straight at him for the first time. Her eyes were clear orange-brown, like dark topaz or amber. They were strange eyes, right on a level with his own.

'I'm sorry too,' he said, trying to speak carelessly, lightly.

'She's Irian of Westpool's mare. You're the wizard, then?'

He bowed. 'Ivory, of Havnor Great Port, at your service. May I –'

She interrupted. 'I thought you were from Roke.'

'I am,' he said, his composure regained.

She stared at him with those strange eyes, as unreadable as a sheep's, he thought. Then she burst out: 'You lived there? You studied there? Do you know the Archmage?'

'Yes,' he said with a smile. Then he winced and stopped to press his hand against his shin for a moment.

'Are you hurt too?'

'It's nothing,' he said. In fact, rather to his annoyance, the cut had stopped bleeding. The woman's gaze returned to his face.

'What is it – what is it like – on Roke?'

Ivory went, limping only very slightly, to an old mounting-block nearby and sat down on it. He stretched his leg, nursing the torn place, and looked up at the woman. 'It would take a long time to tell you what Roke is like,' he said. 'But it would be my pleasure.'

'The man's a wizard, or nearly,' said Rose the witch, 'a Roke wizard! You must not ask him questions!' She was more than scandalized, she was frightened.

'He doesn't mind,' Dragonfly reassured her. 'Only he hardly ever really answers.'

'Of course not!'

'Why of course not?'

'Because he's a wizard! Because you're a woman, with no art, no knowledge, no learning!'

'You could have taught me! You never would!'

Rose dismissed all she had taught or could teach with a flick of the fingers.

'Well, so I have to learn from him,' said Dragonfly.

'Wizards don't teach women. You're besotted.'

'You and Broom trade spells.'

'Broom's a village sorcerer. This man is a wise man. He learned the High Arts at the Great House on Roke!'

'He told me what it's like,' Dragonfly said. 'You walk up through the town, Thwil Town. There's a door opening on the street, but it's shut. It looks like an ordinary door.' The witch listened, unable to resist the lure of secrets revealed and the contagion of passionate desire. 'And a man comes when you knock, an ordinary-looking man. And he gives you a test. You have to say a certain word, a password, before he'll let you in. If you don't know it, you can never go in. But if he lets you in, then from inside you see that the door is entirely different – it's made out of horn, with a tree carved on it, and the frame is made out of a tooth, one tooth of a dragon that lived long, long before Erreth-Akbe, before Morred, before there were people in Earthsea. There were only dragons, to begin with. They found the tooth on Mount Onn, in Havnor, at the centre of the world. And the leaves of the tree are carved so thin that the light shines through them, but the door's so strong that if the Doorkeeper shuts it no spell could ever open it. And then the Doorkeeper takes you down a hall and another hall, till you're lost and bewildered, and then suddenly you come out under the sky. In the Court of the Fountain, in the very deepest inside of the Great House. And that's where the Archmage would be, if he was there . . .'

'Go on,' the witch murmured.

'That's all he really told me, yet,' said Dragonfly, coming back to the mild, overcast spring day and the infinite familiarity of the village lane, Rose's front yard, her own seven milch-ewes grazing on Iria Hill, the bronze crowns of the oaks. 'He's very careful how he talks about the Masters.'

Rose nodded.

'But he told me about some of the students.'

'No harm in that, I suppose.'

'I don't know,' Dragonfly said. 'To hear about the Great House is wonderful, but I thought the people there would be – I don't know. Of course they're mostly just boys when they go there. But I thought they'd be . . .' She gazed off at the sheep on the hill, her face troubled. 'Some of them are really bad and stupid,' she said in a low voice. 'They get into the School because they're rich. And they study there just to get richer. Or to get power.'

'Well, of course they do,' said Rose, 'that's what they're there for!'

'But power – like you told me about – that isn't the same as making people do what you want, or pay you –'

'Isn't it?'

'No!'

'If a word can heal, a word can wound,' the witch said. 'If a hand can kill, a hand can cure. It's a poor cart that goes only in one direction.'

'But on Roke, they learn to use power well, not for harm, not for gain.'

'Everything's for gain some way, I'd say. People have to live. But what do I know? I make my living doing what I know how to do. But I don't meddle with the great arts, the perilous crafts, like summoning the dead,' and Rose made the hand-sign to avert the danger spoken of.

'Everything's perilous,' Dragonfly said, gazing now through the sheep, the hill, the trees, into still depths, a colourless, vast emptiness like the clear sky before sunrise.

Rose watched her. She knew she did not know who Irian was or what she might be. A big, strong, awkward, ignorant, innocent, angry woman, yes. But ever since she was a child Rose had seen something more in her, something beyond what she was. And when Irian looked away from the world like that, she seemed to enter that place or time or being beyond herself, utterly beyond Rose's knowledge. Then Rose feared her, and feared for her.

'You take care,' the witch said, grim. 'Everything's perilous, right enough, and meddling with wizards most of all.'

Through love, respect, and trust, Dragonfly would never disregard a warning from Rose; but she was unable to see Ivory as perilous. She didn't understand him, but the idea of fearing him, him personally, was not one she could keep in mind. She tried to be respectful, but it was impossible. She thought he was clever and quite handsome, but she didn't think much about him, except for what he could tell her. He knew what she wanted to know and little by little he told it to her, and then it was not really what she had wanted to know, but she wanted to know more. He was patient with her, and she was grateful to him for his patience, knowing he was much quicker than she. Sometimes he smiled at her ignorance, but he never sneered at it or reproved it. Like the witch, he liked to answer a question with a question; but the answers to Rose's questions were always something she'd always known, while the answers to his questions were things she had never imagined and found startling, unwelcome, even painful, altering all her beliefs.

Day by day, as they talked in the old stableyard of Iria, where they had fallen into the habit of meeting, she asked him and he told her more, though reluctantly, always partially; he shielded his Masters, she thought, trying to defend the bright image of Roke, until one day he gave in to her insistence and spoke freely at last.

'There are good men there,' he said. 'Great and wise the Archmage certainly was. But he's gone. And the Masters . . . Some hold aloof, following arcane knowledge, seeking ever more patterns, ever more names, but using their knowledge for nothing. Others hide their ambition under the grey cloak of wisdom. Roke is no longer where power is in Earthsea. That's the Court in Havnor, now. Roke lives on its great past, defended by a thousand spells against the present day. And inside those spell-walls, what is there? Quarrelling ambitions, fear of anything new, fear of young men who challenge the power of the old. And at the centre, nothing. An empty courtyard. The Archmage will never return.'

'How do you know?' she whispered.

He looked stern. 'The dragon bore him away.'

'You saw it? You saw that?' She clenched her hands, imagining that flight.

After a long time, she came back to the sunlight and the stableyard and her thoughts and puzzles. 'But even if he's gone,' she said, 'surely some of the Masters are truly wise?'

When he looked up and spoke it was with a hint of a melancholy smile. 'All the mystery and wisdom of the Masters, when it's out in the daylight, doesn't amount to so much, you know. Tricks of the trade – wonderful illusions. But people don't want to believe that. They want the mysteries, the illusions. Who can blame them? There's so little in most lives that's beautiful or worthy.'

As if to illustrate what he was saying, he had picked up a bit of brick from the broken pavement, and tossed it up in the air, and as he spoke it fluttered about their heads on delicate blue wings, a butterfly. He put out his finger and the butterfly lighted on it. He shook his finger and the butterfly fell to the ground, a fragment of brick.

'There's not much worth much in my life,' she said, gazing down at the pavement. 'All I know how to do is run the farm, and try to stand up and speak truth. But if I thought it was all tricks and lies even on Roke, I'd hate those men for fooling me, fooling us all. It can't be lies. Not all of it. The Archmage did go into the labyrinth among the Hoary Men and come back with the Ring of Peace. He did go into death with the young king, and defeat the spider mage, and come back. We know that on the word of the king himself. Even here, the harpers came to sing that song, and a teller came to tell it.'

Ivory nodded gravely. 'But the Archmage lost all his power in the land of death. Maybe all magery was weakened then.'

'Rose's spells work as well as ever,' she said stoutly.

Ivory smiled. He said nothing, but she knew how petty the doings of a village witch appeared to him, who had seen great deeds and powers. She sighed and spoke from her heart – 'Oh, if only I wasn't a woman!'

He smiled again. 'You're a beautiful woman,' he said, but plainly, not in the flattering way he had used with her at first, before she showed him she hated it. 'Why would you be a man?'

'So I could go to Roke! And see, and learn! Why, why is it only men can go there?'

'So it was ordained by the first Archmage, centuries ago,' said Ivory. 'But . . . I too have wondered.'

'You have?'

'Often. Seeing only boys and men, day after day, in the Great House and all the precincts of the School. Knowing that the townswomen are spell-bound from so much as setting foot on the fields about Roke Knoll. Once in years, perhaps, some great lady is allowed to come briefly into the outer courts . . . Why is it so? Are all women incapable of understanding? Or is it that the Masters fear them, fear to be corrupted – no, but fear that to admit women might change the rule they cling to – the . . . purity of that rule.'

'Women can live chaste as well as men can,' Dragonfly said bluntly. She knew she was blunt and coarse where he was delicate and subtle, but she did not know any other way to be.

'Of course,' he said, his smile growing brilliant. 'But witches aren't always chaste, are they? Maybe that's what the Masters are afraid of. Maybe celibacy isn't as necessary as the Rule of Roke teaches. Maybe it's not a way of keeping the power pure, but of keeping the power to themselves. Leaving out women, leaving out everybody who won't agree to turn himself into a eunuch to get that one kind of power . . . Who knows? A she-mage! Now that would change everything, all the rules!'

She could see his mind dance ahead of hers, taking up and playing with ideas, transforming them as he had transformed brick into butterfly. She could not dance with him, she could not play with him, but she watched him in wonder.

'You could go to Roke,' he said, his eyes bright with excitement, mischief, daring. Meeting her almost pleading, incredulous silence, he insisted: 'You could. A woman you are, but there are ways to change your seeming. You have the heart, the courage, the will of a man. You could enter the Great House. I know it.'

'And what would I do there?'

'What all the students do. Live alone in a stone cell and learn to be wise! It might not be what you dream it to be, but that, too, you'd learn.'

'I couldn't. They'd know. I couldn't even get in. There's the Doorkeeper, you said. I don't know the word to say to him.'

'The password, yes. But I can teach it to you.'

'You can? Is it allowed?'

'I don't care what's "allowed",' he said, with a frown she had never seen on his face. 'The Archmage himself said, *Rules are made to be broken*. Injustice makes the rules, and courage breaks them. I have the courage, if you do!'

She looked at him. She could not speak. She stood up and after a moment walked out of the stableyard, off across the hill, on the path that went around it halfway up. One of the dogs, her favourite, a big, ugly, heavy-headed hound, followed her. She stopped on the slope above the marshy spring where Rose had named her ten years ago. She stood there; the dog sat down beside her and looked up at her face. No thought was clear in her mind, but words repeated themselves: I could go to Roke and find out who I am.

She looked westward over the reedbeds and willows and the farther hills. The whole western sky was empty, clear. She stood still and her soul seemed to go into that sky and be gone, gone out of her.

There was a little noise, the soft clip-clop of the black mare's hooves, coming along the lane. Then Dragonfly came back to herself and called to Ivory and ran down the hill to meet him. 'I will go,' she said.

He had not planned or intended any such adventure, but crazy as it was, it suited him better the more he thought about it. The prospect of spending the long grey winter at Westpool sank his spirits like a stone. There was nothing here for him except the girl Dragonfly, who had come to fill his thoughts. Her massive, innocent strength had defeated him absolutely so far, but he did what she pleased in order to have her do at last what he pleased, and the game, he thought, was worth playing. If she ran away with him, the game was as good as won. As for the joke of it, the notion of actually getting her into the School on Roke disguised as a man, there was little chance of pulling it off, but it pleased him as a gesture of disrespect to all the piety and pomposity of the Masters and their toadies. And if somehow it succeeded, if he could actually get a woman through that door, even for a moment, what a sweet revenge it would be!

Money was a problem. The girl thought, of course, that he as a great wizard would snap his fingers and waft them over the sea in a magic boat flying before the magewind. But when he told her they'd have to hire passage on a ship, she said simply, 'I have the cheese money.'

He treasured her rustic sayings of that kind. Sometimes she frightened him, and he resented it. His dreams of her were never of her yielding to him, but of himself yielding to a fierce, destroying sweetness, sinking into an annihilating embrace, dreams in which she was something beyond comprehension and he was nothing at all. He woke from those dreams shaken and shamed. In daylight, when he saw her big, dirty hands, when she talked like a yokel, a simpleton, he regained his superiority. He only wished there were someone to repeat her sayings to, one of his old friends in the Great Port who would find them amusing. '"I have the cheese money,"' he repeated to himself, riding back to Westpool, and laughed. 'I do indeed,' he said aloud. The black mare flicked her ear.

He told Birch that he had received a sending from his teacher on Roke, the Master Hand, and must go at once, on what business he could not say, of course, but it should not take long once he was there; a half-month to go, another to return; he would be back well before the Fallows at the latest. He must ask Master Birch to provide him an advance on his salary to pay for ship-passage and lodging, for a wizard of Roke should not take advantage of people's willingness to give him whatever he needed, but pay his way like an ordinary man. As Birch agreed with this, he had to give Ivory a purse for his journey. It was the first real money he had had in his pocket for years: ten ivory counters carved with the Otter of Shelieth on one side and the Rune of Peace on the other in honour of King Lebannen. 'Hello, little namesakes,' he told them when he was alone with them. 'You and the cheese money will get along nicely.'

He told Dragonfly very little of his plans, largely because he made few, trusting to chance and his own wits, which seldom let him down if he was given a fair chance to use them. The girl asked almost no questions. 'Will I go as a man all the way?' was one. 'Yes,' he said, 'but only disguised. I won't put a semblance-spell on you till we're on Roke Island.'

'I thought it would be a spell of Change,' she said.

'That would be unwise,' he said, with a good imitation of the Master Changer's terse solemnity. 'If need be, I'll do it, of course. But you'll find wizards very sparing of the great spells. For good reason.'

'The Equilibrium,' she said, accepting all he said in its simplest sense, as always.

'And perhaps because such arts have not the power they once had,' he said. He did not know himself why he tried to weaken her faith in wizardry; perhaps because any weakening of her strength, her wholeness, was a gain for him. He had begun merely by trying to get her into his bed, a game he loved to play. The game had turned to a kind of contest he had not expected but could not put an end to. He was determined now not to win her, but to defeat her. He could not let her defeat him. He must prove to her and himself that his dreams were meaningless.

Quite early on, impatient with wooing her massive physical indifference, he had worked up a charm, a sorcerer's seduction-spell of which he was contemptuous even as he made it, though he knew it was effective. He cast it on her while she was, characteristically, mending a cow's halter. The result had not been the melting eagerness it had produced in girls he had used it on in Havnor and Thwil. Dragonfly had gradually become silent and sullen. She ceased asking her endless questions about Roke and did not answer when he spoke. When he very tentatively approached her, taking her hand, she struck him away with a blow to the head that left him dizzy. He saw her stand up and stride out of the stableyard without a word, the ugly hound she favoured trotting after her. It looked back at him with a grin.

She took the path to the old house. When his ears stopped ringing he stole after her, hoping the charm was working and that this was only her particularly uncouth way of leading him at last to her bed. Nearing the house, he heard crockery breaking. The father, the drunkard, came wobbling out looking scared and confused, followed by Dragonfly's loud, harsh voice – 'Out of the house, you drunken, crawling traitor! You foul, shameless lecher!'

'She took my cup away,' the Master of Iria said to the stranger, whining like a puppy, while his dogs yammered around him. 'She broke it.'

Ivory departed. He did not return for two days. On the third day he rode experimentally past Old Iria, and she came striding down to meet him. 'I'm sorry, Ivory,' she said, looking up at him with her smoky orange eyes. 'I don't know what came over me the other day. I was angry. But not at you. I beg your pardon.'

He forgave her gracefully. He did not try a love-charm on her again.

Soon, he thought now, he would not need one. He would have real power over her. He had finally seen how to get it. She had given it into his hands. Her strength and her willpower were tremendous, but fortunately she was stupid, and he was not.

Birch was sending a carter down to Kembermouth with six barrels of ten-year-old Fanian ordered by the wine merchant there. He was glad to send his wizard along as bodyguard, for the wine was valuable, and though the young king was putting things to rights as fast as he could, there were still gangs of robbers on the roads. So Ivory left Westpool on the big wagon pulled by four big carthorses, jolting slowly along, his legs dangling. Down by Jackass Hill an uncouth figure rose up from the wayside and asked the carter for a lift. 'I don't know you,' the carter said, lifting his whip to warn the stranger off, but Ivory came round the wagon and said, 'Let the lad ride, my good man. He'll do no harm while I'm with you.'

'Keep an eye on him then, master,' said the carter.

'I will,' said Ivory, with a wink at Dragonfly. She, well disguised in dirt and a farmhand's old smock and leggings and a loathsome felt hat, did not wink back. She played her part even while they sat side by side dangling their legs over the tailgate, with six great halftuns of wine jolting between them and the drowsy carter, and the drowsy summer hills and fields slipping slowly, slowly past. Ivory tried to tease her, but she only shook her head. Maybe she was scared by this wild scheme, now she was embarked on it. There was no telling. She was solemnly, heavily silent. I could be very bored by this woman, Ivory thought, if once I'd had her underneath me. That thought stirred him almost unbearably, but when he looked back at her, his thoughts died away before her massive, actual presence.

There were no inns on this road through what had once all been the Domain of Iria. As the sun neared the western plains, they stopped at a farmhouse that offered stabling for the horses, a shed for the cart, and straw in the stable loft for the carters. The loft was dark and stuffy and the straw musty. Ivory felt no lust at all, though Dragonfly lay not three feet from him. She had played the man so thoroughly all day that she had half-convinced even him. Maybe she'll fool the old men after all! he thought, and grinned at the thought, and slept.

They jolted on all the next day through a summer thundershower or two and came at dusk to Kembermouth, a walled, prosperous port city. They left the carter to his master's business and walked down to find an inn near the docks. Dragonfly looked about at the sights of the city in a silence that might have been awe or disapproval or mere stolidity. 'This is a nice little town,' Ivory said, 'but the only city in the world is Havnor.'

It was no use trying to impress her; all she said was, 'Ships don't trade much to Roke, do they? Will it take a long time to find one to take us, do you think?'

'Not if I carry a staff,' he said.

She stopped looking about and strode along in thought for a while. She was beautiful in movement, bold and graceful, her head carried high.

'You mean they'll oblige a wizard? But you aren't a wizard.'

'That's a formality. We senior sorcerers may carry a staff when we're on Roke's business. Which I am.'

'Taking me there?'

'Bringing them a student – yes. A student of great gifts!'

She asked no more questions. She never argued; it was one of her virtues.

That night, over supper at the waterfront inn, she asked with unusual timidity in her voice, 'Do I have great gifts?'

'In my judgement, you do,' he said.

She pondered – conversation with her was often a slow business – and said, 'Rose always said I had power, but she didn't know what kind. And I . . . I know I do, but I don't know what it is.'

'You're going to Roke to find out,' he said, raising his glass to her. After a moment she raised hers and smiled at him, a smile so tender and radiant that he said spontaneously, 'And may what you find be all you seek!'

'If I do, it will be thanks to you,' she said. In that moment he loved her for her true heart, and would have forsworn any thought of her but as his companion in a bold adventure, a gallant joke.

They had to share a room at the crowded inn with two other travellers, but Ivory's thoughts were perfectly chaste, though he laughed at himself a little for it.

Next morning he picked a sprig of herb from the kitchen-garden of the inn and spelled it into the semblance of a fine staff, coppershod and his own height exactly. 'What is the wood?' Dragonfly asked, fascinated, when she saw it, and when he answered with a laugh, 'Rosemary,' she laughed too. They set off along the wharves, asking for a ship bound south that might take a wizard and his prentice to the Isle of the Wise, and soon enough they found a heavy trader bound for Wathort, whose master would carry the wizard for goodwill and the prentice for half-price. Even half-price was half the cheese money, but they would have the luxury of a cabin, for *Sea Otter* was a decked, two-masted ship.

As they were talking with her master a wagon drew up on the dock and began to unload six familiar halftun barrels. 'That's ours,' Ivory said, and the ship's master said, 'Bound for Hort Town,' and Dragonfly said softly, 'From Iria.'

She glanced back at the land then. It was the only time he ever saw her look back.

The ship's weatherworker came aboard just before they sailed, no Roke wizard but a weatherbeaten fellow in a worn sea-cloak. Ivory flourished his staff a little in greeting him. The sorcerer looked him up and down and said, 'One man works weather on this ship. If it's not me, I'm off.'

'I'm a mere passenger, Master Bagman. I gladly leave the winds in your hands.'

The sorcerer looked at Dragonfly, who stood straight as a tree and said nothing.

'Good,' he said, and that was the last word he spoke to Ivory.

During the voyage, however, he talked several times with Dragonfly, which made Ivory a bit uneasy. Her ignorance and trustfulness could endanger her and therefore him. What did she and the bagman talk about? he asked, and she answered, 'What is to become of us.'

He stared.

'Of all of us. Of Way, and Felkway, and Havnor, and Wathort, and Roke. All the people of the islands. He says that when King Lebannen was to be crowned, last autumn, he sent to Gont for the old Archmage to come crown him, and he wouldn't come. And there was no new Archmage. So he took the crown himself. And some say that's wrong, and he doesn't rightly hold the throne. But others say the king himself is the new Archmage. But he isn't a wizard, only a king. So others say the dark years will come again, when there was no rule of justice, and wizardry was used for evil ends.'

After a pause Ivory said, 'That old weatherworker says all this?'

'It's common talk, I think,' said Dragonfly, with her grave simplicity.

The weatherworker knew his trade, at least. *Sea Otter* sped south; they met summer squalls and choppy seas, but never a storm or a troublesome wind. They put off and took on cargo at ports on the north shore of O, at Ilien, Leng, Kamery, and O Port, and then headed west to carry the passengers to Roke. And facing the west Ivory felt a little hollow at the pit of his stomach, for he knew all too well how Roke was guarded. He knew neither he nor the weatherworker could do anything at all to turn the Roke-wind if it blew against them. And if it did, Dragonfly would ask why? Why did it blow against them?

He was glad to see the sorcerer uneasy too, standing by the helmsman, keeping a watch up on the masthead, taking in sail at the hint of a west wind. But the wind held steady from the north. A thunder-squall came pelting on that wind, and Ivory went down to the cabin, but Dragonfly stayed up on deck. She was afraid of the water, she had told him. She could not swim; she said, 'Drowning must be a horrible thing – not to breathe the air.' She had shuddered at the thought. It was the only fear she had ever shown of anything. But she disliked the low, cramped cabin, and had stayed on deck every day and slept there on the warm nights. Ivory had not tried to coax her into the cabin. He knew now that coaxing was no good. To have her he must master her; and that he would do, if only they could come to Roke.

He came up on deck again. It was clearing, and as the sun set the clouds broke all across the west, showing a golden sky behind the high dark curve of a hill.

Ivory looked at that hill with a kind of longing hatred.

'That's Roke Knoll, lad,' the weatherworker said to Dragonfly, who stood beside him at the rail. 'We're coming into Thwil Bay now. Where there's no wind but the wind they want.'

By the time they were well into the bay and had let down the anchor it was dark, and Ivory said to the ship's master, 'I'll go ashore in the morning.'

Down in their tiny cabin Dragonfly sat waiting for him, solemn as ever but her eyes blazing with excitement. 'We'll go ashore in the morning,' he repeated to her, and she nodded, acceptant. She said, 'Do I look all right?'

He sat down on his narrow bunk and looked at her sitting on her narrow bunk; they could not face each other directly, as there was no room for their knees. At O Port she had bought herself a decent shirt and breeches, at his suggestion, so as to look a more probable candidate for the School. Her face was windburned and scrubbed clean. Her hair was braided and the braid clubbed, like Ivory's. She had got her hands clean, too, and they lay flat on her thighs, long strong hands, like a man's.

'You don't look like a man,' he said. Her face fell. 'Not to me. You'll never look like a man to me. But don't worry. You will to them.'

She nodded, with an anxious face.

'The first test is the great test, Dragonfly,' he said. Every night he lay alone in this cabin he had planned this conversation. 'To enter the Great House: to go through that door.'

'I've been thinking about it,' she said, hurried and earnest. 'Couldn't I just tell them who I am? With you there to vouch for me – to say even if I am a woman, I have some gift – and I'd promise to take the vow and make the spell of celibacy, and live apart if they wanted me to –'

He was shaking his head all through her speech. 'No, no, no, no. Hopeless. Useless. Fatal!'

'Even if you –'

'Even if I argued for you. They won't listen. The Rule of Roke forbids women to be taught any high art, any word of the Language of the Making. It's always been so. They will not listen. So they must be shown! And we'll show them, you and I. We'll teach them. You must have courage, Dragonfly. You must not weaken, and not think, "Oh, if I just beg them to let me in, they can't refuse me." They can, and will. And if you reveal yourself, they will punish you. And me.' He put a ponderous emphasis on the last word, and inwardly murmured, 'Avert.'

She gazed at him from her unreadable eyes, and finally said, 'What must I do?'

'Do you trust me, Dragonfly?'

'Yes.'

'Will you trust me entirely, wholly – knowing that the risk I take for you is greater even than your risk in this venture?'

'Yes.'

'Then you must tell me the word you will speak to the Doorkeeper.'

She stared. 'But I thought you'd tell it to me – the password.'

'The password he will ask you for is your true name.'

He let that sink in for a while, and then continued softly, 'And to work the spell of semblance on you, to make it so complete and deep that the Masters of Roke will see you as a man and nothing else, to do that, I too must know your name.' He paused again. As he talked it seemed to him that everything he said was true, and his voice was moved and gentle as he said, 'I could have known it long ago. But I chose not to use those arts. I wanted you to trust me enough to tell me your name yourself.'

She was looking down at her hands, clasped now on her knees. In the faint reddish glow of the cabin lantern her lashes cast very delicate, long shadows on her cheeks. She looked up, straight at him. 'My name is Irian,' she said.

He smiled. She did not smile.

He said nothing. In fact he was at a loss. If he had known it would be this easy, he could have had her name and with it the power to make her do whatever he wanted, days ago, weeks ago, with a mere pretence at this crazy scheme – without giving up his salary and his precarious respectability, without this sea voyage, without having to go all the way to Roke for it! For he saw the whole plan now was folly. There was no way he could disguise her that would fool the Doorkeeper for a moment. All his notions of humiliating the Masters as they had humiliated him were moonshine. Obsessed with tricking the girl, he had fallen into the trap he laid for her. Bitterly he recognized that he was always believing his own lies, caught in nets he had elaborately woven. Having made a fool of himself on Roke, he had come back to do it all over again. A great, desolate anger swelled up in him. There was no good, no good in anything.

'What's wrong?' she asked. The gentleness of her deep, husky voice unmanned him, and he hid his face in his hands, fighting against the shame of tears.

She put her hand on his knee. It was the first time she had ever touched him. He endured it, the warmth and weight of her touch that he had wasted so much time wanting.

He wanted to hurt her, to shock her out of her terrible, ignorant kindness, but what he said when he finally spoke was, 'I only wanted to make love to you.'

'You did?'

'Did you think I was one of their eunuchs? That I'd castrate myself with spells so I could be holy? Why do you think I don't have a staff? Why do you think I'm not at the School? Did you believe everything I said?'

'Yes,' she said. 'I'm sorry.' Her hand was still on his knee. She said, 'We can make love if you want.'

He sat up, sat still.

'What are you?' he said to her at last.

'I don't know. It's why I wanted to come to Roke. To find out.'

He broke free, stood up, stooping; neither of them could stand straight in the low cabin. Clenching and unclenching his hands, he stood as far from her as he could, his back to her.

'You won't find out. It's all lies, shams. Old men playing games with words. I wouldn't play their games, so I left. Do you know what I did?' He turned, showing his teeth in a rictus of triumph. 'I got a girl, a town girl, to come to my room. My cell. My little stone celibate cell. It had a window looking out on a back-street. No spells – you can't make spells with all their magic going on. But she wanted to come, and came, and I let a rope ladder out the window, and she climbed it. And we were at it when the old men came in! I showed 'em! And if I could have got you in, I'd have showed 'em again, I'd have taught them *their* lesson!'

'Well, I'll try,' she said.

He stared.

'Not for the same reasons as you,' she said, 'but I still want to. And we came all this way. And you know my name.'

It was true. He knew her name: Irian. It was like a coal of fire, a burning ember in his mind. His thought could not hold it. His knowledge could not use it. His tongue could not say it.

She looked up at him, her sharp, strong face softened by the shadowy lantern-light. 'If it was only to make love you brought me here, Ivory,' she said, 'we can do that. If you still want to.'

Wordless at first, he simply shook his head. After a while he was able to laugh. 'I think we've gone on past . . . that possibility . . .'

She looked at him without regret, or reproach, or shame.

'Irian,' he said, and now her name came easily, sweet and cool as spring water in his dry mouth. 'Irian, here's what you must do to enter the Great House . . .'

3. Azver

He left her at the corner of the street, a narrow, dull, somehow sly-looking street that slanted up between featureless walls to a wooden door in a higher wall. He had put his spell on her, and she looked like a man, though she did not feel like one. She and Ivory took each other in their arms, because after all they had been friends, companions, and he had done all this for her. 'Courage!' he said, and let her go. She walked up the street and stood before the door. She looked back then, but he was gone.

She knocked.

After a while she heard the latch rattle. The door opened. An ordinary-looking middle-aged man stood there. 'What can I do for you?' he said. He did not smile, but his voice was pleasant.

'You can let me into the Great House, sir.'

'Do you know the way in?' His almond-shaped eyes were attentive, yet seemed to look at her from miles or years away.

'This is the way in, sir.'

'Do you know whose name you must tell me before I let you in?'

'My own, sir. It is Irian.'

'Is it?' he said.

That gave her pause. She stood silent. 'It's the name the witch Rose of my village on Way gave me, in the spring under Iria Hill,' she said at last, standing up and speaking truth.

The Doorkeeper looked at her for what seemed a long time. 'Then it is your name,' he said. 'But maybe not all your name. I think you have another.'

'I don't know it, sir.'

After another long time she said, 'Maybe I can learn it here, sir.'

The Doorkeeper bowed his head a little. A very faint smile made crescent curves in his cheeks. He stood aside. 'Come in, daughter,' he said.

She stepped across the threshold of the Great House.

Ivory's spell of semblance dropped away like a cobweb. She was and looked herself.

She followed the Doorkeeper down a stone passageway. Only at the end of it did she think to turn back to see the light shine through the thousand leaves of the tree carved in the high door in its bone-white frame.

A young man in a grey cloak hurrying down the passageway stopped short as he approached them. He stared at Irian; then with a brief nod he went on. She looked back at him. He was looking back at her.

A globe of misty, greenish fire drifted swiftly down the corridor at eye level, apparently pursuing the young man. The Doorkeeper waved his hand at it, and it avoided him. Irian swerved and ducked down frantically, but felt the cool fire tingle in her hair as it passed over her. The Doorkeeper looked round, and now his smile was wider. Though he said nothing, she felt he was aware of her, concerned for her. She stood up and followed him.

He stopped before an oak door. Instead of knocking he sketched a little sign or rune on it with the top of his staff, a light staff of some greyish wood. The door opened as a resonant voice behind it said, 'Come in!'

'Wait here a little, if you please, Irian,' the Doorkeeper said, and went into the room, leaving the door wide open behind him. She could see bookshelves and books, a table piled with more books and inkpots and writings, two or three boys seated at the table, and the grey-haired, stocky man the Doorkeeper spoke to. She saw the man's face change, saw his eyes shift to her in a brief, startled gaze, saw him question the Doorkeeper, low-voiced, intense.

They both came to her. 'The Master Changer of Roke: Irian of Way,' said the Doorkeeper.

The Changer stared openly at her. He was not as tall as she was. He stared at the Doorkeeper, and then at her again.

'Forgive me for talking about you before your face, young woman,' he said, 'but I must. Master Doorkeeper, you know I'd never question your judgement, but the Rule is clear. I have to ask what moved you to break it and let her come in.'

'She asked to,' said the Doorkeeper.

'But . . .' The Changer paused.

'When did a woman last ask to enter the School?'

'They know the Rule doesn't allow them.'

'Did you know that, Irian?' the Doorkeeper asked her.

'Yes, sir.'

'So what brought you here?' the Changer asked, stern, but not hiding his curiosity.

'Master Ivory said I could pass for a man. Though I thought I should say who I was. I will be as celibate as anyone, sir.'

Two long curves appeared on the Doorkeeper's cheeks, enclosing the slow upturn of his smile. The Changer's face remained stern, but he blinked, and after a little thought said, 'I'm sure – yes – it was definitely the better plan to be honest. What Master did you speak of?'

'Ivory,' said the Doorkeeper. 'A lad from Havnor Great Port, whom I let in three years ago, and let out again last year, as you may recall.'

'Ivory! That fellow that studied with the Hand? Is he here?'

the Changer demanded of Irian, wrathily. She stood straight and said nothing.

'Not in the School,' the Doorkeeper said, smiling.

'He fooled you, young woman. Made a fool of you by trying to make fools of us.'

'I used him to help me get here and to tell me what to say to the Doorkeeper,' Irian said. 'I'm not here to fool anybody, but to learn what I need to know.'

'I've often wondered why I let the boy in,' said the Doorkeeper. 'Now I begin to understand.'

At that the Changer looked at him, and after pondering said soberly, 'Doorkeeper, what have you in mind?'

'I think Irian of Way may have come to us seeking not only what she needs to know, but also what we need to know.' The Doorkeeper's tone was equally sober, and his smile was gone. 'I think this may be a matter for talk among the nine of us.'

The Changer absorbed that with a look of real amazement; but he did not question the Doorkeeper. He said only, 'But not among the students.'

The Doorkeeper shook his head, agreeing.

'She can lodge in the town,' the Changer said, with some relief.

'While we talk behind her back?'

'You won't bring her into the Council Room?' the Changer said in disbelief.

'The Archmage brought the boy Arren there.'

'But – but Arren was King Lebannen –'

'And who is Irian?'

The Changer stood silent, and then he said quietly, with respect, 'My friend, what is it you think to do, to learn? What is she, that you ask this for her?'

'Who are we,' said the Doorkeeper, 'that we refuse her without knowing what she is?'

'A woman,' said the Master Summoner.

Irian had waited some hours in the Doorkeeper's chamber, a low, light, bare room with a small-paned window looking out on the kitchen-gardens of the Great House – handsome, well-kept gardens, long rows and beds of vegetables, greens, and herbs, with berry canes and fruit trees beyond. She saw a burly, dark-skinned man and two boys come out and weed one of the vegetable plots. It eased her mind to watch their careful work. She wished she could help them at it. The waiting and the strangeness were very difficult. Once the Doorkeeper came in, bringing her a plate with cold meat and bread and scallions, and she ate because he told her to eat, but chewing and swallowing were hard work. The gardeners went away and there was nothing to watch out the window but the cabbages growing and the sparrows hopping, and now and then a hawk far up in the sky, and the wind moving softly in the tops of tall trees, on beyond the gardens.

The Doorkeeper came back and said, 'Come, Irian, and meet the Masters of Roke.' Her heart began to go at a carthorse gallop. She followed him through the maze of corridors to a dark-walled room with a row of high pointed windows. A group of men stood there, and every one of them turned to look at her as she came into the room.

'Irian of Way, my lords,' said the Doorkeeper. They were all silent. He motioned her to come farther into the room. 'The Master Changer you have met,' he said. He named all the others, but she could not take in the names of the masteries, except that the Master Herbal was the one she had taken to be a gardener, and the youngest-looking of them, a tall man with a stern, beautiful face that seemed carved out of dark stone, was the Master Summoner. It was he who spoke, when the Doorkeeper was done. 'A woman,' he said.

The Doorkeeper nodded once, mild as ever.

'This is what you brought the Nine together for? This and no more?'

'This and no more,' said the Doorkeeper.

'Dragons have been seen flying above the Inmost Sea. Roke has no Archmage, and the islands no true-crowned king. There is real work to do,' the Summoner said, and his voice too was like stone, cold and heavy. 'When will we do it?'

There was an uncomfortable silence, as the Doorkeeper did not speak. At last a slight, bright-eyed man who wore a red tunic under his grey wizard's cloak said, 'Do you bring this woman into the House as a student, Master Doorkeeper?'

'If I did, it would be up to you all to approve or disapprove,' said he.

'Do you?' asked the man in the red tunic, smiling a little.

'Master Hand,' said the Doorkeeper, 'she asked to enter as a student, and I saw no reason to deny her.'

'Every reason,' said the Summoner.

A man with a deep, clear voice spoke: 'It's not our judgement that prevails, but the Rule of Roke, which we are sworn to follow.'

'I doubt the Doorkeeper would defy it lightly,' said one of them Irian had not noticed till he spoke, though he was a big man, white-haired, raw-boned, and crag-faced. Unlike the others, he looked at her as he spoke. 'I am Kurremkarmerruk,' he said to her. 'As the Master Namer here, I make free with names, my own included. Who named you, Irian?'

'The witch Rose of our village, lord,' she answered, standing straight, though her voice came out high-pitched and rough.

'Is she misnamed?' the Doorkeeper asked the Namer.

Kurremkarmerruk shook his head. 'No. But . . .'

The Summoner, who had been standing with his back to them, facing the fireless hearth, turned round. 'The names witches give each other are not our concern here,' he said. 'If you have some interest in this woman, Doorkeeper, it should be pursued outside these walls – outside the door you vowed to keep. She has no place here nor ever will. She can bring only confusion, dissension, and further weakness among us. I will speak no longer and say nothing else in her presence. The only answer to conscious error is silence.'

'Silence is not enough, my lord,' said one who had not spoken before. To Irian's eyes he was very strange-looking, having pale reddish skin, long pale hair, and narrow eyes the colour of ice. His speech was also strange, stiff and somehow deformed. 'Silence is the answer to everything, and to nothing,' he said.

The Summoner lifted his noble, dark face and looked across the room at the pale man, but did not speak. Without a word or gesture he turned away again and left the room. As he walked slowly past Irian, she shrank back from him. It was as if a grave had opened, a winter grave, cold, wet, dark. Her breath stuck in her throat. She gasped a little for air. When she recovered herself she saw the Changer and the pale man both watching her intently.

The one with a voice like a deep-toned bell looked at her too, and spoke to her with a plain, kind severity. 'As I see it, the man who brought you here meant to do harm, but you do not. Yet being here, Irian, you do us and yourself harm. Everything not in its own place does harm. A note sung, however well sung, wrecks the tune it isn't part of. Women teach women. Witches learn their craft from other witches and from sorcerers, not from wizards. What we teach here is in a language not for women's tongues. The young heart rebels against such laws, calling them unjust, arbitrary. But they are true laws, founded not on what we want, but on what is. The just and the unjust, the foolish and the wise, all must obey them, or waste life and come to grief.'

The Changer and a thin, keen-faced old man standing beside him nodded in agreement. The Master Hand said, 'Irian, I am sorry. Ivory was my pupil. If I taught him badly, I did worse in sending him away. I thought him insignificant, and so harmless. But he lied to you and beguiled you. You must not feel shame. The fault was his, and mine.'

'I am not ashamed,' Irian said. She looked at them all. She felt that she should thank them for their courtesy but the words would not come. She nodded stiffly to them, turned round, and strode out of the room.

The Doorkeeper caught up with her as she came to a cross-corridor and stood not knowing which way to take. 'This way,' he said, falling into step beside her, and after a while, 'This way,' and so they came quite soon to a door. It was not made of horn and ivory. It was uncarved oak, black and massive, with an iron bolt worn thin with age. 'This is the back door,' the mage said, unbolting it. 'Medra's Gate, they used to call it. I keep both doors.' He opened it. The brightness of the day dazzled Irian's eyes. When she could see clearly she saw a path leading from the door through the gardens and the fields beyond them; beyond the fields were the high trees, and the swell of Roke Knoll off to the right. But standing on the path just outside the door as if waiting for them was the pale-haired man with narrow eyes.

'Patterner,' said the Doorkeeper, not at all surprised.

'Where do you send this lady?' said the Patterner in his strange speech.

'Nowhere,' said the Doorkeeper. 'I let her out as I let her in, at her desire.'

'Will you come with me?' the Patterner said to Irian.

She looked at him and at the Doorkeeper and said nothing.

'I don't live in this House. In any house,' the Patterner said. 'I live there. The Grove – ah,' he said, turning suddenly. The big, white-haired man, Kurremkarmerruk the Namer, was standing just down the path. He had not been standing there until the other mage said 'Ah.' Irian stared from one to the other in blank bewilderment.

'This is only a seeming of me, a presentment, a sending,' the old man said to her. 'I don't live here either. Miles off.' He gestured northward. 'You might come there when you're done with the Patterner here. I'd like to learn more about your name.' He nodded to the other two mages and was not there. A bumblebee buzzed heavily through the air where he had been.

Irian looked down at the ground. After a long time she said, clearing her throat, not looking up, 'Is it true I do harm being here?'

'I don't know,' said the Doorkeeper.

'In the Grove is no harm,' said the Patterner. 'Come on. There is an old house, a hut. Old, dirty. You don't care, eh? Stay a while. You can see.' And he set off down the path between the parsley and the bush-beans. She looked at the Doorkeeper; he smiled a little. She followed the pale-haired man.

They walked a half-mile or so. The Knoll rose up full in the western sun on their right. Behind them the School sprawled grey and many-roofed on its lower hill. The grove of trees towered before them now. She saw oak and willow, chestnut and ash, and tall evergreens. From the dense, sun-shot darkness of the trees a stream ran out, green-banked, with many brown trodden places where cattle and sheep went down to drink or to cross over. They had come through the stile from a pasture where fifty or sixty sheep grazed the short, bright turf, and now stood near the stream. 'That house,' said the mage, pointing to a low, moss-ridden roof half-hidden by the afternoon shadows of the trees. 'Stay tonight. You will?'

He asked her to stay, he did not tell her to. All she could do was nod.

'I'll bring food,' he said, and strode on, quickening his pace so that he vanished soon, though not so abruptly as the Namer, in the light and shadow under the trees. Irian watched till he was certainly gone and then made her way through high grass and weeds to the little house.

It looked very old. It had been rebuilt and rebuilt again, but not for a long time. Nor had anyone lived in it for a long time, from the feel of it. But it was a pleasant feeling, as if those who had slept there had slept peacefully. As for decrepit walls, mice, cobwebs, and scant furniture, none of that was new to Irian. She found a bald broom and swept out a bit. She unrolled her blanket on the plank bed. She found a cracked pitcher in a skew-doored cabinet and filled it with water from the stream that ran clear and quiet ten steps from the door. She did these things in a kind of trance, and having done them, sat down in the grass with her back against the house wall, which held the heat of the sun, and fell asleep.

When she woke, the Master Patterner was sitting nearby, and a basket was on the grass between them.

'Hungry? Eat,' he said.

'I'll eat later, sir. Thank you,' said Irian.

'I am hungry now,' said the mage. He took a hardboiled egg from the basket, cracked, shelled, and ate it.

'They call this the Otter's House,' he said. 'Very old. As old as the Great House. Everything is old, here. We are old – the Masters.'

'You're not,' Irian said. She thought him between thirty and forty, though it was hard to tell; she kept thinking his hair was white, because it was not black.

'But I came far. Miles can be years. I am Kargish, from Karego. You know?'

'The Hoary Men!' said Irian, staring openly at him. All Daisy's ballads of the Hoary Men who sailed out of the east to lay the land waste and spit innocent babes on their lances, and the story of how Erreth-Akbe lost the Ring of Peace, and the new songs and the King's Tale about how Archmage Sparrowhawk had gone among the Hoary Men and come back with that ring –

'Hoary?' said the Patterner.

'Frosty. White,' she said, looking away, embarrassed.

'Ah.' Presently he said, 'The Master Summoner is not old.' And she got a sidelong look from those narrow, ice-coloured eyes.

She said nothing.

'I think you feared him.'

She nodded.

When she said nothing, and some time had passed, he said, 'In the shadow of these trees is no harm. Only truth.'

'When he passed me,' she said in a low voice, 'I saw a grave.'

'Ah,' said the Patterner.

He had made a little heap of bits of eggshell on the ground by his knee. He arranged the white fragments into a curve, then closed it into a circle. 'Yes,' he said, studying his eggshells, then, scratching up the earth a bit, he neatly and delicately buried them. He dusted off his hands. Again his glance flicked to Irian and away.

'You have been a witch, Irian?'

'No.'

'But you have some knowledge.'

'No. I don't. Rose wouldn't teach me. She said she didn't dare. Because I had power but she didn't know what it was.'

'Your Rose is a wise flower,' said the mage, unsmiling.

'But I know I have – I have something to do, to be. That's why I wanted to come here. To find out. On the Isle of the Wise.'

She was getting used to his strange face now and was able to read it. She thought that he looked sad. His way of speaking was harsh, quick, dry, peaceable. 'The men of the Isle are not always wise, eh?' he said. 'Maybe the Doorkeeper.' He looked at her now, not glancing but squarely, his eyes catching and holding hers. 'But there. In the wood. Under the trees. There is the old wisdom. Never old. I can't teach you. I can take you into the Grove.' After a minute he stood up. 'Yes?'

'Yes,' she said uncertainly.

'The house is all right?'

'Yes –'

'Tomorrow,' he said, and strode off.

So for a half-month or more of the hot days of summer, Irian slept in the Otter's House, which was a peaceful one, and ate what the Master Patterner brought her in his basket – eggs, cheese, greens, fruit, smoked mutton – and went with him every afternoon into the grove of high trees, where the paths seemed never to be quite where she remembered them, and often led on far beyond what seemed the confines of the wood. They walked there in silence, and spoke seldom when they rested. The mage was a quiet man. Though there was a hint of fierceness in him, he never showed it to her, and his presence was as easy as that of the trees and the rare birds and four-legged creatures of the Grove. As he had said, he did not try to teach her. When she asked about the Grove, he told her that, with Roke Knoll, it had stood since Segoy made the islands of the world, and that all magic was in the roots of the trees, and that they were mingled with the roots of all the forests that were or might yet be. 'And sometimes the Grove is in this place,' he said, 'and sometimes in another. But it is always.'

She had never seen where he lived. He slept wherever he chose to, she imagined, in these warm summer nights. She asked him where the food they ate came from; what the School did not supply for itself, he said, the farmers round about provided, considering themselves well recompensed by the protections the Masters set on their flocks and fields and orchards. That made sense to her. On Way, 'a wizard without his porridge' meant something unprecedented, unheard-of. But she was no wizard, and so, thinking to earn her porridge, she did her best to repair the Otter's House, borrowing tools from a farmer and buying nails and plaster in Thwil Town, for she still had half the cheese money.

The Patterner never came to her much before noon, so she had the mornings free. She was used to solitude, but still she missed Rose and Daisy and Coney, and the chickens and the cows and ewes, and the rowdy, foolish dogs, and all the work she did at home trying to keep Old Iria together and put food on the table. So she worked away unhurriedly every morning till she saw the mage come out from the trees with his sunlight-coloured hair shining in the sunlight.

Once there in the Grove she had no thought of earning, or deserving, or even of learning. To be there was enough, was all.

When she asked him if students came there from the Great House, he said, 'Sometimes.' Another time he said, 'My words are nothing. Hear the leaves.' That was all he said that could be called teaching. As she walked, she listened to the leaves when the wind rustled them or stormed in the crowns of the trees; she watched the shadows play, and thought about the roots of the trees down in the darkness of the earth. She was utterly content to be there. Yet always, without discontent or urgency, she felt that she was waiting. And that silent expectancy was deepest and clearest when she came out of the shelter of the woods and saw the open sky.

Once, when they had gone a long way and the trees, dark evergreens she did not know, stood very high about them, she heard a call – a horn blowing, a cry? – remote, on the very edge of hearing. She stood still, listening towards the west. The mage walked on, turning only when he realized she had stopped.

'I heard –' she said, and could not say what she had heard.

He listened. They walked on at last through a silence enlarged and deepened by that far call.

She never went into the Grove without him, and it was many days before he left her alone within it. But one hot afternoon when they came to a glade among a stand of oaks, he said,

'I will come back here, eh?' and walked off with his quick, silent step, lost almost at once in the dappled, shifting depths of the forest.

She had no wish to explore for herself. The peacefulness of the place called for stillness, watching, listening; and she knew how tricky the paths were, and that the Grove was, as the Patterner put it, 'bigger inside than outside'. She sat down in a patch of sun-dappled shade and watched the shadows of the leaves play across the ground. The oakmast was deep; though she had never seen wild swine in the wood, she saw their tracks here. For a moment she caught the scent of a fox. Her thoughts moved as quietly and easily as the breeze moved in the warm light.

Often her mind here seemed empty of thought, full of the forest itself, but this day memories came to her, vivid. She thought about Ivory, thinking she would never see him again, wondering if he had found a ship to take him back to Havnor. He had told her he'd never go back to Westpool; the only place for him was the Great Port, the King's City, and for all he cared the island of Way could sink in the sea as deep as Soléa. But she thought with love of the roads and fields of Way. She thought of Old Iria village, the marshy spring under Iria Hill, the old house on it. She thought about Daisy singing ballads in the kitchen, winter evenings, beating out the time with her wooden clogs; and old Coney in the vineyards with his razor-edge knife, showing her how to prune the vine 'right down to the life in it'; and Rose, her Etaudis, whispering charms to ease the pain in a child's broken arm. I have known wise people, she thought. Her mind flinched away from remembering her father, but the motion of the leaves and shadows drew it on. She saw him drunk, shouting. She felt his prying, tremulous hands on her. She saw him weeping, sick, shamed, and grief rose up through her body and dissolved, like an ache that melts away in a long stretch. He was less to her than the mother she had not known.

She stretched, feeling the ease of her body in the warmth, and her mind drifted back to Ivory. She had had no one in her life to desire. When the young wizard first came riding by so slim and arrogant, she wished she could want him; but she didn't and couldn't, and so she had thought him spell-protected. Rose had explained to her how wizards' spells worked 'so that it never enters your head nor theirs, see, because it would take from their power, they say'. But Ivory, poor Ivory, had been all too unprotected. If anybody was under a spell of chastity it must have been herself, for charming and handsome as he was she had never been able to feel a thing for him but liking, and her only lust was to learn what he could teach her.

She considered herself, sitting in the deep silence of the Grove. No bird sang; the breeze was down; the leaves hung still. Am I ensorcelled? Am I a sterile thing, not whole, not a woman? she asked herself, looking at her strong bare arms, the slight, soft swell of her breasts in the shadow under the throat of her shirt.

She looked up and saw the Hoary Man come out of a dark aisle of great oaks and come towards her across the glade.

He stopped in front of her. She felt herself blush, her face and throat burning, dizzy, her ears ringing. She sought words, anything to say, to turn his attention away from her, and could find nothing at all. He sat down near her. She looked down, as if studying the skeleton of a last-year's leaf by her hand.

What do I want? she asked herself, and the answer came not in words but throughout her whole body and soul: the fire, a greater fire than that, the flight, the flight burning –

She came back into herself, into the still air under the trees. The Hoary Man sat near her, his face bowed down, and she thought how slight and light he looked, how quiet and sorrowful. There was nothing to fear. There was no harm.

He looked over at her.

'Irian,' he said, 'do you hear the leaves?'

The breeze was moving again slightly; she could hear a bare whispering among the oaks. 'A little,' she said.

'Do you hear the words?'

'No.'

She asked nothing and he said no more. Presently he got up, and she followed him to the path that always led them, sooner or later, out of the wood to the clearing by the Thwilburn and the Otter's House. When they came there, it was late afternoon. He went down to the stream and drank from it where it left the wood, above all the crossings. She did the same. Then sitting in the cool, long grass of the bank, he began to speak.

'My people, the Kargs, they worship gods. Twin gods, brothers. And the king there is also a god. But before that and after are the streams. Caves, stones, hills. Trees. The earth. The darkness of the earth.'

'The Old Powers,' Irian said.

He nodded. 'There, women know the Old Powers. Here too, witches. And the knowledge is bad – eh?'

When he added that little questioning 'eh?' or 'neh?' to the end of what had seemed a statement it always took her by surprise. She said nothing.

'Dark is bad,' said the Patterner. 'Eh?'

Irian drew a deep breath and looked at him eye to eye as they sat there. '"Only in dark the light,"' she said.

'Ah,' he said. He looked away so that she could not see his expression.

'I should go,' she said. 'I can walk in the Grove, but not live there. It isn't my – my place. And the Master Chanter said I did harm by being here.'

'We all do harm by being,' said the Patterner.

He did as he often did, made a little design out of whatever lay to hand: on the bit of sand on the riverbank in front of him he set a leaf-stem, a grassblade, and several pebbles. He studied them and rearranged them. 'Now I must speak of harm,' he said.

After a long pause he went on. 'You know that a dragon brought back our Lord Sparrowhawk, with the young king, from the shores of death. Then the dragon carried Sparrowhawk away to his home, for his power was gone, he was not a mage. So presently the Masters of Roke met to choose a new Archmage, here, in the Grove, as always. But not as always.

'Before the dragon came, the Summoner too had returned from death, where he can go, where his art can take him. He had seen our lord and the young king there, in that country across the wall of stones. He said they would not come back.

He said Lord Sparrowhawk had told him to come back to us, to life, to bear that word. So we grieved for our lord.

'But then came the dragon, Kalessin, bearing him living.

'The Summoner was among us when we stood on Roke Knoll and saw the Archmage kneel to King Lebannen. Then, as the dragon bore our friend away, the Summoner fell down.

'He lay as if dead, cold, his heart not beating, yet he breathed. The Herbal used all his art, but could not rouse him. "He is dead," he said. "The breath will not leave him, but he is dead." So we mourned him. Then, because there was dismay among us, and all my patterns spoke of change and danger, we met to choose a new Warden of Roke, an Archmage to guide us. And in our council we set the young king in the Summoner's place. To us it seemed right that he should sit among us. Only the Changer spoke against it at first, and then agreed.

'But we met, we sat, and we could not choose. We said this and said that, but no name was spoken. And then I . . .' He paused a while. 'There came on me what my people call the *eduevanu*, the other breath. Words came to me and I spoke them. I said, *Hama Gondun!* And Kurremkarmerruk told them this in Hardic: "A woman on Gont." But when I came back to my own wits, I could not tell them what that meant. And so we parted with no Archmage chosen.

'The king left soon after, and the Master Windkey went with him. Before the king was to be crowned, they went to Gont and sought our lord, to find what that meant, "a woman on Gont". Eh? But they did not see him, only my countrywoman Tenar of the Ring. She said she was not the woman they sought. And they found no one, nothing. So Lebannen judged it to be a prophecy yet to be fulfilled. And in Havnor he set his crown on his own head.

'The Herbal, and I too, judged the Summoner dead. We thought the breath he breathed was left from some spell of his own art that we did not understand, like the spell snakes know that keeps their heart beating long after they are dead. Though it seemed terrible to bury a breathing body, yet he was cold, and his blood did not run, and no soul was in him. That was more terrible. So we made ready to bury him. And then, by his grave, his eyes opened. He moved, and spoke. He said, "I have summoned myself again into life, to do what must be done."'

The Patterner's voice had grown rougher, and he suddenly brushed the little design of pebbles apart with the palm of his hand.

'So when the Windkey returned, we were nine again. But divided. For the Summoner said we must meet again and choose an Archmage. The king had had no place among us, he said. And "a woman on Gont", whoever she may be, has no place among the men on Roke. Eh? The Windkey, the Chanter, the Changer, the Hand, say he is right. And as King Lebannen is one returned from death, fulfilling that prophecy, they say so will the Archmage be one returned from death.'

'But –' Irian said, and stopped.

After a while the Patterner said, 'That art, summoning, you know, is very . . . terrible. It is . . . always danger. Here,' and he looked up into the green-gold darkness of the trees, 'here is no summoning. No bringing back across the wall. No wall.'

His face was a warrior's face, but when he looked into the trees it was softened, yearning.

'So,' he said, 'now he makes you his reason for our meeting. But I will not go to the Great House. I will not be summoned.'

'He won't come here?'

'I think he will not walk in the Grove. Nor on Roke Knoll. On the Knoll, what is, is so.'

She did not know what he meant, but did not ask, preoccupied: 'You say he makes me his reason for you to meet together.'

'Yes. To send away one woman, it takes nine mages.' He very seldom smiled, and when he did it was quick and fierce. 'We are to meet to uphold the Rule of Roke. And so to choose an Archmage.'

'If I went away –' She saw him shake his head. 'I could go to the Namer –'

'You are safer here.'

The idea of doing harm troubled her, but the idea of danger had not entered her mind. She found it inconceivable. 'I'll be all right,' she said. 'So the Namer, and you – and the Doorkeeper?'

'– do not wish Thorion to be Archmage. Also the Master Herbal, though he digs and says little.' He saw Irian staring at him in amazement. 'Thorion the Summoner speaks his true name,' he said. 'He died, eh?'

She knew that King Lebannen used his true name openly. He too had returned from death. Yet that the Summoner should do so continued to shock and disturb her as she thought about it.

'And the . . . the students?'

'Divided also.'

She thought about the School, where she had been so briefly. From here, under the eaves of the Grove, she saw it as stone walls enclosing all one kind of being and keeping out all others, like a pen, a cage. How could any of them keep their balance in a place like that?

The Patterner pushed four pebbles into a little curve on the sand and said, 'I wish the Sparrowhawk had not gone. I wish I could read what the shadows write. But all I can hear the leaves say is change, change . . . Everything will change but them.' He looked up into the trees again with that yearning look. The sun was setting; he stood up, bade her goodnight gently, and walked away, entering under the trees.

She sat on a while by the Thwilburn. She was troubled by what he had told her and by her thoughts and feelings in the Grove, and troubled that any thought or feeling could have troubled her there. She went to the house, set out her supper of smoked meat and bread and summer lettuce, and ate it without tasting it. She roamed restlessly back down the streambank to the water. It was very still and warm in the late dusk, only the largest stars burning through a milky overcast. She slipped off her sandals and put her feet in the water. It was cool, but veins of sunwarmth ran through it. She slid out of her clothes, the man's breeches and shirt that were all she had, and slipped naked into the water, feeling the push and stir of the current all along her body. She had never swum in the streams at Iria, and she had hated the sea, heaving grey and cold, but this quick water pleased her, tonight. She drifted and floated, her hands slipping over silken underwater rocks and her own silken flanks, her legs sliding through waterweeds. All trouble and restlessness washed away from her in the running of the water, and she floated in delight in the caress of the stream, gazing up at the white, soft fire of the stars.

A chill ran through her. The water ran cold. Gathering herself together, her limbs still soft and loose, she looked up and saw on the bank above her the black figure of a man.

She stood straight up in the water.

'Get out!' she shouted. 'Get away, you traitor, you foul lecher, or I'll cut the liver out of you!' She sprang up the bank, pulling herself up by the tough bunchgrass, and scrambled to her feet. No one was there. She stood afire, shaking with rage. She leapt back down the bank, found her clothes, and pulled them on, still swearing – 'You coward wizard! You traitorous son of a bitch!'

'Irian?'

'He was here!' she cried. 'That foul heart, that Thorion!' She strode to meet the Patterner as he came into the starlight by the house. 'I was bathing in the stream, and he stood there watching me!'

'A sending – only a seeming of him. It could not hurt you, Irian.'

'A sending with eyes, a seeming with seeing! May he be –' She stopped, at a loss suddenly for the word. She felt sick. She shuddered, and swallowed the cold spittle that welled in her mouth.

The Patterner came forward and took her hands in his. His hands were warm, and she felt so mortally cold that she came close up against him for the warmth of his body. They stood so for a while, her face turned from him but their hands joined and their bodies pressed close. At last she broke free, straightening herself, pushing back her lank wet hair. 'Thank you,' she said. 'I was cold.'

'I know.'

'I'm never cold,' she said. 'It was him.'

'I tell you, Irian, he cannot come here, he cannot harm you here.'

'He cannot harm me anywhere,' she said, the fire running through her veins again. 'If he tries to, I'll destroy him.'

'Ah,' said the Patterner.

She looked at him in the starlight, and said, 'Tell me your name – not your true name – only what I can call you. When I think of you.'

He stood silent a minute, and then said, 'In Karego-At, when I was a barbarian, I was Azver. In Hardic, that is a banner of war.'

'Thank you,' she said.

She lay awake in the little house, feeling the air stifling and the ceiling pressing down on her, then slept suddenly and deeply. She woke as suddenly when the east was just getting light. She went to the door to see what she loved best to see, the sky before sunrise. Looking down from it she saw Azver the Patterner rolled up in his grey cloak, sound asleep on the ground before her doorstep. She withdrew noiselessly into the house. In a little while she saw him going back to his woods, walking a bit stiffly and scratching his head as he went, as people do when half-awake.

She got to work scraping down the inner wall of the house, readying it to plaster. But before the sun was in the windows, there was a knock at her open door. Outside was the man she had thought was a gardener, the Master Herbal, looking solid and stolid, like a brown ox, beside the gaunt, grim-faced old Namer.

She came to the door and muttered some kind of greeting. They daunted her, these Masters of Roke, and also their presence meant that the peaceful time was over, the days of walking in the silent summer forest with the Patterner. That had come to an end last night. She knew it, but she did not want to know it.

'The Patterner sent for us,' said the Master Herbal. He looked uncomfortable. Noticing a clump of weeds under the window, he said, 'That's velver. Somebody from Havnor planted it here.

Didn't know there was any on the island.' He examined it attentively, and put some seedpods into his pouch.

Irian was studying the Namer covertly but equally attentively, trying to see if she could tell if he was what he had called a sending or was there in flesh and blood. Nothing about him appeared insubstantial, but she thought he was not there, and when he stepped into the slanting sunlight and cast no shadow, she knew it.

'Is it a long way from where you live, sir?' she asked.

He nodded. 'Left myself halfway,' he said. He looked up; the Patterner was coming towards them, wide awake now.

He greeted them and asked, 'The Doorkeeper will come?'

'Said he thought he'd better keep the doors,' said the Herbal. He closed his many-pocketed pouch carefully and looked around at the others. 'But I don't know if he can keep a lid on the ant-hill.'

'What's up?' said Kurremkarmerruk. 'I've been reading about dragons. Not paying attention. But all the boys I had studying at the Tower left.'

'Summoned,' said the Herbal, drily.

'So?' said the Namer, more drily.

'I can tell you only how it seems to me,' the Herbal said, reluctant, uncomfortable.

'Do that,' the old mage said.

The Herbal still hesitated. 'This lady is not of our council,' he said at last.

'She is of mine,' said Azver.

'She came to this place at this time,' the Namer said. 'And to this place, at this time, no one comes by chance. All any of us knows is how it seems to us. There are names behind names, my Lord Healer.'

The dark-eyed mage bowed his head at that, and said, 'Very well,' evidently with relief at accepting their judgement over his own. 'Thorion has been much with the other Masters, and with the young men. Secret meetings, inner circles. Rumours, whispers. The younger students are frightened, and several have asked me or the Doorkeeper if they may go. And we'd let them go. But there's no ship in port, and none has come into Thwil Bay since the one that brought you, lady, and sailed again next day for Wathort. The Windkey keeps the Roke-wind against all. If the king himself should come, he could not land on Roke.'

'Until the wind changes, eh?' said the Patterner.

'Thorion says Lebannen is not truly king, since no Archmage crowned him.'

'Nonsense! Not history!' said the old Namer. 'The first Archmage came centuries after the last king. Roke ruled in the kings' stead.'

'Ah,' said the Patterner. 'Hard for the housekeeper to give up the keys when the owner comes home.'

'The Ring of Peace is healed,' said the Herbal, in his patient, troubled voice, 'the prophecy is fulfilled, the son of Morred is crowned, and yet we have no peace. Where have we gone wrong? Why can we not find the balance?'

'What does Thorion intend?' asked the Namer.

'To bring Lebannen here,' said the Herbal. 'The young men talk of "the true crown". A second coronation, here. By the Archmage Thorion.'

'Avert!' Irian blurted out, making the sign to prevent word from becoming deed. None of the men smiled, and the Herbal belatedly made the same gesture.

'How does he hold them all?' the Namer said. 'Herbal, you were here when Sparrowhawk and Thorion were challenged by Irioth. His gift was as great as Thorion's, I think. He used it to use men, to control them wholly. Is that what Thorion does?'

'I don't know,' the Herbal said. 'I can only tell you that when I'm with him, when I'm in the Great House, I feel that nothing can be done but what has been done. That nothing will change. Nothing will grow. That no matter what cures I use, the sickness will end in death.' He looked around at them all like a hurt ox. 'And I think it is true. There is no way to regain the Equilibrium but by holding still. We have gone too far. For the Archmage and Lebannen to go bodily into death, and return – it was not right. They broke a law that must not be broken. It was to restore the law that Thorion returned.'

'What, to send them back into death?' the Namer said, and the Patterner, 'Who is to say what is the law?'

'There is a wall,' the Herbal said.

'That wall is not as deep-rooted as my trees,' said the Patterner.

'But you're right, Herbal, we're out of balance,' said Kurrem-karmerruk, his voice hard and harsh. 'When and where did we begin to go too far? What have we forgotten, turned our back on, overlooked?'

Irian looked from one to the other.

'When the balance is wrong, holding still is not good. It must get more wrong,' said the Patterner. 'Until –' He made a quick gesture of reversal with his open hands, down going up and up down.

'What's more wrong than to summon oneself back from death?' said the Namer.

'Thorion was the best of us all – a brave heart, a noble mind.' The Herbal spoke almost in anger. 'Sparrowhawk loved him. So did we all.'

'Conscience caught him,' said the Namer. 'Conscience told him he alone could set things right. To do it, he denied his death. So he denies life.'

'And who shall stand against him?' said the Patterner. 'I can only hide in my woods.'

'And I in my tower,' said the Namer. 'And you, Herbal, and the Doorkeeper, are in the trap, in the Great House. The walls we built to keep all evil out. Or in, as the case may be.'

'We are four against him,' said the Patterner.

'They are five against us,' said the Herbal.

'Has it come to this,' the Namer said, 'that we stand at the edge of the forest Segoy planted and talk of how to destroy one another?'

'Yes,' said the Patterner. 'What goes too long unchanged destroys itself. The forest is for ever because it dies and dies and so lives. I will not let this dead hand touch me. Or touch the king who brought us hope. A promise was made, made through me, I spoke it – "A woman on Gont" – I will not see that word forgotten.'

'Then should we go to Gont?' said the Herbal, caught in Azver's passion. 'Sparrowhawk is there.'

'Tenar of the Ring is there,' said Azver.

'Maybe our hope is there,' said the Namer.

They stood silent, uncertain, trying to cherish hope.

Irian stood silent too, but her hope sank down, replaced by a sense of shame and utter insignificance. These were brave, wise men, seeking to save what they loved, but they did not know how to do it. And she had no share in their wisdom, no part in their decisions. She drew away from them, and they did not notice. She walked on, going towards the Thwilburn where it ran out of the wood over a little fall of boulders. The water was bright in the morning sunlight and made a happy noise. She wanted to cry but she had never been good at crying. She stood and watched the water, and her shame turned slowly into anger.

She came back towards the three men, and said, 'Azver.'

He turned to her, startled, and came forward a little.

'Why did you break your Rule for me? Was it fair to me, who can never be what you are?'

Azver frowned. 'The Doorkeeper admitted you because you asked,' he said. 'I brought you to the Grove because the leaves of the trees spoke your name to me before you ever came here. *Irian*, they said, *Irian*. Why you came I don't know, but not by chance. The Summoner too knows that.'

'Maybe I came to destroy him.'

He looked at her and said nothing.

'Maybe I came to destroy Roke.'

His pale eyes blazed then. 'Try!'

A long shudder went through her as she stood facing him. She felt herself larger than he was, larger than she was, enormously larger. She could reach out one finger and destroy him. He stood there in his small, brave, brief humanity, his mortality, defenceless. She drew a long, long breath. She stepped back from him.

The sense of huge strength was draining out of her. She turned her head a little and looked down, surprised to see her own brown arm, her rolled-up sleeve, the grass springing cool and green around her sandalled feet. She looked back at the Patterner and he still seemed a fragile being. She pitied and honoured him. She wanted to warn him of the peril he was in. But no words came to her at all. She turned round and went back to the streambank by the little falls. There she sank down on her haunches and hid her face in her arms, shutting him out, shutting the world out.

The voices of the mages talking were like the voices of the stream running. The stream said its words and they said theirs, but none of them were the right words.

4. Irian

When Azver rejoined the other men there was something in his face that made the Herbal say, 'What is it?'

'I don't know,' he said. 'Maybe we should not leave Roke.'

'Probably we can't,' said the Herbal. 'If the Windkey locks the winds against us . . .'

'I'm going back to where I am,' Kurremkarmerruk said abruptly. 'I don't like leaving myself about like an old shoe. I'll join you this evening.' And he was gone.

'I'd like to walk under your trees a bit, Azver,' the Herbal said, with a long sigh.

'Go on, Deyala. I'll stay here.' The Herbal went off. Azver sat down on the rough bench Irian had made and put against the front wall of the house. He looked upstream at her, crouching motionless on the bank. Sheep in the field between them and the Great House blatted softly. The morning sun was getting hot.

His father had named him Banner of War. He had come west, leaving all he knew behind him, and had learned his true name from the trees of the Immanent Grove, and become the Patterner of Roke. All this year the patterns of the shadows and the branches and the roots, all the silent language of his forest, had spoken of destruction, of transgression, of all things changed. Now it was upon them, he knew. It had come with her.

She was in his charge, in his care, he had known that when

he saw her. Though she came to destroy Roke, as she had said, he must serve her. He did so willingly. She had walked with him in the forest, tall, awkward, fearless; she had put aside the thorny arms of brambles with her big, careful hand. Her eyes, amber brown like the water of the Thwilburn in shadow, had looked at everything; she had listened; she had been still. He wanted to protect her and knew he could not. He had given her a little warmth when she was cold. He had nothing else to give her. Where she must go she would go. She did not understand danger. She had no wisdom but her innocence, no armour but her anger. Who are you, Irian? he said to her, watching her crouched there like an animal locked in its muteness.

His friend came back from the woods and sat down beside him on the bench a while. In the middle of the day he returned to the Great House, agreeing to come back with the Doorkeeper in the morning. They would ask all the other Masters to meet with them in the Grove. 'But *he* won't come,' Deyala said, and Azver nodded.

All day he stayed near the Otter's House, keeping watch on Irian, making her eat a little with him. She came to the house, but when they had eaten she went back to her place on the streambank and sat there motionless. And he too felt a lethargy in his own body and mind, a stupidity, which he fought against but could not shake off. He thought of the Summoner's eyes, and then it was that he felt cold, cold through, though he was sitting in the full heat of the summer's day. We are ruled by the dead, he thought. The thought would not leave him.

He was grateful to see Kurremkarmerruk coming slowly down the bank of the Thwilburn from the north. The old man waded through the stream barefoot, holding his shoes in one hand and his tall staff in the other, snarling when he missed his footing on the rocks. He sat down on the near bank to dry his feet and put his shoes back on. 'When I go back to the Tower,' he said, 'I'll ride. Hire a carter, buy a mule. I'm old, Azver.'

'Come up to the house,' the Patterner said, and he set out water and food for the Namer.

'Where's the girl?'

'Asleep.' Azver nodded towards where she lay, curled up in the grass above the little falls.

The heat of the day was beginning to lessen and the shadows of the Grove lay across the grass, though the Otter's House was still in sunlight. Kurremkarmerruk sat on the bench with his back against the house wall, and Azver on the doorstep.

'We've come to the end of it,' the old man said out of silence.

Azver nodded, in silence.

'What brought you here, Azver?' the Namer asked. 'I've often thought of asking you. A long, long way to come. And you have no wizards in the Kargish lands, I think.'

'No. But we have the things wizardry is made of. Water, stones, trees, words . . .'

'But not the words of the Making.'

'No. Nor dragons.'

'Never?'

'Only in some very, very old tales. Before the gods were. Before men were. Before men were men, they were dragons.'

'Now that is interesting,' said the old scholar, sitting up straighter. 'I told you I was reading about dragons. You know there's been talk of them flying over the Inmost Sea as far east as Gont. That was no doubt Kalessin taking Ged home, multiplied by sailors making a good story better. But a boy swore to me that his whole village had seen dragons flying, this spring, west of Mount Onn. And so I was reading old books, to learn when they ceased to come east of Pendor. And in one I came on your story, or something like it. That men and dragons were all one kind, but they quarrelled. Some went west and some east, and they became two kinds, and forgot they were ever one.'

'We went farthest east,' Azver said. 'But do you know what the leader of an army is, in my tongue?'

'*Edran*,' said the Namer promptly, and laughed. 'Drake. Dragon . . .' After a while he said, 'I could chase an etymology on the brink of doom . . . But I think, Azver, that that's where we are. We won't defeat him.'

'He has the advantage,' Azver said, very dry.

'He does. So . . . So therefore, admitting it unlikely, admitting it impossible – if we did defeat him – if he went back into death and left us here alive – what would we do? What comes next?'

After a long time, Azver said, 'I have no idea.'

'Your leaves and shadows tell you nothing?'

'Change, change,' said the Patterner. 'Transformation.'

He looked up suddenly. The sheep, who had been grouped near the stile, were scurrying off, and someone was coming along the path from the Great House.

'A group of young men,' said the Herbal, breathless, as he came to them. 'Thorion's army. Coming here. To take the girl. To send her away.' He stood and drew breath. 'The Doorkeeper was speaking with them when I left. I think –'

'Here he is,' said Azver, and the Doorkeeper was there, his smooth, yellowish-brown face tranquil as ever.

'I told them,' he said, 'that if they went out Medra's Gate this day, they'd never go back through it into a House they knew. Some of them were for turning back, then. But the Windkey and the Chanter urged them on. They'll be along soon.'

They could hear men's voices in the fields east of the Grove.

Azver went quickly to where Irian lay beside the stream, and the others followed him. She roused up and got to her feet, looking dull and dazed. They were standing around her, a kind of guard, when the group of thirty or more men came past the little house and approached them. They were mostly older students; there were five or six wizard's staffs among the crowd, and the Master Windkey led them. His thin, keen old face looked strained and weary, but he greeted the four mages courteously by their titles. They greeted him, and Azver took the word – 'Come into the Grove, Master Windkey,' he said, 'and we will wait there for the others of the Nine.'

'First we must settle the matter that divides us,' said the Windkey.

'That is a stony matter,' said the Namer.

'The woman with you defies the Rule of Roke,' the Windkey said. 'She must leave. A boat is waiting at the dock to take her, and the wind, I can tell you, will stand fair for Way.'

'I have no doubt of that, my lord,' said Azver, 'but I doubt she will go.'

'My Lord Patterner, will you defy our Rule and our community, that has been one so long, upholding order against the forces of ruin? Will it be you, of all men, who breaks the pattern?'

'It is not glass, to break,' Azver said. 'It is breath, it is fire.'

It cost him a great effort to speak.

'It does not know death,' he said, but he spoke in his own language, and they did not understand him. He drew closer to Irian. He felt the warmth of her body. She stood staring, in that animal silence, as if she did not understand any of them.

'Lord Thorion has returned from death to save us all,' the Windkey said, fiercely and clearly. 'He will be Archmage. Under his rule Roke will be as it was. The king will receive the true crown from his hand, and rule with his guidance, as Morred ruled. No witches will defile sacred ground. No dragons will threaten the Inmost Sea. There will be order, safety, and peace.'

None of the mages answered him. In the silence, the men with him murmured, and a voice among them said, 'Let us have the witch.'

'No,' Azver said, but could say nothing else. He held his staff of willow, but it was only wood in his hand. Of the four of them, only the Doorkeeper moved and spoke. He took a step forward, looking from one young man to the next and the next. He said, 'You trusted me, giving me your names. Will you trust me now?'

'My lord,' said one of them with a fine, dark face and a wizard's oaken staff, 'we do trust you, and therefore ask you to let the witch go, and peace return.'

Irian stepped forward before the Doorkeeper could answer.

'I am not a witch,' she said. Her voice sounded high, metallic, after the men's deep voices. 'I have no art. No knowledge. I came to learn.'

'We do not teach women here,' said the Windkey. 'You know that.'

'I know nothing,' Irian said. She stepped forward again, facing the mage directly. 'Tell me who I am.'

'Learn your place, woman,' the mage said with cold passion.

'My place,' she said, slowly, the words dragging, 'my place is on the hill. Where things are what they are. Tell the dead man I will meet him there.'

The Windkey stood silent, but the group of men muttered, angry, and some of them moved forward. Azver came between her and them, her words releasing him from the paralysis of mind and body that had held him. 'Tell Thorion we will meet him on Roke Knoll,' he said. 'When he comes, we will be there. Now come with me,' he said to Irian. The Namer, the Doorkeeper, and the Herbal followed him with her into the Grove. There was a path for them. But when some of the young men started after them, there was no path.

'Come back,' the Windkey said to the men.

They turned back, uncertain. The low sun was still bright on the fields and the roofs of the Great House, but inside the wood it was all shadows.

'Witchery,' they said, 'sacrilege, defilement.'

'Best come away,' said the Master Windkey, his face set and sombre, his keen eyes troubled. He set off back to the School, and they straggled after him, arguing and debating in frustration and anger.

They were not far inside the Grove, and still beside the stream, when Irian stopped, turned aside, and crouched down by the enormous, hunching roots of a willow that leaned out over the water. The four mages stood on the path.

'She spoke with the other breath,' Azver said.

The Namer nodded.

'So we must follow her?' the Herbal asked.

This time the Doorkeeper nodded. He smiled faintly and said, 'So it would seem.'

'Very well,' said the Herbal, with his patient, troubled look; and he went aside a little, and knelt to look at some small plant or fungus on the forest floor.

Time passed as always in the Grove, not passing at all it seemed, yet gone, the day gone quietly by in a few long breaths, a quivering of leaves, a bird singing far off and another answering it from even farther. Irian stood up slowly. She did not speak, but looked down the path, and then walked down it. The four men followed her.

They came out into the calm, open evening air. The west still held some brightness as they crossed the Thwilburn and walked across the fields to Roke Knoll, which stood up before them in a high dark curve against the sky.

'They're coming,' the Doorkeeper said. Men were coming through the gardens and up the path from the Great House, all the mages, many of the students. Leading them was Thorion the Summoner, tall in his grey cloak, carrying his tall staff of bone-white wood, about which a faint gleam of werelight hovered.

Where the two paths met and joined to wind up to the heights of the Knoll, Thorion stopped and stood waiting for them. Irian strode forward to face him.

'Irian of Way,' the Summoner said in his deep, clear voice, 'that there may be peace and order, and for the sake of the balance of all things, I bid you now leave this island. We cannot give you what you ask, and for that we ask your forgiveness. But if you seek to stay here you forfeit forgiveness, and must learn what follows on transgression.'

She stood up, almost as tall as he, and as straight. She said nothing for a minute and then spoke out in a high, harsh voice. 'Come up on to the hill, Thorion,' she said.

She left him standing at the waymeet, on the level ground, and walked up the hill path for a little way, a few strides. She turned and looked back down at him. 'What keeps you from the hill?' she said.

The air was darkening around them. The west was only a dull red line, the eastern sky was shadowy above the sea.

The Summoner looked up at Irian. Slowly he raised his arms and the white staff in the invocation of a spell, speaking in the tongue that all the wizards and mages of Roke had learned, the language of their art, the Language of the Making: 'Irian, by your name I summon you and bind you to obey me!'

She hesitated, seeming for a moment to yield, to come to him, and then cried out, 'I am not only Irian!'

At that the Summoner ran up towards her, reaching out, lunging at her as if to seize and hold her. They were both on the hill now. She towered above him impossibly, fire breaking forth between them, a flare of red flame in the dusk air, a gleam of red-gold scales, of vast wings – then that was gone, and there was nothing there but the woman standing on the hill path and the tall man bowing down before her, bowing slowly down to earth, and lying on it.

Of them all it was the Herbal, the healer, who was the first to move. He went up the path and knelt down by Thorion. 'My lord,' he said, 'my friend.'

Under the folds of the grey cloak his hands found only a huddle of clothes and dry bones and a broken staff.

'This is better, Thorion,' he said, but he was weeping.

The old Namer came forward and said to the woman on the hill, 'Who are you?'

'I do not know my other name,' she said. She spoke as he had spoken, as she had spoken to the Summoner, in the Language of the Making, the tongue the dragons speak.

She turned away and began to walk on up the hill.

'Irian,' said Azver the Patterner, 'will you come back to us?'

She halted and let him come up to her. 'I will, if you call me,' she said.

She reached out and touched his hand. He drew his breath sharply.

'Where will you go?' he said.

'To those who will give me my name. In fire not water. My people.'

'In the west,' he said.

She said, 'Beyond the west.'

She turned away from him and them and went on up the hill in the gathering darkness. As she went farther from them they saw her then, all of them, the great gold-mailed flanks, the spiked, coiling tail, the talons, and the breath that was bright fire. On the crest of the Knoll she paused a while, her long head turning to look slowly round the Isle of Roke, gazing longest at the Grove, only a blur of darkness in darkness now. Then with a rattle like the shaking of sheets of brass the wide, vaned wings opened and the dragon sprang up into the air, circled Roke Knoll once, and flew.

A curl of fire, a wisp of smoke drifted down through the dark air.

Azver the Patterner stood with his left hand holding his right hand, which her touch had burnt. He looked down at the men who stood silent at the foot of the hill, staring after the dragon. 'Well, my friends,' he said, 'what now?'

Only the Doorkeeper answered. He said, 'I think we should go to our House, and open its doors.'

THE
RIFTWAR
SAGA

RAYMOND E. FEIST

THE
RIFTWAR
SAGA

RAYMOND E. FEIST

Raymond E. Feist's Riftwar fantasy series begins with the adventures of two boys, Pug and Tomas, each wishing to rise above his lowly station in life. Pug desires to become a magician, Tomas a great warrior. Each achieves his dream through outside agencies and their own natural abilities; Pug is kidnapped during the Riftwar, discovered to have magic abilities, and is trained to greatness. Tomas stumbles upon a dying dragon who gives him a suit of armour imbued with an ancient magic, turning him into a warrior of legendary might.

As Pug and Tomas undergo their transformations and become more adept at controlling the powers that have been granted them, the scope of the novel expands to reveal more about the two worlds upon which the conflict known as the Riftwar takes place: Midkemia and Kelewan. Midkemia is a young world, vibrant and conflict-ridden, while Kelewan is ancient and tradition-bound, but no freer of conflict. The militaristic

Tsurani, from Kelewan, have invaded the Kingdom of the Isles on Midkemia to expand their domain and seize metals common on Midkemia but rare at home. The only way open between these worlds is a magic Rift, and through that portal in space-time the invaders have established a foothold in the Kingdom. Gradually Tomas learns that he has become invested with the power of a Valheru, one of the mystical creatures who are legends in Midkemia. The Dragon Lords were near-godlike beings who once warred with the gods themselves. The action in the first trilogy comes to a climax in *A Darkness at Sethanon*, with the resolution of the war between the Kingdom and the invading Tsurani, Tomas gaining control over the ancient magic that sought to conquer him, and Pug returning to the homeland of his youth.

The Empire Trilogy concerns itself with conflict back on the Tsurani home world, where for much of the first and second books we see 'the other side of the Riftwar'. Lady Mara of the Acoma, a girl of seventeen in the first book, is thrust into a murderous game of politics and ritual, and only through her own genius and ability to improvise does she weather unrelenting attacks on all sides. Aided by a loyal group of followers, including a Kingdom slave named Kevin, whom she comes to love more than any other, Mara rises to dominate the Empire of Tsuranuanni, even facing down the mighty Great Ones, the magicians who are outside the law.

The latest series, the Serpentwar saga, is the story of Erik, the bastard son of a noble, and Roo, a street boy who is his best friend. The Kingdom again faces invaders, but this time from across the sea. The story of the two young men is set against the Kingdom's hurried preparation for and resistance against a huge army under the banner of the Emerald Queen, a woman who is another agent of dark forces seeking dominion over the world of Midkemia. More of the cosmic nature of the battle between good and evil is revealed and Pug and Tomas again have to take a hand in the struggle.

Feist sees Midkemia as an objective, virtual world, even though a fictional one. He regards all the tales set in Midkemia as historical novels and stories of this fantastic realm. 'The Wood Boy' is a tale from the early days of the Riftwar, when the Tsurani first were establishing their foothold in the Kingdom.

◆

THE WOOD BOY

BY RAYMOND E. FEIST

The Duke looked up.

Borric, Duke of Crydee and second-in-command of the Armies of the West, acknowledged the captain at the door of his command tent. 'Your Grace, if you have a minute and could come outside?'

Borric stood up, envying his old friend Brucal, who was now probably sitting before a warm fire somewhere in LaMut while he wrote long letters of complaint to the Prince of Krondor about supplies.

The war was leaving its second winter and a stable front had been established, with Borric's headquarters camp located ten miles behind the lines. The Duke was a seasoned campaigner, having fought against goblins and the Brotherhood of the Dark Path – the dark elves – since boyhood, and every bone in his body told him this was going to be a long war.

The Duke donned his heavy cloak, and wrapped his scarf around him. He exited his tent and a strange tableau greeted him.

In the distance, a group of figures could barely be seen as they approached the camp. Through the swirling snow Borric could see them slowly take shape. Grey figures against the dull white, surrounded by a haze of snowflakes, they approached at a steady rate. Finally, the figures resolved themselves into a patrol escorting someone.

The soldiers marched slowly, for the figure they surrounded was pulling a heavy sled, plodding along at a steady pace despite what appeared a heavy burden. As they came close,

Borric could see it was a peasant boy who laboured to haul the sled to the camp. He moved with steady purpose, coming at last to stand before the commander of the King's Armies of the West.

Borric looked at the lad, who had obviously been through an ordeal. He was bareheaded, his blond hair encrusted with ice crystals. About his neck and face he wore a heavy scarf wrapped several times around. He wore a heavy jacket and trousers, and thick sturdy boots. His simple wool coat was stained dark with blood.

He had been pulling a sled, laden with odd cargo. A large sack had been secured with ropes atop the sled, and over that two bodies had been lashed down. A dead man stared up at the sky with empty eyes, his lashes sparkling with frozen tears. He had been a fighter, from the look of him, and he wore leather armour. His scabbard hung empty at his side and his left glove was missing. Beside him lay a girl, under blankets, so that it appeared she was sleeping. She had been a pretty girl in life, but in death her features were almost porcelain, near perfection in their pale whiteness.

'Who are you, boy?'

The boy said, 'I am the Wood Boy.' His voice was faint and his eyes were vacant, as if he stared inward, though they were fixed on Borric.

'What did you say?' asked the Duke.

The boy seemed to gather his wits. 'Sir, my name is Dirk. I am the servant of Lord Paul of White Hill. It's the estate on the other side of the Kakisaw Valley.' He pointed to the west. 'Three days' walk from here. I carry firewood.'

Borric nodded. 'I know the estate. I've visited Lord Paul many times over the years. That's thirty-five miles from here, and twenty behind enemy lines.' Pointing to the sled, he asked, 'What is this?'

Weary, the boy said, 'It is my master's treasure. She is his daughter. The man is a murderer. He was once my friend.'

'You'd better come inside and tell me your story,' said Borric. He motioned for two soldiers to take the ropes that the boy used as a harness to pull the sled out of the way, and indicated that another man should help the exhausted youth.

The Duke led the boy inside and let him know it was permissible to sit. He signalled for an orderly to get the boy a cup of hot tea and something to eat, and as the soldier hurried to obey, Borric said, 'Why don't you start at the beginning, Dirk?'

Spring brought the Tsurani. They had been reported in the Grey Tower Mountains the year before, bringing dire warnings of invasion from both the Kingdom rulers on the other side of the mountains and some of the more important merchants and nobles in the other Free Cities. But the tales that accompanied the warning, of fierce warriors appearing out of nowhere by some magic means, had been met with scepticism and disbelief. And the fighting seemed distant, up in the mountains between Borric of Crydee's soldiers, the dwarves, and the invaders.

Until the first warning by the Rangers of Natal – who had quickly ridden on to warn others – followed a day later by a column of short men in their brightly-coloured armour who appeared on the road approaching the estate at White Hill.

Lord Paul had ordered his bodyguards to stand ready, but to offer no resistance unless provoked. Dirk and the rest of the household stood behind the Lord of White Hill and his armed guards.

Dirk glanced at his master and saw he stood alone, his daughter still in the house. Dirk wondered what extra protection the master thought that afforded his young daughter.

Dirk found the master's pose admirable. The stories of Tsurani fierceness had trickled down from the early fighting, and the Free Cities would be wholly dependent upon the Kingdom for defence. Areas like White Hill and the other estates around Walinor were simply on their own. Yet despite no hope of successful resistance, Lord Paul stood motionless, without any sign of fear, in his formal robe, the scarlet one with the ermine collar. No hereditary title had been conferred on any citizen since the Empire of Great Kesh had abandoned its northern colonies a century before, yet those families with ancient titles used them with pride. Like other nobles in the Free Cities, he held in disdain other men's claims on title while treasuring his own.

As the invaders calmly marched into view, it was obvious that any resistance would have been quickly crushed. Paul had a personal bodyguard and a score of hired mercenaries who acted as wagon guards and protection against roving bandits. But they were a poor band of hired cut-throats next to the highly-disciplined command that marched across the estate. The Tsurani wore bright orange and black armour, looking like lacquered hide or wood, nothing remotely like the metal armour worn by the officers of the Natal Defence Force.

Paul repeated the order that no resistance was to be mounted and when the Tsurani commander presented himself, Paul offered something that resembled a formal salute. Then, with the aid of a man in a black robe, the leader of the invaders gave his demands. The property of White Hill, as well as the surrounding countryside, was now under Tsurani rule, specifically an entity named Minwanabi. Dirk wondered if that was a person or a place, like a Kingdom Duchy. But he was too frightened to imagine voicing the question.

The leader of this group of Tsurani – all short, tough-looking veteran soldiers – could be differentiated from his men only by a slightly more ornate helm, graced with what Dirk took to be some creature's hair. The black fall reached the officer's shoulders.

Dirk tried to guess what the role of the black-robed man might be; the officer seemed extremely polite and deferential to him as he translated the officer's words for him.

The officer was called Chapka, and his rank was Hit Leader or Strike Leader, Dirk wasn't sure which.

He shouted orders and the black robe said, 'Only the noble of this house may bear arms, and his personal man.' Dirk took that to mean a bodyguard. That would be Hamish. 'All others put weapons here.'

The estate guards looked at Lord Paul, who nodded. They stepped forward and put their weapons in a pile, slowly, and then when they were done, they stepped back. 'Any other weapons?' asked the man in black.

One of the guards looked at his companions, then came forward and took a small blade from his boot, throwing it in the pile. He stepped back into line.

The officer shouted an order. A dozen Tsurani soldiers ran forward, each searching the now unarmed guards. One Tsurani stood, holding up a knife he had found in a guard's boot, and the officer indicated the man be brought forward. He spoke rapidly to the man in black, who said, 'This man disobeyed. He hid a weapon. He will be punished.'

Lord Paul slowly said, 'What shall you do with him?'

'The sword is too honourable a death for a disobedient slave. He will be hanged.'

The man turned pale. 'It was just a small one; I forgot I had it!'

The man was struck hard from behind and collapsed. Dirk watched in dread fascination as two other Tsurani soldiers dragged the guard – a man Dirk hardly knew, named Jackson – to the entrance to the barn. A hoist hung over the small door to the hayloft – there was one at each end of the barn – from which a long rope dangled. The unconscious man had the rope tied around his neck and was hoisted quickly up. He never regained consciousness, though his body twitched twice before it went still.

Dirk had seen dead men before; the town of Walinor where he grew up had known a few raids by bandits and the Brotherhood of the Dark Path, and once he had stumbled across a drunk who had frozen to death in the gutter outside an inn. But this hanging made his stomach twist, and he knew it was as much from fear over his own safety as from any revulsion over Jackson's death.

The black-robed man said, 'Any slave with weapon – we hang.'

Then the officer shouted an order, and Tsurani warriors ran off in all directions, a half-dozen into the master's house, others into the outbuildings, and still others to the springhouse, the barn, and the root cellar. Efficient to a degree that astonished Dirk, the Tsurani returned in short order and started reporting. Dirk couldn't understand them, but from the rapidity of the exchanges, he was certain they were listing what they found for their officer.

Others returned from the barn and kitchen carrying dozens of commonplace items. The officer, with the aid of the black-robed man, began interrogating Lord Paul about the nature of various common household items. As the master of the estate explained the use of such common tools as a leather punch or iron skillet, the Tsurani officer indicated one of two piles, one on a large canvas tarp. When two of the same items were displayed, one instantly went into one pile, while the other might join it or be separated.

Old William, the gardener and groundskeeper, said, 'Look at that,' as two Tsurani soldiers picked up the tarp, securing the larger of the two piles, and carried it off.

'What is it?' whispered Dirk, barely loud enough for the old man to hear.

'They're queer for metal,' softly said the old man with a knowing nod. 'Look at their armour and weapons.'

Dirk did so, and then it struck him. Nowhere on any Tsurani could a glint of sunlight on metal be seen. Their armour and weapons all appeared to be hide or wood cleverly fashioned and lacquered, but there were no buckles, blades, or fasteners of metal in evidence. From their cross-gartered sandals to the tops of their large flared helmets, the Tsurani appeared devoid of any metal artefacts.

'What's it mean?' whispered Dirk.

'I don't know, but I'm sure we'll find out,' said the old man.

The Tsurani continued their investigation of Lord Paul's household until almost sundown; then the household servants were ordered to gather their personal belongings and move them into the barn or kitchen, as the Tsurani would be occupying the servants' quarters. In a move that puzzled Dirk, the Tsurani officer stayed in the same building with his men, leaving Paul and his daughter alone in the big house.

It was but the first of many things that would puzzle Dirk over the coming year.

Alex lay curled up, his face a mask of pain while Hamish shouted, 'Don't get up!'

The Tsurani soldier who had struck the young man in the stomach stood over him, his hand a scant inch from the hilt of his sword. Alex groaned and again Hamish shouted to the young man to remain still.

Dirk stood near the entrance to the barn while those servants nearby stood anxiously watching, expecting the worst at any moment. The Tsurani had revealed themselves as strict but fair masters in the two months since arriving at White Hill, but there was occasionally some breach of etiquette or honour that took the residents of White Hill by surprise, often with bloody consequences. An old farmer by the name of Samuel had got drunk on fermented corncob squeeze a month earlier and had struck out at a Tsurani who had ordered him back into his home. Samuel had been beaten senseless and hanged as his wife and children looked on in horror.

Alex continued to groan but did as he was bid by Hamish until the Tsurani soldier seemed satisfied he wasn't going to move. The soldier said something in his alien language, spat in contempt upon the workman, turned, and walked away.

Hamish hesitated a moment, then he and Dirk hurried over to help Alex to his feet. 'What happened?' asked Dirk.

'I don't know,' said Alex. 'I just looked at the man.'

'It's how you looked at him,' said Hamish. 'You smirked at him. If you'd looked at me that way, I'd have done the same.' The burly old soldier inspected Alex. 'I had my fill of smirking boys in the army and knocked down a few in my time before I retired. Show these murderers some respect, lad, or they'll hang you just because they can and it's a slow day for amusements.'

Rubbing his side, Alex said, 'I won't do that again, you can bet.'

'See that you don't,' said Hamish. The old soldier motioned

for Drogen, his senior guard, to come over. 'Pass the word that the bastards seem touchy. Must have something to do with the war. Just make sure the lads know to keep polite and do whatever they're told.'

Drogen nodded and ran off. Hamish turned to inspect Alex again, then said, 'Get off with you. You'll live.'

Dirk helped Alex for a few steps. Then the man's legs seemed to steady and Dirk let go of his arm. 'They don't seem to take kindly to any sort of greeting,' said Dirk.

'I think keeping your eyes down or some such is what they want.'

Dirk said nothing. He was scared most of the time when he was around the Tsurani and didn't look at them for that reason. That was probably a wise choice, he judged.

'Can you take the wood?' asked Alex.

'Sure,' said Dirk before he realized that he was being asked to carry wood to the Tsurani quarters. Dirk picked up the fallen bundle and wrestled with it a moment before getting the unwieldy load under control. He moved to the door of the outbuilding and hesitated, then rolled the wood back on his chest and reached out to pull the latch rope.

The door opened slightly and Dirk pushed it open with his foot. He entered, blinking a moment to get his eyes used to the darkness inside.

A half-dozen Tsurani warriors sat on their beds, speaking in quiet conversation as they tended their arms and armour. Upon seeing the serving boy enter, they fell silent. Dirk went to the woodbox next to the fireplace situated in the centre of the rear wall and deposited his load there.

The Tsurani watched him with impassive expressions. He quickly left the room. Closing the door behind him, he could hardly believe that just weeks before the bed in the farthest corner had been his own. He and the other workers had been turned out to the barn, except for the house staff who now slept on the floor in Lord Paul's kitchen.

There was little need for wood save for cooking, as the warm nights of summer made sleeping fires unnecessary. The Tsurani used their fires primarily for cooking their alien food, filling the area nearby with strange yet intriguing aromas.

Dirk paused a moment and glanced around, taking in the images of White Hill; familiar, yet cast in alien shadow by the invaders. Mikia and Torren, a young couple engaged the week before at the Midsummer's festival, were approaching the milking shed, hand in hand, and the invaders could be invisible for all the distraction they provided the young lovers.

From the kitchen voices and the clatter of pots heralded the advent of the noon meal. Dirk realized he was hungry. Still, he needed to carry firewood to the other buildings before breaking to eat, and he decided the sooner started, the sooner done. As he turned to the woodshed, he caught a glimpse of a soldier in black and orange moving towards the barn. He idly wondered if the time would come when the invaders would be driven from White Hill. It seemed unlikely, for there was no news of the war, and the Tsurani were settling in at White Hill as if they were never leaving.

Reaching the woodshed, Dirk opened the door and saw Alex in the back of the shed cutting more wood. The still-bruised man said, 'You can carry, lad. I'll cut.'

Dirk nodded and went in the shed, to get another arm-ful of firewood. He sighed. As youngest boy in service, the worst jobs fell to him, and this would just be another task added to his burden, one which would not free him from any other.

Before coming to White Hill, Dirk had been nothing, the youngest son of a stonecutter who had two sons already to apprentice. His father had cut the stone for Lord Paul's home, and had used that slight acquaintanceship to gain Dirk a position in Paul's household.

With that position was the promise that eventually he would have some sort of rank on the estate, perhaps a groundsman, a kennel master, or a herdsman. Or he might gain a farm to work, with a portion of his crops going to his landlord, even eventually earning the rank of Franklin, one who owned his own lands free of service to any lord. He had even dared to imagine meeting a girl and marrying, raising sons and daughters of his own. And perhaps, despite the Tsurani, he still might.

Reminding himself he had much to be thankful for, he lifted the next load of wood destined for the fireplaces of the invaders.

Fall brought a quick change in the weather, with sunny but cool days and cold nights. Apples were harvested and the juice presses were busy. The Tsurani found the juice a wonderful delicacy and commanded a large quantity for themselves. A portion was put aside for fermenting and the air around the kitchen was spicy with the smell of warm pies.

Dirk had got used to hauling wood to the Tsurani, and now was the one designated to keep all the woodboxes on the property filled, while Alex still did most of the chopping. Everyone began calling him 'Wood Boy', rather than his name.

Dirk also worked the woodpile, and the constant labour was broadening his shoulders and putting muscle on him by the week. He could now lift as much as the older boys and some of the men.

He found that as the nights cooled his workload increased, for now he had to help plan for the coming winter. The sheep pens were repaired. The herd needed to be kept close, as starving predators would come down from the mountain to hunt. The cattle would be brought down from the higher meadows as well.

Fences needed repairing and the root cellar and springhouse needed stocking. The winters in the foothills of Yabon came quickly and the snow was often deep after the first fall, lasting until the thaw of spring.

Dirk worked hard and enjoyed those infrequent moments he could steal to relax, joke with the older boys and young men, and talk to Litia, an old woman who had once been in charge of the poultry and lambs. She was kind to the awkward boy and told him things that helped him understand the world that seemed to be changing around him by the day.

Dirk now was faced with the realization that life's choices were down to a precious few. Before the Tsurani's arrival, he had stood a chance of learning to be a herdsman or farmer, and perhaps meeting a girl and starting a family on the edge of Lord Paul's estates, having land and a share of the harvest. Or he might save the tiny sum allotted him over and above his keep and someday attempt to start a trade of his own; he knew the rudiments of cutting stone and perhaps might pay a mason to apprentice him.

But now he feared he was doomed to be a servant until death took him. There was no payment of wages above his keep; the Tsurani had taken all of Lord Paul's wealth – though it was rumoured he had two parts in three safely hidden from the Tsurani. Even if the rumour was true, he wasn't about to risk hanging to pay a lowly servant boy his back wages.

And there were no girls his own age on the estates, save Lord Paul's daughter.

The Midwinter's festival was supposed to be the time to meet the girls from town or the nearby estates, but the Tsurani had forbidden such travel for the Midsummer's festival, and Dirk doubted they would change their mind for the winter festival. Lord Paul's household had celebrated Banapis on Midsummer's Day by themselves, with little enthusiasm, because of the poor food and drink, and the isolation.

At least, thought Dirk, Midwinter's Day was likely to be a little livelier, as there was a good supply of fermenting applejack laid in. Then, remembering how morose his father could get when drinking, Dirk wondered if that was a good thing. Hamish had been known to drink himself into a dark and blind rage in the depths of winter.

Putting aside his own misery, he attacked the tasks the day put before him and was judged a hardworking if unremarkable boy by those of the household.

The festival was a pale shadow of its former self. Traditionally the towns turned out, with those living on the neighbouring estates coming in for the parties. A townsman would be selected to play the part of Old Man Winter, who would come into town on a sled pulled by wolves – usually a motley collection of dogs pressed into playing the part, often with comic results. He would pass out sweets to the children, and the adults would exchange small gifts and tokens. Then everyone would eat too much food and many would drink too much wine and ale.

And many young couples would be married.

This year the Tsurani had forbidden travel, and Dirk stood at the edge of a small crowd in the barnyard watching Mikia and Torren getting married under the watchful eyes of Lord Paul and his daughter. The Tsurani had let Dirk travel to the shrine of Dala and return with a priest of that order, so that the wedding could be conducted.

The couple looked happy despite the frigid surroundings, made slightly more bearable by the large bonfire Dirk and the others had built earlier in the day. It roared and warmed whichever side was facing it, but otherwise it was a cold and bitter day for a wedding, with low grey skies and a constant wind off the mountains.

The meal was the best that could be managed under the circumstances, and Dirk had his first encounter with too much to drink, consuming far too much applejack and discovering that his stomach would inform him of its limits before any of his friends would. The other boys stood around in amusement as Dirk leaned against the wall behind the barn, sick beyond belief, his head swimming and his pulse pounding in his temples as his stomach tried to throw up drink no longer there.

He had somehow managed to find his way back to the loft in which he now slept. Because he was the youngest boy in the household, he got the worst pallet, next to the hay door, which meant a draughty, frigid night's rest. He passed out and risked freezing to death without the other boys' warmth nearby.

Late that night, he stirred as a shout from outside rang through the silent darkness. Dirk stirred as did the other boys, and Hemmy said, 'What's that?'

Dirk pushed open the hay door. In the moonlight a drunken figure stood waving a sword with his right hand, while holding a jug of applejack with the left. He shouted words that the boys couldn't understand, but Hemmy said, 'He's fighting some old battle, for sure.'

Suddenly Alex said, 'The Tsurani! If Hamish wakes them with all that shouting, they'll kill him. We've got to get him to shut up.'

'You want to go and try to talk to him while he's waving that sword around,' said Hemmy, 'you go ahead. I'll take my chances up here. I've seen him drunk before. Puts him in a dangerous dark temper, it does.'

'We've got to do something,' said Dirk.

'What?' asked Hemmy.

'I don't know,' admitted Dirk.

Then two Tsurani ran into view and stopped when they saw the drunken old soldier in the moonlight, his breath forming clouds of steam in the frigid night air.

'You stinkin' bastards!' shouted Hamish. 'You come on and I'll show you how to use a sword.'

The two Tsurani slowly drew weapons, and one spoke to the other. The second man nodded and stepped back, putting his sword away. He turned and ran off.

'They're going to get some help,' whispered Dirk, afraid to be overheard by the Tsurani.

'Maybe they'll just make him put up his sword and go to bed,' said Hemmy.

'Maybe,' echoed Dirk.

Then a half-dozen Tsurani, led by the officer, came into view. The officer shouted at Hamish, who grinned like a grizzly wolf in the stark white moonlight. 'Come and sing to me, you sons of dogs!' shouted the drunken old man.

The Tsurani officer seemed more irritated by the display than anything else, and said something briefly to the men. He turned and walked off without a glance back.

'Maybe they're going to let him alone,' said Hemmy.

Suddenly an arrow sped through the darkness and struck old Hamish in the chest. He looked down in disbelief and sank to his knees. Then he fell off to the right, still holding his sword and jug of applejack.

'Gods!' whispered Dirk.

The Tsurani turned as one and walked away, leaving the dead bodyguard lying in the moonlight, a black figure against the white snow.

'What do we do?' whispered Dirk to the older boys.

'Nothing,' said Alex. 'Until the Tsurani tell us to get out tomorrow and bury him, we do nothing.'

'But it's not right,' said Dirk, fighting back tears of frustration and fear.

'Nothing is right these days,' said Hemmy, reaching out to shut the hay door.

Dirk lay in the loft, huddled against a cold far more bitter than winter's night.

'Let me help you with that,' said Drogen, as Dirk tried to close the kitchen door with a kick. The wind outside howled and this had been Dirk's fifth trip to the woodbox.

Dirk said, 'Shut the door, please.'

The new bodyguard to Lord Paul did as Dirk asked, and Dirk said, 'Thanks. I've got to get this to the great hall.' He hurried with the heavy bundle of wood and made his way through the big house. He entered the great hall, where Lord Paul ate dinner with his daughter Anika.

Dirk was very deliberate in arranging the new firewood, as it gave him a moment to watch Anika from beside the fireplace. She was a year younger than Dirk. Fifteen last Midsummer's Day, she was perfection embodied to the young kitchen boy. She had delicate features, a small bow of a mouth, wide-set blue eyes, and hair of pale gold. Her skin held a faint touch of the sun in summer and was flawless pink in winter. Her figure was ripening, yet not voluptuous like the kitchen women, still possessing a grace when she moved that set Dirk's heart to beating.

Dirk knew she didn't even know his name, but he dreamed of somehow earning rank and fame someday, and winning her love. Her image filled his mind every waking moment of the day.

'Is something wrong, Wood Boy?' asked Lord Paul.

'No, sir!' said the boy, standing up and striking his head on the mantel. The girl covered her mouth as she laughed, and he blushed furiously. 'I was just putting the wood away. I'm done, sir.'

'Then get back to the kitchen, lad,' said the Lord of the house.

Lord Paul was an Elector of the City. Before the Tsurani had come, Lord Paul had voted on every important matter confronting Walinor and had once been the delegate from the city to the General Council of Electors for the Free Cities of Natal. He was by any measure one of the wealthiest men in the city. He had ships plying the Bitter Sea and farms and holdings throughout the west, as well as investments in both the Kingdom of the Isles and the Empire of Great Kesh.

And Dirk was now hopelessly in love with his daughter.

It didn't matter she didn't know his name, or even notice he was there, he just couldn't stop thinking of her. For the last two weeks, since Hamish's death, he had found his mind turning constantly to thoughts of Anika. Her smile, how she moved, the tilt of her chin when she was listening to something her father was saying.

She wore only the finest clothing and her hair was always put up with combs of fine bone or shell from the Bitter Sea, or left down with ringlets that softly framed her face. She was always polite, even to the servants, and had the sweetest voice Dirk had ever heard.

When he was back in the kitchen, Jenna the old stout cook said, 'Getting a peek at the girl, were we?'

Drogen laughed and Dirk blushed. His infatuation with Lord Paul's daughter was a well-known source of amusement in the kitchen. Dirk prayed Jenna said nothing to any of the other boys, for if it became obvious to the boys in the barn, Dirk's already miserable existence would become even blacker than it presently was.

'She's a pretty girl,' said Drogen with a smile at Dirk. 'Most men would look more than once.'

Dirk liked Drogen. He had been just one of Lord Paul's men-at-arms until Hamish had been killed for disturbing the Tsurani on Midwinter's Night. Since then he had become a fixture in the main house and Dirk had found several chances to talk to him. Unlike Hamish, who had been given to bouts of ill-humour, Drogen was a quiet fellow, saying little unless answering a direct question. Easy-going, he was reputed to be one of the best men with a sword in the Free Cities, and he had an open and friendly manner. He was handsome in a dark fashion, and Dirk had heard gossip that more than one of the serving women had snuck off with him on a thin pretext, and there were several tavern girls in the city who waited for his next visit. Dirk thought the man a nice enough fellow, though Jenna often had acid comments on Drogen's inability to think of much besides women.

Dirk stood and said, 'I have to get more wood over to the Tsurani.' He left the warm kitchen and, back out in the cold, wished he hadn't. He hurried to the woodpile.

Dirk picked up a large pile of wood and moved to the first of the three buildings. He pushed open the door and found the Tsurani as he always did. Quietly they rested between patrols or other duties which might take as many as half the garrison away for days, even weeks at a time. Occasionally they would return carrying their wounded. When resting they slept in their bunks, tended their odd, black and orange armour, and talked quietly. Some played what appeared to be a gambling game of some sort involving sticks and rocks, and others played what looked to be chess.

Most were off on some mission for their master, leaving less than a dozen in residence at White Hill. They looked on impassively as he filled the woodbox. He left and serviced the other two woodboxes. When he was finished, he sighed audibly in relief. No matter how many times being the Wood Boy forced him to enter the buildings occupied by the Tsurani, having witnessed their capacity for ruthless murder brought Dirk to the edge of blind panic when he encountered them alone. When he knew he had done with them for another night, he felt as if he was entering a safe place for some hours to come.

Done with his outside chores for the night, he returned to the kitchen and ate his meagre supper, a watery stew and coarse bread. The very best of the foodstuffs not taken by the invaders was served to Lord Paul and his daughter. He had overheard Anika complain about the food, only to hear her father reply it wasn't too bad, all things considered. Dirk thought by the standards he was used to, it was a feast. Drogen and the other workers in the house got the pick of leftovers and there was never anything for a mere Wood Boy.

Dirk returned to the barn and ignored the moaning that came from under a blanket in the first stall. Mikia and Torren seemed unconcerned their privacy was non-existent. Still, Dirk reasoned, they were dairy people, a herdsman and milkmaid, and he found farm people far more earthy and unconcerned with modesty than townspeople.

Litia sat in the corner of the next stall, her slight form shivering under a blanket as she sat on the dirt floor, huddled close to the warmth of a small fire. Dirk waved and she returned a toothless smile. He went over and said, 'How are you?'

'Well enough,' she said, and her voice was barely more than a whisper.

Dirk was concerned the old woman might not last the winter, given the scant food and warmth, but others in the household seemed indifferent. You got old, then you died, they always said.

'What gossip?' asked the old woman. She lived for tidbits of news or rumours. Dirk always kept his ears open for something to enliven the old woman's evening.

'Nothing new, sorry to say,' he replied.

With a wide, gummy grin, the old woman said, 'And has the master's daughter favoured you with a glance yet, my young buck?'

Dirk felt his face flush and he said, 'I don't know what you mean, Litia.'

'Yes you do,' she chided him playfully. 'It's all right, lad. She's the only girl your age here and it wouldn't be natural if you didn't feel a tug towards her. If those heathens who took our beds relent and let us visit with neighbours in the spring, the first young farm lass you meet will get your mind off my lord's wicked child.'

'Wicked child?' said Dirk. 'What do you mean?'

Litia said, 'Nothing, sweet boy. She's a wilful girl who always gets what she wants, is all. What you need is a good strong lass, a farm girl with broad hips who can bear you sons who will take care of you in your old age.'

The bitterness in Litia's words was not lost on Dirk, even if he was young. He knew her only son had died years before in a drowning accident and that she had no one left to care for her. Dirk said, 'I'll try to get you another blanket from the house tomorrow.'

'Don't get yourself into trouble on my account,' said the woman, but her expression showed she appreciated the offer.

Dirk left her and climbed the ladder to the loft, where the young men slept. He was the youngest up there, for the boys younger than he stayed with their family. Alex, Hans, and Leonard were already resting. Hemmy and Petir would be up shortly. Dirk wished for another blanket himself, but knew that he would have to depend upon the ones allotted to him. At least one side of him would be warm at a time, as he would huddle next to Hemmy, the next older boy. He would turn a few times in the night to ward off the freezing air.

And spring was but two months away. Hemmy and Petir climbed up and took their places in the loft, and Dirk snuggled down as best he could in his blankets and went to sleep.

It was an odd sound, and Dirk couldn't quite make sense of it as he came awake in the dark. Then it registered: someone had cried out. It had been a muffled sound, but it had been a cry. Dirk listened for a moment, but the sound wasn't repeated. He tried to go back to sleep.

Just as he was drowsy again, he heard a creak and the sound of someone moving in the barn. A dull thud and a strange gurgling noise made him lift himself up on his right elbow, listening in the dark. He strained to hear something, but he couldn't make out the sounds. Assuming it was Mikia and Torren again, he rolled over and tried to go back to sleep.

Again he was almost dozing when he realized something was

wrong. As he turned over, he saw something moving rapidly towards him in the gloom, a large dark shape. He sat up, reflexively pulling away from what was coming towards him.

Two things happened at once. Someone slashed at him, a blade cutting into the fabric of his coat below his collarbone, and he struck the hay door with his back. He choked out an inarticulate cry, unable to speak for the terror which overwhelmed him. Then another body slammed into him with a strangled cry and he felt the door latch behind him give.

Never too sturdy, the latch parted as the weight of two bodies struck it, and with a muffled cry, Dirk fell out of the hay door, down to the snow-covered ground below. He landed with a thud that drove the breath out of him.

Then the other body landed on him, and Dirk was knocked senseless.

He awoke as the sky was lightening. He was freezing and barely able to breathe. His left eye seemed glued shut and something on top of him held him firmly to the ground.

Dirk tried to move, and discovered that Hemmy lay atop him. 'Hey, get off!' he said, but his voice was weak and strangled. A burning pain below his throat caused him to gasp when he moved.

His legs were numb from the cold, and he lay in a hole in the snow. He wiggled his bottom and managed to work his way upright and realized Hemmy was dead. The older boy's face was white, and his throat was cut. Terror galvanized Dirk and he lifted the corpse enough to get out from beneath him, forcing numb legs to do his bidding.

He pulled himself out of the snow and his muscles screamed at being forced to move. He climbed out of the hole and saw he was drenched in blood, Hemmy's blood.

'What happened?' he whispered.

As he staggered towards the barn, he saw the morning sun was still an hour from cresting the eastern horizon. His legs became wobbly and he leaned against the barn, looking up to see the rear hay door still opened. He paused a moment to get control over his frozen, stiff legs, walked around to the front, and looked at the large doors thrown open to the cold. He glanced down at the snow before the door and saw no unusual number of footprints. But off to the south side of the entrance, where snow remained uncleared, he saw a single set of footprints and the parallel impression left by a sled's runners. Someone had pulled the large sled out of the barn. The depth of the runner tracks in the snow told him it was heavily loaded. The horses were long gone, having been eaten by the Tsurani the winter before, so whoever had moved the sled was pulling it.

Dirk went inside the barn and saw Mikia and Torren lying in each other's arms, their throats cut. Old Litia also lay dead in her own blood, her eyes open wide. Everywhere he looked, he saw death.

Who did this? Dirk wondered in panicked confusion. Had the Tsurani who occupied Lord Paul's estate gone mad and killed everyone? But if they had, there would have been footprints in abundance outside in the snow, and there was none. Most of them were gone on some mission or another, leaving only a few in the outbuildings this week. Then Dirk's thoughts turned to the manor house. 'Anika!' he said in a hoarse whisper.

He hurried through the pre-dawn gloom to the kitchen and found the door open. He stared in mute horror at the carnage in the room. Everyone who slept in the kitchen was as dead as those in the barn.

He hurried upstairs and, without knocking, entered Anika's room. Her bed lay empty. He peered under it, afraid she might have crawled under it to die. Then he realized there was no blood in the room.

He got up and ran to her father's room, and pushed open the door. Lord Paul lay in a sea of blood on his bed. Dirk didn't need to see if he lived. Beside the bed a secret door was opened, a door painted to look like a section of the wall. Dirk looked through the door into the small hiding-place and realized here had been where his master had kept his wealth. The invaders had demanded every gold, silver, and copper coin held by those living in the occupied region, yet it was well documented they had no concept of wealth on this planet. The servants had speculated that Lord Paul had turned over only one part in three of his wealth and the rest had remained hidden. Perhaps they had found he had hidden wealth and this was their way of punishing everyone. If the Tsurani had gone on a rampage . . .

'No,' he said softly to himself. The Tsurani hanged those without honour. The blade was for honourable foes. Whoever did the killing had moved with stealth, as if afraid to raise an alarm and be overwhelmed, and had cautiously killed all the servants one at a time. The killer had been armed . . .

Drogen!

Only Drogen and the Lord of the House, of all those who weren't Tsurani, were permitted arms. Dirk closed the secret door, too stunned to appreciate how clever it was. Once closed, it appeared indistinguishable from the wall.

He hurried down to the large dining hall and saw over the fireplace the two swords hung there, heirlooms of Lord Paul's family. He considered taking one down, then remembered that should the Tsurani find him with a sword in his possession, he would be hanged without any opportunity to explain.

He returned to the kitchen and took a large boning knife from the butcher's block next to the stove. That was something he had handled many times before and the familiarity of the handle was reassuring to Dirk.

He had to do something about finding Anika, but he didn't know what. Drogen must have taken her with the gold. He ran back to the barn to see if anyone else might have survived. Within minutes he knew only he and Anika survived.

And the Tsurani, of course.

Panic struck Dirk. He knew that if one of them stuck his head outside one of the huts he would be hanged for carrying a kitchen knife, no matter what the reason.

He put the knife in his tunic, and climbed into the loft. He went to the canvas bag that served as his closet, holding his few belongings. He removed his only coat, and saw a long cut below the collar. Drogen had lashed out at him first, because he had awakened. He must have thought Dirk's throat cut. Then he had killed Hemmy, pushing him atop Dirk, causing them to fall through the hay door. Only the darkness and the fall had saved Dirk's life, he knew. Had he not fallen out of the barn, Drogen would certainly have ensured the boy was dead.

Dirk put on his extra shirt for warmth, ignoring the sticky blood soaked into his undershirt and the shirt he already wore. Wearing the extra layers of clothing might be the difference between life and death. He considered pulling a tunic off one of the other boys, but he couldn't bring himself to touch the bodies of his dead friends.

He again donned his coat and took his only pair of gloves from the bag, along with a large woollen scarf Litia had knitted for him the year before. He put them on and checked the bag for his other belongings: there was nothing else there he could imagine would help him.

He hurried down the ladder. The only thing he could think of doing was following the murderer. He was terrified of waking the Tsurani, and not certain they would care about the murder of people they obviously felt were inferior to themselves. They might blame Dirk and hang him, he feared.

Drogen. He had to find Drogen and rescue Anika and get the gold back for her. The boy knew that without gold the girl would be at the mercy of the townspeople. She would be forced to depend on the generosity of relatives or friends. But he was terrified enough he couldn't move. He stood in the barn aisle, rooted with indecision.

After a time he heard a shout from across the compound. The Tsurani were up and one had seen something. A confusion of voices sounded from outside, and Dirk knew they would be in the barn in moments.

He hid himself in the darkest corner of the stall most removed from the door, and lay shivering in fear and cold as men came into the barn, speaking rapidly in their odd language. Two walked past where Dirk lay, one casting a quick glance in his direction. He must have simply assumed Dirk was another dead boy, for he said nothing to his companion, who climbed the ladder to the hayloft. After a moment, he shouted down, and the other responded. He heard the man return down the ladder and the two of them left the barn. Dirk waited until it grew quiet again, then got out of the straw. He hurried to the door and peered out. From his vantage point he saw one Tsurani instructing others to search the area.

Uncertain of what to do next, Dirk waited. A Tsurani he knew to be of some rank came out and pointed to the tracks in the snow. There was some sort of debate, and the man who had sent the others searching seemed to be indicating that someone should follow the murderer.

Then the leader spoke in commanding tones and the other man bowed slightly and turned away. Dirk realized no one was going to follow Drogen. He was going to get away with killing more than two dozen people and kidnapping Anika and taking all of Lord Paul's gold. The Tsurani soldier in charge seemed content to leave this matter to his own officer, when the bulk of the command returned from their mission.

Dirk knew if anyone was to save Anika, it would have to be him. Dirk slipped out of the barn, and around the side and when he was certain no one was nearby, he slipped down the hill behind the barn and made his way into the woods. He hurried along through the birch and pines until he found the sled tracks. He turned to follow them.

Dirk slogged his way through the snow, his breath a white cloud before him. His feet were numb and he felt weak and hungry, but he was determined to overtake Drogen. The landscape was white and green – the boughs of pines and firs peering out from mantles of snow. A stand of bare trees stood a short distance away, and Dirk knew he had left the boundary of Lord Paul's estate.

The murderer was making good time, despite having to pull the heavy sled. He knew that he gained on Drogen each time he had to pull the sled up a hill, but each time he went down the next slope, Drogen probably gained some of that time back.

Dirk stopped to rest a moment. His best chance of finding

the murderer, he knew, was to catch him at night. Dirk glanced
around. He had no idea how much time had passed; a good part
of the day, he realized, but he couldn't tell from the grey sky
where the sun was and when darkness would arrive.

A rabbit poked his head above a nearby ridge and sniffed. Dirk
wished he had some sort of weapon, or the time to rig a snare,
for a rabbit cooked over an open fire would be welcome, but he
knew such wishes would go ungranted.

He continued on.

It began to snow as darkness came, and it came quickly. Dirk's
plan of following through the night vanished along with the
sled tracks. Dirk tried to follow the tracks, but there was no
light. It was the blackest night he could remember, and he was
terrified.

He found a small clump of trees overhung by a large pine
bower thick with snow that acted like a roof, and he crawled
in for the meagre shelter it provided. He built up a low snow
wall around him, having been taught as a boy it would shelter
him from the wind. He dozed but didn't sleep.

A soft sound woke him. He heard it again. He poked his head
out from under the pine bower and saw that snow had fallen
from a branch in a large clump.

He crawled out and looked for tracks. There were places where
the snow had fallen lightly, and he could barely see the tracks,
but they were there, and they pointed the way.

Dirk began again to hunt down the murderer.

At sundown he saw the light of the fire, high on a ridge to the
east. Drogen was making his way towards the city of Natal. It
was free of the Tsurani invaders. Once there, Drogen could make
his way to Ylith and from there to anywhere in the world: the
Kingdom, Kesh, or the Island Empire of Queg. How Drogen was
going to cross the frontier, Dirk didn't know, but he assumed the
man had a plan. Maybe he just counted on the Tsurani holding
tight to their campfires and not having too many men in the

field in the dead of winter. From what he had heard, there had been almost no fighting between them and the Free Cities and Kingdom forces since the first heavy snow of winter.

Dirk slogged his way towards the fire.

He finally reached a place where he could get a glimpse of the site. Slowly approaching as quietly as he could, Dirk saw a single man resting on the sled, warming his hands at the fire. Drogen must have thought himself free of pursuit, for he had taken no pains to hide his whereabouts. At his feet, Anika lay in a bundle of furs. Dirk had aired them out every fall after fetching them out of storage, so he knew the girl was well protected from the cold. She appeared to be asleep – probably exhausted from terror, Dirk thought.

Dirk stopped, again rooted by fear. He had no idea how to proceed. He made up and discarded a dozen plans to attack the murderer. He couldn't imagine how to attack a trained warrior, one who was paid to fight.

Dirk stood freezing his feet, watching the fire grow dimmer. Drogen ate, and still Dirk remained motionless. Cold, exposure, hunger and fear were on the verge of reducing him to tears.

Then Drogen threw more wood on the fire and wrapped a blanket around himself. He lay down on the ground between the sled and Anika, who moved, but didn't awake. He was going to sleep!

Dirk knew that he could only rescue Anika and regain Lord Paul's gold by sneaking up on Drogen and killing him as he slept. Dirk had no compunction about the act; Drogen had killed everyone Dirk had known since leaving his family to work at the master's estate, in their sleep, and he deserved no more than they got. Dirk just feared he wouldn't be up to the task, or would inadvertently wake up the killer.

Dirk moved his legs, trying to regain circulation in the freezing night, and eventually he judged it safe to approach the camp. Stiff legs and an inability to catch his breath drove Dirk to a heart-pounding frenzy. He found his hands shaking so badly he could barely manage to get the heavy knife out from within his jacket.

The familiar handle was suddenly an alien thing that resisted fitting comfortably in his palm. He crept forward and tried not to let panic overwhelm him.

He stopped on the other side of the sled, uncertain which way to approach. He decided that he'd approach Drogen's head.

Dirk held the knife high, and crept around the sled, slowly, moving as carefully as he could so as not to make noise. When he was just a few feet away, Drogen moved, shifting the blanket around his shoulders. He snuggled down behind Anika, who didn't move.

Fear overwhelmed Dirk. He knew if he didn't move now, he would never move. He struck down hard with the knife and felt the point dig into the murderer's shoulder.

Drogen shouted in pain and convulsed, almost pulling the knife out of Dirk's hand. Dirk yanked it back, and struck out again as Drogen tried to rise. The point again dug deep into his shoulder, and he howled in pain.

Anika awoke with a scream and kicked off the furs, then leaped to her feet, spinning around and trying to understand what was happening. Dirk pulled the blade out and was ready for a third strike, but Drogen charged, driving his shoulder into Dirk, knocking him aside.

The boy rolled on the ground and found Drogen sitting atop his chest, his hand poised to deliver a blow. 'You!' he said as he saw the boy's face in the dim light of the dying fire. Drogen hesitated.

Dirk lashed out with his knife and struck Drogen in the face, cutting deeply. Drogen reared back, his hand to his cheek as he cried out in pain. Dirk acted without thought. He pushed hard with his knife, driving it deep into Drogen, just under his ribcage.

Drogen loomed above Dirk in the dim light, his eyes wide in silent astonishment. His left hand dropped from where it had momentarily touched his cheek. With his right hand he grabbed Dirk's tunic, as if he was going to pull him upright to ask him something. Then he slowly toppled backward. He didn't release his grip on Dirk's coat and he pulled the boy upright, then forward.

Dirk's legs were pinned under Drogen, and he was forced to bend forward.

Dirk frantically pried the dying man's fingers from his coat. He fell back and the pain in his side was a searing agony. He saw the blade of the knife protruding from Drogen's coat and his head swam. Using his elbows, he pulled himself back and got his legs free of Drogen's weight. Dimly he was aware of a sobbing voice saying, 'No.'

Dirk was in a fog as he reached down and pulled out the knife from Drogen's body. He turned as a girl's voice again said, 'No! You killed him!' screamed Anika as she rushed towards Dirk. The disoriented boy stood uncertain of what was occurring. He tried to focus his eyes as his head swam from pain. 'I –' he began, but the girl seemed to fly at him.

'You killed him!' she screamed again as she fell upon him.

He stepped back, his heel striking Drogen's body and he fell, the girl suddenly atop him. She landed heavily upon Dirk, her eyes wide in shock. She pushed herself up and looked down between them.

Dirk followed her gaze and saw the knife was still in his hand. Anika had impaled herself upon the blade. Confusion beset her features and she gazed at his face and at last said, softly, 'The Wood Boy?'

She fell atop Dirk. He moved her aside, but held her in his arms, and he sank to the snow, holding her. She looked up at the sky, eyes glassy, and he gently closed them.

Then Dirk felt a hot stabbing pain in his side and bile rose in his throat as he realized that somehow he had been cut. He touched the wound and hot pain shot through his body, and his eyes seemed unwilling to focus. He knew that he couldn't move with the blade there, and reached up to grip the handle again. Mustering all the resolve he could, he pulled the knife from his side, and screamed at the agony of it. After a moment, the pain subsided and was replaced by a throbbing torment, but one which didn't make him feel as if he was going to die. He slowly stood, and turned to confront the girl.

Then he passed out.

Borric said, 'She helped him kill her father and the rest?'

'I don't think so, sir.' Sadly Dirk said, 'I think Drogen tricked her, convinced her to elope with him to gain the secret of where her father's gold was. She was an innocent girl and he was a rake known to have wooed many women. If he killed everyone without awakening her, then bundled her up in those furs and carried her straight to the sled, she wouldn't see. Once away from the Free Cities, she might never have known.' He looked as if he was about to cry, but held his tone steady as he said, 'She fell upon me in a fright, and without knowing what had occurred at home. Else she wouldn't have been so frantic over Drogen's death, I'm certain. Her death was an accident, but it was all my fault.'

'There was no fault in you, lad. It was, as you say, an accident.' After a moment, Borric nodded. 'Yes, it's better to think of it that way. Lad, why did you come here?'

'I didn't know what else to do. I thought if Drogen planned on coming this way, I would, too. I knew the Tsurani would take my master's gold and hang me as likely as not . . . it was all I could think of.'

'You did well,' said Borric softly.

Dirk put the cup down and said, 'That was good. Thank you, sir.' He moved and winced.

'You're hurt?'

'I bound the wounds as best I could, sir.'

Borric called for an orderly and instructed him to take the boy to the healer's tent and have the wound treated.

After Dirk had left, the captain said, 'That was quite a story, Your Grace.'

Borric agreed. 'The boy has special courage.'

'Did the girl know?' asked the Captain.

'Of course she knew,' said Borric. 'I knew Paul of White Hill; I've done enough business with him through my agent in

Bordon, Talbot Kilrane. I've been to his home, and he's been to Crydee.

'And I knew the daughter.' Borric sighed, as if what he thought tired him. 'She's the same age as my Carline. And they're as different as two children could be. Anika was born scheming.' Borric sighed again. 'I have no doubt she planned this, though we'll never know if she anticipated all the murders; she may have only suggested to the bodyguard they steal the gold and flee. With her father behind Tsurani lines and all that gold in her possession, she could have cut quite a social figure for herself back in Krondor or even in Rillanon. She easily could have disposed of the bodyguard – he clearly couldn't admit to anyone his part in this, could he? And if word of the killings reached us, we would assume the Tsurani murdered the household on some pretext.' Borric was silent. Then he said, 'In my bones I know the girl was the one behind all this . . . but we'll never know for certain, will we?'

'No, Your Grace,' agreed the captain. 'What of the bodies?'

'Bury them. We have no means to return the girl to her family in Walinor.'

The captain said, 'I'll detail men to the digging. It'll take a while to dig through the frozen ground.' He then asked, 'And the gold?'

Borric said, 'It's confiscated. The Tsurani would have taken it anyway, and we've an army to feed. Send it under guard to Brucal in LaMut.' He paused a moment, then said, 'Send the boy, too. I'll pen a note to Brucal asking the boy be found some service there at headquarters. He's a resourceful lad and as he said, he has nowhere else to go.'

'Very well, Your Grace.'

As the captain turned to go, Borric said, 'And Captain?'

'Yes, Your Grace?'

'Keep what I said to yourself. The boy doesn't need to know.'

'As you wish, Your Grace,' said the captain as he departed.

Borric sat forward and tried to return his attention to the business at hand, but he found his mind returning to the boy's story. He tried to imagine what Dirk had felt, alone, armed only with the kitchen knife and afraid. He had been a trained warrior for most of his life, but he remembered what it was to be uncertain. He recognized the boy's act for what it had been, an unusual and rare act of heroism. The image of a lovestruck, frightened boy trudging through the snow at night to confront a murderer and rescue a damsel lingered with the duke, and he decided it was best that the boy be left with that one shred of illusion about the girl. He had earned that much, at least.

Assassin's Apprentice
Book One of The Farseer Trilogy
Robin Hobb

A new legend begins . . .

In a faraway land in which members of the royal family are Named for the virtues they embody, one young boy will become a walking enigma.

Born on the wrong side of the sheets, Fitz, son of Chivalry, is a royal bastard, cast out into the world, friendless and lonely. Only his magical link with animals – that old art known as the Wit – gives him solace and companionship. But the Wit, if used too often, is a perilous magic, and one abhorred by the nobility.

So when Fitz is taken from his warm stable and finally adopted into the royal household, he must give up his old ways and learn a new life: weaponry, scribing, courtly manners; and how to kill a man secretly, as he trains to become a royal assassin.

'Refreshingly original'   JANNY WURTS

'I couldn't put this book down'   *Starburst*

ISBN 0 00 648009 8

Magician
Raymond E. Feist
New Revised Edition

Raymond E. Feist has prepared a new, revised edition, to incorporate over 15,000 words of text omitted from previous editions so that, in his own words, 'it is essentially the book I would have written had I the skills I possess today'.

At Crydee, a frontier outpost in the tranquil Kingdom of the Isles, an orphan boy, Pug is apprenticed to a master magician – and the destinies of two worlds are changed forever. Suddenly the peace of the Kingdom is destroyed as mysterious alien invaders swarm through the land. Pug is swept up into the conflict but for him and his warrior friend, Tomas, an odyssey into the unknown has only just begun. Tomas will inherit a legacy of savage power from an ancient civilisation. Pug's destiny is to lead him through a rift in the fabric of space and time to the mastery of the unimaginable powers of a strange new magic. . .

'Epic scope . . . fast-moving action . . . vivid imagination'
Washington Post

'Tons of intrigue and action'
Publishers Weekly

ISBN 0 586 21783 3

WIN A TRIP TO NASA

worth over £2,000 with *Voyager*Direct

The book you're holding now is just one of the many fantastic titles you could be getting direct to your door. What's more, order our new catalogue today and you could be heading for Florida.

Exclusive offers, big savings, signed copies and free books! *Voyager*Direct – A whole new world direct to your door

---

Yes! Send me a *Voyager*Direct catalogue today

Name ....

Address ....

....

....

Postcode ....

Send to Jeremy Millington, *Voyager*Direct, 77–85 Fulham Palace Road, Hammersmith, London W6 8JB.

Membership is free and there is no obligation to buy at any time.

 Voyager

www.voyager-books.com